YOU PEOPLE ARE MONSTERS

BOOK 3 OF
THE CONVENTION OF FIENDS

by

Benjamin Gorman

Trigger Warning for
The Convention of Fiends
Series

As a school teacher, I learned that just about anything can be a trigger for an anxiety/PTSD attack for someone out there. I was once showing the most innocuous of films, and a student had a PTSD attack because, she realized during the movie, it was the exact one which had been playing when she experienced a traumatic event. So no list like this is ever complete.

That being said, I do think trigger warnings identifying some common triggers are valuable in case you, Dear Reader, are aware of some content which could threaten your mental health. Your health is more important than my story, and I want to give you this list for the entire series so you don't get invested and then find you shouldn't have taken these books on right now.

But some of you may read this list and think, "That sounds right up my alley." And that's fine. Warnings are also invitations to mischief.

Some of these triggers take the form of comments by the antagonists, so they are obviously things I oppose, but you should be aware they exist in the text:

- references racism, sexism, religious bigotry
- a description of an attempted sexual assault
- trolls waggling their naughty bits non-consensually

Most of the sexuality is loving and consensual, but if you are not in a mental place to read about it, this series does contain:

- lesbian sex
- sexual encounters between a human woman and vampire (arguably bestiality)
- a sexual encounter between a human woman and a dragon (bestiality)

And, though I didn't set out to write a story with so much violence, it turns out, when monsters are involved, one ends up with:

- vampires killing people
- werewolves killing people
- werewolves and vampires killing one another
- people killing a vampire
- merfolk killing people
- people killing merfolk
- a minotaur killing a person
- lots of other monsters attempting to kill people
- trolls attempting to kill monsters by flinging flaming feces
- vampires being tortured by trolls
- a dragon killing lots of other monsters
- panicked trolls stampeding upon, and almost certainly killing, one another
- gun violence
- sword violence
- hand-to-hand violence
- biting
- a warlock seducing people while glamoured (which is, technically, a form of sexual assault)

- a giant tentacle monster killing and consuming like … tons of people (and merfolk)
- a golem punching a Nazi to death

Perhaps most challenging, our protagonist struggles with
- depression
- suicidal ideation

Oh, and characters use "bad words." (There's no such thing. But they do use words some people find offensive.)

Take care of yourself. You were warned!

Novels by Benjamin Gorman

The Sum of Our Gods

Corporate High School

The Digital Storm:
A Science Fiction Reimagining of
William Shakespeare's The Tempest

Don't Read This Book
Book 1 of The Convention of Fiends

You Were Warned
Book 2 of The Convention of Fiends

You People Are Monsters
Book 3 of The Convention of Fiends

Poetry Collections

When She Leaves Me:
A Story Told In Poems

This Uneven Universe

Non-Fiction

Dear America: A Breakup Letter

YOU PEOPLE ARE MONSTERS

**BOOK 3 OF
THE CONVENTION OF FIENDS**

Dedication

We will all die, yet
Some will choose to love harder.
Maybe that's enough.

"I think cinema, movies, and magic have always been closely associated. The very earliest people who made film were magicians."

-Francis Ford Coppola

Chapter 1

How many stories are about secrets? So many hinge on the thing unsaid, that fateful kernel of information which, if shared, could have allowed the characters to avoid the whole mess.

This story is the other kind.

This is the kind about a secret revealed. Not quite a confession, but almost. And given freely, not coaxed or cajoled or tortured out of some reluctant keeper of unutterable knowledge. Quite the opposite. This story threw itself at the listeners, begging to be believed, valued, purchased. But it wasn't.

In those secret-style stories, the truth would set everyone free. But humans don't always want to be free. Even if the truth could be served for thirty bucks with a gallon of soda, a bag of popcorn coated with a heart attack of butter and salt, and Dolby Surround sound to drive it into their stupid human ears. Humans don't want to know some things.

A truth rejected does not qualify as a secret. Just a failure.

Three humans who didn't want to know any secrets sat around three sides of a rectangular table in a conference room in Burbank, California, and, in a way, they were the people most prepared to hear the story and most prepared to reject it. Listening to good stories was a big part of their job, but saying, "No," was the bigger part.

"So, who is next?" Joyce asked. William Joyce's friends called him "Bill." His colleagues called him "Mr. Joyce" or just "Joyce" if they got promoted high enough. And people in the industry who pretended to be his friends and colleagues called him "Big Bill" which he hated but tolerated because it clearly identified them as people who would never be his friends nor colleagues. He *was* big, heavy set by L.A. standards, and important by industry standards. But people who are heavyset or important do not need to be called "big."

Carol and Kim got to call him "Joyce."

Kim looked at their notes. Kim was a non-binary person who leaned toward male presenting but wore eye makeup and painted nails, and they tapped those expensive, light blue nails on the manila folder in front of them. "This guy's treatment came to us from Warner, so there's already some interest. Weird thing: It doesn't include his name. All part of the schtick, like the story is some big, top-secret expose, but it's clearly a monster movie, so that's a clever framing device."

Carol rolled her eyes. "Or cheesy. We'll see." She had dyed magenta hair, cat-eye black-rimmed glasses, and that well-practiced eye roll, which should have made her look like fun, but her frown mostly matched her severe business pantsuit.

Joyce just nodded at her. Then he pressed the intercom button. "Martha, send the unnamed gentleman in, please."

"Right away, Mr. Joyce," a pleasant voice chirped.

The three sat in a brief, uncomfortable silence while they waited. Kim opened the folder in front of them, looked at the film treatment, then decided not to have it open during the pitch and closed it.

The man who walked into the conference room wore a tailored gray suit, somewhat too warm and far too formal for L.A. His hair was a dirty blond and looked like he'd had it styled on Rodeo Drive with the explicit instruction to make it look ruffled by a breeze on a yacht. Clean shaven and with movie-star cheekbones, he flashed a smile that was a little too white, a little too friendly, and a little too confident for a man who should have been appearing, hat in hand, to beg these producers to consider making his movie.

"Mr. Joyce, Mx. Quinlan, and Ms. Doyle, thank you

for meeting with me today." He didn't offer to shake their hands and didn't ask if he should sit.

"Nice to meet you, Mr. ...?" Carol provided the fill-in-the-blank question.

"I'm just the messenger, so let's go with 'Emissary.' Feel free to use it as a first name or last name." He flashed that smile again. "Or both."

Kim smiled, but there was a bit of Carol's eye roll in their voice when they said, "Alright, Emissary Emissary, what have you got for us today?"

The emissary repositioned his feet, signaling he was launching into a rehearsed pitch and revealing he had some acting training like every third person in Hollywood. "There's some backstory, which will be revealed within the story itself. Or maybe in a crawl at the beginning. But, of course, the story can't start with all of that as an infodump. For our purposes now, suffice it to say that it's set in the modern day in our world, but there is a secret organization of monsters — think werewolves and vampires and witches and Merfolk — and they have been around for thousands of years doing things behind the scenes, which we'll learn about later. But the movie itself starts with two beautiful women on screen and ..." He held up his hands and mimicked a clapperboard snapping shut, and, as his hands connected, he shouted, "... action!"

Chapter 2

Bel and Lena were also headed into a meeting.

The mansion sat just inside the north side of Monaco, almost on the French side of the border. The tiny city-state on the Mediterranean coast was well known as a playground for the wealthy and a headache for global tax regulators.

Bel drove the rented Lamborghini up the long driveway and through the wide round-about in front of the house. After parking in front of the steps leading to the front door, she raised her upswing door and snaked one pale leg out. The high slit on the left side of her black cocktail dress made sure to capture some attention.

As Bel tossed the keys to the valet, Lena swung her door up and mimicked Bel's dramatic exit, the high slit on her bright red dress conveniently located on the right side, her brown leg contrasting against her dress's sequins. The couple had coordinated their outfits carefully because it was part of the fun; they could walk in with every sign screaming they were together, and at this particular party (and in so many other settings), the humans would presume they were two single, straight friends.

Bel had grown her hair out over the last few months until it came down to her jawline, still shaved short on the sides and the back but now swept over on one side instead of being gelled up. For tonight's occasion, she'd dyed it a bright fire-engine red to complement Lena's sequins. Lena, for her part, wore black sequined gloves, large black tiffany art deco earrings, and an ornate black necklace to match Bel's dress.

The pair hooked their arms as they ascended the steps together, almost walking on point like ballerinas because of the heels they'd chosen for the occasion. But even paired that way, bare shoulders pressing together on a warm, humid Mediterranean night, they could feel the armed security guards—two at the foot of the stairs, two at the door, two in the foyer, and the final pair in the ballroom—all evaluating them as potential sexual targets. Even the most subtle and professional of the guards gave himself away with his elevated heart rate and the change in the smell of his sweat, though he barely gave them a moment's glance. And Bel knew the difference, the way humans—male, female, and everything in between—reacted differently to potential partners than to those they immediately dismissed as unavailable halves of coupled pairs.

Lena was learning to detect that, too, though she'd only had her new senses for a few months. After catching one of the humans eyeing them in that way, she'd squeeze Bel closer, maybe shoot her a glance, and then point the person out with her eyes. The couple would laugh, a laugh that would be interpreted as two single straight women out on the town, looking to get drunk and pair off with single straight men, or men who were single for the evening, maybe even security guards at the end of their shifts. The humans were invested in imbuing Lena and Bel with extremely specific, self-serving plans for the evening's adventures.

Bel and Lena had their own plans.

The ballroom was only three-quarters as full as the hosts would have liked. They would have sneered at the ratio of white-suited serving staff to guests. But the number of heavily armed guards made the hosts feel comfortable, and the ratio of women to men pleased them.

Part of the challenge of throwing a party like this was to invite enough single women to entertain the foreign VIPs without getting the attention of too many authorities. Notice of the party had been spread carefully, with professional party planners recruiting at dance clubs for weeks beforehand, passing out flyers, buying drinks, giving out pills in little bags or bumps of cocaine in bathrooms. Most of the guests were not professional sex workers, though there were a few. The bulk of the guests were aspiring social media influencers; the taking of selfies on the dance floor so ubiquitous it could have been considered a dance move of its own. The DJ, a Moroccan who was decently famous back home and gaining notoriety internationally, leapt back and forth between turntables on stage as colored spotlights pinwheeled over him and the ornate marble double staircase behind him. Luckily for Lena and Bel, those stairs were not roped off, and guests who wanted to watch the DJ and catch a breather from the dancing stood above and behind him holding champagne flutes and shouting at one another to make pleasant conversation.

Lena did not have to shout for Bel to hear her over the music, but she chose her words carefully in case anyone was reading lips. "I count eight in here."

"Same. Stairs?"

"Yeah, let's see if they'll take us right in."

The pair made their way through the middle of the dance floor, gyrating their hips to the rhythm to remain inconspicuous. Both enjoyed the dancing. It was freeing to wear the layer of disguise. They weren't under any obligation to dance well, since they were merely playing the roles of partygoers, so they could laugh at themselves and, in their silliness, dance better than if they'd felt the need to impress one another with their cool moves. They laughed about their shimmies, steps, and electric slides which drove them closer to the stage. Lena, who had the butt for it, did not twerk, but Bel, who did not, made a committed attempt, and Lena found that hilarious. She got up on that and spanked Bel further toward the stage, much to the amusement of the nearest dancers who whooped and cheered for the ludicrous display. When they neared the stage, Lena and Bel grabbed one another's hands, feigned exhaustion, and made their way around to the staircase, then up halfway where they found a few free steps next to the railing. They stood there for a moment, laughing in character but also authentically, watching the DJ below, clocking the guards at the top of the stairs out of the corners of their eyes.

A server in a white suit coat carrying a tray of champagne flutes swept by. Bel guessed the woman probably didn't speak Norwegian but would believe someone as pale as Bel herself might, so, while she took two glasses off the tray, she chose that language to try to start a conversation about where they could find a bathroom. After the woman explained, in French, that she didn't speak Norwegian, Bel switched to a halting, broken French to thank her.

"What was that about?" Lena asked in English.

Bel spoke a dozen languages fluently and could mimic dialects to play a Parisian, a Lyonnaise, a Nantais, or a person from rural France well enough to fool most people. "I wanted to figure out what language to use when talking to the guards."

Lena bit her lip. "Will it be French when we get inside,

too? How am I going to deliver my quips and catch phrases?" It was only her second visit to Europe, the first having been a whirlwind. She hadn't even had time to learn enough French to say, "Holy shit! I'm in the catacombs of Paris being attacked by a skeleton army while I try to save the world from an evil Necromancer," before she was hopping on a ship and sailing to Central America.

She'd grown up in an English- and Spanish-speaking household in Oregon and had lived for a year in Costa Rica, so her two native tongues were impeccable, but she'd only had 29 years to master those, while her girlfriend had been traveling around the globe for the last eight centuries. Bel started off speaking a dialect of Welsh, one that preceded the existence of Wales as a distinct country and which wasn't spoken by anyone anymore, not even in modern Wales. Bel would be able to handle the languages once they got inside, but Lena worried she would have to ask for translations.

"I'm sure they'll speak English. In fact, that's probably what they use when they're doing business. But their guards might not understand your one-liners."

Lena scowled. "Fuck, man. I have some good material I'm planning on trying out."

"Did you just call me 'man'?" Bel asked. "I'm deeply offended."

Lena didn't miss a beat. "No, I called you my 'fuckman.' It's like a 'fuckboi,' but slightly more respectful. If I'd gone with "fuckwoman,' that would've been flattering, but I'm trying to be professional when we're at work."

Bel shook her head. "Too many syllables. How about 'fuckgal'?"

Lena pushed away from the railing and stood very stiffly. "Ew, no, I do not like the sound of that."

Bel nodded. "Yeah, that sucks. 'Fuckpartner' has the same syllable problem as 'fuckwoman'." She flashed a toothy smile at Lena. "'Fuckbroad'? 'Fucktoots'?"

"I'm liking all of this less and less. You have to stop."

"Fine, I'll leave the wordsmithing up to the writer, man!" Bel drew out the last word.

Lena smiled. "I love you."

"I love you, too. You ready to do this?"

Lena became pensive, but only briefly. "I think so, yeah. Let's do it."

The two carried their untouched champagne flutes up to the top of the stairs. There, a guard in a black suit with an M-16 hanging on his shoulder and the bulge in his coat failing to conceal the Glock stepped into the middle of the space leading to the balcony around the ballroom.

"Ladies," he said in French, "I'm sorry, but this area is off limits."

Bel chose a Parisian accent because it felt most dismissive. "Yes, of course, but my friend just needs to use the ladies' room, and the waiter said it was up here." She continued to walk past him.

"No, no, no," the man tried "They should not have told you this. The restrooms for guests are on the first floor."

"Our presence was requested for the meeting on the

second floor," Bel said, "but my friend needs to use the restroom first. So, point us to the bathroom, and then you can check and see that they want us to come to the meeting. Oh, but here, will you take these first?"

Bel shoved their champagne flutes into the guard's hands. He tried not to accept them, but she pushed them into the crooks of his arms, then turned to join Lena, who'd already walked past him.

"Mademoiselle, no, you cannot continue up here. This is off limits."

Lena turned to him and walked backwards as she spoke in English. "So, the bathroom is this way?"

The guard switched to English and followed her while Bel kept pace with him. "No, Miss, you cannot be up in this part of the house." He shifted one flute to hold both by the stems in one hand, then gestured fervently with the other, like he was trying to fan a flame to leave its candlewick and burn elsewhere. "You must come back to the party."

Lena made it to the bathroom door. "I really need to use the bathroom. But you can stand guard out here or come inside or whatever you want. I just need to pee."

The guard tried to stop her, but the door swung away from him, so when he reached out his free hand, all he could do was bang it open rather than closed, and then the woman was inside, and the other one, with the bright red hair, was edging around him to go inside as well.

"In or out, we don't care," she said in her haughtiest Parisian French. "If you want to ask them about taking us to the meeting, go do that, and if you want to come in and watch us pee, that's fine, but make up your mind."

"No, no, ma'am, no," he said, and pushed his shoulder into the door's frame to block her passage. Bel gently rested a hand on his shoulder and held him back just as forcefully as if he'd been leaning on the doorframe itself. The shock of her strength dislodged the rifle's sling off his shoulder. When the weight of the gun caught in the crook of his elbow, the champagne in the flutes sloshed up and splashed onto his jacket, shirt, and shoes. As he examined the damage, the door closed in his face.

"*Merde*," he said. Flustered, the guard looked for a place to set the flutes and what remained of the champagne. Spying an end table, he hiked the rifle back onto his shoulder, stepped quickly over and deposited the glasses, and then hurried back to the bathroom door. Moving fast, he planned to slow and knock, but just as he approached, the door opened, and the woman in the black dress grabbed a fistful of his shirt and used his own momentum to pull him inside.

Three minutes later, lipstick carefully reapplied, Lena and Bel stepped out of the bathroom, walked purposefully around the balcony to a hallway, and headed towards the office where their targets were meeting. All the doors might have delayed them. They would've heard and smelled the meeting's attendees behind the right one eventually, but the door flanked by two men was the clear winner. These two were more serious. They held their machine guns in their hands.

As Lena approached, she remembered following Matteo down the hall in The Venetian Hotel and Casino in Las Vegas only three months earlier, walking towards two similarly stationed guards outside the office belonging to Cassius, the one who had stolen her manuscripts. Those two guards hadn't been holding any weapons, but they'd been far more dangerous than these two. She'd been so nervous that day, terrified mostly about the danger to the werewolf pups, less so about the danger to the entire human race, least of all for herself. Now she walked down the hall towards the guards with a nonchalance she couldn't have imagined only three months ago. She was a very different kind of person.

The guard furthest away stepped around so the two men blocked the width of the hall. "This area is off limits," he said. The other tightened his grip on his rifle, edging the barrel towards them, making it clear he was preparing to aim without actually doing so..

Bel pointed back down the hall with such conviction that one of the guards looked over her shoulder. "They told us to come up here to provide some extra company. You can ask downstairs or ask the men inside." Then she made a show of translating this into English for Lena, which wasn't all for show since Lena really hadn't caught the French, but it gave the men one more complication to deal with.

Lena noted the way Bel kept giving guards multiple options to contemplate to keep them distracted. I'll have to remember that trick, she thought.

One guard looked to the other. "Do we interrupt or call downstairs?" he asked in French.

Bel turned to Lena. "He's asking if they should call

downstairs or interrupt the meeting."

"Oh," Lena said. Then, quicker than any human could move, she lunged forward and yanked the guns out of both men's hands. It happened so fast, they literally stared down at their open palms, mouths agape, and still hadn't looked up when Bel punched both simultaneously. She didn't jab with her nails extended the way she normally would have when intending to maim or kill, partly because she didn't want to be covered in blood (yet), but partly for Lena's sake. Still, she didn't pull her punches much.

A blow to the face must be pretty hard to render a human unconscious, and the same number of pounds of pressure can kill just as easily as knocking a person out. In the movies, the good guys always find that perfect balance, knocking out the guards when they want to in order to keep the audience on their side. In reality, the best way to make sure they didn't make any noise was to kill them. Bel hit both men so hard, one died immediately. The other managed to moan as he fell, so she crouched over his body and delivered a second blow, one that proved fatal as well.

She looked up at Lena and shrugged. "I tried."

Lena shrugged, too, bouncing the two seven-pound rifles in her hands like they were feathers. "I appreciate the effort." Using one toe, she removed one of her heels, then switched feet and removed the other so the shoes stood next to one another like the last sad pair of creatures waiting in line for Noah's ark. Then, as quickly as she snagged the guns, Lena sprinted down the hall to a door far enough away to be out of human earshot, turned the handle with enough force to pop the lock, and opened it. She dashed inside the bedroom without turning on the light, laid the rifles on the bed, and sprinted back, passing Bel who was already barefoot and fireman-carrying one body. Lena hoisted the other onto her shoulder and followed Bel. Once both guard's corpses were flopped down next to their rifles on the bed, the women picked up their heels, positioned themselves in front of the office door, and knocked gently.

"Yes?" a voice called.

Bel shoved the door open, and Lena stepped through, holding her heels up. "We're here!" she said in English. "They said you guys wanted us to come up to party."

Five people occupied the room. Elmer Madsen, the mansion's owner and party's host, sat behind a large desk in front of a wall-to-wall bookcase filled with antique books. Someone once told Bel he was more of a collector, less a reader. As a respected billionaire business tycoon, Madsen made his legal money from open pit mines that produced a lot of the rare earth metals needed for cell phones. He also pocketed gobs of illegal cash connecting criminals like the two sitting across from him. Ironically, illegal arms sales killed fewer people than his legitimate businesses. Elmer Madsen spent a ridiculous amount of that money on plastic surgery, dieticians, personal trainers, tailors, and hairdressers, so at sixty, he could pretend the two women reclining on the couch were interested in him because of his body and his good looks rather than his money.

The couch sat facing the desk on the other side of the room, separating Elmer's study and receiving area from his bedroom. A decorative table on the other side of the desk behind the couch held a crystal vase filled with fresh-cut flowers, replaced daily so they were the first things Elmer's overnight guests saw when leaving his bedroom in the morning. The women on the couch were not interested in Elmer's body, his good looks, of the flowers. They weren't specifically interested in his money, either. They were big fans of the drugs purchased with his money, and, at present, they were so loaded, they were only vaguely aware Lena and Bel had come into the room. For Elmer, these women were mostly decorative as well, and they were replaced frequently, though less regularly than the flowers.

Two men sat across from Elmer's desk in chairs between the desk and couch. These men were very aware of Lena and Bel. Leon Vogt was a former officer of the Stasi, the East German security services, and when the Berlin Wall fell, he'd left with enough truckloads of Russian Kalashnikov rifles to start multiple armed rebellions in Africa and the Middle East. He also had a well-known fetish for women's high heeled shoes, so he couldn't take his eyes off the pairs in Lena and Bel's hands.

Ayşe Kaplan was a representative of the Turkish secret service, and he'd been sent by Recep Tayyip Erdoğan to purchase off-the-books military equipment which would then be handed over to the Saudis who would use them to outfit American mercenaries to kill

Yemeni civilians. Then they would tell the American government they were not involved and continue to receive the American guns. The Saudis didn't mind the cost, especially if it repaired the relationship with Turkey's president and kept the Americans happy. The flood of cash meant Madsen stood to make a killing (by facilitating lots of killing) just by brokering the deal. But the deal was currently delayed by Kaplan's less well-known fetish for women's bare feet.

Vogt stared at the shoes. Kaplan stared at Lena's and Bel's feet. Madsen stared at the now closed door. "Where are …? What did my men tell you at the door? Who called for you?" He composed himself. "I don't mean to be rude. Of course, such lovely ladies are welcome, and you can see these gentlemen are both grateful for your arrival, but we take security here very seriously, so I must ask—"

"It's kind of a funny story," Bel interrupted. She walked between Vogt and Kaplan. She had to turn sideways to squeeze between the chairs facing Madsen's desk. She carefully set her shoes down on the desk. "You see, we didn't get sent up here by the staff, and the guards didn't seem happy about it, either."

"Nope," Lena agreed. "In fact, we didn't even receive a formal invitation." She walked around the desk and set her shoes in front of Madsen. Then she ran a fingernail gently up his chin, then tapped the end of his nose with her index finger. "I'm a little offended that you forgot us, frankly."

"But we were invited, in a way," Bel said. She turned

to the two women on the couch. "You two might want to leave for this part. Big, important secrets."

One of the women didn't seem to hear Bel at all. The other, who had been staring at the ceiling, snapped her head down and tilted it to the side. She spoke in English, but with a thick Russian accent. "Fuck you, bitch. We were here first. This is our party. Tell her, Elmer. These men are ours." She didn't mind Vogt and Kaplan sitting their backs to them, but she did not want to be turned out by these interlopers.

Bel looked at Lena. Lena shrugged. Then Bel looked at Madsen. "It's fine with us if they stay."

"Alright." He called over Bel's shoulder, "You girls can stay. It's fine." Then to Vogt and Kaplan, "It's fine if they all stay, right? The more the merrier."

The distracted men only nodded.

Madsen looked back at Lena, "But I still don't understand—"

"Actually, it was Mr. Vogt who got my attention first," Lena explained. She walked around Madsen's chair, running her nails gently over his shoulders as she passed behind him and rounded to Vogt's end of the desk. "I wanted to sit down with you and discuss your business dealings. You just seemed special to me, Mr. Vogt. A very clear, cut-and-dry case of 100% moral depravity. That's what I was looking for."

"Yes," Bel jumped in, "but then we found out you would all be here together."

Lena touched her hip against Vogt's arm, and it was almost enough to pull his eyes away from the shoes on the desk. "Yeah, you three are not the easiest people to meet with, and you aren't really the best host, Mr. Madsen."

"Oh, is the party not to your taste, Miss …?"

Lena ignored him. She had a line to get to. "Did you notice, Bel?"

"I couldn't help but notice, Lena."

Lena looked at Madsen. "You didn't offer us seats at the table, Elmer."

"Oh, I'm sorry. I can…" His voice trailed off, and he scowled, confused. There was no table for them to sit around.

"Do you know what they say, Mr. Vogt?" Lena asked.

For the first time, he tore his eyes away from the shoes. "What?" He didn't seem to be asking about what they say, specifically. It was more of a general question.

"They say, 'If you don't have a seat at the table…'" Lena leaned down and put her lips near Vogt's ear. "… 'you're the meal.'" Then she unhinged her jaw, retracted her human teeth, and extended the concentric rows of thin, hollow needle teeth. When she plunged her lips around his neck, the teeth went to work opening the tissue, and she drank.

Both Madsen and Kaplan shouted curses loosely related to gods they didn't believe in. Kaplan grabbed for the pistol in his shoulder holster and managed to get his hand around the grip before Bel sucked enough blood out of his neck to cause him to lose consciousness. Quieter and more controlled than her punches in the hall; if only heroes in movies could quickly drain blood from the bad guys they didn't want to kill, they could knock them out more effectively. Elmer yanked open the top drawer of his desk and pulled out his pistol. He chose to aim for Lena rather than Bel, perhaps because he'd seen her teeth before she bit Vogt.

This turned out to be a terrible choice for everyone in the room.

In his terror, he fired wildly. Lena saw the gun coming up from the desk and had plenty of time to move, so she'd seemingly vanished, leaping to his side faster than he could make his eyes move. Madsen's choice to aim for Lena did not work out well for Vogt. He was still alive, if only barely, and hadn't had time to slump over, when Madsen put the first bullets into his head, shoulder, and chest.

Another thing the movies often get wrong; bullets don't just stop when they've hit a target . So, as Madsen kept pulling the trigger, aiming at the space where Lena had been, he managed to put 19 of his 21 rounds into the two women on the couch behind Vogt, and five of those bullets had passed through Vogt and the back of his chair before hitting the women (and the couch behind them, and the decorative table behind the couch, and the wall behind the table, and the mirror in Madsen's bedroom on the other side of the wall…). The bullets hit the table behind the couch at just the right angle to cause it to buckle and collapse. The heavy vase with the cut flowers fell forward towards the couch first, splashing the dying women with one last insult as it bounced on the top of the couch, then flipped the other way and shattered in the doorway of Elmer's bedroom. So Madsen's choice to aim for Lena did not work out well for the two women on the couch.

Although Bel saw Lena had safely dodged out of the way, she felt absurdly protective. They had been in a relationship for only a few months, and Lena had been a vampire for about that long. She threw the unconscious body of Kaplan down and launched herself at Madsen. In her haste, she didn't save any of her meal for later. Kaplan's head hit the edge of Madsen's desk with about as much force as a human normally produces when splitting logs with an eight-pound maul, a trifle for Bel but certainly not what Kaplan would have wished for that morning while sipping his Turkish coffee.

Bel pounced on Madsen like a cat, her feet landing on his lap, her weight and momentum driving the chair back on its little wheels. Her nails punctured his shirt, the cartilage of his sternum, and his lungs beneath. Her teeth sank into his throat, but she didn't waste time drinking, just yanked her head back and ripped a chunk free, then leapt again so that she landed on her feet in front of him as his chair continued to slide back into the wall.

The gentle thunk of the chair's leather back against the bookcase, muted compared to the drama of Elmer's demise, was enough to knock a shelf askew. That one fell onto the next, a slightly louder thunk, just heavy-against-soft, and then the antique books rained down, clapping and plonking onto their deceased owner, his chair, and his hardwood floor in a cacophony that kept going on and on.

22

Madsen's choice to aim for Lena resulted in the sound of 21 gunshots, a crashing end table, a shattering vase, a breaking mirror, and the clatter of 64 heavy, decorative antique books falling onto a hardwood floor.

"How long before more security gets here?" Lena asked.

"Long enough. Longer than anyone in here will have a heartbeat, anyway, and then they get really hard to drink. Quick, you see if there's much left of Madsen, and I'll see if one of the women still has a pulse."

The two vampires went to work sucking as much as they could from the room's occupants, but Madsen had nearly bled out from his neck and chest wounds, and the girls were both nearly dead when Bel got to them. Madsen's imprecise aim had stopped Vogt's heart, as had Kaplan's brief encounter with the desk. Once the heart stopped beating, Lena and Bel had to suck and chew to get more blood, and it verged on the sensation of eating meat, something neither could stomach anymore. Plus, their vampire senses, perhaps due to some vestigial supernatural form of evolution, perhaps due to something deeper and more purely magical, rejected corpses as sources of food. As soon as the people died, both women felt waves of revulsion if they kept trying to feed.

Their super-sensitive ears picked up the clumping of heavy boots on the stairs and the carpeted hallway.

"Time's up," Bel said.

"Which way?"

"Sorry to ditch the Lambo, but we're going to have to

go out Elmer's balcony window, through the back yard, and out to the Boulevard d'Italie, then north into France, and—"

"I don't know the fucking street names yet, Bel!" Lena said, and she laughed. "Just lead the way and I'll follow you."

They sprinted into Madsen's bedroom. Lena stopped to look back when the broken mirror caught her eye. The myth about vampires not casting a reflection wasn't true. Since her transformation, she'd enjoyed dressing up with Bel and prepping in the mirror. It was one of the elements of hunting she liked most, like every meal came with a costume party. Now, seeing herself reflected in a broken mirror, with a distended jaw and rows of wriggling needles, she couldn't escape the idea that the bloody woman looking back at her was a broken version of her human self.

She pouted in the mirror, mad that the transformation hadn't altered her figure. In fact, she'd put on weight, regaining all she'd lost during her period of deep depression in Costa Rica and then some. She looked like the version of herself who had been doing all that emotional eating back when her only form of exercise was writing short stories to exchange for rejection letters in her failed writer days. She turned sideways and sucked in her stomach.

"We talked about this," Bel said. "It doesn't make you into what Madison Avenue says you should look like. It makes you look like the most seductive version of yourself. You need to get over the bullshit you were taught about how women are supposed to look and accept that this is the version humans will most easily be seduced by. Not twiggy, stick-figure Lena…" Bel wrapped an arm around Lena's waist and pulled her gently towards the window, "… but meat-on-her-bones, voluptuous Lena."

"Then why are you so skinny?"

"I put on a lot more weight when I changed than you did, Lena. I was a starving milkmaid on a medieval farm, remember? And I was glad to put on the weight. I understood that humans like a girl who looks like she isn't starving. It tricks their brains into thinking it means she's more ready to have babies. Beauty standards are really all about evolution and procreation and babies, babies, babies, Lena. Except some countries said, 'Keep 'em skinny so they are too fragile to run away, and we'll get more babies out of them,' and your fucked-up culture said, 'Keep 'em skinny and weak so they don't look like Black women who work all day.' Give it a few hundred years, and you'll get over all that fucked-up-ness they taught you."

Lena looked hard at Bel. "Really? I'll get over all of it?"

Bel shook her head. "No, probably not, but you'll certainly have a better chance to deal with body-image issues if we piss off right now and don't get caught by…" she paused and counted footsteps, "fourteen guys with machine guns. You haven't been shot yet. It won't kill you, but it hurts like … well, like getting shot, so let's avoid that."

She opened the sliding door to the balcony just as the men in the hall kicked in the office door. Lena watched and mimicked Bel leaping up onto the balcony railing, then dropping silently into the courtyard next to the pool. Before the men could run the twenty-five feet to the balcony, both women had raced around the pool and across the lawn, jumped over the hedge, scaled the wall, and were walking briskly up the Boulevard d'Italie while Bel called for an Uber on her phone.

As the couple stood in the darkness, waiting for the car to arrive, Bel took two wet-wipes out of her tiny purse and handed one to Lena so they could clean the blood off their faces. She tried to offer a generous smile, but something in the expression tipped Lena off that her girlfriend was disappointed. Adopting a teacher-student relationship with a romantic partner is complicated in any circumstance. Theirs was worse because Bel was, objectively, the cause for Lena's need to learn how to be a vampire. Oh, and there was the nearly eight-hundred-year age difference. It was weird.

Bel did her best to maintain her patience. She found Lena's desire to kill those she identified as deeply immoral immature. Humans were food. Bel didn't need to morally evaluate cattle back when she'd been human, and she'd learned not to morally evaluate humans as a vampire. But she recognized her girlfriend needed this justification to feed. She owed Lena this as recompense for turning her without her consent. It was just damned inconvenient.

"I'm sorry," Lena said, apologizing for her performance, not the real reason Bel was irritated.

"It's okay," Bel lied.

That's often how love sounds.

"We cannot solve problems with the kind of thinking we employed when we came up with them."

- Albert Einstein

Chapter 3

Tisina, Queen of the Sirens, Lord over all the Merfolk, Rider of the Leviathan, Ruler of the Depths and Heights of the Sea, struggled Not in the political sense, though her leadership was certainly in question now. Not in the emotional sense, either. Her feelings were always inscrutable to others, and she was frequently unsure of them herself. But today she felt a strikingly binary ambivalence, and she was comfortable with that. She wasn't struggling physically as she had during childbirth, though one could say she was struggling with the consequences of childbirth. Not the physical injuries caused by pushing a monster out of her womb. Those had been considerable, but she was, herself, a monster, and she healed with supernatural speed. Sometimes a person feels like the walls are crumbling all around them and they are doing everything they can to keep from being buried, but that's generally figurative. In Tisina's case, this was quite literal.

She sounded much as she had during childbirth, straining and pushing, but the tentacles which normally hid underneath the jellyfish bell masquerading as the skirt of her royal gown (which was, in fact, a part of her flesh) were splayed across her bedroom, holding up the walls. And the gorgon tentacles which pretended to be her hair pressed upwards, holding the ceiling in place. She was trapped between.

Tisina could only attempt to hold on a little longer.

There wasn't much left of the room to hold up. The once enormous space, so large it made even the huge four-poster bed in the center look like a dollhouse decoration, was now mostly filled with rubble. When two of the walls had buckled, they'd folded inward, crushing the bed entirely.

Tisina had been lucky to be awake and fretting about the noises outside her room when it happened, and she was an incredibly fast swimmer, able to balloon out her bell and tentacles, then snap them together and propel herself like a rocket. She'd launched from the center of her bed, darted around a huge chunk of falling wall, and made her way to the highest point in the vaulted ceiling.

When the third wall came down, the corner she hid in also collapsed, but she rode it down. Objects fall more slowly under the ocean, and she was able to reach out in every direction and guide some of the debris, heavy as it was. When the room's ceiling descended onto the rubble on the floor, she created a small space and kept it from collapsing.

At first, she reminded herself she was the queen, that a rescue would come promptly, that she just had to hold on for long enough and someone would pull one of the pieces of the ceiling away and set her free. It was only a matter of time.

Only it wasn't. Hours went by. She pushed and strained and sucked water in through her mouth and out through the gills along her jawline, ripping away every bit of oxygen she could get to her lungs and pumping it to the muscles all the way at the ends of her tentacles. She listened for the sounds of the expected rescue. Instead, she heard a nightmare.

Her city, the capital of the Merfolk, was located at the top of an undersea mountain, one that would have been a part of the Mariana Islands if it broke the ocean's surface. This gave the residents a home filled with sea life and the light and warmth of the sun, but close enough to the Mariana Trench that they could hide there from humans if they were ever in need. But now Tisina knew they would never have to abandon the city because of humans. The merpeople, her people, those who counted on her leadership and who she was entrusted to protect, were screaming and dying on the other side of the walls she held up, but there were no humans involved.

The cracks in the walls provided her with enough moving seawater that she didn't deoxygenate it and suffocate herself, but those same cracks let in the sounds of devastation, the crashing buildings, the terrified wails, the keening of the injured, and, above it all, the roars of the monster, like the bellows of a bear but shouted underwater and multiplied a thousand times as they came out of every one of the creature's ever-increasing number of mouths.

Tisina wondered how many mouths it had now. And she decided it needed a name. It was her child, after all. She had the right to give it a name, even if the creature would never know it, never answer to it, never even hear it if the walls collapsed around her. She had the right to give her child a name even if that name would only live in her head and die with her. She wanted something grand enough for the rightful heir to the throne of all Merfolk, but also something that would fit a creature who killed its older twin while he was suckling at his mother's breast, a creature who immediately fled from its mother to chase down a fleeing handmaiden, then slaughtered everyone it could find in the palace as it grew and grew and grew.

Tisina remembered her handmaiden's last desperate attempt to flee the room. Oh, my sweet Devushka, she thought. Perhaps you saved my life by drawing it away. And maybe that was no mercy. What would you have wanted me to name such a child? If it had a name, you would have fallen before it and pled for your life. It would not have slowed my child. Not this monster, created in this way, for this purpose. Whatever name you would have screamed and prayed and whispered in your last seconds, that is the fitting name for such a great king of all Merfolk.

Tisina thought of all the languages she knew, human and monster. She ran through possible words, translating them, while she listened to an orchestra of carnage. She organized the languages alphabetically using the proto-Cyrillic alphabet the Merfolk had used before they were first banished to the sea millennia ago. She'd think of a word, then run it through a thousand languages. She didn't know all of them well enough to remember each translation, but she needed something to occupy her time while she held the walls in place. With each new translation, she would take three quick gulps of breath, then say the next word, like an ever-changing mantra.

A silence fell outside. The wailing and crying persisted, and pieces of buildings continued to fall, rumbling the seabed with each mini-quake. But the roaring ceased, and it was only in its wake Tisina realized how loud it had been. The pieces of stone she held up had been vibrating with it, and now they stilled. She knew two things immediately. This was her last chance to save herself. And she knew her child's name.

She tested the walls, pressing outwards with her lower tentacles, first more on one side, then another, then a third, until she found the wall that most wanted to fall outwards and the two wanting to fall in. She ran the tentacles on her head along the lip of the ceiling closest to the wall that wanted to fall outward, the east wall, and she found enough purchase for the tiny tips of those smaller tentacles to worm their way into the cracks. She took three quick gulps of breath. Then three more. The last she held in her cheeks, a sight that would have been comical if anyone could see her. She counted to three, forced the water in her mouth out through her gills, and heaved, pressing against the east wall and letting what remained of the others fall inwards. As they did, Tisina lifted the piece of ceiling sufficiently so the tentacles on her head reached into the growing gap. Then she yanked herself upwards while her lower tentacles shoved the ceiling back. It was just enough space, and her bell convulsed to launch her through.

The stone walls crumbled in behind her. A blinding pain lanced her as rocks smashed two of her tentacles. One was caught between two slabs, but the other was severed almost completely, the pain excruciating.

She was almost free, and almost free is worse. In a rage, she spun and wrapped her hands around the healthy portion of the trapped tentacle. Her other appendages—both those below and those from her head—snaked themselves around her wrists and forearms. She yanked, felt her flesh tearing, not cleanly or quickly, but in slow, ragged starts, like some complex tapestry being rudely rent. Blood, like smoke, wafted around her from the new wound and from her first severed tentacle which could only dance to the rhythm of her straining.

She wrenched the second tentacle free and saw pieces of her own meat float away from the tip of the severed limb. Her eyes stung with a vestigial pain, reminding her of an epoch when her ancestors' only ocean was in their tears.

She forced her face into a calm composure. She was, after all, the queen. The people, if any remained, needed to see her unfazed.

Her lower tentacles spiraled on the remains of her palace, and so she gracefully turned to survey the remains of her city. When she came almost fully around, she looked up at her child and fought off the urge to embody the worst stereotype of her species. She refused to gape like a fish.

The enormity of the creature boggled Tisina's mind. Roughly spherical, its exterior was covered in a mass of writhing tentacles. How big was the body beneath those tentacles? Tisina wondered. Two hundred feet in diameter? Three hundred? No, on closer inspection she realized those weren't tentacles growing out of some planet-shaped body. The tentacles *were* the body. It was all tentacles looping and sliding over one another, a Siphonophore of distinct organisms.

Each tentacle undulated, calm now, not attacking or thrashing. Each tentacle ended in a fine-pointed bulge shaped like a barb, But Tisinia had seen what these really were. Each could bisect and snap, like claws. And inside each claw hid a mouth waiting to swallow whatever it could cut off. The closed claws also functioned like eyelids, the open mouths smelling the water and serving as sense organs. Tisina hoped the claws or tentacles also contained some kind of tympanic membranes. She wanted her child to hear her, if only for the last time.

Though she could swim with great speed and agility, she had to aim head-first when she did so. Now she wanted to present herself with as much regal grace as she could muster. Walking like an octopus on the ocean floor, she let her tentacles leap-frog one another and pull her along while she seemed to float—back straight, chin slightly up—across the ruins of her palace and into the central thoroughfare which aimed her directly at the creature.

As she carried herself down the street, she saw merpeople out of the corners of her eyes. Most were corpses, or so injured they soon would be. She passed smaller buildings which had been spared and saw some of her soldiers hiding inside. They kept their backs to the walls protecting them from the creature, their tridents held in front of them like bouquets or votives or their own dicks. Cowards, Tisina thought. What real soldier would choose to live while their country lay in ruins?

As she passed, some looked down, others beckoned to her with rough gestures, and a few swam out to form a phalanx behind her. These gave others courage, and the group grew. Tisina didn't look back at them. She hated them all. An army of cowards hiding behind their queen, pretending to be led into battle after they'd already hidden while the battle was lost. If she'd turned to look at them, she would have spit, another vestigial human gesture which was more potent for the Merfolk. It meant, "I shouldn't have to breathe the same water you live in."

Sharks and other carrion feeders prowled the city's streets. When they smelled the blood trailing behind Tisina from her two severed tentacles, they left off the corpses they'd found and began to follow, hoping to incapacitate her. The corpses weren't going anywhere. A particularly brave Great White, large for a male at 13 feet but smaller than the 16-foot females wending their way through the city, circled once at a ten-foot radius, then lunged at her bleeding tentacles. Tisina didn't slow her stride. One of her larger, lower tentacles shot out like lightning and wrapped around the shark, just behind its eyes, then squeezed and wrenched. The whole front of the shark's face tore free. Tisina kept sauntering forward. The other sharks fell on the corpse of the decapitated male, and the soldiers following Tisina gave the bloody feast a wide berth, shouldering along the buildings on either side of the road before falling in behind her again.

Two more small fish darted up and pecked at Tisina's wounds. For a moment, she let them. The tiny nibbles were ticklish. But one hit a nerve and made her wince. She grabbed both fish and broke their backs, then flung them behind her. No other life bothered her on the rest of the slow trek toward her child.

The creature floated above Tisina like some obscene copy of a heavenly body falling from orbit, then halting, suspended fifty feet from the ocean floor. Tisina calculated by the angle of her head. Tisina understood optics and power dynamics. She knew she would need to look up at the thing, but she didn't want to be shouting at its underside from directly below. When she was less than a hundred feet away and where she looked up 45 degrees into the center of the thing's bulk, she stopped. To her surprise, a few of the soldiers swam parallel to her and aimed their tridents at the monster. She considered telling the Merfolk to lay down their weapons, then decided to ignore them. They were beneath her contempt, and if the creature decided they were a threat and killed them all, that was acceptable. She just wanted a tiny bit of time to speak.

Tisina opened her mouth. Not the small one on her face used for polite conversation, but the one she hid just beneath her ribcage.

"I am Tisina," she shouted with this grotesque maw. Her subjects rarely heard her speak and never heard her call out in an elevated voice. She was famous for her silence. And most never saw her eat, though they knew sirens kept similar mouths hidden in the same place as gorgons. But now Tisina needed every decibel of power she could muster. When the soldiers started at the sound and sight of her, her shoulders and head thrown back at an inhuman angle, sound roaring out of her abdomen, Tisina knew she'd found the right volume.

"I am Queen of the Sirens, Lord over all the Merfolk, Rider of the Leviathan, Ruler of the Depths and Heights of the Sea, and I am your mother. I command you to hear me!"

It did. A thousand tentacles sprang to life. Claws lanced towards her, then stopped. They opened, and the mouths inside gaped. Whether this was to improve hearing or expedite feeding, she couldn't tell, but she felt compelled to hurry.

"I surrender my city to you. All my true subjects would lay down their lives and the lives of their children to serve me, and I give them to you as a sacrifice. Take all of us who remain if you wish, but then go."

She pointed an arm out like a weather vane, directly east. The direction wasn't really important to her. She had targets in mind, but they were all around them. "Go and do what you were born to do. Fulfill your calling. Attack the surface dwellers and kill anyone in your path. Spare only those who bow down and worship you as a god, and even these you may kill at your leisure. Feast until you have eaten all you want and have grown as large as you can. For I am your mother, Tisina, Queen of the Sirens, Lord over all the Merfolk, Rider of the Leviathan, Ruler of the Depths and Heights of the Sea, and it is my right to command you and give you your name. I name you Lord Varr, The Grave that Devours, Prince of the Merfolk, The Destroyer of Humans, The Swimming Apocalypse. Go!"

As she shouted, she pointed firmly again. "Go and bring with you the final ruin as I have planned, the extermination of humanity all Merfolk have dreamt about for generations. I, Tisina, have given you life and a name and a purpose. Now go, Lord Varr, and end their world!"

Despite her confidence she'd spoken every word exactly as planned, Tisina was a bit surprised when her child heard and obeyed. The claws twisted and aimed to the east, and then, one by one, they flicked backwards, some as large as the towers on her palace, propelling the mass away and creating such a strong current in its wake that Tisina's own lower tentacles had to flatten against the cobbled street and hold on while her head tentacles were pushed uselessly to the west. Behind her, the soldiers leaned into the current and kicked their powerful tails to hold their positions, their gleaming scales flashing in the dim glow of the noonday sun.

As Lord Varr swam away, Tisina turned to address her subjects. The flashing of their tails camouflaged another glint of light. The trident struck her in the abdomen. Positioned vertically, all three tines pierced her torso, pinning the mouth there closed. She looked down at the hilt of the spear, her face wearing an unusually clear expression of utter incomprehension. When the soldier charged at her, its powerful tail rippling, she didn't look up at first, but her tentacles grabbed for him just as they had the Great White. Only he'd seen that and was ready.

The knife in his hand lopped off both the tentacles that came for him in one stroke. When the pain hit Tisina's brain, her head snapped up to face him. By then he was on her, grabbing the trident's hilt and pushing her back and down. She made a last effort and wrapped a tentacle around his tail, trying to yank him away, but he angled the spear sharply so her effort only gave him more leverage. He bucked against her remaining tentacles using all the might his tail possessed. His strength lifted her off the street for a moment, then drove her onto her back. The trident's tines wedged into the spaces between the cobblestones like a climber's pitons, pinning Tisina. Exhausted, she loosened her grip on the soldier's tail and waited for him to come at her with the knife.

He didn't. Instead, he used his hands to swirl around and see which soldier would attack him in return. Tisina looked at the soldier, then lifted her head as far as the trident would allow and scanned the others.

No one moved.

A soldier near the front gave a quick nod.

Another made a show of pulling his trident away and aiming it back toward the ruined palace.

Then, one by one, the Merfolk swam off to tend to their wounded.

But Tisina was not left alone. She watched the soldiers swim away, their tails sparkling, until the school became a blur on the dark street, then disappeared in the ever-present darkness of the depths. She didn't know the name of the soldier who had betrayed her, the treacherous assassin who had dared to strike down his queen. But she understood. She'd declared them all forfeit to her son, sentenced them all to be sacrifices, and when Lord Varr had spared them, one rose up. She was surprised, but not shocked. More than anything, she was offended. While the assassination seemed justified, Tisina felt they owed her a clean death, not this dismissive abandonment, pinned to the street of her own city while these lowly soldiers swam off to recover whatever members of their peasant families lingered in the rubble. She was the queen. Killing her should have been the highest priority.

It was too dark to identify the shadows of the sharks circling above her, but she knew they were there. Some would come at her from above, but others would attack from the sides. She could not fight them all, could not intimidate them once the feeding frenzy began.

She was trapped. Tisina could only attempt to hold on a little longer.

"Evil people always support each other; that is their chief strength."

- Aleksandr Solzhenitsyn

Chapter 4

For hundreds of years, The Convention held its annual meeting to choose leadership, approve bylaws, make resolutions, and identify policies it would implement the next year. Despite being populated by monsters, the organization obeyed the same universal forces that compel all institutions. It got organized. It built bureaucracy. It elevated those who could most effectively navigate that bureaucracy. Seemingly isolated events became traditions which became laws.

And then, last year, it blew up. To be more specific, in the middle of the annual meeting, a human tried to assassinate a vampire who was presenting a new business item, a giant luck dragon tore up the place and then flew away through the ceiling, and the perpetrators escaped. In the ensuing chaos, The Convention could not complete its business. Everything was a mess.

Some organizations have contingency plans for specific scenarios. For example, though it didn't address attacks by dragons specifically, The Convention did have policies in place allowing the current elected officials to remain in office for an extended term in extreme circumstances where elections were prevented by events outside of their control. The Convention still had individuals in charge and a clear order of succession to maintain the power structure. But it didn't have any document that said, "If everything really goes tits up, maybe step back and take a breath and figure out if an organization of supernatural monsters even makes sense anymore." Institutions rarely, if ever, have plans for their own dissolution. The underlying principle of every living thing is: "Continue existing," and institutions, as collective expressions of their constituents' wills, always fall back on this same principle at their core.

So, even without clear direction about what they ought to accomplish before the next annual meeting, the various dignitaries, elected officials, and bureaucrats of The Convention scheduled the same planning meetings they'd held the year before, and each division of the organization hoped some other would get their shit together and tell them what to do. The largest burden of these expectations fell on CimBim, the Convention Inquisition of Major Breaches and Minor Infractions, the judge, jury, and executioner of violations of The

Convention's central document (confusingly also called "The Convention"). Clearly, someone had fucked up, so the monsters assumed the group most able to right the ship would be the one responsible for dishing out punishments. Of course, anyone who has ever interacted with any group in charge of punishing people knows those are the last people who should be in charge of a response to a crisis. Punishment is inherently backwards looking. But punishment requires authority, so the punishers are often mistaken for people who can take charge and solve problems. Cassius was the perfect example of this error.

There are some men (mostly men) who believe denying their own luck makes them deserving of the benefits of their luck. This not only puffs them up; it allows them to look down on everyone else who isn't born as lucky while these men do everything they can to make sure no one else has access to the benefits luck has brought them. Cassius was such a man, only after almost a millennium of privilege, his star of self-regard had grown to the brightness of a super-giant, and his opinion of all other beings, human and monster alike, had shrunk to a burnt little asteroid which couldn't be spotted in an ecliptical position without losing one's sight.

For such men, any setback is an existential threat, no matter how small, because it strikes at the conceit that all successes are deserved. For a nearly thousand-year-old vampire, this impulse was proportionally magnified. When multiplied by a situation as truly disastrous as the complete cock-up that was last year's convention, his fear-fueled rage was sustained and terrifying.

To make matters worse, he'd lost a lot of his staff. Three of his crew had been blown up in Costa Rica trying to recover Lena's first book. He'd managed to acquire the book with the help of the imp Apraxis, and then his longtime personal assistant, Mildred, leapt out a window and burned in the Las Vegas sun after reading Lena's sequel. When Lena came to steal her books back, two of Cassius' oldest and most faithful guards had been ripped apart by werewolves right in front of his office. Even his new temp hire, Ann, the office assistant who'd seemed promising, had also fallen out a window. Cassius mistakenly believed she'd at least managed to take a werewolf with her. Most frustrating, Cassius' best operatives, Nando and Bel, had been missing for more than a year, and then Bel had shown up just in time to help some human, Esau, shoot Cassius on the floor of The Convention in front of everybody who mattered. For a vampire, being successfully shot by anyone was mildly embarrassing, and to have a human get away with it in front of the people Cassius most respected was positively mortifying.

Cassius didn't have enough people to yell at to make him feel better. Instead, when people called him for direction, he had to placate them, convince them he would handle everything, and simultaneously enlist their help so he had enough people-power to do the work, all while figuring out what that work was going to be. He had no master plan, since everything had gone so spectacularly pear-shaped. But now things seemed to be coming together bit by bit.

First, he wanted to get his hands on Lena's books

again. They were still the two giant pieces left on the board: a book that could incapacitate, derange, or kill any human who read it; and a sequel that could do the same to any monster. Of course, the testing of the first novel had been incomplete. Cassius had seen the reports of the human trials, and the efficacy rates had been very high, but footnotes pointed out the weapon had only been tested on middle-class and wealthy white men. Still, Cassius felt certain eliminating this group, the group of humans he'd once been a part of himself, would reduce the rest of the human population to the stone age in short order.

Lena's sequel hadn't been tested much at all. It had been discovered by accident when Mildred thought she was making copies of the first manuscript, read it, and leapt to her death. To Cassius, the effectiveness of both books was a secondary concern. He didn't need his nuclear bombs to work. He just needed everyone to know he had them and they might work. That would be enough to give him empire-building power in The Convention.

Of course, creating the first book had been the boondoggle that had gotten the necromancer, Nigel Marion, the most powerful werewolf Apocalumus Kreshnik, and the vaunted Pictish warlock Erdogan Ueda killed. Cassius had already invested most of his people in finding, acquiring, and losing the books. Having his nuclear options would be nice, but he didn't want to sacrifice himself to find them again. And while he was pretty sure he was the hottest shit in existence, he knew he was no match for a dragon. So he'd called up his CimBim counterpart in the Asia region to get some help with his dragon problem.

"Yes, I understand you're upset," Cassius said into his cellphone, and he leaned back in his chair and put his very expensive shoes up on his desk to console himself that he was still in control despite the fact that he was as close to apologizing and groveling as a man like Cassius can get. "I'm pissed, too. But it was a dragon. A mother-fucking dragon, Larry! You know the security protocols we have in place at The Convention. We're ready for a lot of things, but not a dragon going ape-shit and smashing up everything."

Ryou-Ryou Daiō's deep, resonant voice came clearly through the phone. It was accompanied by a constant crackle easily mistaken for static. In fact, the yokai was standing in his own office, a large room which looked like a carefully manicured Japanese garden with a pond in the middle, except the pond was on fire and he paced on its surface amidst three feet of crackling flames. King Ryou-Ryou was not happy. He was a spirit ogre with the responsibility to rule over other spirits and crush them with a magical iron club when they got out of line, so he was accustomed to being irritated and experienced at channeling that irritation into brutal action. Cassius was right to be wary of him and take his calls. "I get that, Cassius. Dragons are above my pay grade, too. I've had my people looking to identify him, and we're fairly certain he's a Chinese luck dragon who goes by the name Lóng … which might be his idea of a joke because it just means 'Dragon' in Mandarin."

Cassius detected some complicated tension in Ryou-

Ryou Daiō's voice when he said "Mandarin." Those who prefer to speak Japanese and those who prefer Mandarin have a complicated history filled with legitimate grievance, reluctant interdependence, and competing senses of superiority. This history's attendant feelings are magnified when the beings involved have experienced much or all that history since their conflicting narratives' origins of the world. Also, yokai don't like spirits they can't control, and dragons sometimes prey upon yokai, though not consistently.

Ryou-Ryou Daiō resented that he had to work with the dragons in the Asian delegation at all, and he was now embarrassed that monsters from the other five regions might associate him with the dragon who wrecked last year's convention. He wanted the dragon held accountable by CimBim even more than Cassius did. "The rumor is that he used to live in the Hengduan Mountains, then spent most of his time in his human form in Hong Kong, but some of my sources say he may have been further south, maybe even as far as Laos or Cambodia. It's a lot of ground to cover, but we're looking for him. I'll take care of the Lóng problem. He probably isn't part of some master plan related to your books. Or maybe he is, but if so, his plan is much longer-term than anything a group of humans and vampires cooked up. No offense."

"None taken, Larry," Cassius lied. Ryou-Ryou Daiō's name best translated to "King Larry" in English. Ryou-Ryou allowed Cassius to call him Larry because he felt it polite to let an interlocutor speak to him in his own language. Cassius could speak passable Japanese and could have called Ryou-Ryou Daiō by his real name and title, but Cassius thought King Larry sounded stupid in English, and Cassius was the kind of person who liked to dictate other people's names to make himself feel superior.

"I'm not saying vampires don't have longer-term plans than humans," Ryou-Ryou Daiō mused, sounding more academic than defensive. He was the kind of person who could tolerate some insolence from lesser men as long as both of them knew Ryou-Ryou Daiō could bash the other man's head in with an iron club if he felt like it. "I'm just saying dragons do things for reasons the rest of us don't understand, yokai included. Who knows why Lóng attacked The Convention? It might have nothing to do with Nigel Marion's NBI and the books you're looking for. Maybe he just thought it sounded like fun. Maybe he sees time backwards. That's some people's theory about dragons. I don't know. They aren't just petty mischief-makers like the gremlins or slightly more complex chaos agents like the trolls. I deal with oni like those yahoos all the time, but the dragons are ... they're different. It's best not to try too hard to understand them. Because, let's face it, Cassius: You have a bigger problem."

"Bigger than a sixty-foot-long luck dragon smashing everything at The Convention?"

"Not literally bigger. More consequential," Ryou-Ryou Daiō said. He smiled at his concession, and even over the phone Cassius could hear that smile. Vampires don't get the chills very often, but the sound of a smile spreading that far around a creature's head was unnerving. Sure, Cassius could unhinge his jaw and open his mouth to an inhuman size when feeding. Vampires were creatures of the supernatural, their physiology not limited to nor dictated by evolution. But they were made of solid stuff, even if that matter did things matter shouldn't. In contrast, Larry's dark red, almost purple skin wasn't matter in any way Cassius could understand. The yokai could not only stretch his mouth from ear to ear, he could move that mouth around his body's surface if he wanted, or cover his body in little mouths, or make extra eyes appear, or stretch out its limbs in strange, liquid ways, or turn into smoke or slime. Cassius found Larry's yokai-ness too disturbing to think about, and Cassius had been drinking the blood of live human prey for the last thousand years, so that was really saying something.

"You mean the books." Cassius didn't inflect his voice because he was sure he was correct.

"No, not the books." Larry shook his head as he paced on his pond of flames. "I must admit, Cassius, sometimes you vampires sound very much like humans, and I must remind myself you're only few millennia old. Your obsessions with magical weapons. Your secret spells. Your plans to backstab one another to rise up in the ranks."

Cassius almost laughed. "What are you talking about, Larry? You do the exact same thing! You knocked out how many other lords and earls and kings to get where you're at?"

"Yes, and sometimes I even used a magic weapon to do it. But do you know what I needed to do before I got to use whatever magic weapon to cut down the people who stood in my way? First, I needed to be in the room. I had to play the part, bow low enough to the right people and not too low to the wrong people, get next to the target at just the right time, and then put the knife in his back. And if it had to be a magic knife, fine, fuck it, I found the right magic knife. But I had to make sure that when I pulled the knife out, the people left standing respected and honored and feared me. Meanwhile, you vampires just kick in the door, rip your enemy's head off, and wonder why the next guy is going to do the same thing to you in only 80 or 90 years. Look around you, Cassius. You're worried about some magic books. You think, if you have them, people will respect you. Meanwhile, your own spawn helped a human shoot you in the face in front of everybody. A human. A human shot you in the face."

If Cassius could have blushed, his face would have been beet red. And he would have masked it as a flush of rage because he was the kind of man who converts shame into anger and then violence quickly enough to convince himself he never felt shame in the first place. Only he couldn't lash out at Ryou-Ryou Daiō because A) they were on a long distance phone call, B) Ryou-Ryou Daiō was in his hall of judgment in his own pocket dimension where people were only allowed by invitation (mostly misbehaving oni about to get their heads smashed in), and C) Ryou-Ryou Daiō was his peer in rank in CimBim, and Cassius had called the guy for help. So, he filed away his rage, but he would never forget it, hoping someday to have an opportunity to hurt Ryou-

Ryou Daiō physically or humiliate him because that's how people like Cassius process embarrassment. For now, he swallowed it. "I know. What do you suggest?"

"Forget the books. They aren't your main priority. And forget the dragon. I'll deal with him here if I can find him. Focus on finding your spawn, her human girlfriend, and the human who shot you."

"So your advice is to become obsessed with revenge?"

"Yes! We're not Buddhist monks, Cassius. We're monsters! Find them, capture them, and then make sure there's a large audience when you rip them apart in the scariest way you can imagine so everyone watching remembers you are not to be fucked with for the next thousand years. I know it's more of a style thing, but I suggest getting a big iron club." Ryou-Ryou Daiō kept his phone to his ear with his left hand, brought up his club with his right, and smashed it down on the surface of the flaming pond again and again, sending out giant splashes of fire. "Smash! Their fucking! Skulls! To paste!" He calmed and began pacing once again. "And the audience part is important. If your spawn loves this human, make her watch while you kill the human first. Or the other way around. And make sure your other rivals are there to hear them scream. The pageantry matters, Cassius. Make it a big production number." He swept his iron club around at the hall Cassius couldn't see through the phone. "A nice backdrop. Costumes. Masks are cool. I can make my face look like just about anything, and I'll still put on a scary mask from time to time. Then take it off to reveal an even scarier face. It adds some nice panache."

"Fine," Cassius said. "Good plan. I like it." He hated admitting this, so he ran ahead. "But last time I hired an outside consultant, an imp named Apraxis, to help me find and kidnap someone, the results were mixed. Who would you recommend to locate Bel and her Lena and this Esau guy?"

"Well, there are a number of monsters you could turn to, but consider this idea: This Esau human fancies himself a professional monster hunter, right? Maybe you can enlist him to hunt some monsters for you, and then, when he delivers them, you have all three."

"Your advice is that I should hire the guy who shot me in the face to find the women who helped him shoot me in the face?"

"Probably best if he doesn't know he's working for you. Who does he work for?"

"Hell if I know, Larry."

"Well, do some research. It's not like you lack resources. And you don't need to sleep. Trust me, this would not be the first time monster hunters worked for monsters. Capitalism is a monster's best friend."

"I am more than what others want of me. I am more than what society expects of me. I will not let my life be defined by a box meant to hold me down."

- Trixi Anne Agiao, writing as The Thoughtful Beast

Chapter 5

The train cut through the French countryside at a speed Lena would once have found very impressive, less so now that she could now run about half as fast as the train from Monaco to Paris which moved at over 100 kilometers per hour. Lena couldn't run as fast as Bel and didn't think she ever would be able to. It wasn't a matter of training but something intrinsic and mystical and maybe genetic; Bel was just the faster of the two of them. When Lena learned she could run a bit faster than the greatest human sprinter, could sustain that top speed for longer than the greatest human marathon runner, and didn't need to breathe or sweat while doing so, cars and trains and even planes lost a bit of their luster. She still needed them to get around. Though she could run for the 19 hours it would have taken her to get from Monaco to Paris, she couldn't fit 19 hours into the protection of night, so a red-eye and a reservation for a safely darkened hotel room were necessary.

She found the view out the train's window much sweeter than her previous train trip through France, when she'd been a human heading from London to Paris to confront a necromancer who had stolen her book. Then, she was too terrified to enjoy the scenery. Now she chided herself. It would have been wiser to absorb beauty out of desperation. Why hadn't she seen the view from that train window as a kind of last meal for her eyes, savored it, memorized it? She could barely remember the trip now. Had it been morning or evening? she wondered. What had the sunlight looked like? What a shame humans can see so little and are too afraid to hold on to the little they can see. Now Lena could pick out the rows of grapes in the moonlight, the soil beneath them clearly beige to her eyes and not the shadow in shadow a human would have seen, the spring leaves bright green, the moon's reflection a haunting silver, each row a flicker of a fan blade relative to the speeding train but caught by her vampire eyes like a child studying the fan on a boring hot summer's day. She wished she could open the window and stick her head out like a happy dog in a car, inhale the smell of the fields rushing by, enjoy the smell of the grapes in a way she never could have as a human. Perhaps she would even open her mouth and stick out her tongue, catching the taste of the pollen in the air. She smiled and almost laughed aloud at the vision of herself, a seeming-human hanging her head out of the train window like a dog after she'd punched a hole in the window, the other passengers screaming and Bel hissing, "What the fuck do you think you're doing?"

But then Lena imagined the taste of the wind, and her stomach turned. Any taste, particles of diesel and oil from the roads, even the hint of the future wine that would come from those tart little red grapes, made her stomach turn. All tastes fell into two categories now. There were things she had to identify, to stomach no matter how revolting in order to find her way to human blood. And then blood, the only thing she wanted to drink.

Even the taste of Bel's skin was diminished. As a human, there were so many tastes she'd liked, and licking a beautiful woman's skin turned her on. The taste was so closely associated with pleasure. Now, when her tongue touched Bel's skin, it was a gift to Bel and an exchange for the joy Lena took in Bel's pleasure, but the taste was not the same immediate reward it had been. This hadn't adversely affected their sex life, at least not measured by frequency or intensity, but Lena admitted it was different, and she mourned that slight change. There were so many tiny changes to mourn, and the euphoria of the taste of human blood could not fill all the small sadnesses. Lena continued looking out the window, but she leaned her head on Bel's shoulder.

Bel turned away from the book she was reading and pressed her cheek against the top of Lena's head. "Hey," she whispered. "What was that?"

"What was what?"

"Something amused you, and then you got sad. What are you thinking about?"

Lena smiled. "I thought you might be irritated with me if I punched a hole in the window and stuck my head out to smell the wind." Then she scowled. "And then I thought the smell would make me sick anyway. And that made me sad. Weird, huh? To miss the taste of diesel exhaust in the air, a taste I wouldn't have noticed or even been able to identify, and now I can and feel sad that I can't enjoy it?"

Bel kissed the top of Lena's head. "Yes, you're weird. And I love you. And I'm sorry."

"Love you, too. And you don't have to be sorry. I don't blame you." Lena said these words and wanted them to be as true as she tried to make them sound.

"Okay," Bel said, and she wanted that to be true, also.

"So," Lena announced, sitting up and looking at Bel, "please explain why we are risking letting Cassius know where we are by taking a job for CimBim when we know he's high up in CimBim? Because that sounds really unwise to me."

"First, I've only been in touch with The Archduke, and he hates Cassius, so I'm not too worried about him telling Cassius which subcontractors he hired to do a job in the Archduke's territory. Still, there's always a risk.

We could just lay low and not do any CimBim work until things blow over with Cassius. But that's how long? A decade? A century? A girl's gotta work."

"Technically, no she doesn't. A girl is loaded because of 700 years of compound interest. She does not have to do anything."

"Okay, but a girl has to have some fun. And you have to keep training. The witches said I had to get you ready for some … something that's coming. But we don't know what it is or when, so I want you to be the best fighter I can make you in the shortest time possible. Again, is that a decade? A century? Who knows? Damned witches. Could have been a spot more specific."

"Okay, but why CimBim jobs? Why not more jobs like Monaco?"

"Monaco wasn't really a job. Not for money. I just picked out a really bad human because I know you prefer them that way. That was a meal, and not even a good one. We made a mess of it, and we didn't get to drink them all dry because we allowed them to get wounded first. Also, they were all humans. That's good training for dealing with humans, but if you're going to be even better, you need to start going up against monsters. Some will be faster than humans. Some will be stronger. Some will heal as fast as you do, maybe faster."

Lena raised her eyebrows, then frowned. "Am I ready for that?"

"Nope!" Bel laughed. "But we're going to start off easy, and then you'll get better and better. The next job is just one sad, pretty pathetic monster." She reached down into her backpack and pulled out her laptop. "And also, this is our mess to clean up."

Ludwig didn't know much when he woke up. For one thing, he didn't know his name had been Ludwig.

He didn't open his eyes because he didn't have any. Instead, he became aware that he could see. Bones. That was all he could see. Bones in darkness. Human bones. Under him, on him, all around him. He was buried in human bones.

His first impulse was a normal human reaction to such a situation. He panicked. He tried to flail and shake them off. That's when Ludwig learned he didn't have a complete body. This did not help him calm down.

He bucked his head and shook his shoulders and ribcage. He couldn't feel his arms or legs. He wanted to scream, but he couldn't draw breath. He didn't feel any pain in his lungs from the absence of breath because … he didn't have lungs. He stopped struggling and took inventory. He had no lungs, no beating heart, no stomach muscles to tighten in his fear, no testicles constricting up into his scrotum because he had no scrotum. He had no flesh he could feel. But somehow he knew he *did* have arms and legs. They just weren't properly attached. He could identify them in just the way he'd once been able to feel the locations of his hands even when they weren't touching anything. And somehow, he knew they were nearby. He just wasn't absolutely positive of their locations.

He started panicking again, but this time he was thinking about his arms and legs, so when he started flailing, he noticed their movement. One pile of bones near his face was quivering in the darkness. Where was the light coming from? Ludwig wasn't seeing them because of any light bouncing off them, through his pupils, into his lenses, then flipped by his brain and read like a map. The bones did not have light sides and dark sides, no shadows. They had solidity, rough surfaces he could feel like braille, but from a distance. It was radar, he deduced. Or echolocation, like bats.

What was radar? he wondered. What were bats? How did he know of such things and not know his own name or location or how he came to be there?

Time was also moving strangely. How long had it been since he'd awakened? An hour? Days? When he shook and the piles shook with him, it didn't seem they were moving quickly. If he could really get hopping, a bone might roll on the pile or be tossed into the air, and he could watch it fall. If anything, it seemed to fall slowly, so he knew he was able to observe things more quickly than … than what? Than before? When he'd had eyes? Yes, he realized, at some point he'd had eyes! And lungs! And testicles! And his arms and legs had been attached. What had happened? He guessed it was *ein schreckliches ereignis*. A terrible event of some kind. He was thinking in German, but Ludwig didn't know that.

But time could also pass by without it bothering him.

Despite his hyperawareness, he didn't get hungry or tired. He wanted to move, but that was his only annoyance. Otherwise, he was fairly content to remain in his pile. He'd shake some, just to try to flip a bone into the air and watch it fall, but then he'd lie dormant for days, trying to remember. Trying and failing.

One day, while wondering about what he didn't know and discovering he still didn't know it, he idly shook his shoulder and his arm at the same time. This was tricky because his arm was three feet away. The movement of both dislodged enough bones that the arm rested on the top of the pile. Ludwig's head was still buried, but he could feel his arm was now completely free. He bent his wrist and held his fingers up in the air, then wiggled them to assure himself they were completely unencumbered. The hand was liberated! It could do things!

At first he couldn't decide what the hand should do. He tried wiggling his fingers a lot, but that got boring. He tried tapping them on the bones in front of them. At first he tapped with all of them at the same time. That also turned out to be boring. Then he tapped them in a sequence, first his pinky, then his ring finger, then the middle, then the index. Repeat. A classic expression of boredom, yet it was the most exciting thing he'd experienced in … years? he wondered. Certainly the most exciting thing he'd managed since awakening in the pile of bones.

Then his fingers started moving in a different order, tapping on the bone before him in a way that first seemed random, then revealed itself to be a complex pattern. This was the product of some kind of muscle memory, he realized, only how did he know that? How did he even know what muscles were, let alone muscle memory, since he had neither? Yet his fingers were playing a song. Yes, a song, he realized. They were tapping on the bone in front of them just as those fingers had once played the keys on a piano. Piano! He knew how to play piano. But he also knew he didn't know how to play it well. At some point he'd learned, but he'd stopped learning long before he got very good at it. When was that? He couldn't remember.

In frustration, he reached forward with the free hand and wrapped the fingers around the bone that had been his piano keyboard, then tilted his hand back at the wrist. Luckily the bone was someone else's rib, and it wasn't connected to anything. If it had been heavier than his arm bones, his hand would only have lifted his own elbow into the air. Instead, he was able to raise the rib, then toss it across the room like a basketball player shooting a free-throw. He felt the rib roll as it danced up his fingers, felt it touch the last tips of his fingers, then Ludwig curled his hand in and aimed it forward. He'd done all this without thinking about it. He could throw something! Ludwig found this terribly exciting.

He spent the next few days throwing bones. He found he could pull his whole arm forward using his finger, then find another bone light enough to pick up and throw. It was fun. He didn't pay too much attention to where he was taking his arm. It worked just fine whether it was three feet away from his buried head or five, but eventually he crawled the hand back toward his own head because it just felt right to have it close by. Then he wondered if his fingers could find his skull. He spent some time throwing the lighter bones that were above his head, then prying off the bones that were heavier, and eventually he could bend the wrist down and touch his own skull. This told him how far down he was buried; about a hand's length. He scratched his skull, contemplating this new fact. With a great deal of effort, he calculated, he could dig his skull out of the pile. But it would take a long time. Then he had another idea.

Ludwig grabbed onto the heaviest thing he could reach, a whole rib cage resting on top of his head. He laced his fingers in between the ribs. He squeezed with his fingers until he was sure his hand would not move, then lifted up the rest of his arm by pivoting at his wrist and elbow joints. He found he could lift his whole arm up this way, and in triumph, he made the arm point straight up like an exclamation point. He held it there for a while. The joints did not get tired. The muscles holding the arm upraised did not burn because there were no muscles. This was interesting … for a second. Then it got boring, and he remembered his plan. With a great deal of care, he aimed the shoulder joint down like the head of a snake. It pointed through the bones, finding just the right gaps, until it found its way to his shoulder socket. He felt a tingle when they got close together. Suddenly, he constricted, like a person with abdominal muscles contracting them, or a person with lungs inhaling sharply. But he had no muscles or lungs. Instead, something magical happened, and the shoulder socket sucked in the ball joint.

And then he had an arm attached to his body. Only he was still trapped. For a moment, he felt more trapped than ever. He couldn't find bones to throw which were five feet away if his arm was stuck to his body. What would he do all day? He panicked again, and this time, he started grabbing bones which were larger and heavier than his arm and pushing them away. He had the weight of his own ribcage and spine and pelvis and skull as a counterweight, he realized. Now he could lift much heavier things. In fact, by throwing out an elbow and then chicken-winging in again, he could lift his torso up. Just a little at first, but as he calmed and became more systematic, he found he could remove the bones above him.

He began tossing them away and dragging himself to the surface of the pile. At one point he grabbed a bone and prepared to heave it, and then he realized it was his own leg. With great care, he placed the ball of that joint next to the socket in his pelvis, then inhaled again. Pop! He had a right arm and a left leg. Using the leg, he pushed himself out of the pile completely, then sat on the top of the pile for a second, his spine righted, his head turning around, examining the room.

Everything was bones. There were bones beneath him. And the walls were made of bones, too. They'd been organized like bricks. Many were skulls, but the other bones were there, too, layered with great care, with some scant soil between as mortar. He looked up. Above him, there was a ceiling, but it was made of something else. He couldn't understand the difference at first, just that it was a brighter white than the bones and shaped like bricks. It seemed everything in this place was painted white. *Ich bin ein bisschen irritiert*, Ludwig thought, but then he remembered his next task.

He thought about his other leg and arm, wriggled them a bit, and discovered them buried in nearby piles. Using one hand, his pelvis, and his foot, he crab-walked to them, dug them out, and set them in front of himself. First, he popped his right leg into place. Then his left arm. Then he realized it would have been easier to do it in the other order.

With care, he stood up. It wasn't difficult because of any stiffness in his joints or lack of coordination, but because he was still standing on a shifting pile of bones. Once he found his footing, he began to walk around the hallway, then jump a bit, then nearly dance with joy. He could move around as easily as … before? When he'd had flesh on his bones? When had that been? He couldn't remember having flesh, but he knew there was a time when his body wasn't just bones.

Then something caught Ludwig's eye. He immediately identified it as a rifle, but it didn't look like any rifle he'd ever seen before. And when had he seen a rifle before? He didn't know. But this one was different because of its coloring. The barrel was a very bright white, the brightest, whitest thing in the nearly all-white cave. But the stock (how did he know that was the stock?

he wondered) was slightly gray, a darker color than anything else in the room. And that was when he pieced it together. He wasn't seeing. Not really. He was identifying objects by their density. The air between him and the walls had no color at all, and he hadn't noticed that because air didn't have color back when he'd had eyes. The bones were white, and he hadn't noticed that because bones had been white back when he had eyes. The walls were white because they were covered in bones. The few visible bricks and the ones in the ceiling were roughly the same shade of white as the bones because bones and bricks are of similar densities. And when he looked up and down the cavern, it seemed he was looking into darkness in the distance just because there wasn't anything but air for a long time, not because the cave was bright around him and dark far off. The stock of the rifle was a darker gray than the barrel because it was made of wood rather than metal. And when he looked down the barrel, the hole in the center wasn't black. It was still brighter than the bones around him, just slightly darker than the exterior of the barrel because the metal inside was farther away.

Ludwig found he was seeing the world without depth perception and had to move and compute the relative brightness of the objects around him in order to orient himself. This made him a bit twitchy and awkward; it was hard to judge just how far away a wall was, or the floor, or even his own hands unless he moved them, but he was getting the hang of it. *Ich glaub ich spinne*, he thought to himself, then realized he was not going crazy at all. He was becoming more sane. The world was making more sense. Sort of.

As he walked around his section of the cave, he found some other objects which were not the same density (and thus the same whiteness) as the bones on the floor and in the walls. Some of the other skeletons, all of which were broken in some way, were wearing fabric. It was much darker than the bones, like a hole he could fall into but not quite as dark as the points off in the distance. When he'd touch these dark patches, he'd realize they were closer than the floor. They were clothes, he realized. These skeletons were wearing clothes. And as he inspected them, he had another realization. He could identify some of the clothes, and even when he couldn't, his mind placed the others in a category, too. Some of the uniforms he clearly recognized as "German." He didn't know what that meant, but the label came to him immediately. *Deutsch*, he thought. And all the clothing that did not match was similarly labeled with a single word, but that word was, "*Französische*." Why were the similar clothes German, and the mismatched ones French? he thought. He couldn't tell. But somehow he knew this.

And then he heard a sound. It was very faint, so distant he couldn't hear it when his skull was buried in the pile. He continued walking and heard the sound more clearly. Then another. Then a lot of sounds. He couldn't clearly remember ever hearing sounds before, but he remembered that a piano made sounds, and he knew these new sounds he heard were certainly not made by a piano. As he listened, he identified footsteps on the floor, but not on piles of bones. Someone was walking on a different surface than he was. It sounded smoother and less musical than a pile of bones. He looked up. Yes, it sounded like someone was walking on those bricks. He imagined multiple skeletons who looked just like him, only they were walking on the ceiling. He could tell they were coming from one side of the tunnel rather than the other. He decided to go find these skeletons and see if they would be his friends. Perhaps they could tell him where he was and how he'd come to be here. How would they do that? he wondered. He couldn't speak, so they probably couldn't either. What was speaking? he asked himself. Oh! he realized, that's the other sound. He could clearly hear someone speaking!

"*Mesdames et Messieurs, sur les murs, vous verrez des inscriptions datant de l'époque où les Catacombes étaient utilisées comme carriers…*" a voice was saying.

This meant absolutely nothing to Ludwig, but again, his mind cried out, "*Französische.*" But how could this also be French when French was clothing and now French was speaking? He continued to walk toward the voices.

He passed beyond his pile of bones and found he was walking on dirt, then bricks. Only his feet made a slightly different sound than the other feet on bricks. Perhaps they were not skeletons, and perhaps they were on the floor rather than on the ceiling, since bricks could be both places. This must be why they can speak and I cannot,

Ludwig mused. They are something other than skeletons. But what?

As he neared the end of his tunnel, Ludwig saw what they were, though he couldn't understand it at first. Unlike the walls which were white and got whiter and brighter the closer he got to them, these creatures were gray like the fabric of the German uniforms and French clothing. Like the French clothing, these creatures were wearing non-matching shirts and pants and shoes. Some even had diaphanous skirts which looked even darker than the other clothes because they were so lightweight. A few of the creatures held very bright things in their hands. One held a cylindrical metal canister that was almost as blinding white as the barrel of the rifle had been. A metal water bottle, Ludwig realized, though he thought of it as an oddly shaped canteen. Most held something else, almost as white as the water bottle but smaller, rectangular, and nearly flat. Ludwig had no idea what those were except that they appeared to be made of something almost as solid as a gun's barrel and demanded a lot of the creatures' attention. The creatures were looking at the objects they held, then up at the walls, then back at their objects. Ludwig couldn't make any sense of this behavior. He continued approaching.

Then one of the people holding one of the pieces of rectangular metal pointed it in his direction. The creature looked up above their doohickey and stared right at him. He could see the features of the person's face very clearly by identifying the density of the parts. The cheeks were darker than the cheekbones, for example, because there was no bone behind them. The nose was not like the skulls he'd seen before. Instead, it looked like a skull had been covered in gray clay, and someone had gotten lazy and left a big clump of slightly darker clay right in the middle of the face. The eyes were darker than the skin of the cheeks, but not dark pits of emptiness followed by solid white like the skulls he'd examined. They looked like dark gray clay had been shoved in the eye sockets, and in those two dark clumps were two black tunnels almost as empty as the air.

And then the dark eyes grew in their sockets, and the pupils expanded. And while they did so, Ludwig raised his hand and waved.

Though he'd never tried it, he felt an urge to say, "*Hallo. Wie geht es dir heute*?" He moved his jaw up and down. His teeth didn't touch, and there was no breath to push out the words, no lips or tongue to shape them, so he just stood there waving with his jaw moving up and down slightly.

Then the creature, who Ludwig had identified as a "person" and then a "woman" (but a *person* and a *frau*, of course), opened her own mouth and made a new sound which did not sound like speaking at all.

Bel handed Lena one of her headphones as she opened the computer, and Lena plugged it into her ear while Bel found the email and clicked on the attachment.

The video opened up. At first, it showed only a shot of a strange green building on a city street, but when passersby stopped to look at the door, she realized she didn't have any sound.

"It's muted," Lena said.

Bel apologized by shooting out her fingers and pinching in her shoulders in embarrassment, then found the sound button. When the computer and the headphones made friends, Lena heard the sounds getting the attention of the people on the sidewalk. Someone inside that green building was screaming. Many someones. The screams attracted the attention of whoever was taking the video, and they were narrating in a language Lena couldn't understand. Something Scandanavian or Eastern European, she guessed, and she felt guilty for her ignorance.

"Language?" she said aloud.

"Estonian," Bel said. "Don't feel bad. Less than two million speakers. I don't speak it, either. Don't worry. You won't need the commentary."

She was right. When fifty or sixty panicked tourists came pouring out of the green building's two front doors (entrance and an exit), they were pushing past one another, some hyperventilating, others screaming, others blank with terror. A few of the people were wearing uniforms of some kind, but the uniformed people weren't helpful in any way. If anything, as they knocked the tourists aside, Lena guessed they were the most frightened of all.

After the last person ran out, there was a lull, and the

nervous camera operator remained, as curious as Lena watching from the safety of the train. A hush fell over the observers on the street, but Lena could hear the voices of the tourists sporadically shouting in different languages. Then even these fell away, and now Lena could hear the sounds of traffic, car horns in the distance, city noise the cellphone barely picked up. She was straining so hard to listen that when the door suddenly framed an animated skeleton, she started so much she bounced in her seat.

"Holyshitthatscaredme," she whispered loudly to Bel.

The video stopped seconds after the skeleton's appearance. The person holding the cellphone had decided not to stick around to interview the monster coming out of the caves under the city.

Bel smiled at Lena. "Really? That's scary? You've seen these before."

"Um, yeah, and I didn't have my vamp superpowers at the time, remember? That was one of the scariest moments of my whole life."

Bel nodded. "I admit, when they grabbed us and held us down, I thought I was going to die within minutes of you, vampire powers or not."

"Yeah, Josef saved our bacon." She felt a deep sadness remembering the golem who Matteo had captured in a ball of magic, thrown through a window, and then buried in the Colorado River in the deepest part of the Grand Canyon. Josef had been her only companion for almost a year of her life, her constant protector, and a true friend until Cassius had somehow mind-controlled it to guard her books and fight against her. She understood

Matt had needed to kill Josef, but she would never fully forgive him for it. She had some other reasons to be angry with Matt, but the loss of Josef was high on her list.

"This may be one of the very ones you met before," Bel said.

"Really? But how? I thought they all died when Nigel died. All died again. Returned to being dead?"

"I thought so, too. But…" Bel gestured to the screen. "Paris catacombs. Same entrance we took."

"So what's the mission?"

"This is a very clear breach of The Convention. A monster, undisguised, just walking out among a bunch of humans, causing a panic. And the rules are the rules. So we've got to put him down."

"What about the humans who saw him?"

"That's on a case-by-case basis, and in this case, we haven't been assigned any. The eyewitnesses sometimes decide no one will believe them and stop talking about it. We don't have to kill them. When there's a video like this, we have to shut it down. Mostly. You would be surprised how easy that is. When it comes to the big social media platforms, they have really great software for identifying videos and removing them. They are afraid of getting sued for sharing copyrighted material. So we just have to trick the algorithms into flagging these videos as Disney properties, basically. Not too hard. And then they shut it all down. And did you know your phone company can even remove videos directly from your phone?"

"I did not."

"Good. You're not supposed to. But let's say you had government nuclear secrets on your phone. You think Uncle Sam can't just call up Verizon or Apple and say, 'Sure would be a shame if that phone had some technical difficulties.'"

"Without a warrant?"

"A warrant for what? The pictures or videos you no longer have and can never complain to anyone that you had in the first place?" Bel knocked on an imaginary door in front of her. "'Hello, officer?'" she said in a silly, deep voice. "'I had some highly illegal videos on my phone, and now my phone is busted, and I think it's fishy and want you to arrest my phone company.' As long as we have the right people in the right offices in governments and corporations, it's pretty easy to scrub stuff out of most locations, and we have people throughout the news media who can bury a story if it does leak out. That used to be the easier way, but now it's pretty easy for a video of a vampire or werewolf to spread without showing up on the 6 o'clock news, so we had to learn how to keep it off TikTok, too."

"Lots of humans trust TikTok more than the evening news," Lena said.

"Yeah, but a lot of that is because the trolls do a good job of spreading misinformation. It's easy to lose trust and hard to gain it, so if we can trick a news outlet into carrying enough lies, people stop taking it seriously even if it tells a true story. Better yet, if the trolls can convince people their 'team' doesn't trust 'the media,' like *all of it*, then the humans close themselves off to any truth and only believe what the trolls tell them. Those trolls are good at their part of protecting The Convention, I'll give them credit for that.

"But on the dark web? That's a different story. People can get away with spreading videos like this one, peer to peer, pretty easily. And we don't want to stop all of them. As long as they are easily dismissed as crackpots, they do us a favor. They basically find these violators of The Convention for us and point us at them. We pretend to be a monster hunter fan club. We pay enough that the humans who collect these videos come to us first with anything juicy they've found. After they've given us the information we need, we let them tell their little group of obsessives, but if they get too famous and start talking to more important people who might believe them, we have to eliminate them. And we know exactly where to find those human monster hunters because they tell us where to send the checks. Until then, the internet monster hunters don't know it, but they are working for the monsters." She shrugged. "Capitalism is a monster's best friend."

Bel patted Lena's knee. "And since I know you still hold a tender place in your heart for the humans, I thought this would be the perfect job for us. Individually, the skeletons aren't that hard to kill. We just have to find it, take it down, and crush it or burn it so it can't put itself back together." Then Bel put a hand on Lena's cheek and looked into her eyes. "But if our skeleton friend doesn't go back into the catacombs or cause another big scene like this, it might take a few nights of walking the streets to sniff it out, so you will need to be ready to eat some meals while we're in Paris. There are not enough international gun smugglers in the world to keep us going, Lena."

Lena looked down somberly, then snapped her head back up and gave a decisive nod. "We'll hold hands and walk the streets. The racists and homophobes and catcallers will identify themselves."

Finding food on the streets of Paris had been as easy as Lena expected, and she found the catcallers went down as smoothly as heavily buttered French pastries. But while the hunting was easy, finding their real target was not. They couldn't find a scent at the scene of the original video's documentation of the initial violation of The Convention. They had a rough sense of where the skeleton took to the streets, but no solid leads on where it had gone from there. Bel acknowledged the possibility it had returned to the catacombs (meaning they would never sniff it out among the other bones unless it revealed itself), but she suspected it remained topside.

"Once a monster violates The Convention," she explained, "it usually just keeps right on doing it. It's not like our system gives them a lot of wiggle room to get back in CimBim's good graces. We have a zero-tolerance policy."

Lena raised an eyebrow. "And we know how well

those work."

Bel shrugged. "In a weird way, this helps. Once a monster is visible, they tend to stay visible until we show up and put them down. If they suspected we would forgive them if they went back into hiding, more monsters might make a flashy public spectacle of themselves thinking they could just hide out long enough afterwards. But why hide once you're guaranteed to be caught and killed? Zero-tolerance makes our job easier."

Lena looked around the small, mostly empty street. "This is easy?"

"I admit, this case is weird." Bel ran a hand over the stubble on the back of her head. "In the video, it didn't look like it was trying to attack anyone. So maybe it's not making any kind of calculation that it's going to get caught. Maybe it doesn't understand how any of this works."

"But it obviously is hiding. No more humans screaming through the streets."

"True." Bel turned around in a slow circle. "So, if I were an animated skeleton in Paris, where would I hide?"

Lena shrugged. "Cemetery, right?"

"Maybe, but it came from the catacombs. Would it go back to a cemetery?"

"What do we know about the particular skeletons that attacked us? They had weapons and uniforms, so…"

"Soldiers!"

"So the skeleton used to be a soldier. It's wandering

the streets. Where does it go? It might not even know it's dead. It's just a soldier wandering through the city."

Bel raised an eyebrow. "I have a guess. Probably not correct, but it's something to check out."

The pair had no trouble finding the campus. The chapel's dome used to be the tallest point in Paris before the Eiffel Tower's construction, and its gold top reflected the city's lights and quite a few tourists' flashbulbs throughout the night. The big draw was the chapel itself, which served at the tomb of Napoleon. The name of the street, the Avenue de Tourville, was not a joke about tourists, but it might as well have been. Bel led Lena away from gawkers with cellphone cameras, around to the Boulevard des Invalides and then a little stretch of the Rue de Varenee, and from there they made their way onto the back side of the complex, which still served as a veteran's hospital.

"I figure, he might think of himself as a severely injured veteran. So he looks for a hospital, right?"

"But wouldn't there have been a trail of screaming humans leading us here?"

"Maybe. Or maybe he got here and found some veterans to hang with who were in the same shape he is. How many humans would he run into on his way to the morgue? If he timed it just right, he may have only terrified a few people. Maybe he even slipped in unseen."

"Which is what we need to do, right?"

"Nope. Advantage of looking like humans. Tonight, we're grieving daughters who've come to identify our dead dad."

Lena frowned. "Sisters?"

Bel smiled. "Okay, maybe two dads? Or one dad, two moms? Who is going to bother grieving daughters who seem to know where they are going?"

"For our appointment at three in the morning?"

"Trust me. They won't ask."

Bel was right. She had a cursory conversation with a nurse at a counter, but mostly the couple walked right in, found their way to the morgue, and discovered it empty. Outdated pale green and white tiles ringed the room, and though it was spotless and bleached, the smell of formaldehyde had seeped into the yellowing grout. Silence echoed off the tiles in French.

"Now what?"

"We check all the slabs, I guess." Bel grabbed a drawer handle, yanked it out, found it empty, and slid it back into place. She reached for another.

"Um, Bel, honey. Oh, sweetie. You dear, sweet, summer child."

"What?"

"How the fuck do you think a skeleton is going to

open a drawer, climb onto a slab, and then close the drawer without help?"

Bel tried to demonstrate her theory with some rudimentary motions of her shoulders and arms, pretending to lie back and then pull herself forward, but halfway through the strange dance she realized it wouldn't work.

"Okay, so the VA morgue was a bad idea."

"I didn't say that," Lena said. "Just not the slabs. Plus, if he thinks he's a very injured soldier, would he come to the morgue? That's not where injured people go."

"The ER?"

"Let's go see if there's a place near the ER where a very scared person who is hiding from people might wait for a doctor to come outside."

They made their way back, sniffling over their pretend loss, thanked the nurse on duty, then walked around the exterior of the building until they found the entrance to the parking lot marked for ambulances, and followed that to the round-about ER entrance.

"Okay, so I show up here, but I know every person who sees me goes off screaming, so I need to find a place where I might find a doctor alone." As she spoke, Lena pulled her pack of cigarettes out of her pocket, tapped one out, and freed it from the box with her lips. As she fished her lighter out of the other pocket, Bel's eyes brightened.

"Where do the doctors smoke?"

"The doctors smoke?"

"Lots of doctors smoke. Even more in France."

They found the spot. It was empty of humans, but a row of coffee cups stood on top of a railing on a wheelchair ramp by a side exit, and there were cigarette butts in every one. The vampires didn't even have to see into the cups to know; the rancid smell of wet butts mildewing in coffee with curdled creamer alerted them before they even turned into the alley containing the dumpster.

The dumpster itself smelled unusually clean. It wasn't used for food waste, since it wasn't near the cafeteria, nor for biomedical waste which went out through a different service. Lena and Bel could smell the paper goods inside. And 206 human bones.

"We got him," Bel said. She opened the lid on one half of the dumpster, leaning it against the alley's red brick walls, looked inside, and said, "C'mon out of there."

Nothing.

"Can you see him?" Lena asked, and she opened the other side.

The bin was about half filled with little bags containing the contents of small trash cans in offices and waiting rooms, some loose papers, a few coffee cups and aluminum cans.

Then a skull rose up out of the trash. It wasn't attached to a spine, just held in a skeletal hand. It turned back and forth, the empty sockets examining the two women, and then the head retreated back into the trash.

"We just saw you, too, dude," Lena said. "We know you're there." She looked up at Bel. "The periscope thing was pretty cool, though. Okay, so what do we do now? Last time you were cutting them down with a sword, but that doesn't seem to have kept this guy down."

"Burn the bones, I guess?" Bel asked. "Not going to walk around scaring people as a pile of dust." And then Bel saw the way Lena's face fell and caught her error. "Oh, I'm so sorry, honey. I didn't..."

"I know. Not your fault. I just miss Josef, you know? It wasn't fair."

"There's still hope, right? I mean, when that warlock got rid of him in Scotland, he came back. So another warlock gets rid of him in Vegas, he's bound to come back, right?"

"Maybe. But I doubt it." Lena was acutely aware of the difference. In Scotland, Josef wanted to come back to them. In Vegas, it had been fighting them, enslaved by Cassius. Lena didn't know the imp, Apraxis, was involved at all, let alone that Apraxis had truly enslaved her golem friend and forced it to pretend to serve Cassius.

Bel felt Lena's sadness like the kinds of physical injuries she hadn't experienced in decades. Only this didn't heal as quickly as a stab wound or bullet hole, so she entered into the next debate compromised by pity.

"If the skeleton doesn't understand what's going on, it didn't really mean to break The Convention, right?" Lena said.

Bel shook her head. "Doesn't matter. We're judge, jury, and executioner, but we're also pest control. If a monster threatens to reveal our existence, The Convention doesn't allow them to risk any other monster's safety just because they don't know any better. We put them down. That's why all the monsters sign on. They know the rules are straightforward and strict."

"And kinda' monstrous."

Bel shrugged.

"Fine," Lena lied. She looked down into the dumpster. "Okay, buddy, c'mon out. Time to get burned up."

"We could just light everything in there on fire," Bel said. "Easier." She hopped up against the metal box, doubled over at the waist, and grabbed some loose papers, then kicked her feet, righted herself, and landed softly on her Doc Martens. She held the paper out toward Lena. "Light?"

Lena pulled her lighter out of her pocket, cupped her hand around a portion of the papers' edges and lit them, but she didn't take them from Bel, and Bel accurately read this as an expression of reluctance on her girlfriend's part. She chose not to comment on it, held the papers inside the dumpster to let them get going shielded from the night's gentle breeze. When she felt confident, she dropped them into the pile.

Ludwig leapt out of the trash like a cricket, catching on the corner of the raised lid leaning against the wall. Of course, even without muscles or skin, Ludwig weighed more than a cricket. Ludwig would have been appalled to learn he'd dropped down to only 14 kilos, but 30 pounds of pressure is more than enough to pull down the plastic lid of a dumpster. He also didn't know he could move at superhuman speed, but in the comically slow moment when the lid began to fall, he realized his danger (his eye sockets widening to exactly the same size as always), and he twisted and lunged for the far side of the bin, then yanked himself out into the alley between Lena and Bel. He landed on all fours, his elbows and knees higher than his spine like a spider, and he rotated in quick half-circles, examining both his attackers.

Bel crouched, claws out only slightly faster than Lena, and both women circled, ready to attack.

Then Ludwig stood up straight. He looked at Lena, unsure what to make of the pretty woman with the large, curly hair. If he could have, he would have blinked.

Then his left arm fell off. Whatever magic kept his bones in place faltered, and the ball fell out of the socket at the shoulder. This wasn't the first time. As he'd re-learned to move his limbs, his shoulder was his recurring injury, and he'd learned to recognize the change in weight almost immediately and catch the arm as it fell, manipulating his right arm and the upper portion of his left so his right hand and humerus came together like magnets. (He didn't think of the pun because "humorous" is *humorvoll* in German, but he did find the whole thing amusing.) Now, performing this trick with an audience for the first time, he also felt embarrassed, so he sank into a shrug and waved apologetically at Lena. With his left hand. The one at the end of the arm held by his right hand. To his great relief, Lena rose out of her crouch and laughed.

"Okay," she said, "that was adorable."

"What?" Bel asked.

Ludwig didn't need to understand English to translate their exchange. He turned to the other woman. Both women's skin was the same density, so it looked an equivalent gray to Ludvig. He mostly distinguished this one by her short, straight hair which was not magenta to him but the same light gray as Lena's. He waved at Bel with the loose arm, then reattached it.

"Cute," Bel conceded. "But we still need to kill him."

"Really?" Lena said. "He's not hurting anyone. He might not even know why he's scaring people." She made a pouty face and blinked at Bel. "Can we keep him?"

"He's not a pet, Lena."

"And we're not humans. Humans have dogs and cats. Maybe vampires have skeletons."

"We don't."

"But we could," Lena almost sang.

"No. I'm putting my foot down. No reanimated skeleton pets." But Bel thought of the way Lena grieved the loss of Josef, and her voice carried a hint of her indecision.

"C'mon," Lena begged.

"No."

"C'mon!"

"No."

Then the smoke detectors picked up the fire raging in

the dumpster next to them and set off alarms throughout the VA wing of Les Invalides.

"Oh, shit," Bel said. "C'mon."

Lena brightened. "Yes?"

"Yes. No. Later. Just c'mon. Before humans arrive and we have to kill ourselves for violating The Convention."

"Okay!" Lena turned to Ludwig. "C'mon!"

To Ludwig's "ears" (such as they were), this word *kamen* the women kept repeating sounded like the German word for "arrived" conjugated for "they" and in the past tense, so he had no idea who had been doing all this arriving or when, but when the pretty woman with the big hair smiled at him and gestured for him to follow, he presumed he was not part of "they" and instead he was part of the new "we" getting the hell away from whoever "they" were, so he followed the women as they ran across the Rue de Talleyrand, hopped a fence, and took cover in a little private park behind the Korean embassy.

In the deep dark under the trees, beyond the reach of the moon and the city's lights, Bel recovered some of her resolve. "We cannot keep him, Lena. We came to Paris on a very clear mission. It's our job to—"

"Okay, but just hear me out," Lena said.

Ludwig looked from one whispering woman to the other.

"Fine. I'm listening."

"We came to Paris. We found that skeleton. It was with a bunch of other skeletons reanimated by Nigel. That part is sort of true. And we burned that skeleton up.

Punished. Done. But while we were at it, we found this *other* skeleton. Maybe he helped us find the one who broke The Convention, and that's how we became friends. So when we left Paris, we took our new friend with us."

Bel shook her head slowly. "Lena, you know I'm already on very thin ice with CimBim. Killing all those werewolves in London could have gone either way if we hadn't had the Archduke on our side, and then I hid from Cassius for a year before showing up and very publicly helping him get shot in the face. The Archduke is trying to clean up that mess and has been succeeding only because Cassius is AWOL, but if he shows up and starts pointing fingers, we're fucked. And if they haul me and my only recently turned girlfriend in for an investigation, and I show up with a skeleton pet when my last mission was to eliminate a skeleton who terrorized humans in broad daylight in the middle of Paris, how is that going to look?"

"'Kay, A) In that case the skeleton is going to be the least of your problems, and B) They probably won't send someone to take you in. If they call, you don't have to bring him along. But if they send someone, the monster who shows up will be some other agent of CimBim sent to kill us, right? And in that case, wouldn't it be better to have a skeleton friend who never sleeps watching out for us while we're unconscious during the day?"

"So now he's less of a pet and more of a familiar? Do you want to name him Renfield?"

Lena shook her head. In such darkness, the gesture

would have been meaningless to a human, but Bel could see her and even hear the muscles in Lena's neck and the breeze in her hair. "No, but he does need a name. How about Jim Reaper?"

Lena could likewise hear Bel's eyes roll. "Oh, please don't do this."

"Doug Up? Ben Rattling? Cat A. Comb?"

"I am undead, and this is still killing me."

Lena was on fire now. "Helter Skelator? McRibs? Oh, how about pop culture. Like Indiana Bones?"

"No."

"Eddie Deader? Jon Bone Jovi?"

"I don't get those."

"Too new for you? Maybe Pelvis Costello?"

"I still don't get it."

"Okay, older then. Albert Spinestein? Clarence Marrow? Teddy Bones-evelt? Thomas Deadison?"

"Okay, I get all of those. And no."

"How about famous actors? Val Killmore? Christopher Walken Dead? Grim Carey? Bruce Killis? Owen Killson?"

Bel frowned so hard Lena could hear the muscles in between her eyes. "Do we even know he's a killer? He doesn't seem particularly kill-y to me."

"See, you're getting into it."

"I'm not," Bel lied.

"Antonio Bone-deras."

"Yeah, that's pretty good. How about Armand Bone-el?"

"I don't get that one," Lena said.

"You know, Armand Borel? Famous Swiss mathematician? Won the Brouwer Medal from the Royal Dutch Mathematical Society and the Royal Netherlands Academy of Sciences in 1978? Taught at Princeton? The Borel subgroup H is named after him."

"Never heard of him."

"Too bad because the pun is a double. Arm and Bone."

"Yeah, but no," Lena said. "How about Killem Dafoe?"

"Also a double, but also with the killing."

"Fine. Maybe an artist? Vincent Van Bone?"

"It's not even close to 'Gogh,'" Bel said, pronouncing "Gogh" correctly like a pedant or a Dutch person.

Lena looked at Ludwig. "You aren't helping. Did you have a name back when you were human? That could give us something to go on."

Ludwig shrugged. He didn't understand her, couldn't remember his own name, and couldn't speak. But the timing of the shrug convinced Lena he could hear her just fine. "Do you understand what I'm saying?" she asked in English.

Ludwig shrugged again.

"*Parlez-vous français*?" Lena asked with such a thick American accent that Bel winced.

Ludwig shook his head.

Lena bounced a little. "Okay, he doesn't speak French, but he understood that!"

"*Parli italiano*?" Bel asked. "*Spreek je Nederlands? Taler du dansk? Mówisz po polsku? Sprechen Sie Deutsch?*"

Ludwig shrugged through most of her questions, then started nodding enthusiastically and pointing at her and at himself.

"German!" Bel said.

"Ask him if he was German or if he just speaks German," Lena suggested.

Bel asked. Ludwig shrugged, then rapped his knuckles on his skull, then opened his empty hand. Bel spoke some more, and Luwig nodded.

"What?" Lena asked.

"He doesn't remember. He speaks German but doesn't remember if he was German."

"Probably was," Lena said. "Ask him if he remembers his name."

Bel asked.

Ludwig shook his head.

"Ask him if he was a soldier."

Ludwig shrugged a reply.

"I'm guessing he was," Bel told Lena in English. "Not only was he a German in the French catacombs, but his first impulse was to go to a VA hospital.

"Maybe. Or a church. Or a museum. It's both. Maybe he's religious. Or really into Napoleon."

"That's it!" Bel almost shouted.

"What?"

"Napoleon Bone-apart! We even found him at Napoleon's tomb."

Lena frowned. "But we just found out he's German."

"So what?" Bel said. "Napoleon was Corsican, and Corsica only became a part of France the year Napoleon was born, so he was barely French anyway. I wasn't a big fan of Napoleon. You know he was elected 'First Consul' for life in 1802 before being crowned Emperor in 1804. It really did seem like he would bring peace to Europe for a little while there. Which was bad for me. The Reign of Terror had been an easy time to make humans disappear. 'Where did that family of nobles go?' 'Must have run off to escape the guillotine. Couldn't possibly have been eaten by that new serving girl who just started working in their kitchen.' Good times. And then Napoleon came in with his codes and basically outlawed getting anything by inherited title, ending the nobility, and declared freedom of religion, and everything kind of chilled out for a bit. So I moved to Spain which was less stable at the time." She turned to Ludwig. "*¿Has viajado alguna vez a España?*"

Ludwig shook his head.

"*Entiendes español?*" Lena asked him.

Ludwig nodded.

"*Eres español o alemán?*" she asked.

Ludwig didn't know if he had been Spanish or German. He just understood both languages.

Lena was very relieved. She'd worried about depending on Bel for translation and, if she was totally honest, she'd started to feel jealous that her new pet skeleton might like Bel better if the two of them shared a language.

"Okay, we have a skeleton from France who understands German and Spanish but not French, and we've named him Napoleon." Lena asked Ludwig if he minded his new name and explained they'd found him at Napoleon's tomb. He shrugged. She wasn't sure if he knew who Napoleon was, but she decided that was better than the skeleton feeling offended. "Napoleon it is!" she declared, and clapped a hand on Ludwig's scapula.

His arm fell out of the socket again. He caught it.

"I'm so sorry!" Lena said, then realized she was still speaking English. "*¡Lo siento mucho!*"

Ludvig raised the arm he held in his right hand and made a thumbs-up with his left.

"See?" Lena asked Bel. "We have to keep him!"

"Sure," Bel said. "What could possibly go wrong?"

"'It was a mistake,' you said. But the cruel thing was, it felt like the mistake was mine, for trusting you."

-David Levithan

Chapter 6

It had been a rough year for Augy and Bob. At last year's convention, they'd been blinded by a warlock and ripped limb from limb by a bunch of toddler werewolves. That was unpleasant. Then their boss, Cassius, got shot in the face with a bullet full of liquid silver in the middle of the convention in front of all the monster delegations, and if that wasn't embarrassing enough, a dragon had appeared and wrecked everything. Cassius had to go into hiding, and he'd brought the body parts of Bob and Augy with him so they could all heal up together.

Cassius was not a kind boss, and he turned out to be a terrible hospital roommate, too. Bob and Augy were laid up in beds in a windowless room to minimize the chance any sunlight would slow their healing. Their torsos and what remained of their scalped heads were set in the center of the beds, and what remained of their arms and legs were set in place in the hopes that they would reconnect. Bob was lucky. One of his arms and one of his legs reconnected and didn't need to be completely re-grown. Augy's left leg seemed like it might reattach, but the putrefaction won out, and that leg had to be re-amputated, so he had to grow all his limbs back from scratch.

As they lay there re-growing body parts, Cassius worked the liquid silver out of his system. In ancient times this would have been a process of years, maybe decades, but with a modern variation on a dialysis machine, his vampire doctors were able to infuse new blood and filter out the silver more quickly. The process was painful and painfully boring, and Cassius took his frustration out on the two people closest at hand.

"Baby werewolves?" he shouted. "You were beaten by babies! I am never going to let you live this down. I don't know why I'm wasting blood on the two of you right now. Do you have any idea how much your recuperation is costing me? I have to hire the people who track down the victims we drain to get the blood to heal you two up. You think they like hunting humans and then having to turn the blood over to me? Of course not. And do you think I like having to share it with two worthless lumps of gnawed meat who used to be my toughest soldiers? Maybe I should have just let this be your retirement. Your swan song. The gold watch. You get beaten by a bunch of toddlers, that's it for you, and you're better off turning to dust right then and there. But they didn't stake you or cut off your heads because they thought they could avoid breaking The Convention on some technicality. And guess what? They were right! No one is hunting down those baby werewolves. They're too cute and too weak and no one cares! It's too embarrassing for the both of you. What, are they going to bring you in as witnesses? 'Tell us, Mr. Augustus, what happened on the day a bunch of fucking children jumped on your back and tore all your limbs off? And Mr. Roberto, do you have anything to add about your humiliating defeat?'"

"No, Boss," Bob groaned.

"It was rhetorical! I'm not actually asking you to say anything, Bob. You can be silent for a few more months until your vocal cords repair themselves."

"Thanks, Boss," Bob said.

Augy discovered enough of the muscles in his ocular cavities had healed to allow him to roll both eyes, though his left eyelid was still too thin and scabby to allow even that much movement without intense pain. He sucked his teeth, and that hurt where his lungs were still growing back beneath his ribcage. "Dammit, Bob," he muttered.

"Shut up, both of you," Cassius barked. "Now I've lost my place. Where was I? Oh, yes, your attack isn't being investigated by CimBim because it's too embarrassing. And they aren't sure what to do about Bel and her crew because I'm not there. And I'm not sure what to do because if I send CimBim after her, they might kill her for violating The Convention, but they won't bring the human's books to me afterwards, and that's the whole point.

"So I have to let the werewolves and the human and my own betraying spawn get away with shooting me and unleashing a dragon and ruining my whole plan. Years of work! Fucking years! And they get away with it because I need what they have. I need those books. So I'm going to heal you two up. And then, instead of making you stand guard, since you're obviously too incapable to do that even after a thousand fucking years of practice, I'm going to send you out into the field. Remember what happened to Nicobar and Gunnar and Blake in Costa Rica? When the human blew up her own fucking house to get rid of anyone who got close to her books? I'm going to send you after her. And after Bel. And after the werewolves. I'm going to put you in the most dangerous situations I can think of. That will be your punishment. You'll either redeem yourselves, or you'll get killed, and I'm being totally transparent with you right now; I hope it's the latter."

Augy managed to look over at Cassius. The boss wore his usual stylish shoes, dark slacks, and an Italian button-up shirt that would have been dashing if it wasn't marred by a splash of blood from the half of his face that was still oozing. Tubes from the dialysis machine were jammed into each of his arms, and the pressure of the dark, fresh blood and his own purified blood channeling into his right arm exceeded the amount that could be drained from his left, so some of the silver-tainted blood was continuously dripping out of his ears, his eyes, the thin skin in his nose, and the gumline around his teeth. Also, the cavity where his cheekbone was growing back in, and the more prominent hole in the back of his head which Augy couldn't see from his vantage point. There must have also been a good deal of internal bleeding, because as Cassius ranted, he wheezed a bubbly, wet gurgle when breathing in. Cassius made a conscious choice not to cough, not out of any sense of propriety or concern about infecting or disgusting his roommates, but because it was one of the few areas of his existence where he could exert self-control, his favorite type of exercise.

So, hanging out with the boss was no fun. Then he got better and was upstairs in his new office most of the time while Augy and Bob continued to heal in the basement, so they didn't hear the conversation where Ryou-Ryou Daiō gave Cassius the idea of hiring Esau to find Lena and Bel. But sure enough, six months later Augy and Bob found themselves in a high-rise parking structure in Shanghai, standing on their brand new, fully functional legs, with their brand new, fully functional arms raised up in the air, with twenty-five little dancing red laser lights wavering all over their torsos and heads.

The lights of the surrounding skyscrapers pierced in over the concrete exterior walls, and the dim fluorescent bulbs overhead did their dramatic, infrequent blinking, but the lasers on their bodies captured Bob and Augy's attention. The mercenaries aiming rifles at them were tense but not terrified in the way Augy thought they ought to be, and he found that unnerving. Bob, a fan of online conspiracy theories, reveled in this new cloak and dagger role because it reinforced his belief that the less he understood about what was going on, the more it proved he was right for believing the things he'd heard on YouTube.

Bob, a head taller than Augy, leaned toward his partner and whispered, "See? I bet they came here in silent, black helicopters. With chemtrails."

Augy didn't look away from the mercenaries. "What are chemtrails?"

"I don't know," Bob admitted. "I've never really understood that part. Something bad. And secret. CIA, probably."

"You think these guys are CIA?"

"We're not CIA," a new voice said. It preceded the man coming up the flight of stairs. "We're not FBI or DoD or NSA or Mossad or MI5 or DGSI or Kremlin or MSS or ASIS. Torreblanca, who am I missing?"

Esau stepped around a parked SUV and into view, and his lieutenant followed just behind. "Te Pā Whakamarumaru," she said. "That's New Zealand's secret service. Maori name meaning 'Sheltering Citadel.' By far the coolest name of any country's secret service agency."

"Agreed," Esau told her, then spoke to the vampires again. "We're not Te Pā Whakamarumaru, either. We do not work for any government. Because we know you have your tentacles in all of them. And we don't want to work for monsters. And then you reach out and ask us to come work for you. So why, when we have gone to so much trouble to avoid working for you, would you think we'd be interested in what you're offering?"

"Mr. Esau Sullivan. Ms. Anahí Torreblanca. Thank you for meeting with us," Augy said. "First, may we lower our arms so we can all talk more comfortably?"

"Nope," Esau said.

The vampires kept their hands up. "Alright. I understand this whole arrangement is very unusual, seeing as we're vampires and you're …"

"Hunters who kill vampires."

"Right, and—"

Torreblanca stepped up next to Esau. "We kill all monsters. Including a pair of them in a Shanghai parking garage."

Augy tilted his head. "Yes, ma'am. I understand that. But you haven't always killed all of them, have you? You have been known to make exceptions."

"One exception. Singular. And that was to save the whole human race from a vampire. Seemed like a good deal."

"We want to offer you something similar," Augy said. "If you'll hear us out, we believe you'll consider our offer and decide that a second exception needs to be made in this case as well."

Esau looked at Torreblanca, then nodded. "Alright. I'm listening."

"Oh, I'm sorry. I was unclear. When I said 'you,' I meant your organization. And when I said 'we,' I meant my employer. I am not at liberty to give you the details tonight. We, and by that I mean my associate and myself, are only empowered to arrange a meeting between your employer and ours. They will work out whether the deal is mutually beneficial."

Torreblanca twisted on her heels and looked at Esau. "So we have two vamps here offering us nothing in particular and expecting to walk out of here alive?"

Augy risked lowering one hand slightly and extending only his index finger into the air. "If I may clarify, *you believe* you have two vampires in your custody expecting to walk out of here alive. And while that may be the case, it's also possible we have 27 humans pointing 25 rifles at two vampires who are actually in the custody of a number of vampires you can't determine with your limited human senses, and those vampires don't need little lasers giving away their positions to eliminate all of you if you decide not to convey our employer's desire for civil negotiations to your employer. Just sayin' it's a possibility worth considering."

Esau smiled. "If that's a bluff, you have a pair of steel testicles, buddy."

Augy shrugged, then lowered his arms slowly. "I'm almost six centuries old. They shrivel up and harden with age."

"Really?" Torreblanca said.

Bob spoke for the first time in the exchange. "No, not really. Mine are pretty much the same as they were in the 1400s, but I had to regrow them a couple times due to serious injuries."

"I wasn't talking to you." She looked at Esau. "Really? We've got two vamps in our sights, and you're having a discussion about who has the biggest balls?"

"Technically about who has the hardest balls," Bob said. "More a discussion of density."

Augy shrugged. "I said mine were shriveled, but maybe increased density implies increased mass."

Torreblanca shook her head. "Esau, what the fuck?"

"You're out of line, soldier. We'll discuss it later."

"I'm out of line? You're considering negotiating!"

"I'm considering the possibility there are a bunch of vamps just over those walls, waiting." He scanned around the garage. They were on the 26th floor, but that didn't preclude the possibility they were surrounded. Or on the floor above, ready to jump down. There was no way of knowing for sure.

"Okay, but they don't need two vampires to send a message to their boss. We could kill one," Torreblanca said.

"True, but we don't need to leave 27 of you alive to contact your employers. We could kill 26."

"Fuck," Torreblanca said.

"If I may," Augy said, "I'd like to suggest you allow me to slowly reach into my coat pocket, pull out a business card and a burner phone, deposit them carefully on the ground here in front of me, and then let me and my associate here walk over to the entrance to the stairwell you all just came up. From there, we will go up or down or both to inform our colleagues that we have not been killed, and they can allow you all to leave unscathed, and you can continue the discussion you clearly want to have once we're out of earshot." He smiled, a snide leer. "But remember, we can hear very well, so you'll want to give us a good amount of time to leave before you say anything you don't want us to hear."

Esau nodded. "Set the stuff down and fuck off."

Augy did as he was told.

When the vampires exited through the door to the stairwell, Torreblanca immediately shouted at Esau: "The fuck?"

"It's my fault. I should have had the whole building guarded, top to bottom. We scouted it earlier, but it wasn't until they were standing right here that I considered the possibility the vamps had leapt onto the roof from another building."

"Or maybe there were no other vamps."

"Exactly. And it's my fault we didn't know that. I fucked up, Torreblanca. But so did you. You're forgetting the chain of command. Talking out of turn. They can certainly hear us both right now. You don't have the authority to negotiate with them."

"Do you?"

"I'm going to run it by my higher-ups," Esau said.

"And who are they?"

"You're way out of line, Torreblanca," Esau said.

"No, Esau. I don't think I am. I think I was out of line when I agreed to work for you without knowing exactly who was giving you your marching orders. I think I was out of line when I learned you had a vendetta against a single monster because he fucked you over and broke your heart, and you were letting that personal relationship compromise your judgement. I think the moment you shot Lena, a *human woman*, because you wanted to kill Matt, I should have walked. I'm starting to think I need to rethink a lot of things, Esau."

Esau's voice was almost as much a growl as a whisper.

"I think this is the wrong place for us to discuss this, and I think you know that."

"Convince me, Esau. Convince me we're still hunting monsters and not just killing anybody who gets between you and the guy who dumped you."

"First of all, Lena was not the first civilian casualty we've ever suffered. This is war, and sometimes civies get caught in the crossfire. You know that. You were in the sandbox. Shit happens. You know full well I was aiming at a monster when I took that shot. And you know the only reason I agreed to work with any monsters on that mission was because of the books. If it hadn't been for those damned books, I would have executed every single wolf in that camp, including the puppies. You know that's true."

"So who are we working for, Esau?" Torreblanca's voice quavered, a pleading sound she hated. "Just tell me who is giving the goddamned orders. Tell me they signed off on the mission in Vegas. Tell me they know about Lena's murder. I will believe you, because even though you withheld information from me, you never lied to me. So tell me the truth."

Esua looked down at the sealed concrete, breathed deeply through his nose, and then paced to one side. "Okay. Here's what I can tell you, Torreblanca. I can tell you that we don't work for monsters. We work for humans. I can tell you that I will never reveal their identities because the whole organization is built on the knowledge that the only way we keep it from getting taken over by The Convention is by keeping their identities a secret. I will remind you that you knew that from the beginning." He turned his back on her. "I will tell you, honestly, that it has been my honor to serve with you, and that I hold you in the highest respect. I will tell you, honestly, that I hate to do this."

He turned towards her, and when his right hand was obscured by his body, he pulled the pistol, his nickel-plated Desert Eagle, out of his thigh holster.

Torreblanca saw it, but too late. She reached for the pair of Rugers in her shoulder holsters, crossing her arms on her chest.

When Esau's bullet hit her, a perfect center-mass shot that should have pierced the right side of her heart, it clipped the bones in her wrist and was driven down into her lower torso, passing through her liver and kidney and ending in her gall bladder. No surgeon in the world could repair that much damage, but Esau didn't take a chance. Torreblanca stumbled backwards, more from the surprise than the impact. Esau lunged forward as she fell and kicked her once, side-snap style, knocking her onto her back, then swiped back with his heel over her body, smacking her pistols out of her hands. As he did so, he aimed his gun at her face.

Then he hesitated. "You also knew what happens to people who ask about the chain of command. Or threaten to go AWOL. Field punishment ranging from demotion to execution." He looked up at the other soldiers, quickly identifying how they were holding their rifles and where they were pointed. None of the men were training theirs on him. Seven held theirs in low ready position, and ten held theirs in patrol carry position, and eight had their rifles trained on Torreblanca. Esau took careful note of each, though he knew there were distinct explanations for why a man might want to show he wasn't engaged in a fight or was clearly taking a side. He'd have to do some interviewing of each when they debriefed. But in that moment, he needed some quick reassurance. "Does everyone understand Torreblanca's violation of the rules?"

"Yessir." some shouted. Most spoke clearly. No one whispered.

"We do not kill humans. That's a rule. We do not disobey orders. That's a rule. We do not threaten to desert. That's a rule. And we do not attempt to expose the identities of the higher ups. That's a rule. I hope you all are seeing the priority of the rules of engagement. I will kill a human to preserve field discipline if I consider it necessary to do so, and I will sure as shit kill a human to protect the identities of the higher ups, because if we compromise on that, we could end up working for The Convention, and then nothing else matters. We will not work for monsters. We may, at times, be ordered to work alongside them in order to trick them, manipulate them, use them to kill other monsters. But we will not make peace with them. We will not join their ranks. We will not serve them. We are monster hunters. And anyone who jeopardizes that is a legitimate target. Is that understood?"

"Yessir."

Esau looked down at Torreblanca. She was gasping for air, not because the bullet had punctured a lung, but out of absolute shock and terror. Esau wasn't sure if she could even hear him anymore. He lowered his gun from her face to her chest. "I never wanted this. And you know I'm telling you the truth." Then he raised his gun again, aimed at her forehead, and pulled the trigger twice.

He watched long enough for his brain to identify blood, and then he pinched his eyes closed and turned away. He didn't mind that his men would see how agonizing it was for him; he wanted them to know he cared for them, too, and would be pained to have to employ field justice in this way. As long as they knew he wouldn't hesitate to do it, knowing he didn't want to do it was beneficial.

"What should we do with her body, sir?" one of the soldiers asked.

Without turning, Esau said. "Leave her. I don't like it, but it will raise less suspicion than if we moved her. The authorities will just assume it was a drug deal gone bad. We're not Army or Marines anymore. We're monster hunters. People get left behind."

Esau, still concerned they might be surrounded by vampires, led his men out of the garage quickly without looking back at his closest colleague and friend. But averting his gaze meant he didn't notice something important.

Some events, like winning the lottery or being hit by an asteroid, are statistically unlikely for an individual at a given time but near certainties given enough time and space. Other events are unlikely regardless of the scale, like the speed of light changing, or time travel. And then there are phenomena which can only occur thanks to the direct intervention of the supernatural, like a dead person returning to life as a vampire. One such event is a bullet passing through a human skull, into the brain, then changing direction 180 degrees and popping back out, only to have the damaged material instantly return to its previous state. That's not the way bullets work, the way skulls work, or the way brains work.

In fact, it's so unlikely, it would be easier to create a magical fabrication of the individual by magical means, place the false version almost exactly where the real person lay, but with the head in a slightly different position, allow the bullets to pass through empty air, and decorate the false version of the person with some deceptively realistic blood spatter.

But if any monster were capable of creating such an illusion, there's no reason why they would need to also redirect the bullets. The confluence of the illusion and the nearly infinitely improbable bullet redirection would only occur if two monsters were involved.

The illusion of the false version of Torreblanca required the brilliant warlock pulling off the trick.

And even then, that magical achievement wouldn't change the fact that Torreblanca had a very real, very lethal bullet wound in her torso which no glamour could heal.

For that, she'd need help from the second supernatural monster, a monster able to make her impossibly lucky.

"A story has no beginning or end: arbitrarily one chooses that moment of experience from which to look back or from which to look ahead."

-Graham Greene

Chapter 7

The emissary waved his hand in a dramatic arc over his head. "Flashback," he shout-whispered.

"Wait, hold on," Mr. Joyce said. "I'm sorry to interrupt, but will the audience know these characters at this point? Like, this monster hunter guy who shot the other monster hunter girl in the face? It seems like we're walking into a sequel here and don't have all the backstory we need to make sense of everything. Will the flashback explain all that?" He turned and looked at Carol and Kim. "Are you two following all of this? Is it just me?"

Kim nodded but looked puzzled, their brow knitted, and then they tapped one of their bright blue nails on their cheek. "I think I'm getting it all, but I'm not sure how much I'm filling in and how much is really being made explicit."

Carol shrugged. "And maybe that's okay, to some extent. If we're talking art-house, maybe it's okay to demand a little more from the audience. If we're thinking blockbuster, we'll need to spell things out." She looked at the emissary, "Like, I'm gathering the hunter guy, what was his name?"

"Esau Sullivan."

"Yes, he's some hard-ass who teamed up with the vampires at some point. The hot ones from the first scene. And his girlfriend, this woman he shot."

"Anahí Torreblanca," the emissary said. "His lieutenant. Not a romantic relationship."

Carol didn't slow down. "Okay, but maybe we can add that. Anyway, she was opposed to working with monsters, and he did that, and then she questioned him publicly, and he shot her. But there's this ominous sense that there was some other woman involved."

"A man, actually," the emissary said.

"Spicier. I like it," Kim said. "But it might not play in Arkansas."

"As long as it works with teenage boys in Beijing, Guangzhou, Shenzhen, Chengdu, Tianjin, Chongqing, Nanjing, Wuhan, Xi'an, Hangzhou, Shenyang, and Wuhan, that's all that matters." Joyce rattled off the names in a passable Chinese accent despite not being able to speak Mandarin. William Joyce knew his business. "Not being political," he explained. "Just twelve cities in China have more potential moviegoers than all the red states put together. So fuck Arkansas."

Kim smiled at this. It was a fake smile, because they knew Joyce would also cut every non-binary character if his market research said the people buying tickets didn't like non-binary characters tomorrow. Joyce could take a principled stand and fight for it tenaciously against all the big egos in Hollywood, but he had only one principle, and that was the box office number.

"Okay, so the monster hunter is a jilted lover, and now he's back to his monster hunting but has some mysterious employer to be revealed later. Got it. But there's a hint this Torreblanca isn't dead, because we CGI her forehead shitting out the bullets. So that's what we need the flashback for, right?"

"Well, sort of."

"Sort of?"

"We need the flashback to understand the Torreblanca part, but it's not going to make much sense to the viewers because it introduces new characters, The Weird Sisters McElroy, who have been intervening and manipulating this since well before this story began, going back a few years to when a necromancer named Nigel Marion made Lena write a book that would kill off the human race."

"Who is this Nigel Marion?" Carol asked.

"Unimportant. He's dead."

"But he's a necromancer, so he comes back in this

one?"

"Nope. Punched to death by the golem, Josef."

"Who is he?"

"'It.' It's non-binary and uses 'it/its' pronouns."

Kim made a startled look of disgust. "I don't like that at all. We'll have to change those to they/them."

The emissary raised his palms up. "It's not a person. If it wants to express that part of its identity with it/its pronouns, shouldn't we respect that?"

Kim shook their head. "Won't test well." They looked at Joyce. "Even in Beijing."

"I'm sorry," Joyce told the emissary, "but I feel like you're resistant to taking feedback, and that's going to be a problem down the line, so…" He nodded slowly, his head pointing toward the door, but the emissary was directly in that path, obscuring the motion's meaning, so he chose to interpret it as a cue to continue.

"Of course. I think it will all make more sense in the end. If I may?" He didn't hesitate for permission, just waved his hand in an arc above his head. "Flashback!"

Chapter 8

Matteo Bernusconi (or Matt Bern depending on where he traveled) stood on the back deck of his yacht, the *Exclamation*, blowing bubbles. A warlock of considerable power, he fed on the emotions of humans, and that afternoon he'd riled up the patrons in a crowded bar in Portland by arguing both that homeless people were ruining the city and houseless persons deserved dignity and government assistance, then that sex workers were legitimate small business owners and also homewreckers destroying monogamous relationships. In less than an hour, he'd started seven heated discussions, two shouting matches, a near-fistfight, and a serious talk that would result in a breakup (interestingly, not over the sex workers but over the houseless persons). Matt gained more from the quietest witnesses who were wracked by their own discomfort or seethed in silent fury at friends' comments. The fistfight was less emotional and thus less of a meal for him, more of a strong after-dinner mint than a main course. The whole experience had been very satisfying, and even hours later, once he'd returned by car and tender to his ship, he was still full to bursting.

As he'd learned, the best way to handle the excess magical power he acquired in these binges was to generate very small creations which allowed him to control the burn until he'd vented only the surplus and retained all the power he'd need until the next meal. To do this, he created bubbles of magical power which floated away. Only they did not obey the wind but seemed to choose directions of their own volition. And they couldn't be popped. No matter what projectile was aimed at them, they simply swirled or looped as though buffeted by a different breeze and resumed their course unhurt and unimpeded. Matt had been launching the bubbles for hundreds of years, but he had no idea where they traveled or why. He didn't care. That wasn't the point. Once they'd served their purpose, they were no longer his concern. Kind of like the humans he'd manipulated to generate them in the first place.

Only, unlike the bubbles, one of those humans had crossed his path again. Worse, despite Matt's best effort to be unaffected by the encounter, he found himself bothered by his former victim's attempt to kill him. Sure, he was mildly disturbed that Esau, in an effort to shoot Matt, had accidentally shot the human, Lena, standing behind the glamour of himself Matt had generated in order to make a silent retreat from an uncomfortable situation. That was one of his favorite tricks. He'd just create a false version of himself which humans could see, make himself invisible, and walk out of tight spots, then turn off the glamour, seeming to disappear dramatically when he'd really slunk away in a manner less becoming.

And maybe, he now considered, that was part of what was bothering him. That very day he'd done something far more hands-on and heroic than usual. He'd confronted, confined, and disposed of a raging golem to save some werewolf pups, a human, and, by virtue of rescuing Lena's two novels, the entire human race and all of monster-kind. Or maybe most humans and most monsters. Matt liked to think he'd saved them all. But he resented his own pride in his heroism.

He didn't want to want that role. He was a monster, after all. He wanted to feed on his victims and forget them, not save them. This vestigial concern for others was an itch on a phantom limb.

He frowned as he made his magical crystalline excretions and sent them floating on their way. Their gentle drifting calmed him. The events of the summer were past, and the rainy winter of the Pacific Northwest had washed enough of his worries away. Matt was pretty sick of the Oregon Coast, and that's why he'd pushed inland to Portland. Now that he was filled up, he'd head down to southern California, maybe to Baja, maybe down along the coast of Central America again. He could leave all this behind and put extra distance between himself and his uncomfortable run-in with Esau.

Matt cast his last impervious bubble, set it aloft, and was turning in for the evening when he caught something out of the corner of his eye. His bubble popped.

Shocked, he spun and found three women standing behind him, near the ship's prow. They stood around a cauldron which glowed, though it lacked any obvious source of heat or light. The light came from within the cauldron rather than a fire beneath it. The green glow illuminated the three faces. One of the women was old, hunching into the traditional role of The Crone. Another appeared young, though Matt knew better. Her blond hair was tied in a tight braid that ran down the back of her head and hung over one shoulder, and she bounced that shoulder at him flirtatiously. The other sister was the middlest. She had a brown bouffant hairstyle and wore a man's bowler hat resting on top. Even the unusually gentle breeze of the evening should have tossed the hat overboard, but it sat there, defiant and dramatic like its owner. In addition to her hat, Taravissa also held an umbrella. She'd pointed it up in the air and popped Matt's magical bubble as it floated by.

Matt threw his arms wide and stepped towards the women as though he might embrace them all. "The Weird Sisters McElroy! As I live and breathe. How long has it been? Two hundred and fifty years? More?"

"Not long enough," Justinia said.

"Two hundred and sixty-seven years, to be exact," Taravissa said.

Garifinia made a pouty face. "I can't believe you don't remember our night of passion, Matty!"

"Oh, I'm sure I would have remembered if that actually occurred, dear, luscious Garifinia."

"I hate the way he flirts," Justinia told her middle sister. "It's slimy. Drippy."

"Your moistness is my goal, sweet, lovely Justinia."

That got a laugh from Taravissa and Garifinia.

Justinia sneered. "I'm going to barf on your boat."

Now Matt was offended. "It's a ship, not a boat."

"You're a dick and a cock," Justinia replied.

Matt nodded. "I would think you fine ladies would be admirers of great ships. Your ancestors must have made their way to Scotland from the Continent by boats of some kind. Where would you be without nautical travel?"

"My ancestors never came to Scotland," Justinia said. "I walked across the ice during the last ice age all by myself."

"Uphill both ways," Taravissa added. "And she never lets us forget it."

Matt looked at Garafinia and Taravissa. "So did you two follow later? By ship, perhaps?"

"I floated there using my umbrella," Taravissa said.

"I hiked up my skirts and ran really fast on the surface of the English Channel," Garifinia said.

"I rode there in the first submarine," Justinia said.

"Ooo, I took that car that M makes for Bond in *The Spy Who Loved Me*, the one that changes into a submarine. What kind of car was that? A Porsche?"

Matt shook his head. "A Lotus Esprit S1. Did you know that was an actual working sub made just for that movie?"

"Of course I know. My ancient ancestors took that to get to Scotland, douchebag. Show some respect!"

"My humblest apologies," Matt said. "So, to what do I owe the pleasure of your visit to the *Exclamation*, ladies?"

"For the record, I didn't want to come," Justinia said.

"Noted," Matt said, then looked to Taravissa and Garifinia for an explanation.

But Justinia continued: "I voted we just let you die."

"Die?"

"Yes. You're going to die. Very soon."

"How soon?"

Garifinia raised her eyebrows. "Not tonight. So if you're down to clown, you have a little time to get some of this, but not much."

"Just so I know how long we have to enjoy one another's company, are we talking about days? Weeks? Months?"

"Who can say?" Justinia said.

"We could," Taravissa said.

"Unless…" Garafina started.

"Unless?" her sisters chorused.

"Unless we can't tell him because it would allow him

to change his behavior in a way that would prevent his death. We couldn't tell him then, could we?"

Taravissa looked to her older sister. "We still could, but…"

Justinia frowned down into the cauldron. "But then we'd be saving his life, and that's exactly what I voted against."

Matt inclined his head. "Maybe if you just gave me a little information, it wouldn't be a sure thing, and then you could watch and see if I survive, and it would be more fun? Maybe money could even change hands. Not a bribe from me, of course. I know you're above that. But maybe a friendly wager between sisters to see if I can get through this with some clues. How does that strike you all?"

"Hmm." When Justinia seemed to be considering it, her sisters looked at her, slightly surprised. "I find that intriguing, frankly, but I don't think it would work. Here, come over and look into the cauldron, and you'll see your future." She waved him over, suddenly excited.

Matt crossed the deck in long strides, stepped up to the cauldron, and peered inside. It was filled with a green liquid that was, in fact, glowing brightly. He couldn't see anything beyond the flat green color and the light emanating from it, and the deeper he looked, the more the light stood out against the evening's falling darkness. He couldn't tell if the contrast produced the strain, or if his eyes were crossing from the effort. "I don't see anything but the … soup? Is it soup?"

The three women burst out laughing. "I do love that

joke," Taravissa said.

"Every time."

"They're so stupid."

Taravissa explained, "Normally we get people to just stare at stew. Some last longer than you did."

"Impatient. Unimpressive stamina," Garafinia mumbled.

"This time we knew we'd be dealing with a warlock of some ability…"

"Some," Justinia said.

"…so we bought a bunch of those green glow sticks at Tesco."

"Three different Tescos!" Garafinia whined.

"And then we cut them open and poured the goo in the cauldron." Taravissa said. "Come to think of it, we may not be able to use this for stew anymore."

Justinia shook her head. "Non-toxic. I looked it up. Might cause mild upset stomach if ingested, but so does Garafinia's stew."

"Hey!"

Taravissa stared down into the bowl, then up at Matt. "It does look cool, doesn't it?"

"Certainly, but it doesn't convince me that my demise is as imminent as you made it out to be."

"Of course not. For that, you'd need our eyes," Garafinia said. And then, without hesitation, she reached up and grabbed one of her mismatched eyes (the green one), plucked it out of her head, and held it out to him.

"What am I supposed to do with that?"

"Well," Justinia said, "if you really wanted to see the

future, you'd have to pluck both your own eyes out, replace them with a couple of ours, and then stare into the cauldron—"

"Or anywhere, really. Just focus on something that could serve as a screen," Taravissa interrupted.

"—and if you learned how for a couple hundred years, you'd eventually be able to pick out your own future and evaluate the likelihood of that occurrence based on the clarity of the image."

"We're really good at it," Garafinia said. "We watch future episodes of TV shows to hone our skills. A lot more efficient than it used to be when we'd have to go out and talk to people to find out if our predictions were correct. That blew."

"Peopling," Justinia agreed.

"I loved that part," Taravissa said.

"You would."

"I did!"

"Um, so should I take the eye?" Matt asked, looking down at it resting in Garafinia's outstretched hand

"Hell no," Justinia said. "Put that back, Garafinia. He'd just drop it in the glowing goo. He doesn't have the time to learn to use it, anyway."

"Good point." Garafinia stuck the eyeball back in her socket, winced and groaned as she rolled it into place, blinked until it righted itself, and then looked at Matt. "You have nice eyes. You should keep those."

Taravissa shrugged. "They're fine."

"So, about me dying."

"Yes, you're just going to have to trust us on this

part," Taravissa said.

"Somebody's going to kill you," Garafinia said. "Painfully. Violently. Like, excessively violently. Like, still stabbing and cutting and biting after you're dead kind of overkill-y murder-y murder."

"Who?" Matt asked.

Taravissa leaned towards him. "Well, who do you think would want you dead, Matt?"

"Oh, there are any number or people I've angered over the years."

"And what does that tell you, Matt?" Justinia asked.

"I'm a monster?"

Taravissa nodded. "And an asshole. Aren't you, Matt?"

"It kind of comes with the territory."

"Yes, and so does getting thoroughly killed by someone you've been an asshole to," Garafinia said. "Just part of the game. Haters gonna hate, and…" She looked up at the night sky, trying to find the right phrase. "Jerk's gonna get jerked? That doesn't work."

"Dick's gonna get dicked?" Taravissa tried. "Seems like it has sexual connotations that don't really apply."

"Fucker's going to get fucked up," Justina said.

"Better, but it's too close to FAFO," Garafinia said.

"We'll workshop it later," Taravissa told her younger sister.

"Yes," Garafinia agreed, then turned to Matt. "Just pretend I said something really cool. We'll edit it in post."

"Right, but just to put a pin in this for a moment, this

fucker would like to know which fucker is going to fuck him up."

"See, I don't like it," Taravissa said. "I'm not being a prude. It just gets hard to follow."

"Agreed," Garafinia said. "And it's Bel."

"You got her girlfriend shot by your angry ex who was aiming for you, so she holds you partly responsible," Taravissa explained.

"Fair, right?" Justinia asked.

Matt shrugged. "Fair enough. So, Bel is looking for me?"

"Nope. You'll just cross paths. And when she sees you, you're screwed," Taravissa said.

"Donezo," Justinia said.

Garafinia shook her head slowly. "And she just keeps going even after you're dead. It's really awful. She's obviously still pretty upset about the whole thing."

"Yeah, it sounds unpleasant. I'd prefer to avoid it. If you could give me some sense of where this will occur, I might be able to change my itinerary to be as far away from that place as possible."

"Good thinking," Taravissa said.

"But it won't work," Justinia explained. "Wherever you go, that's where she'll be."

"This will happen," Garafinia said

Justinia raised an eyebrow. "Unless..."

"Unless?" Taravissa asked.

They all waited.

"Unless?" Matt echoed.

"When she comes across you, she kills you, right? But

what if you sought her out and had something to offer which might cause her to hesitate long enough for you to employ that used-car-salesman technique of yours to convince her not to kill you."

"Would that work?"

Taravissa shook her head. "It's almost impossible."

"Almost?"

"So many things will have to fall into place. You'll have to complete a number of very difficult tasks."

"Very difficult," Garafinia agreed. "Like Hercules' Labors level difficulty. Nightmare mode."

"And even then it probably won't work. And even if all those things do work out, Bel will probably still kill you. If I may," Taravissa frowned conspiratorially, "can I just suggest that you don't even try. It's all going to be exhausting and probably pointless. Frankly, it makes me tired just thinking about it."

"All that work," Justina said.

"Right?" Taravissa barked. "So much easier to just live your life to the fullest. You're rich and spoiled. Keep pampering yourself. Do whatever makes you happiest. And just know, all the time, that at any instant an angry vampire is going to spot you and rip you apart in a fit of rage. But other than that, live your best life. That's my advice, anyway."

Matt nodded. "It doesn't sound like good advice. I've been living my best life for quite some time now, and having the Sword of Damocles hanging over my head will put a damper on my fun. But I have to admit, you're probably right. I'm not really the Seven Labors kind of guy. Just for the sake of argument, what would my seven labors be?"

"Four," Justina said.

"What would they be for?"

"No. Four. There would be four labors. First, you'd need to find a dragon in his lair."

"And they don't like to be bothered at home. So that's kind of an Indiana Jones thing," Garafinia said.

"More Bilbo Baggins, don't you think?" Taravissa said.

"Too on-the-nose. It looked more like that temple from Raiders to me."

Taravissa acquiesced. "It did, didn't it? Not dwarven at all. And very little gold."

"Okay, so I find a dragon. Then what?"

"Then you convince the dragon to go with you to help you save a human from your ex-boyfriend," Justinia said.

"Shanghai a dragon in Shanghai," Garafinia said.

"Stupid," Justinia muttered.

"Esau doesn't kill humans," Matt said. "Does he?"

"Sometimes," Taravissa said. "He will again. Unless you stop him."

"Okay, then what?"

"You find the golem, Josef, and reach out to Bel and tell her where to find it."

"You'll meet her there. That's where she might just let you live. She has a soft spot for Josef." Garafinia shot a conspiratorial look at her sisters. "For reasons."

"Okay, so that's only three."

"Yeah, and then she'll still kill you unless you promise

to do one more thing."

"What?"

Justinia raised her palms upwards and shrugged. "We can't tell you that yet."

"It wouldn't make any sense, anyway," Taravissa said.

"Complicated," Garafinia said.

"But you can try telling Bel you'll do one more thing, the thing we'll tell you about later, and if she believes you, maybe she'll let you live."

"Oh, and you may need to get Bel a helicopter. And a private plane flight. And whatever else she needs. But those don't count as labors. Just business expenses."

"Probably tax deductible," Justinia said. "Not heroic if they're write-offs."

"Not even really charity, if you think about it," Taravissa said. "Like when they ask you to round up for a charity when you're buying something at a business. It's really a way to keep profits in-house and buy PR instead of paying taxes."

Justinia nodded sagely. Garafina mumbled, "Scam."

"Oh, and one more thing, and this is important," Taravissa started.

"Very important," Garafinnia agreed.

"Vitally important," Justina said.

"Don't let Esau see you. You'll cross paths with him again. If he sees you, he'll shoot you. He won't miss this time. But if he doesn't see you, he won't shoot you. You'll walk away from the encounter unscathed. So just don't reveal yourself to him. Remember that."

Matt nodded. "Note to self: Don't tell the guy who tried to shoot me before that I'm standing right in front of him. Pretty straightforward. I can do that one."

Justinia waggled a finger. "Doesn't count as a labor. Just an omission. But worth remembering."

"Got it. Four labors, one to be named later, plus some business expenses and an act of omission. I have to say, compared to being ripped to shreds, this sounds preferable."

Justinia looked down into the glowing bowl. "I look forward to asking you if you still think so if you survive."

Matt followed her gaze. "I guess I look forward to surviving to tell you."

"Politics is the art of looking for trouble, finding it everywhere, diagnosing it incorrectly and applying the wrong remedies."

-Ernest Benn

Chapter 9

The King of Trolls sat on his throne on the dais in his lair beneath 1211 Avenue of the Americas. New Yorkers called Avenue of the Americas "Sixth Avenue." Americans, if they thought of it at all, thought of the building as the skyscraper housing Fox News. And the King of Trolls, 45 stories beneath the street, thought about how everything seemed to be going fine and was, in fact, all going to shit. He felt deeply conflicted about this.

Chaos was his bread and butter, literally his food

supply. Trolls, for millennia, had generated outrage and terror, feeding on the human emotions and only settling for human flesh reluctantly as a last-ditch means to stay sated or as an appetizer to bring about the main course.

Over a hundred years ago, the King himself had discovered that radio, then moving pictures, and then television could sow the seeds of chaos and produce outrage in much greater quantities than bands of roving trolls attacking wayfarers or single trolls frightening passersby on bridges. And then, in the ass-end of the 20th century, the humans had given him their greatest gift: the Internet.

Now, stretched out before him in rows reaching each side of the enormous room and repeating as far back as the eye could see into the shadows of the cavernous space, trolls sat at computer screens, their horrible faces illuminated by the gamma glow, their fingers clicking on caps-locked keyboards, each doing their best to enrage some human who made the billy-goat mistake of peering under the bridge into the comments section. The trolls hardly ever ventured above anymore, nor did they eat human flesh. Instead, they ate Cheetos (an increasing number favoring the "Flamin' Hot" variety), drank energy drinks (initially Red Bulls, but the King provided Rebels and Monsters to his wingless, obedient monsters as well), and worked in three overlapping 18 hour shifts. And they were happy to do it. Or, if they weren't, the King, far larger than his subjects, would grab the nearest pouty-faced troll and rip off a limb or hurl him through the air, or both, so the trolls did their best to express high levels of job satisfaction at every performance review.

Despite the occasional need to motivate his subjects with a public dismemberment, the whole underground office ran as a well-oiled machine, generating high returns in outrage, growing the troll population, and increasing the King's power within The Convention. A few years back, he'd been named the Parliamentarian at the annual meeting, and he'd used the authority that came from ruling on questionable actions vis-à-vis Robert's Rules of Order to further entrench his authority in that larger organization. The King had even managed to make a deal with the Archduke of the vampires to work together to sideline the upstart Cassius, who was threatening both their positions.

Then the whole meeting had been thrown into an uproar when Cassius announced he had a weapon that could kill all monsters, then got shot in the face by a human infiltrator, and the whole room was overturned by a rampaging dragon. Now Cassius was AWOL, nobody was really sure who was running CimBim, and there were lots of potential inroads to improve the position of the trolls in the organization. The chaotic end of last year's annual meeting hadn't harmed the King much. Though trolls couldn't feed on chaos among monsters the way they did with humans, they were comfortable in disordered environments, recognizing fear and anger as opportunities to exploit. The King should have been happy. And that made him nervous. And that made him irritable.

"Egg!" he bellowed.

Egg knew he was the King's new favorite, and sometimes that made him overwhelmingly proud. Sometimes it also made him bruised, and it pretty much always made him exhausted. His eyes popped open in the darkness of the warren where he slept in a pile with a random assortment of other trolls. Some of his bunkmates groaned when he sat up quickly and began scrabbling over their sleeping bodies, and one made a halfhearted attempt to bite him as he passed, but Egg dodged away, slapped his sibling hard enough to generate a loud clap, and continued to the cave's small aperture. From there, he sank his claws into the stalactite which descended into the main hall where all the working trolls hammered away at their keyboards.

Egg's warren could be reached by a stalactite and a stalagmite which didn't quite connect. Some years ago a tired troll at the end of a shift had tried to make the leap from the top of the pointy stalagmite to the bottom of the stalactite, missed, and had been impaled. That had been nice for the others because it gave them a handhold and platform when climbing up and down each day. But poor Grep had rotted away eventually, so everyone had to make the risky jump again. Egg was fairly certain he could get permission to move warrens from the King now, but all his new roommates would resent him for using the King's favoritism to invade their space. He'd made the calculation that a daily risk of death was better than sleeping in a pile of trolls who wanted to bite him. Now he reconsidered. If the King was going to call for him at odd hours and make him take the leap more often, maybe it made sense to move.

Egg let go of the stalactite and managed to grab onto the stalagmite as he fell, ran across the floor of the great hall, scrambled up the steps of the stage, and stopped, panting, next to the King's throne. "Yessir?"

"What, were you sleeping?"

Egg tried to decide if it was better to admit he was sleeping when the King ordered his shift to sleep, or if it was best to pretend the King hadn't awakened him. He decided on neither. "Came as soon as I heard you call, sir!"

"Good job, shit-splat. But be faster next time. I want to talk to somebody. Get me my computer."

"Right away, sir. Who do you want to talk to."

"Who is in charge over at CimBim?'

"Unclear. Maybe the Archduke knows?"

The King of Trolls sneered. "Probably. I hate that guy."

"And he's your favorite non-troll, so that's saying something," Egg said. He hoped he was reminding the King that he was his favorite troll-troll.

The King nodded. "True. Get him on the line, Egg."

Egg barked at the computer crew. One brought a tower computer, and two more carried a large television monitor, crab walking their way onto the stage in comic fits and starts as it teetered above their heads. A fourth troll followed behind with a roll of orange extension cords he dolloped out like a flower girl trailing a bride with rose petals. Once the tower was placed, the two holding the monitor did their best to keep it upright in front of the King, and Egg directed the cord techie to stand next to the throne. Then he gently placed a foam mouse pad on the troll's head. Egg had been in that role before, and he'd learned it was kind to give a fellow troll the mousepad so the mouse's laser didn't hit it in the eyes when the King got frustrated with his technology. It was also a kindness he did himself; by offering the mousepad to one of the crew, he saved himself from being assigned the job.

The King smacked the mouse onto the mousepad troll's head a few times and clicked the button impatiently until the computer woke up. He opened the Zoom icon, and Egg typed for him on a wireless keyboard. Soon the screen was ringing. The King made faces at himself, his green and purple scales clashing with his bright pink tongue, so when the Archduke and his butler, Jeeves, opened the call that was the first thing they saw.

The Archduke yanked at a lock of his hair which remained standing at an angle when he lowered his hands. "Your Highness. Always such a pleasure. But really, it's not a great time."

"Yeah, you look like hell, Arch-Dookie," the King said. He turned to Egg. "What time is it?"

Egg read the clock at the bottom of the screen. "3:30 in the afternoon, sir."

"Oh, I woke you up? Sorry, Archie."

The Archduke's hand found its way back to the shock of hair, patted it down, and then pulled it back up again. "It's not the sleep issue, really. I mean, yes, you are calling during daylight hours which is inconsiderate, but you aren't the paragon of manners, now are you?" The Archduke turned toward Jeeves who stood at attention just behind his shoulder. "He's always been a rude sort, hasn't he, Jeeves."

"Compulsively uncouth, sir."

"So I'm used to that. Unfazed, really, at this point. But I've got a great deal going on here, if you must know. Terribly busy."

The King considered expressing his usual disdain for the concerns of others, then saw that the Archduke's problems might align with his. "I wonder if we're dealing with some of the same things. What's going on with you?"

"Oh, what one would expect when there's a power vacuum."

"Suckage?" the King said.

"Of a sort. Our vampire contingent is a mess. CimBim is a mess. Monsters are breaking The Convention, being seen by humans, and the backlog is getting long enough they think they've gotten away with it. Cassius had ambitions that were problematic, and you and I were working on a successor, but we understood he couldn't just disappear, or there would be problems in the organization. But then, after his humiliation, he vanished anyway, and here we are picking up the pieces."

"Well, he probably wanted to avoid the limelight for a while because half his face was gone."

"Nonsense," the Archduke said. "His whole position was behind the scenes. He could have continued with all his duties while healing."

"Doodies," the King muttered.

Egg snickered, his head bouncing up and down at the bottom of the King's box on the screen.

"And the werewolves are still in disarray, so they can't be called upon to help enforce The Convention. CimBim called me because they have resorted to sending out teams of minotaurs with warlocks keeping them in glamours so they can move about amongst the humans, and you know how much warlocks charge for their services, so the cost overruns... CimBim has blown through its annual budget and rainy day fund, and there will be hell to pay at the budget hearing at the next annual meeting, I promise you."

"Minotaurs? Topside?"

"Yes, yes, far from the perfect solution, but what were we going to do? Some monsters just aren't fighters, and others are too conspicuous. I did manage to track down one of our most consistent operatives, Jezebel Shipwright, and sent her out into the field, but after reporting back on the completion of that one job, she hasn't taken another. Too focused on training her newly turned partner, Magdalena Wallace, I suppose."

"Wait," the King said. "*The* Magdalena Wallace? The one who wrote the book? Both books?"

"Yes, she's one of ours, now," the Archduke said.

The King of Trolls didn't know if the Archduke meant "ours" as in "belonging to monsters" or "one of the vampires" or "belonging to the two of us," and he suspected that was intentional.

"And the books?"

"Destroyed. And she has no interest in making more since she no longer wants all monsters to die and never did want all humans to die. And as a vampire being trained to fight by Jezebel Shipwright, she'll be quite safe from any more attempts to compel her to produce more of her little genocidal novels, so that's one less headache for me."

The King only hummed thoughtfully at this, but he set one of his huge hands on Egg's head and tapped his claws on Egg's bald scalp in a contemplative sequence, like a flute player practicing scales, up and back down, up and back down.

Egg caught the meaning but said nothing.

Finally, the King spoke, but he immediately changed the subject. "So, CimBim is a shit-show. It will get itself back in order soon enough under your leadership. My bigger worry is Tisina."

The Archduke raised an eyebrow. "Oh, have you heard from her?"

The King shook his head, a tight, swift shake that made his huge ears wobble. "No, and that's the problem. I've only communicated with her a few times, but in the last four months I've reached out repeatedly, and I haven't heard back. And neither have any of my contacts. Have you heard from anyone in her entire kingdom? Any gorgons? Any sirens? Any Merfolk at all?'

The Archduke looked back at Jeeves, and when he turned back around, he'd shifted gears from frazzled to frightened. When the King took in the Archduke's expression, he realized the old vampire was thinking three moves ahead of him, and the fear became contagious.

"What?" the King breathed.

"We're not prepared," the Archduke said.

"Not prepared for what?"

"Tisina has been planning to invade the human world for a long time. Since before she became queen, probably. I assumed she would wait until her heir had come of age. She was plotting to give the world to him, have him lead her armies, conquer the humans."

"She was knocked up the last time I spoke with her," the King said.

"But maybe she wants to give him the world as a birthday gift. Or maybe he's been born and is already magically an adult. I don't know how gorgon gestation works. Do you?"

"I presumed they grew up more slowly than humans because they live so much longer. But who knows?"

"Regardless, if she is starting her invasion, that means the entire contingent of undersea monsters are about to break The Convention and appear on land. Just when CimBim is in disarray and doesn't have the numbers to repel an attack. It will be on every human newspaper headline and TV screen. And when the other monsters see The Convention is no longer enforced, they will do what monsters do when presented with a loaded banquet table and no guardrails."

"Feeding frenzy."

"Exactly. Who wants to be last in line at the buffet and

find out it's not really all-you-can-eat after all?"

"And the humans will retaliate."

"Yes. Not the little groups of monster hunters who drove us into hiding back when The Convention was signed. Nations. Armies. The kinds of weapons we cannot survive."

"You think they'll use nukes?"

"Wouldn't you? Every kind of monster suddenly comes out of hiding all at once? You'd decide it was an existential threat and bring out your biggest guns."

"Even if that meant I died, too? You think they'll see some monsters and decide to go out in a blaze of glory?"

"We're not talking about the kind of people with the courage and morality and strategic thinking necessary to retreat, regroup, and start picking off disorganized monsters. We're talking about the second most cowardly humans in the world, politicians, and the most cowardly, demagogues.

"Politicians live in constant fear that they'll lose the thing they value most, the validation that comes from winning regularly scheduled popularity contests. And the demagogues live in constant fear that everyone around them hates them and wants to kill them because everyone around them hates them and wants to kill them.

"The politicians will do what they think will make them popular, and the demagogues will do what they think makes them frightening. Neither will tell people to retreat behind castle walls until daylight and then go out to stake the vampires. Both will yell, "Charge!" and lead the army out when it's darkest. Trust me. I've been fighting humans more directly than you have for millennia. You can count on them to make impulsive, suicidal moves when careful ones would be more likely to succeed but might look too hesitant. I think it's their short lifespans. Maybe. It's certainly the reason I'm still alive. New vampires think our biggest asset in combat is our speed. But they're wrong. It's our patience. If we can't kill an opponent, we can hide for centuries and kill his great-grandchildren. That's why we started The Convention. To get all the monsters to hide, be patient, eat our fill from the shadows. I think Tisina understood this, but she never wanted to really do it. She wanted to wait in the darkness while she gathered her strength, and she was always planning to break The Convention."

The Archduke looked down into his lap and shook his head. "So I've been trying to shore up the institution, to prepare it for this day. When I suspected Cassius was working with Tisina, I reached out to you to form our partnership. I'm sure you thought I was merely protecting my position among the vampires by dealing with an upstart who wanted to take my place. But I was aware you had also been working with Cassius and Tisina before you confirmed that fact. I hope that doesn't offend you."

"No offense taken, dickwad. We all should presume we have more complicated plans in the works."

"Right-O. Jolly good," the Archduke said without enthusiasm. "I thought, if you and I could form an alliance in opposition to Cassius, it would perhaps allow me to throw a monkey wrench into Tisina's plans, but I learned that Cassius had already betrayed her by sending inferior ingredients for whatever spell she was working on. I presumed that would either delay her or cause her to turn on Cassius."

The King of Trolls raised a finger. "We shouldn't discount the possibility one or both of those things has occurred. Tisina hasn't been heard from. We shouldn't leap to the conclusion she is beginning her invasion. Maybe the mix-up with the ingredients did backfire, and maybe that killed her. Or maybe she discovered it, and that's why we haven't heard from Cassius since the annual meeting of The Convention. Maybe she got to him."

"Possible, but unlikely. Both of those theories might explain her lack of communication, but neither would explain why we haven't heard from any other Merfolk or gorgons or sirens recently. The entire delegation is out of communication. I find it more likely the entirety of both species is marching towards their destination as we speak."

"Do they march?" the King asked.

"Swimming in formation. Schooling? That doesn't sound like an army moving to a battlefield."

"Swarming?"

"Perhaps. Regardless, we should prepare. I will task some of CimBim's resources to look for the Merfolk. Human satellites and informants in human governments and such. While vast areas of the oceans are often unobserved, I imagine some fisherman or sailor will cry out for help as an army passes beneath his boat, and if we're listening for that, we might find out where they're headed."

"Good. While you do that, I'll get my whole crew looking around the Internet for any humans talking about anything weird happening on the water. You let me know if you hear anything, and I'll let you know if we hear anything. Deal?"

"Agreed."

"Oh, and stop futzing with your hair when you're anxious. You look like Boris fucking Johnson or something."

The Archduke frowned. "That is the most offensive thing you've ever said to me."

"I'll try to think of something more cutting before we talk again, Boris. Happy hunting, you fanged limey weasel."

"Yes, good luck to you as well, you…" The Archduke stammered, then flapped a hand at his screen. "...big, trollish troll." He clicked the red "Leave Meeting" button, then sighed and turned to Jeeves. "I couldn't think of anything."

"It was appropriately disdainful, sir."

The King of Trolls waved the computer crew off with similar enthusiasm, then turned to Egg. "So, you heard that?"

"Get everyone looking for rumors of an aquatic army?" Egg asked.

"No, forget that. I'm not making thousands of trolls go hungry just to find one crazy mermaid."

"Gorgon," Egg corrected.

"Whatever. Fish lady."

"More of a cephalopod lady."

The King scowled.

Egg swallowed.

"Anyway, did you catch the other thing? The human woman who wrote the books is now a vampire. That's a big advantage for the vamps. Like being the only ones with a cure when there's a potential global disease."

Egg nodded. "More like being the only ones with a vial of the disease."

"If the Merfolk are going to break The Convention, and then everybody is going to go hog wild on the humans, it might be a good time to release that disease. Better than a nuclear war, right?"

Egg was fairly certain he recalled hearing that dissemination of Lena's books would result in the death of all humans and all monsters, so he questioned whether that would really be better than or merely equal to thermonuclear war, but he decided not to argue the math with his boss.

"So here's what you're going to do, Egg," the King continued. "Instead of tasking everybody to search for online posts about underwater armies, I want you to have them keep at their usual work but be on the lookout for any reference to a couple of vampires, and see if you can get some of your best hacker boys to take a break from their usual ID thefts of elderly Boomers learning Facebook. Instead, have them see if they can put a trace on any of Jezebel Shipwright's credit cards. She's got to have some bank accounts going back centuries, right? Shouldn't be too hard to follow the money. Do whatever you have to do, but find her. That's the easy part. Then, I want you to put together a strike force. You'll need a lot of trolls to nab a couple of vampires, especially one who tracks and kills monsters for a living, and a lot of them will probably die, so make sure they're really brawny and not too bright. And then, when you find this Jezebel Shipwright and her girlfriend, I want you to nab them and bring them to me."

Egg swallowed. "Both, your Highness?"

"Both, and both alive. We're a lot more likely to be able to get this recently-human woman to write us books if she's motivated by threats to her girlfriend, and if either are hurt or killed, the other is just going to fight harder, so see if you can convince them to come in without fighting, but bag them and bind them in silver chains just in case. I don't want you to die on this mission, Egg. And, more importantly, I don't want to get killed when you bring them here, so be careful, but bring me that weapon of mass destruction."

"While I see many hoof marks going in, I see none coming out. It is easier to get into the enemy's toils than out again."

-Aesop

Chapter 10

Ludwig still couldn't remember any of his life before waking up in the catacombs beneath Paris, but he was beginning to realize there were a number of things he could identify, like buildings and cars and people, and a seemingly greater number that took him by surprise, like glowing LED advertisements. He took these to be smaller versions of the screens from motion picture shows he must have been aware of before his awakening, only these were far more vivid and didn't seem to be the targets of any projection devices he could see. To him, these screens were all "off", just blank gray like a screen in a movie theater before the show begins. But he noticed people looking at them. He stopped and starred. Something changed, like the movie had begun. He could see motion on the screen. It was still in shades of gray, but he was seeing light instead of density.

He looked ahead of him to his two new friends, Bel, the one with short hair who spoke to him in German, and Lena, the one with the big, curly hair who spoke to him in Spanish. For the first time, he could their skin was different, Lena's a darker gray than Bel's, and their clothes, previously slightly less dense than skin but roughly the same shade on everyone, now appeared distinct. The women were wearing different colored clothes, he realized. He couldn't see the colors, but somehow he was experiencing light reflecting into his eyeless sockets and not just radar of density being read by his bones. Now that he had friends, everything looked different.

The women led him through the streets, stopping him at each corner so they could make sure no one was looking, then hurrying him along. He waited in an alley with Lena while Bel ran ahead for a bit, and then the women escorted him through a fire exit into a building he couldn't identify from the outside but which he recognized as a hotel when he saw all the identical doors with numbers lining the long hallway.

The trio made their way to the room Bel had rented. While she opened the door (not with a key, Ludwig noticed, but with a plastic card), the door on the far side of the hall opened, and a woman stepped out. At first she looked down at the ground, making a show of being uninterested in her neighbors, and turned her back on them to close her door quietly, giving the knob a little twist to make sure it was secure. Then, as she turned to head down the hall, she caught sight of them out of the corner of her eye. She was a middle-aged woman, white, with some grey in her auburn hair and thick black rims on her stylish glasses. When she saw them, she turned so she could take them in fully through the lenses, and then her eyes widened so much they seemed to fill the glasses with the whites of her eyes like a cartoon character.

She opened her mouth and inhaled, preparing to scream. Bel dashed around Lena and Ludwig who were standing there, unsure what to do. Lena held out a hand in a calming gesture, and Ludwig's left arm fell off as he tried to wave hello. In the time it took for his upper arm to descend to his pelvis and be caught by his quick right hand, Bel slammed her palm over the woman's mouth, wrapped her other hand behind the woman's neck, kicked back to push open the door of their room, and yanked the woman inside. Lena shoved Ludwig in after them, then closed the door behind her.

"Quick, before she screams," Bel shout-whispered. She raised a knee to the woman's lower back, forced her back like a 1920's movie star or a tango dancer dipping their partner for a kiss, and then she tilted the woman's head to expose her neck to Lena.

Lena made a sad face and hesitated for a moment.

"Quick!" Bel ordered. She knew she could hold the woman indefinitely, but Lena was more likely to feed if she didn't think about it.

Lena leaned forward, distorted and extended her jaw in the supernatural way that always made her feel a twinge of revulsion, allowed her circular rows of spiney, hollow teeth to pierce through the folds in her gums which hid them, and descended on the woman's neck. The long teeth perforated the soft skin easily, and the blood drew up through each tooth like medicine through a needle. Simultaneously, the sharp sides of the teeth sliced the flesh as they quivered, carving away the skin and allowing more of the woman's blood to flow down Lena's throat.

Bel waited for a few seconds until the woman stopped struggling. Then she slowly lowered the woman to the floor. The woman's legs buckled and bent unnaturally beneath her, but she didn't have the strength to straighten them. The pain from her knees would have been intense if her brain had been able to register it, but just as those signals were passing through her spine, Bel plopped down on all fours and sank her own teeth into the other side of the woman's neck. This caused some pain, but the signals were confused by the lips caressing the skin, the room's sudden cold, and the body's need to pull all the remaining blood to her head and torso. The woman's brain tried to react to an experience that was at once sensual and as traumatizing as breaking through the ice of a frozen lake.

And then, mercifully, the brain decided it was all too much, and she lost consciousness. But her heart continued to beat long enough to give Lena and Bel a full meal before the last, bitter gulp that was just platelets and flesh, the signal to both vampires that there was nothing more to drink.

Lena retracted her teeth, pulled her jaw back into place, and licked her lips. She ran her fingers around her mouth and found she'd done a good job of eating without making a mess of her face, though she would need to reapply her lipstick. She looked down at the woman in front of them. The last dribbles of that sludgy, scabby blood made its best, pathetic effort to fill the gaping holes on either side of her neck. "Just bad timing," she muttered.

"No, honey," Bel said, rising to her feet. She looked down at Lena. "Just timing. Not good or bad. Just a thing that happens at a certain time like everything else."

Lena looked up at her, thought about how to reply, then nodded silently and stood.

"Okay," Bel said, her voice somewhere between businesslike and chipper. "We can leave her here when we check out. I paid in cash. No need to dispose of the body. Maybe stick her in the closet or the bathtub to get her out of the way. I'm going to go shopping for some clothes for Napoleon. Unless you want to come with me?"

"No, I think one of us should stay with him," Lena said. She turned to look at Ludwig.

He was standing with his spine wedged into the far corner of the room, visibly shaking.

Lena held out a calming hand. "*No te preocupes, Napoleón. Todo está bien.*"

But he was worried, and her assurance that everything was fine did not stop his shaking. Unfortunately, when he shook, his bones, uninsulated without cartilage, rattled in their sockets comically, like agitated wooden wind chimes.

Bel managed to avoid laughing at the sound. *"Napoleon, wir sind Vampire,"* she explained. *"Du bist ein Skelett. Bei uns haben Sie nichts zu befürchten."*

Her efforts to explain their relative positions as vampires and a reanimated skeleton did not convince Ludwig he had nothing to fear.

Bel turned to Lena and spoke in English. "Okay, you stay here and try to calm him down. I'll go get him some clothes so he can walk the streets at night without violating The Convention. When I get back, we can talk next steps."

"Good plan," Lena replied, though she kept her gaze on Ludwig. *"Calmate. Todo está bien,"* she told him again.

"Yeah, good luck with that," Bel said. She gave Lena a quick kiss on the cheek, opened the door a crack to make sure the hallway was empty, and slipped out.

Lena looked around the tiny hotel room and discovered the little desk under the window next to the tall wardrobe. She made a mental note to remember to drag the wardrobe in front of the window before they went to sleep for the day, then opened the top drawer of the desk and found a little pad of paper and a pen.

"¿Puedes escribir?" she asked Ludwig, pantomiming writing with the pen.

He didn't respond immediately, just stood there

shaking, staring with his empty sockets at the vampire he'd just watched murder and consume a woman on the hotel floor. Then he made a tight little nod.

"Good!" Lena said, clapping her hands. Switching back to Spanish, she began to ramble in an effort to calm him and (aware of the irony) humanize herself. She explained she'd been a writer once and still thought of herself as a writer, though she hadn't been doing much writing lately. She'd attempted to do a little processing on the page when she'd first been turned, recording some of her feelings and noting some of the early lessons Bel had taught her, and that had been a comfort. She encouraged Ludwig to write a bit, both as a means to communicate with her and to express his feelings.

"You and I, we're not completely dissimilar," she told him in Spanish. "You were once a human, just like me. And then, one day, you woke up to discover you're something else. I had that same experience. Only I woke up just a couple days after I'd died. Many years passed in between your human life and your new life. You see, you're alive now, but you're one of us. We're monsters. Don't be frightened. You don't have much to be afraid of anymore. And, like me, you have people to help you make this transition. Bel and I can help you learn to navigate this new world in which you find yourself. We'll teach you how to hide from the humans, figure out what you need to eat. Maybe you don't eat anything anymore. I know it was shocking to see us feed on that woman. This will take some adjustment, but you will come to learn that we aren't really a part of their species anymore. If I'm being really honest, I'm still struggling a bit with that myself. Even if, as Bel assures me, the humans are like cattle and chickens and pigs to us, I still feel…"

She switched back to English. "How do you say 'squeamish'?"

"…uncomfortable," she continued in Spanish, "with the idea that we just kill them without any regard to their feelings. Like, even then it's cruelty to animals, right?"

She kept talking until Ludwig stopped shaking, and then she sat down on the bed and patted the spot next to her. But she didn't slow down, fearing she'd spook him with silence. She wanted his choice to sit to feel consensual. "…So, while we sleep during the day, you'll need to stand guard. If you feel comfortable in that role. I don't want to compel you. I figure you've had enough of that. That's what brought you back, you know. There was a … I have no idea how to say 'necromancer' in Spanish. Not a word my grandmother taught me. '*Brujo*' is probably closest, but it's not quite right, because there are warlocks, but this guy was a certain kind of monster who brings people back from the dead to work for him. I want you to know, whatever he made you do, that's not your fault. You were … I don't know how to say 'thrall,' either. Under his orders. Yes, you were under his orders. But we defeated him, and it seemed all his skeletons just went back to being dead. But you are still here. And that's great! I'm glad you are still alive, Napoleon. I don't know if you're glad. Would you like to write to me? Or write down your feelings for yourself?"

At this, Ludwig sat next to her and took the offered pad of paper. He took the pen as well, a simple plastic disposable one with the name of the hotel engraved in tacky gold paint. But when he pressed it to the paper, he found the pen slid up between his fingers. He couldn't control it well enough with only bones.

"Hmm," Lena said. "I guess I'd never thought of that. Pens do require skin, don't they."

Ludwig slumped a bit, then sat up straight in a fit of inspiration. He held up the pen and began biting near the end, first with his incisors, then some chewing with his molars, then some poking with his canines, until he'd created some rough holes where the tips of his fingers could pinch.

"Clever!" Lena said.

He wrote, and the pen worked. *"No recuerdo mi vida cuando era un ser humano. ¿Que ano es?"*

Lena smiled. "It's 2025. And it's okay that you don't remember. We'll figure some things out together. For example, we just learned that Spanish is not your first language, probably. You forgot the accent over the 'e,' here." She pointed it out. "And the tilde over this 'ñ.'" She chuckled. "That's an error a native speaker would never make. Without that, it's a very different word." She laughed but did not elaborate.

Ludwig liked hearing the sound of her laugh.

"So, unless we find some other language you understand better, I'm guessing you were German, and you learned Spanish at some point. Do you remember learning Spanish?"

Ludwig did not know he'd learned Spanish in school nor that he'd been stationed in Spain as a consequence before being relocated to the French coast, nor his reassignment to a garrison in Paris, nor his death when ambushed by some resistance fighters hiding out in the catacombs under the city. He shook his head and wrote, "I don't remember any of it."

"But you remember both languages. That's great! And do you know what city we're in now?"

He shook his head sadly.

"That's okay, my friend," Lena said. "We're in Paris. Do you know that name?"

He nodded.

"Do you know what country it's in?"

He shook his head.

"Okay. No problem. Don't be sad about that. Lots to learn. Paris is in France, and France is a country in between Germany and Spain. Those are the countries where your languages come from, so you may have lived in one or both.

"And we don't know quite when you lived as a human, but maybe we'll be able to figure it out based on which kinds of technology you recognize and which you don't." Lena placed her hand on his hand bones. "But Napoleon, here's the important thing: As much as it might be scary right now, you aren't that same person anymore. You're a skeleton. You are a skeleton with two friends who will help you learn what kind of skeleton you want to be, okay?"

Ludwig nodded slowly, considering this. And by the

time his head came to rest, he was no longer Ludwig. Napoleon placed his other hand on top of Lena's, squeezed gently, and then picked up the pen and pad of paper and wrote, "Thank you, my friend."

A few hours later, as Lena started to get anxious about the coming dawn, Bel returned to the room carrying three large bags.

"Phew," Lena said. "I was getting worried." She looked at the bags. "How many clothing stores are open at four in the morning?"

"None," Bel said. "But some have lower security than others. Find a back door, break a padlock, cut the electricity, and shop in the dark. Even if they have video cameras on battery power, they got what? A person in a hoodie carefully choosing clothing and putting them in a bag?"

"Did you leave money on the counter?" Lena asked.

"You know what's weird? I actually did think about doing that. But no."

"Really?" Lena asked. "Like moral qualms or as a joke?"

Bel cocked her head to the side. "More like as a kind of homage to you, or a joke to make you laugh. Either way, not worth the money. No offense."

Lena laughed. "None taken, I think. So, what did you get our boy, here? And did you find any notebooks and pens?"

"Yeah, I got those at a gas station. Paid for them with money!"

"That's sweet of you," Lena said.

"I thought about eating one of the attendants instead, but I wasn't that hungry." She set the bags on the bed and rummaged in one of them, pulling out the spiral notebooks and a couple packages of disposable pens. "Are these for you?"

"No, for Napoleon. He can write in German and Spanish. Well, I didn't see any German, but his Spanish is very obviously second-language Spanish, so he was probably German. We had a good talk about how it really doesn't matter. Now he can write to us, so that will make communication easier." She almost said, "That was what Josef used to do, with his little notepads," but she caught herself.

Bel almost said the same thing and caught herself, too. Silence.

"So," Bel said, "let's see how Napoleon looks in these."

"Damn. Why did you get him so many clothes, Babe?
"Oh, you'll see."

And Lena did. When they helped him into a pair of jeans and a t-shirt, he looked absurd. Even with the slim fits of European men's fashion, or perhaps exaggerated by them, Napoleon looked less like a human and more like an oddly shaped clothesline. "Okay," Bel said, "let's stuff the scarecrow."

Once Napoleon was dressed in twelve pairs of socks under his boots, ten t-shirts wrapped around his legs inside his jeans, another five balled up and stuffed into his abdomen and ribcage, another five shirts over those, a hoodie over that, a pair of knitted gloves under a pair of leather ones, and a long coat to hide the strange bulges, he looked enough like a human to not draw eyes on the street. Unless someone looked inside the hood and saw a skull there.

"Ideas for his face?" Lena asked.

"A couple." She held up a scarf in front of his eyes. "Napoleon," she asked in German, "can you see me through this?"

He shook his head.

"*Donnerwetter,*" she cursed without much passion. Then, to Lena, she said, "I was hoping his vision wasn't really based on light coming into his eye sockets."

"It can't really be, can it?"

Bel shook her head. "A lot of things about monsters don't make a lot of biological sense. We shouldn't be able to move as fast as we can, and our metabolism should be much higher. And there's the whole living-on-a-liquid-diet-but-never-needing-to-take-a-piss thing."

"I always thought that was weird," Lena said. "Or a shit, for that matter. I mean, some of it's got to be solid, right? Do we have, like, portals to another dimension inside of us or something?"

"It's beyond science. And I'm sure his vision is, too. And beyond reason. Like, why would a necromancer give him the ability to move around but then limit him by making it possible to blind him? Seems like a design flaw. But who knows? Maybe the spell depends on the skeletons believing they have flesh-and-blood bodies so they can fight like humans?"

Lena frowned. "I guess that makes a kind of sense,

but…"

"But?"

"…but it doesn't. It's stupid."

"Exactly. Some monsters try to figure out all the magic. They just drive themselves crazy."

"'"Theirs not to make reply / Theirs not to reason why / Theirs is but to do and die,'" Lena quoted.

"I was there, you know?"

"At the charge of the Light Brigade?"

"Well, not during the day, but you would be surprised how many women just followed armies around back then."

"I would not," Lena said. "Did you really, um, do that kind of work?"

"First," Bel said, "no shade to sex workers. I can confidently say their work is more valuable and dignified than the work of a lot of the soldiers they were fucking. Second, you'll learn people taste basically the same whether they are professionals plying their wares behind the battle lines or bleeding out in a battlefield after a day of stabbing and shooting one another, so a warzone is a smorgasbord."

Lena nodded. "I guess finishing off dying soldiers is like mercy killing."

Bel shrugged. "Okay. Anyway, I didn't see the charge like Tennyson did because it happened during the day, but I was right there that night in the camp when the French Marshal Pierre Bosquet famously said, 'C'est magnifique, mais ce n'est pas la guerre. C'est de la folie.'" She sighed wistfully. "Such a great quote. Truth be told, he said it over and over. He was very drunk that night. Still a great quote."

Lena waited, then raised an eyebrow. "I don't speak French, remember?"

"'It is magnificent, but it is not war. It is madness,'" Bel recited. "Of course, he was just talking about the failed charge, but he might as well have been talking about the rationale for that war. A war 172 years ago in what is now Ukraine fighting over who got to mistreat whom in Palestine a thousand miles away. Sound familiar?"

"Yeah, I know," Lena said sadly. "'History doesn't repeat itself, but it rhymes.'"

Bel shook her head. "The lyrics may rhyme sometimes, and sometimes they do repeat, but history is a poorly written song, the background music to a fight scene in an action movie where the hero establishes himself as heroic by killing a lot of people we're told not to care about. Human history is not a song anyone wants to dance to, just fight their way through."

"Oof," Lena said. "That's grim. Even for you."

"Not grim at all for me, Honey. I grew up in the Kingdom of Ceredigion, ankle deep in sheep shit and always five minutes away from death by fever or a Mercian invader's sword. We knew life was hard, and we celebrated making it to every solstice and equinox because a whole year was too long to wait to be grateful. You grew up a Black, Latina, gay woman in a country that said every part of you was less-than, but you still lived better than 99.9% of all humans who ever lived, and somehow they still managed to convince you to believe in human decency and progress and human rights and human dignity. And that's fine. You needed to believe in that to get out of bed each day.

"But you need to let it go now. They're food. Just food. And sometimes they produce beautiful art, and sometimes they love one another, and that's nice, but it's elephants with paint brushes or crows mating for life, and mostly they hurt one another and often kill one another, and that's fine, too. It's a forest filled with tigers and lions and bears, oh my! You'll stop being too surprised by any of it, eventually."

"That kind of cynicism just sounds so depressing, Bel," Lena said. "An eternity of being disappointed?"

"You won't be disappointed. You won't be impressed. You'll get a place of Zen about the humans once you see you're not one of them anymore." She turned and dumped out the last of her night's spoils, then shoved the bags into one another, wadded them all up into a ball, and tossed them unceremoniously on the corpse of the woman stuffed into the bottom of the closet. "I see it's too soon. I need to be patient. It can take a while."

Lena chafed at the implication she was a child who needed to grow into a fuller understanding of the world, but she acknowledged she was a baby-vampire and must have seemed exactly that infantile to her girlfriend. She didn't like what that said about their power dynamic, and she wanted to fix it, even if that meant accepting the very disdain for humans Bel demanded of her. And then she resented needing to make Bel a winner when it came to humans just so the two of them could become equals.

She turned and looked at Napoleon waiting patiently for the next step in his makeover montage. Perhaps, she realized, if she could learn to be patient with his acceptance of his new place in the world, she could more easily accept her own.

"So, what about his face?" she asked.

"Well, I was thinking we'd cover it entirely and put dark sunglasses on him, but that won't work. Still, let's try this." She held up a ball of dark gray fabric that turned out to be a wide scarf with a subtle plaid print of maroon and black lines. Bel pulled Ludwig's hood down, wrapped the scarf around his neck until it had the girth of a human one, then tucked the bottom into the sweatshirt. Next, she wrapped it around his chin, then another time around over his nose, careful to keep his eyes exposed, then around his forehead, and then she pulled the hood back over.

Lena scowled. "He looks like a B-movie ninja with his eyes CGI-ed out. But maybe if we get him a baseball cap or something, it won't be too noticeable at night."

Bel smiled. "I got him this, but just for when we're in private because it won't help in the disguise department." She held up her last acquisition, a cheap tourist version of the bicorne hat Napoleon Bonaparte famously wore sideways so he'd be more distinguishable in portraits and on the battlefield. A stripe of white fake fur ran along the top ridge, curving up and back down again to accentuate the hat's shape, and a plastic gold button on the wearer's left connected a blue strip of ribbon that ran around the back of the hat at a jaunty forty-five-degree angle. "I guess he could wear it straight, the way most generals wore them to keep the sun out of their eyes, and it would hide his eye holes a little, but…"

Lena laughed. "Yeah, no. Not going to help him be inconspicuous. But I love it." She placed the hat on Napoleon's head, sideways like his namesake, and then gestured to the mirror. She wasn't sure if he'd get the reference.

He stepped forward, looked at the hat, then clasped the zipper slider (a struggle since he wore gloves, but easier than if he'd been using his boney fingertips) unzipped his hoodie halfway, and stuck his four fingers into the sweatshirt, then turned and modeled proudly.

Both women laughed, and Bel clapped Napoleon on his shoulder. His arm fell off but remained inside his costume, and he reattached it. That made Bel and Lena laugh harder. And that made Napoleon happy.

He maintained his good mood when they explained his first and most important responsibility in their trio, guarding them while they slept through the day. He didn't really understand why the women giggled a bit when they added that he'd need to sit in the bathroom for about an hour when they first went to bed, then come out and stand in the room while they slept. As far as Napoleon was concerned, the whole ritual was new, and their alone time was merely a normal part of it. He understood their giggling more clearly when he heard the muffled, hotel-room version of their lovemaking through the bathroom door, but while some part of his minimal memory told him listening to this was strange, it was no more or less unusual than much of anything else he'd experienced since coming up out of the catacombs.

He'd brought one of the notebooks with him into the bathroom, and he began writing about his feelings, filling out seven pages with his precise penmanship and technically proficient German prose. Though he wasn't attempting to be anything but clear and direct, the writing would have struck any human as dreamy and poetic because it came from a place of careful noticing unencumbered by prejudicial understanding.

Napoleon was midway through a page when Bel knocked gently on the door, then opened it and told him to go into the bedroom. She was completely naked and unabashed, but Lena stood close behind her and covered herself, smiling shyly and everting her eyes as Napoleon squeezed past her in the doorway. He found they'd moved the dresser in front of the room's only window and then shoved the comforter around the edges. He heard the women talking to one another as they brushed their teeth, speaking in that other language he couldn't understand but somehow could identify as *Englisch* and *ingles*. When they came back out, he motioned to the lamp on the room's tiny desk, clicked it on and off, then on again.

Bel looked at Lena. "Will it keep you awake?"

"Won't bother me, I don't think."

"Go ahead," Lena told Napoleon in German. Then she

turned out the room's overhead light, and the women climbed under the sheet together, curled up in a big-spoon and little spoon, and fell asleep before Napoleon could think of the next word to write.

Yet write he did. In the dim light of the desk lamp, a single bulb under a green glass rectangular cover, Napoleon filled an entire notebook and started a second. He wasn't sure if he was remembering things or extrapolating from what he found most strange and what seemed banal, but it allowed him to deduce a bit about his previous life and begin to explore his new one. For example, he should not have had a basis of comparison, since he knew only two people beyond those who screamed and ran away from him, but he had the sense that he was a person with an exceptionally positive attitude. How would he know this, he reflected, unless he contained some memory that most people he knew in that previous life were less optimistic?

When night fell, and Bel and Lena awoke, they waited in the hotel room together, allowing the streets to empty. While they waited, they discussed their next steps.

After Bel turned Lena, the vampires had been visited by the Weird Sisters McElroy, and the witches had given them dire warnings about a future catastrophe and some vague instructions about how to play a role in preventing it.

"They said we'd be building a team, so maybe Napoleon is part of it?" Lena said.

"He must be. And that's part of what I hate about any kind of seeing-into-the-future magic. When we found him and you wanted to keep him, I couldn't help but wonder if he was part of the witches' plan. But then, maybe that made me more inclined to accept your idea to have him come with us. So is it their prediction coming true, or their prediction altering our choices to make it true?"

"They didn't seem to have any ulterior motives," Lena said.

"Everyone has ulterior motives. I can accept the witches aren't our enemies. I mean, they just appeared. They could do that with wooden stakes in our hearts or silver blades through our necks, too, right? But they are using us. And I believe them; they're using us to stop this world-ending cataclysm. Fine. But I'm sure there's more to it than that. There must be some reason they are sending us and not … I don't know, Nando and his werewolves, or—"

"Maybe they got us because we are the ones who can get them?"

"Get who?"

"I don't know. Everyone we've worked with? Everyone we know?"

Bel frowned. "Maybe. It's not like we have some vast network. And I'm not going to work with Esau and his monster hunters again. If I see them, I'll kill them. They know that. Same with that Matt Bern coward who got you killed and then disappeared. If I see that little shit, he's toast. So who else would we get? I guess we worked with that imp in Ireland who helped us get away from the Fomorians. What was his name?"

"Apraxis. But he betrayed us in Scotland, remember?"

"Right. Guess I'll kill that little motherfucker on sight, too."

"Well, let's start by reaching out to the only people who have always been on our side, and maybe they will have more connections, and so on and so forth."

"Okay, Canada it is," Bel said. She pulled out her phone and started making arrangements for a private plane. One of the benefits of a very long life was the wealth that came from compound interest.

Lena turned to Napoleon and did her best to explain the plan in Spanish. "You're going to have some new experiences. We'll take a plane, fly across the Atlantic Ocean to Toronto, and then travel by car to visit our friend at Camp Bigfoot. He lives in a community of people, and they will all love you so much. You will have lots of new friends!"

Napoleon squeezed her hand and nodded enthusiastically.

Lena turned back to Bel. "But how will we get him to the airport?"

"I'll have someone deliver a rental car. There aren't the standard security checks for private planes. Shouldn't be a problem."

And Bel was mostly right. Her idea of a rental turned out to be an Uber that picked Bel up alone a few blocks from the hotel and managed to lose its original driver by the time it arrived to pick up Lena and Napoleon. Once at the airport, they got onto their little jet without drama, then got a visit from a customs inspector who insisted he be allowed to board the plane and look around. They let him on and allowed him to inspect the cockpit and cabin, but he refused to sign off on his inspection until he'd seen inside the little bathroom. There he found a bundled up skeleton, and he took note of it in case there were any accusations of grave robbing or illegal trafficking in human body parts or ancient relics, but the women assured him they had all the necessary paperwork to transport a classroom prop they'd purchased and dressed up as a gift for a friend back home in Toronto who taught high school biology and anatomy. The inspector believed they had the receipts in the bags in the hold, and since he couldn't figure out any law they'd broken, he allowed the plane to take off.

"Good thinking, playing dead," Bel told Napoleon. "Come take a seat and get your fill of the view before sunrise. We're going to have to duct-tape these shades in a second. I want you to get to enjoy your first time in an airplane. I remember the first time I ever flew. 1911. Little biplane at night. Ohio. Forests below, and rivers winding through it. Seeing those in a way I never had before, in a way almost no one ever had before except birds. Contrary to some accounts, we vampires cannot turn into bats or ravens or any other kind of animal, so I'd never flow before. It's pretty cool. Enjoy it. But the sun is going to come up over the horizon soon. We'll outrun it over the Atlantic and land before dawn in New York, get a hotel room for the day, and then fly to Toronto, then Winnipeg, then rent some ground transport from there. It's going to be a long trip, so settle in." She patted his leg and went back to her seat next to Lena.

Her girlfriend was clearly anxious. Bel could read it in Lena's posture, the way she gripped the armrest and pressed her spine into the seat. Lena wasn't afraid of flying, so Bel didn't understand where the new anxiety was coming from.

"What's up?"

In the same way their intimacy allowed Bel to read Lena's body, Lena could read a different kind of concern and confusion in Bel's two words than usual.

"Oh, it just feels like … like a big change. We've been on this … adjustment vacation training thing, and now we're going back, and I'm nervous about seeing Nando and Lucia and all the people at Camp Bigfoot. Plus, and I know this sounds weird, but it didn't feel strange to be in new cities at night. Like, I'd never been to Monaco during the day before. Or Barcelona. I would have liked to see Barcelona during the day, but it didn't feel wrong to be seeing it at night because I have no basis for comparison. And even Paris didn't feel too strange. Last time I was here, it was this whirlwind. I didn't get to be a tourist. So seeing it at night felt right.

"But at Camp Bigfoot, I was walking around the lake talking with Nando and Lucia in the middle of the afternoon. I was engaging with people during the day. I was very much a human there, even though I was one of the only humans. Maybe even more so because there were only a few humans there. I felt my humanness there. And now, going back, it's just going to be strange. And seeing Nando… Like, will he be pissed that I didn't call sooner? Will he be glad to see me? Even if he is, will I be glad to be seen as I am now?"

Bel took Lena's hand. "Honey, are you ashamed of who you are?"

"Maybe. I had a lot of life experience that was designed to make me ashamed of parts of myself. And I mostly learned to push back against that, to choose to be proud of the things other people wanted me to hate about me. But let's face it, if you have to learn to be proud, to push back, to fight just to be comfortable in your own skin, then you really aren't as comfortable in your skin as other people. You're at war inside that skin, building the defenses, always fighting off the siege. And now I have this new identity, and I don't know how to feel about it myself. And I know you understand, but I can't really talk to you about my discomfort without criticizing your vampire-ness, too, and I don't want to do that."

Bel smiled. "It's okay. I can take it."

Lena shook her head. "No, I know that, and I love that you are so comfortable and confident in who you are. I don't want to take that away, and—"

"You won't. Don't worry. I've had a lot of time—"

"I know, and I'm not worried I'll make you change. I'm worried I'll make you feel guilty or make you see me as …. I don't know, a less reliable partner because I'm struggling to embrace this part of who I am, and … I don't know."

Bel let that uncertainty breathe for a while. "How about one thing at a time, okay? We'll get back to Nando, and then you can worry about that part. We'll need him to meet us in Winnipeg or Saskatoon and then give us a ride from there. Otherwise we'll have to rent a moving truck and stay in a shipping crate each day, or maybe mail Napoleon separately, and that might freak him out."

Lena nodded, "Yeah, no, and I think I'd rather see Nando before we get to Camp Bigfoot, anyway. I'll message him and let him know we're coming and apologize for not being in touch sooner, and maybe that will help me process."

Bel patted her on the knee, then gave her thigh a squeeze. "Okay, I'll get these windows taped, and you start on that, but don't send it until we get to New York. I have an idea."

Lena got to work on her project, and while she composed on her phone, Bel spoke with Napoleon in German. She waited until it seemed Lena finished writing or had gotten stuck, and then she returned to the seat across from her. "I thought of something that might help."

"What's that?"

"I asked Napoleon if I could borrow his journals and share his thoughts with you. Since he's in a similar position. Or similarly new and strange. Do you think that might help?"

"I don't know, but I'm curious to hear what he's been writing, anyway."

They crossed the Atlantic in a multilingual fever, Napoleon composing more observations in German, Bel translating his first notes into English for Lena, and Lena writing her apology and reintroduction to Nando in Spanish. By the time they touched down at the Teterboro Airport in New Jersey (the more common destination for private planes than LaGuardia or JFK), Lena felt ready to hit "Send" on her message to Nando. She chose to send it via text messages rather than email because she knew he didn't check his email frequently. She wanted to make sure he got the message as soon as possible, especially since the satellite internet service in Camp Bigfoot was not always reliable. That choice would prove fortuitous.

Bel reserved rooms at a nice hotel in Newark, ordered an Uber for the trip down there from the airport, and then started working on arranging another private flight from Teterboro to Winnipeg or Saskatoon, hoping to reserve the jet and crew though she didn't have a specific destination nailed down. She made all these reservations with the same credit card, a bit of carelessness that would also prove consequential.

"How are we going to get Napoleon through customs?" Lena asked as she pulled her backpack, her only luggage, down from the carry-on compartment.

"I don't think you're going to like it. I think Napoleon will be fine with it, but I think you'll consider it a bit demeaning."

"Hey, if it doesn't require us to kill every TSA worker here, that's a relief, because that's where I thought you might go."

Bel laughed. "I don't know how we'd do that without being spotted. Lots of eyes in an airport, even in the private wing. So," she turned to Napoleon, "you're going to have to ride out of here in a suitcase."

Napoleon shrugged.

The suitcase was a small, carry-on case, and it turned out he could fit just fine, though some disassembly was required. His head ended up between his pelvis and ribcage, and his legs and arms stuffed around them. With his clothing stuffed in, Lena had to sit on the case while Bel zipped it shut.

Lena carried her own bag through customs, and no one asked about her two manuscripts, the reams of loose typing paper with a neat hole punched through the middle. The blood stains on the paper should have raised eyebrows, but the bomb detector didn't notice them or detect the trace amounts of gunpowder residue on the first page, and the person looking at the stack of pages through the X-ray machine didn't care, either. The TSA tech did care about the human bones, but only enough to squint at Bel.

"My sister teaches high school biology and anatomy," Bel said.

The guard laughed and waved them through.

Out on the street, Bel checked her phone and found the Uber by make, model, and license plate. The driver sat in his seat but waved them in. This struck Lena as a tiny bit odd; they normally waited outside their cars and offered to help load bags. But she decided Bel must have communicated they didn't have much in the way of luggage, or maybe he arrived just as they were leaving the terminal and saw they didn't require assistance.

Bel motioned to the front seat, and the driver nodded. He was middle-aged, medium height and a little on the portly side, olive skinned, short mustache, with straight black hair combed back over a bald spot Lena could see clearly when she climbed into the back seat and set Napoleon down next to her. She noted the way the man was sweating and looking anywhere but at Bel.

The driver, on the other hand, did not notice how gently Lena could set down her heavy suitcase.

Bel gave the driver the name of the hotel, and he plugged it into his phone. When he set the phone on the cradle so the map faced him, he did a little adjusting, tilting it away from Bel slightly, and Lena thought that was very strange. She figured a professional driver would already have the cradle positioned to offer him the clearest view. She tried to catch Bel's eye in the passenger-side mirror, but Bel was looking out the window, seemingly entranced by the skyline of Newark. Lena checked her watch. Then she looked at Google's estimated time of arrival on the driver's phone. They'd make it to the hotel well before dawn. She wondered what Bel was looking for out there in the darkness.

Halfway to downtown Newark, the driver took the Mill Street exit off NJ-21. That was weird, and Lena wasn't the only one to notice. The driver's phone made a scolding sound as it recalculated.

"Um," Lena said.

"Short cut," the driver said.

"But, um, Bel?"

"It's fine," Bel said. She looked at the driver. "Thanks

for saving us some time."

He didn't look back at her, just nodded curtly while staring straight ahead.

"Wha tha fa?" Lena whispered to her suitcase.

Napoleon, hearing this and understanding it exactly as much as Lena understood the driver's new route, pried two fingers into the opening between the zipper sliders, then made the opening a little larger. Lena heard the teeth of the zipper clicking, then saw Napoleon's hand wriggle free. Her first impulse was to shove it into the bag, but she felt anxious enough to need some comfort, so she reached over and held his hand in her own, keeping most of him inside without forcing him. This satisfied Napoleon who gave her hand a little squeeze and then stilled. The driver stayed on Mill through the light on Main and the light on Broadway, then made a left into a parking lot.

Lena squeezed Napoleon's hand.

Then the driver drove around the back of the strip mall and parked behind the Dollar Tree store.

Lena stiffened her other hand as Bel had taught her, curving her fingers only slightly so her nails werebladed points that could puncture or slash.

Lena couldn't see it, but Bel's right hand tensed in the same way, though she continued looking out the window even though she was staring at the beige, painted brick wall next to the dumpsters.

And then, to both of their surprise, the driver grabbed the door handle, swung his door open, and fell out of his car onto the ground.

Bel looked back at Lena. "That was not what I was expecting."

"What were you expecting?"

Bel looked through the windows at the dark alley. Her reply was vaguely directed at Lena but clearly wasn't her primary concern. "I thought he was going to try to mug us. Maybe rape us at gunpoint or something. I thought we'd get a meal out of it and then take his car to the hotel, so I was playing along, looking out the window, pretending not to notice the different route or his flop sweat. I thought he was just working up the courage to do whatever he was going to do, but … it looks like he was doing it all along…"

"What?"

"My new guess?" Bel said. "He was forced to bring us here. Threatened. Sweating like he thought we'd kill him, but he was more afraid of what would happen if he didn't get us here. So why …? Who …?"

She kept scanning the darkness with her superhuman vision and saw nothing out of the ordinary, just a space between the back of the Dollar Tree and the back wall of the warehouse on the other side of the street. The alley wasn't as thin as some urban alleys. It was wide enough for dumpsters behind the strip mall and a normal two-lane road, though not enough for parking or additional pedestrian space. And Bel didn't see anything other than a few dumpsters in the entire length of it.

"I'm getting out of the car to sniff around a bit. You wait in here with Napoleon."

"No way," Lena said. "I can't fight in a car, and if you

can't fight whatever it is, I don't want to not be able to fight it. Better two than one and then a half. I'm getting out."

"Okay, but stay close to me," Bel said.

"I promise."

Lena released Napoleon's hand, then looked into the opening in the bag. "We're just going to look around for a second," she told him in Spanish, "and then we'll be right back. Here." She put her phone into his hand but held onto both. "Take that and call Bel if you need anything." She unlocked it with her code and released it.

Napoleon pulled his hand with the phone back into the suitcase. He couldn't tell her he didn't know how to use it. He couldn't even read the English text on it. He touched it and found it responded to his gloved fingertip. His newly acquired light-sensitive vision allowed him to see the screen. The day before it would have been a bright, white brick. But he had no idea what he was supposed to do with the device and couldn't write a message on paper to ask.

Bel and Lena got out of the car and sniffed the air. Both caught the smell immediately and heard the sounds around them as well. But it was too late.

Then all three of them heard the voice.

It was high-pitched and raspy and unpleasant, like a child's if the child had shouted itself nearly hoarse or had been smoking for a hundred years. The voice was mechanically magnified.

"Miss Shipwright and Miss Wallace," Egg said through the bullhorn. "I'm here to escort you to a very important meeting with a very important person. Your presence has been requested and isn't optional. Now, I know you are not used to taking orders from anyone, so the notion that you have no choice is probably going to make you angry. I get it. So, if it makes you feel any better, you really do have options. You could try to fight us, and you'll probably kill a lot of us, and then we'll rip your arms and legs off and take you in anyway. We both know you'll be fine eventually, but it won't be much fun, and you won't like watching it happen to your girlfriend because of all the screaming and pain and stuff."

Then Bel and Lena heard the giggling of all the other trolls on the rooftops above them. Lena turned in a slow circle, preparing to fight. Bel held still and tried to count them by the giggles and the sounds of their feet and hands on the roofs. One roof was covered in sheets of aluminum, sticky to the touch. The other had a layer of pea gravel, and the little pebbles ground together as the trolls shifted their weight. She could also smell them, the distinct odor of Cheetos and bitter-sweet energy drinks and sweat and snot and feces with a special brimstone tang. They were too close together to be easily distinguished by sound or smell, though. Bel couldn't tell if there were fifty or two hundred. Trolls were not nearly as fast as vampires, but they were strong, at least in the upper body. She had no doubt they could fulfill the promise made through the megaphone and rip their limbs off.

"Here's what I propose," Egg continued. "If you want to fight, just kind of continue doing that stalking-around walk you're doing."

"Got him," Lena hissed. She pointed. Near the far corner of the building, near the origin of the sound, she'd spotted a little mirror on an extending arm, like a dental tool mixed with an old TV antenna.

Bel nodded, then pointed slowly along the roofs of each building until Lena understood and nodded back.

"Okay, they spotted us, boys and girls. We might as well show ourselves," Egg said. "Ollie ollie oxen free!"

Not only did the trolls line both roofs, but after the order, twenty trolls filled up the openings on each side of the alley. The trolls laughed, hooted, waggled their naughty bits, and laughed some more. The groups at either end of the alley began to move towards them in two mobs. The ones on the roofs converged as well, but no attack came.

At the far corner, Egg jumped up on the wall but didn't move closer like the others. "Or, here's the other choice. You could raise your arms up like it's a stick-up, and then pretend you've surrendered until we get close enough, and then attack, right? So let's just start there and see how that goes."

Lena, confused, looked at Bel. Bel shrugged and lifted her arms. Lena couldn't tell if they were planning on fighting back as Egg had directed, so she followed Bel's lead.

Egg spoke into the megaphone again, but this time it was clear he was not speaking to Lena and Bel. "Teams one and two, will you escort our guests to our vehicle?"

The trolls walking towards them from either side of

the alley advanced more quickly, hands out in front of them, dark purple talons and bright green and purple scales catching the glow of their Uber's taillights and headlights so they looked like two distinct armies, one ghostly pale, the other glinting with red menace. When they were just out of arm's reach, Bel caught the eye of a troll who looked up at his compatriots on the roofs. She followed his gaze, but even with her speed, she was too late. A pair of trolls were already descending through the air, fast approaching terminal velocity, their descent slowed only by the parachute they seemed to share. Only it wasn't a parachute exactly. It was a white canvas bag. The trolls landed with a sickening crunch, but the leap was successful; Lena was completely wrapped up. Bel cried out and launched herself toward Lena, her nails aiming to tear open the bag, but the trolls had planned for this, and the pair who leapt down on her aimed to take her motion into account. This second canvas bag fell on her, and then dozens of strong troll hands wrapped around her arms and legs and torso, even her face.

Both women struggled, bucking and kicking, clawing at the canvas as well as they could without much leverage, even trying to bite it with their human teeth since their thin fangs weren't suited to the job.

"Don't you let go," Egg shouted into the megaphone. "If one of them gets loose, you're all gonna be pulled pork and hamburger meat and pink slime in chicken nuggets, and it will serve you right, you lazy keyboard warriors. Prove me wrong! And the rest of you, get those chains on them, quick!"

Lena and Bel, suspended in midair in the grip of the trolls, could feel those meaty hands moving around as bonds were wrapped around the exterior of each of their bags, but only Bel could identify them by sound and smell.

"Lena!" she shouted. "Hold still, honey. Stop fighting."

But Lena was in no state to be calmed. In her flailing, she'd managed to cut a small hole in the bag with her sharp nails, and though she continued to buck with her whole body, she focused on getting a finger through that hole and jabbing the nearest hand, hoping to create a little give. Instead, the chain wrapped over her exposed index finger, trapping it on the outside of the canvas. The silver burned with a ferocity she'd never experienced before, like she'd placed her hand on a stove and held it there until the flesh melted and it stuck. She tried to yank her hand back inside the canvas, but the chains were all around her, so they pinned her elbow to her side and didn't allow enough area of motion to pull the hand away. The silver burned through her flesh, and when it began to burn the bone in her finger, the pain rose to a new height. The heat now radiated inside her, screaming from bone to joint to bone, and she believed, with a faith the most zealous would envy, this would kill her.

Instead of yanking her arm back at the elbow, she managed to twist her pelvis and create enough space for her wrist to bend, and that allowed her to pull the finger upwards and away from the hole. But the chain was now embedded partway into the bone, so she had to yank to create the countervailing force to the inhumanly strong trolls tightening the chain, just so she could force the links to do even more damage as they burned their way out. By the time she slid the finger under the chain and back into the canvas, half the finger was burned off, the wound running the length from near the knuckle to the spot where her nail melted and fell to the pavement.

Bel could hear the sound the nail made when it landed, even under Lena's screaming. All she could do was weep and force herself to hold as still as possible.

Egg didn't need the megaphone. He'd hopped down from the roof and joined the group. "You dipshits are a lot tougher than I expected," he said to the trolls. "You might have even made your ancestors proud. They may have fought every day with their bare hands, but how many bridge trolls could claim to have captured real honest-to-goddamned vampires? Now, don't let go, even in the truck. Hold on like your lives depend on it. Because I promise they do. Fuck this up and they will kill you, or I will kill you, or the King will certainly kill you. And ladies," he said, and Bel and Lena could only deduce he meant them, "I hope you will see I did this as painlessly as I could and not hold me responsible when you inevitably break free and want to hold someone responsible. But if you need to find me and get revenge, my name is Phlegos."

The hand wrapped around Bel's forearm tensed, and a nearby voice said, "Hey, no you're not! I'm Phlegos!"

"My mistake, Phlegos," Egg said. "He's right. The one holding you is named Phlegos. Don't screw this up now,

Phlegos. They know your name."

A chorus of jeering laughter, punctuated by wet snorts, filled the alley, and Bel could feel Phlegos' grip tighten with his shame.

Phlegos was a troll, after all, and trolls almost always lash out when they feel embarrassed. And they generally aim for the nearest women at hand.

"Load 'em up!" Egg said. "Don't keep the King waiting!"

The trolls carried their prisoners into the back of a rented U-haul (rented properly by a guy from Jersey City, then stolen by the trolls), and packed in around them, each holding Bel or Lena in place with one or two hands, depending on their reach in the crowd of troll bodies. Egg climbed into the truck's cab, but he wasn't the driver. Another troll stood up on the driver's seat, operating the wheel, and a second troll crouched down in front of him, operating the pedals with his hands. The one operating the wheel communicated with the second by kicking him in the ears, a soft kick in the right for more gas, a swift, painful kick in the left to slam the brake. It was a functional but imperfect system, and the truck lurched as it turned out of the alley, too fast, stopping too slowly, too fast, making its way to the traffic light, then back to the highway and into the city.

Napoleon, alone in the suitcase in the back of the Uber, turned on Lena's phone. He didn't know how to use the device, but, as with everything, Napoleon approached the task with cheery optimism, and he did his best.

"Intent doesn't matter, she'd say, when you've really injured someone else. You need to be open to their pain and anger if you're ever to make things whole between you."

-Naomi Novik

Chapter 11

Lucia walked into their bedroom and found her boyfriend grabbing clothes out of his dresser and throwing them into his suitcase.

"So you decided to leave?" she asked.

The two of them had been struggling ever since Nando discovered she'd traded the location of Lena's books for Cassius' promise to leave Camp Bigfoot alone. On a purely rational level, he recognized Lucia hadn't understood the danger of her choice. She thought she was betraying a human, a friend of his but a human nonetheless, to a very powerful vampire in order to secure the fledgling utopian werewolf community that was Nando's passion. But on a deeper, emotional level, he knew Lucia made a conscious choice to deceive him. He wasn't angry her deception had risked the lives of just about everyone in the world. He was angry her deception had endangered the community.

Soon after the events in Las Vegas, during one of her tear-filled apologies, Lucia had offered to leave Camp Bigfoot and never return, the kind of exile the community would probably employ as a lesser punishment for a wolf who betrayed the pack. Nando would have been well within his rights to order such a thing, or to take her before the community and let them decide. If some of their pups had died in the heist of the books from Cassius' office, he would have called for that kind of trial. Even if he wouldn't have wanted to, he'd have been forced. The community would have lost faith in his leadership if they thought he was showing favoritism to his girlfriend when everyone else wanted her gone. But all the werewolves who participated in the heist miraculously survived, including the pups' teacher, Miss Rita, who had leapt through the window of a 36th story suite in The Venetian Hotel and Casino and used the body of a burning vampire to cushion her fall. Because all the pups, their teacher, and Tina the getaway driver had made it back alive, most of the members of the community considered the whole event a harmless adventure. They attributed Nando's grim mood to the death of his human friend and the disappearance of his vampire friend who had lived with them for months. Werewolves could smell his melancholy, and they'd been giving him a wide berth lately. They didn't know the reason for Lucia's sadness. Their acute senses could distinguish between guilt and other emotions, but her particular scent was complicated by the fact that she smelled eight months pregnant with triplets.

Lucia had hoped the pregnancy would repair their relationship, but that's not really the way relationships or pregnancies work. Nando had been hoping to become a father before the Vegas mission, and they'd been trying for months, but when Lucia's smell gave her away, he hadn't been happy about the news. That cut her to the core. From Lucia's perspective, she'd broken faith with him in the service of the community, but his inability to be overjoyed about their pending parenthood was a far more grievous sin. She'd tried to talk to him about it a few times, but he'd just turn and go running off into the woods to hunt deer or elk or, once, a moose, return with his kill, and busy himself sharing the meal with the pack, surrounding himself with other wolves so she couldn't force a private conversation.

Then she'd given up, and they'd stopped talking almost entirely, communicating mostly in grunts like roommates who hated one another and shared an apartment because they couldn't break the lease.

And then she caught him packing a bag.

He didn't look back to the doorway. "This isn't about us," he said.

"Then what is it?"

"Not permanent. I just have to go away for a while."

"How long?"

"If I drive straight through and only stop for gas, about 35 hours. Then, however long it will take. Then sleep. Then come back. So, I guess I don't know."

"Where are you going? What's happened?"

"Maybe nothing. But maybe something." He mumbled as he walked past her into their tiny summer-camp cabin bathroom. "I don't know. Have you seen my toothpaste?"

She could smell the artificial peppermint from the door, which confirmed how distracted he was. "It's on my side. I used it last. Sorry." She caught herself. "Why am I apologizing? It's my goddamned toothpaste, too."

"I don't have time to fight," Nando said. He stomped back into the room and threw his little bathroom kit into his suitcase. "I'm taking your toothpaste. Sorry about that."

"It's okay," she said. "It's yours, too."

Nando wasn't listening. He dropped down to the ground, sniffed, and reached into the darkness under the bed. This time he found what he was looking for by smell, pulling out the little safe. Rather than opening it, he threw the whole thing into the suitcase.

Lena could smell the gunpowder and cordite in the little steel box. "Nando, tell me what's going on."

"I…" He broke off, looked at her, and his eyes filled with tears. "I can't tell you because I don't trust you, okay? And that esucks and it's estupid and I hate it." His

Spanish accent flared when he was the most emotional, but Lucia had never seen him like this. This wasn't anger or joy or sadness or any other feeling of Nando's she'd witnessed in their time together. This was a broken heart. "I want to tell you. I want to tell you everything I've been thinking and feeling for the last eight months. You are the person I want to talk to the most in the whole estupid fucking world, okay? But I can't. Especially about this. So, just … I will come back. I will be back here for our children, and … we will figure things out. But right now, I need to go."

"Take me with you," Lucia said.

"No."

"Yes," she said. "I'm coming. I can't betray you if I'm sitting in the car with you. 36 hours to talk and hash this out and if we can't, you can drop me off 36 hours away from here and never see me again."

Nando turned away and pressed his clothes into wrinkled bunches in the suitcase. "Of course not. I'm going to raise my children. We'll figure it out when I get back."

"No," Lucia said.

Nando could tell that word was more packed than his suitcase, but he wasn't sure of all its contents. He turned slightly to face her, though he didn't look her in the eye. "No to what?"

"No to me living here. No to you raising your children. No to a life of the silent treatment. No."

"My children will grow up in this pack," Nando said firmly, a slight growl under his words.

"Not unless their parents learn to live together again. If we're through, I'm leaving." She pointed at her protruding belly. "And in case you haven't noticed, Huey, Dewey, and Louie go where I go. You want to punish me forever for lying to you? Fine. But I don't have to stay here and take it." The room was so small, and Lucia was so big, she had to shove him aside to squeeze between the bed and the dresser. She yanked open the top drawer, grabbed some underwear and socks, pulled two maternity t-shirts out of the next, and a pair of panel jeans out of the third. She threw them all into his suitcase, slammed it shut, then hopped up and sat on the lid while she zipped it closed. "I'm going with you. Now grab this suitcase, because I'm not supposed to carry anything heavy."

She slid off the bed onto her feet, reached into the closet.

"Lucia, what are you—" he tried.

She grabbed her sawed-off shotgun and a box of shells. "This…" She shook the gun in his face, "…isn't heavy. Now, get your ass in the car."

*"For somehow this disease inheres in tyranny,
never to trust one's friends."*

-Aeschylus

Chapter 12

Esau felt more comfortable in a large canvas tent in a FOB built in a rocky valley in a high desert somewhere between Timbuktu, Kalamazoo, and Bum-Fuck, Egypt. He didn't mind cities like Shanghai too much as long as he was on a mission, but he hated the feeling of an ultra-secure base far from action, whether it was a little house made of ticky-tacky in the suburbs of a large city or this particular base built in a standard office building in a medium-sized town. Both felt too sterile, and somehow infantilizing, like the designers wanted to account for his every need. In fact, as he got off the elevator on the ninth floor of the PNC Bank Building in Toledo, Ohio, the first things he saw as he walked down the hall were a water cooler and a hand sanitizer dispenser, as though the physical space were mocking him, cooing, "Now, little Esau, are you staying hydrated? Are your hands dirty? Stay clean and drink lots of water, Little Esau." He snorted in disgust as he walked by.

He didn't mind the cloak-and-dagger stuff. The seventh office door led to a waiting room with no attendant and no decoration, a security measure that would turn away most accidental passersby. Next, a palm scanner to a locked door that would dissuade an intentional but not particularly skilled thief or vandal. Then an optical scanner and a vault door that would impede a real enemy. On the other side of the vault door (which opened automatically), he entered a windowless room containing a simple desk in the middle of the far wall, a single chair, and three laptops, the first and third angled inwards so they created an intimate space but also allowed his employers a complete view of the room through the three cameras.

Esau sat at the desk, tapped the touchpad on the middle computer, and waited. All three came to life without any external hardware to connect them, a fancy way of reminding Esau his employers were onto some next-level shit on their end. A prompt asked him for his code name and password. He thought this was excessive, since he'd just provided his handprint and optical scan. He supposed a monster might be able to fake those or physically force him to interact with those machines, but it would be harder to pry a password out of him, though still not impossible for the right monster. A warlock, for example, could probably do it. Esau did not like thinking of warlocks at all. Except the one he fantasized about killing day and night. But even that one put him in a sour mood.

Esau had no idea the main headquarters of the HCR. were located in an office building across the street. The four-story, non-descript building posed as the regional office of a national chain of senior living care centers. While publicly called the Health Care and Retirement Corporation and a subsidiary of ProMedica Senior Care, the organization was really the Human Conservation Ring, or The Ring for short. The members of The Ring even wore ornate rings to represent their membership in this elite cabal of senior monster hunters. And senior they were, the few who had survived a lifetime of hunting deadly monsters and risen to the highest rank within their organization, a club of 15, 13 men and two women, none of them younger than seventy.

One might presuppose the members of The Ring would be singularly focused on their mission to destroy monsterdom and protect humanity. Not so. First and foremost, they were obsessed with making sure none of the other members of The Ring were monsters, were being controlled by monsters, or were consciously or unconsciously colluding with monsters. The group was collectively and individually paranoid, recognizing, correctly, that none of their good work to protect humanity would amount to a hill of beans if they were secretly being used by some monsters to eliminate others in the greater service of some monster agenda.

When Rob arrived for the meeting in the chauffeured town car sent to pick him up, he pulled the silver chain around his neck out of his shirt, carefully unclasped it, and removed the large, decorated, polished iron ring. He slipped it onto his pinky finger as he stepped into the door to the main lobby, took the elevator to the fourth floor, and began to run the gauntlet of tests he had to pass in order to step into the conference room. The other members of the group were arriving at the same time. This was convenient because they had to test one another in order to be sure they were all who they claimed to be, and none of them could pre-select their evaluator or turn down a test from any other when it was asked of them. This guaranteed that no two members could deceive the rest of the group into allowing one or two monsters in.

"Hey, Rob. How's it going." Gerald did not inflect the greeting into a question.

"Hey, Gerry."

"Salt?" Gerald asked.

"Sure."

Gerald took a pinch of salt from a shelf on the wall in the hallway outside the conference room and threw it at Rob. It landed on his head and shoulders. Rob let it linger there while Gerald scrutinized him. Satisfied, Gerald turned to another member of The Ring.

Rob turned to the woman to his right. "Suzanne, how are you?"

"Hello, Rob. Doing fine."

"Silver cross?"

"Sure."

He picked up a silver cross from the same shelf and gently pressed it to her forehead while he watched for any reaction. She stared back placidly. He lowered the cross, nodded, and turned to another member of The Ring. "Sean? How's it going?"

"Fine."

"Garlic?"

"Okay."

The members of The Ring took turns testing one another until they were all satisfied, then motioned one another into the conference room. Inside, they found their places around a large, round table. Each place setting held a small pad of paper, a larger stack of pages stapled together, a cheap plastic pen, and a metal name placard in a wooden stand. The secretary and the chair both had keyboards in front of their seats. Projection screens were positioned on all four of the square room's walls, but none of them were currently in use. The meeting packet, the notes, and even the pen would be confiscated and disposed of at the end of the meeting while all the members watched, just to be sure none of the others were sneaking out with the trash.

Rob picked up the meeting packet. The front page held the meeting's agenda. The next dozen pages were the notes from the last meeting compiled extemporaneously so nothing ever left the room. The secretary, a position that rotated among the membership annually, was typing even as Paul spoke. Rob, like the others, took a moment to read through the notes. They comported with his memory of events.

"Do we have a motion to approve the minutes?" Paul, the current chair, asked the group. Someone made the motion, someone else seconded it, and the meeting was underway.

"Old business," Paul said. "We got a report on Esau's mission to Shanghai. It's on page 14 of your packet."

"Mission to Shanghai only a partial success," it

reported. "Made contact with vampire associates of Cassius. Names not provided. Ambushed by an unknown number of vampires. Escaped with only one casualty, Lt. Torreblanca, deceased. Before retreat, vampires demanded to communicate directly with superiors. Provided contact information. Awaiting orders."

"Without objection, I think we should skip to the new business portion of the agenda and address this before going back to the other old business. Is that alright with everyone," Paul asked.

The members of The Ring nodded with varying amounts of enthusiasm, and no one voiced an objection.

Suzanne raised her hand and didn't wait to be called on. "I move we direct Captain Sullivan to ignore this request and move on to a different target. We don't work with monsters."

"Second," Bradley said.

"Objections?" Paul asked the question so quickly, it was clear he expected a quick, unanimous vote.

"Hold on," Rob said. "I have an alternate motion. I don't think we should work with monsters, but this seems like essentially free intel. We could just have Esau give us the contact information, and then we could reach out, ask the monsters what they want Esau to do, and maybe use that to find them and eliminate them. If they don't give us anything actionable, it hasn't hurt us or compromised Esau at all. No harm in more information."

Suzanne shrugged, then nodded. "Good point."

"Esau is on the secure line now," Gerald said. "Should we send those orders now?"

"All in favor?" Paul asked.

Everyone raised their hand.

Paul aimed a remote at one of the screens, typed his message to Esau, and looked around the room for approval. Everyone nodded. He hit "send" on the message: "Provide contact information. We will reach out to Cassius and acquire the information needed to formulate your next mission."

A block away, Esau read this and sat back heavily in his chair. "Shit," he muttered. He leaned forward, fingers hovering above the keyboard, then hesitated. He thought about the look on Torreblanca's face when he aimed the pistol down at her as she lay in front of him, already gutshot. Surely his employers, with the vast resources they used to send him and his soldiers all over the world, could eliminate him just as easily if he questioned them. And they wouldn't be haunted by the same guilt which plagued him now since they wouldn't have to see his face, just order one of their other companies to clean up a mess, absorb his troops into another force or two, and go about their mission. Esau carefully considered how to word his reply.

"Here are the email address and phone number I was provided," he wrote, and entered the information from the card Augy had given him. Then he typed, "If Cassius makes contact with me directly and demands to know who is giving me my orders, what information should I give him?" He raised his hand up above the keyboard, read his question three times, then brought his finger down hard on the "Enter" key.

Paul looked around the table. Suzanne raised her hand. "I move we tell Captain Sullivan we will handle all direct communication with Cassius."

Moved and seconded, Paul sent a message to Esau reading: "We will handle all direct communication with Cassius."

Esau read this, pursed his lips, and thought. He ran his fingers through his close cropped, salt-and-pepper crew cut. "Acknowledged," he wrote. "However, there is some concern among the soldiers about who our employer might be. If they believe you are working with a vampire to design our next mission, this may affect morale and group cohesion. Please advise: How can I convince my men they are not working for The Convention if you are contacting Cassius?"

Gerald rolled his eyes. "Captain Sullivan is having a crisis of faith in our organization."

"Yes, or he's masking some other personal crisis as concern for morale."

"He's never had morale problems before," Paul said.

"Yeah, it's bullshit," Bradley said.

Rob only nodded sagely. Everyone at the table knew the stakes. This wasn't just about Esau. It was about whether the HCR could overcome its single greatest obstacle in its ages-long battle against monsterdom.

It would be easy to assume humanity's greatest deficiency in the battle against monsterdom was human physical frailty. Humans cannot move as fast as vampires, do not have the physical strength of minotaurs or trolls, the claws and teeth of werewolves, the ability to disappear and reappear like warlocks and witches, or the power to steal souls like demons. For sixty thousand years, these weaknesses dominated human existence. Humans huddled together in groups of thirty to sixty, faced constant depredation at the whims of rain, drought, fire, and disease. The regular threat of monsters was merely another sign of the gods' disfavor, barely more frightening than plague and less horrific than lightning. Just as humans learned to ward off some of those natural dangers with technology, they developed technological solutions for monsters which overcame human physical frailty. Castle walls. Salt to ward off demons and ghosts. Iron to bind some magical creatures. Wooden stakes and silver blades for vampires. Silver bullets for werewolves. In the large scheme of things, the humans were developing machines of offense and defense against monsters much faster than the monsters' ability to kill them.

Human civilization did not develop in parallel with this monster hunting, but through it. The concrete that kept the monsters out became the walls of human cities, then the foundations of skyscrapers. The ore mined to build the weapons to cut the monsters down became the rockets to the moon. The salt used to ward off certain monsters, season food, and exchange as currency became an essential building block of fire extinguishers, pottery enamels, food preservatives, and the fertilizers that allowed the human population to reach into the billions.

But the most important weapon in the human arsenal was one those early humans could not have imagined. They couldn't have looked at the sand beneath their feet and dreamt it would become the glass windows in their homes (and used to measure and tax their homes), let alone the filaments that would send beams of light around the world and connect over two billion thinking machines. The human race had outpaced monsters' ability to kill them to such a degree that monsters had to form The Convention and work together to remain in hiding. The very existence of The Convention was a testament to humanity's success in repelling the seemingly more powerful creatures who fed upon them.

The greatest weakness was not the human body, but the human mind. It didn't matter if a human held the perfect silver blade or the most advanced firearm loaded with high tech bullets filled with liquid silver. If she could be manipulated by a siren into leaping off the side of a Spanish galleon or a modern 100,000-ton aircraft carrier, she would be just as dead. It didn't matter if a human was protected by a thin line of salt, the walls of a medieval fortress, or the armor of an Abrams tank. If a warlock could trick him into leaving that protection, he was just as vulnerable. Worse, even if all the monster hunters could organize human civilization into their ever-growing assault on monsterdom, it wouldn't do them much good if the monsters could take over the minds of the few remaining humans who remembered monsters existed and were committed to their eradication.

So those humans did something quite exceptional for their species: They put the wellbeing of the human race above their own egos. Monster hunters who had previously entered the business for the glory as much as the thrill now relinquished their identities to The Ring entirely. In fact, only the highest ranking even knew of The Ring's existence, and even they didn't know who sat on the board.

"I recommend telling Captain Sullivan he is free to do what is necessary to convince his soldiers they are serving the cause of eradicating all monsters from the face of the Earth, and he has been given the green light to eliminate any monster while awaiting orders. That should convince them the higher-ups are more committed to the cause than to working with any particular monster," Gerald said.

The people around the table nodded in assent. Paul wrote up the message and sent it.

Esau, the afterthought foot soldier, hated being forced to trust he was not serving monsters, especially when it seemed his employers were willing to talk with a vampire behind his back. He consoled himself that armies are built on faith. Faith in the righteousness of their cause, and faith in their leaders. He decided, if the next mission aimed him at monsters and allowed him to do his work in his way, even if he was killing some monsters to assist a vampire in some Convention intrigue in the short-term, those monsters were dead in the long term. If they aimed him at humans, that would test his faith, bend it to the breaking point. But he'd wait. Humans did not have the lifespans of immortal vampires or nearly immortal warlocks or even long-lived werewolves, but their cause was both eternal and ascendant. The monster hunters would win in the end; they had been gaining ground incrementally for millennia. Esau just wanted to put a few more down before one got to him.

"Acknowledged," Esau typed, then left the office.

The Ring sent Cassius an email. Rob didn't even have to contribute a word. This victory was remarkable because Ryou-Ryou Daiō had specifically tasked him to make it happen.

Rob was not Rob. Rob was a baak, a monster from the

Assan region in India. When the original Rob had traveled to India on behalf of The Ring, the monster had lured him close to a river's edge, pulled him in, drowned him, absorbed his memories, and mimicked his shape. Baaks were capable to producing these near-perfect copies of their victims for the purpose of infiltrating their homes and taking over their lives.

Rob, the baak version, didn't have any particular interest in using his position as a member of The Ring to manipulate the organization. He just wanted to remain in the human world rather than living in a river. This made him susceptible to a specific kind of blackmail. If he crossed Ryou-Ryou Daiō, the yokai could reveal him as a baak, take his stolen life away, and leave him slinking back to his river in India (if he was lucky enough to make it before his human form melted off and revealed a fanged fish monster in the middle of a trans-Pacific flight).

For all their efforts, the Human Conservation Ring had at least one monster on the board. And baaks couldn't be discovered by salt or crosses or silver or magic wards.

Esau was working for a monster.

Chapter 13

Lena tried to judge her surroundings by smell and sound, but her superhuman senses created a jumbled image. Trapped in her bag, she'd been carried from the van to an elevator, then brought into some kind of room and plopped in a chair. Clearly the space was huge. Strange sounds echoed off a ceiling far above her and receded deep into a space to her right, behind, and in front of her, but rebounded off a stone wall just to her left. She could hear trolls shouting and hooting, laughing at one another, thousands of them, but these were coming from odd directions. Some were above her and seemed to be bouncing through rocky tunnels. Most were off to her left, but there was some other sound masking them, a constant whisper of pebbles clinking over one other, like a slow landslide. Closer, she could hear a smaller group of trolls breathing loudly through smiling mouths as they prepared something. She could smell them distinctly, the repulsive stench of unwashed flesh, unwiped asses, unbrushed teeth, salty snot, junk-food sweat, and nervous caffeine stink. The sound of their breathing and their individual smells allowed her to place them all in the space and get a rough sense of their sizes: five little ones scurrying about, clearly the most nervous; a small one standing still; and a large one sitting, his claws tapping on the arms of a large chair of some kind, his feet, complete with their own unique odor, yeasty and cheesy and overripe, swinging in the air, waving that smell around with each kick.

One of the smaller trolls climbed up onto Lena's lap, pushed her head back by smacking her in the forehead and holding his arm out stiff, and grabbed a handful of the bag between her chest and chin. Lena heard the knife piercing the canvas and smelled the silver. She gasped, then held her breath, as though she could escape a stabbing by inflating her lungs and holding them taut. The blade didn't slice her throat. The troll cut a ring around her neck, almost full circle but halting near her right clavicle, then gripped the top of the bag and yanked. He caught a handful of her hair in the process, and when he pulled the fabric away, he pulled the curls out of her scalp. Lena sucked her teeth on instinct, though the pain was less than she'd expected. She hadn't felt the pain of her hair being pulled out since her older brother grabbed a handful while wrestling when she was four. She remembered the pain and reacted accordingly, but compared to the silver chains, this was minimal.

The troll heard the sound of her sharp intake of breath, read it as a hiss, and leapt off her lap. The silver blade glinted as he waved it at her while walking backwards into the laughter of his compatriots. Lena's eyes caught that light and adjusted quickly. Orange flames from torches in sconces around massive columns illuminated the ceiling, but a different glow caught one edge of the knife. Lena looked out to her right, and she blew out the sucked-in breath like exhaling cigarette smoke as she scanned the space. The light came from thousands of computer screens facing away from her illuminating thousands of trolls and the far wall behind them, then bouncing back to wash the room in a cool gamma glow.

Overwhelmed by the numbers, she looked up toward the ceiling and saw columns, some constructed and others the products of stalactites and stalagmites that had mated over eons. Trolls crawled up and down, to and from holes in the ceiling which led up into the small caverns where they made those other noises, fighting and mating but mostly snoring. Her eyes continued back down the wall near her, and she found the source of Bel's slow heartbeat and occasional, shallow breathing. Bel sat in a chair next to Lena, still wrapped in her bag overlaid with silver chains, her head also freed from the material by jagged cuts in the fabric around her neck. She sounded like she was asleep, but her eyes were open, and she stared at the trolls with vicious concentration.

"What's going on?" Lena whispered.

Bel did not let her gaze stray from the King of Trolls. "Don't talk. They want us to talk. Patience." Then she fell silent.

"She's right," the King said. "I do want you to talk. That's why I brought you here. I want to talk with you. You're the writer, right?"

Lena looked at Bel, seeking guidance. Finding no response, she looked back at the King and refused to answer.

"I heard about your books. Both of them. I saw the one Cassius had. At the meeting of The Convention. I was there. Very impressive. Quite an accomplishment, for a human to make something that can scare so many monsters. So, to avoid future unpleasantness, perhaps you could just tell me where you've hidden copies of these books?"

Lena shot another glance at Bel, then said, "It wouldn't make a lot of sense for me to just tell you where the books are without some negotiations first. What do you have to offer me in return?"

Bel scowled and made a tight shake of her head.

"Well, seeing as I have you trussed up like a..." The King of Trolls turned to Egg. "What's the right simile? A Christmas pig?"

"A side of beef in a slaughterhouse?" Egg asked. "Like one that Rocky might tenderize in a training montage?"

The King nodded. "I can see that. Because they are more vertical than horizontal, aren't they?" He turned back to Lena. "So I feel like I have all the leverage here. I can offer you your freedom. That's something I presume you would like."

Lena nodded, then said, "No. Yes, you could offer it, but that only has value as a bargaining chip if you could also make me believe you would follow through. I don't think that's likely, so your promise wouldn't be valuable. It won't get you anything. Do you have something more tangible to offer?"

The King smiled. This was fun. "Alright, how about this? Egg, bring me the box."

Egg winced when the King said his name.

Bel stopped glaring at the King just long enough to catch Egg's eye.

"Aw," Lena cooed. "Bel knows your name now, Egg. Let's put a pin in that, shall we?"

Egg looked down at the stage floor.

"Egg, bring me the goddamned box!" the King roared. "I was in the middle of making a point. A very intimidating point. You're fucking it up. Skedaddle, you shitsplat!"

Egg leapt off the stage and through a side door.

The King looked at Bel. "You've got him pretty scared of you, eh? We'll fix that."

Bel continued to look him in the eye and said nothing.

The King turned his gaze to Lena. "Your girlfriend is scary."

Lena laughed. "You have no idea. You think you have all the leverage here, but the truth is I have a lot more than you do. I'm probably the only person on the planet who can convince Bel not to kill you all."

"Ah, Bel, is it?" the King said.

Bel allowed herself a quick glance at Lena.

Lena winced at her mistake.

"We're getting off topic," the King said. "I was asking you to tell me where your books are located. You were explaining I have no leverage. Bel was…" he waved a hand in Bel's direction dismissively, "…not being helpful and trying to be intimidating." Egg ran onto the stage with a small wooden box. "So I had Egg here bring these to me to illustrate a point." He opened the box and pulled out a plastic tube that looked like an undersized dildo. Then he pinched the cap on one end between two claws and screwed it off, tapped the cigar out into his hand, flicked the plastic tube off the stage into the fourth row of computers below, and put out his hand, waiting. Egg placed a miniature guillotine in his palm. The King used it to nip the cap end of the cigar, then tossed the cutter into the air, this time more gently, so Egg could crouch down like an outfielder, look up, and catch it. While Egg fumbled the catch, picked the cutter up off the floor, and placed it in the box, the King held out his empty hand again. Egg placed an ornate lighter there.

The King leapt down from his throne onto his little legs and walked, back bent and head down, toward the two vampires. They were only a few steps away, but he did his best Columbo, wiggling the cigar up and down as he thought of what to say. Then, immediately in front of Lena, he straightened to his full height. The King was much larger than the average troll, but he still only stood around six feet. Since the women were chained up in chairs, he towered over them. He held the lighter forward, far too close to be practical, so close to Lena's nose she had to cross her eyes to see it. It was topped with an ornate gold head, a stylized version of a dragon or a wolf. The little sculpture reminded Bel of Lung when she'd seen him in his full dragon form at the meeting of The Convention. Lena had been upstairs stealing back her second book, so she hadn't seen the luck dragon reveal himself. She thought of the time she saw Miss Rita charge past Josef as a wolf and then turn into her monstrous half-wolf form to fight the vampire in Cassius' office.

"It looks a little like me, doesn't it?" the King said.

Lena and Bel shared a look but didn't reply.

"It was a gift. Almost a hundred years ago. I'd only been the king for about a hundred years at that point. You know that saying, 'Heavy is the head that wears the crown'? Well, it's kinda' bullshit but kinda' true. On the one hand, being a king is not a burden. Every little turd in here wants to be my best friend, and they do everything I ask. So that's nice. On the other hand, when you put on the diadem…" He tapped the crown with a claw. The silver spikes rising out of the simple ring hummed like the tines of forks. "…you grow to three times your size. Yeah, I was once a micropenis like all these guys. Sucked up to the last king just like they do to me. And the crown can't be removed." He pinched one of the spikes and wiggled it, then yanked his fingers away, stared at the droplets of blood, and stuck the fingers in his mouth. He sucked the wounds clean, then continued. "It's there till I croak. The guy who gave me the lighter? He was my right hand, at the time. My majordomo. My first lieutenant. But he had ambitions to be the next King, and you just can't keep people like that around for too long. You can keep their gifts, though."

Bel made sure the King was staring at Lena and risked a glimpse at Egg. The little troll's eyes were wide. He had not known about his ruler's ascendence to the throne or his magical means to maintain his authority.

The king flipped the ornamental gold cap on the lighter back, revealing a button on a piston over a visible spring next to a tube with the top of a wheel between them. When he pressed down on the button, the wheel's teeth engaged a row of teeth hidden on the side of the piston. The wheel turned and ground a spark out of the flint inside the lighter's casing, and a modest but consistent flame appeared on top of the tube.

"I'm just saying, sometimes what we give away outlives us, and sometimes we get the crown and outlive the gift giver. You could live a very long time." He bit down on the cigar, wrapped his bulbous lips around it, then held the flame to its end. He dragged, puffed, dragged again until the end of the cigar had a strong, glowing cherry. "So, yeah, you give me the books, and maybe that doesn't guarantee your freedom. Maybe it does, and maybe it doesn't. If I decide to set you free, you'll live longer than your gifts. If not, your books will still exist, right? Little monuments that remind more important people you were here, a human who made these magic books that could wipe out humanity, then a vampire who made a magic book that can bring an end to all monsters. Pretty neat tricks, both of them. And I know I don't look like a kind, generous friend of humanity…" He looked over his shoulder at the trolls assembled around his throne, and they chuckled obediently. "…but you can evaluate the incentives involved and rest assured I have no interest in eliminating the humans who feed me or the monsters who include me."

"So you're telling me the books would be safer with you," Lena said flatly.

"Depending on where they are currently, I'd say that's a good bet."

"And once you had them, you'd do everything you could to make sure you kept them safe."

"Of course."

"And everything you could to make sure no one else could produce a copy or possess a similar book, right?"

The King stuck the cigar in his mouth and puffed. "I can see why you might be reluctant to give me any information, Ms. Wallace. But I get the sense you are focusing on your leverage and not taking mine seriously enough." He leaned toward her and blew a giant puff of smoke in her face.

Lena did her best to hold perfectly still, but the smell was so overwhelming to her new heightened senses, she couldn't help but wrinkle her nose.

"You see, I can make your stay only mildly unpleasant. Or..." He leaned forward just a bit further, and the silver crown pressed against her forehead. When the metal made contact, it sizzled against her skin, cooking its way inside. She refused to scream, but she couldn't help but suck in a tense breath. "...I can make it mildly unpleasant. Or..." He reached over with one of his long arms and brought the cigar down on Bel's thigh. The cherry burned through the burlap, then her jeans, and then began to sizzle against her skin. Bel stared at the

King, unflinching, a show for Lena. But Lena could see and even smell the slight hint of tears in her eyes. "...or I can make it very, very unpleasant for you by torturing your girlfriend. I have always wanted to know certain things about vampire healing."

He pulled the cigar out of Bell's leg. Then he swung back to Lena and wrapped one of his huge hands around the back of her head, yanking her forward. Lena strained her back and pressed her feet heavily onto the floor, trying to keep him from touching the crown to her forehead again. Struggling, she closed her eyes, and when she opened them, she found he wasn't angling his head down to headbutt her with those silver spikes. Instead, the King examined the burn marks on Lena's forehead.

"Gone," he said. "No scars. Not a trace."

He let go of Lena's head, and she fell into the back of her chair hard enough to rock it and lift the front legs off the floor, so it fell back with a ponderous double-thud. The King stepped toward Bel and put one of his claws into the hole, and he gently scraped back and forth. "Nothing. Even the ash is probably from the sack and your pants. Skin as smooth and clean as a marble statue."

He was too close. Bel lunged forward and bit his huge ear. She didn't have time to use her real teeth, but her human ones worked fine. She grabbed a chunk the size of the top of a can of soda, bit down hard enough to crunch through the cartilage, and then hauled back, her feet pressing the floor like Lena's had, her back muscles straining, and tore through the few strips of flesh hanging on between her teeth.

The King yelped like a wounded dog and stumbled away, then slapped his hand to his ear and looked at Bel. She turned her head very slowly to the wall and spat. The piece of ear and the troll's purple blood splattered like a thrown sponge full of paint.

"Oh, you motherfucking vamp cocksucking cumguzzling shiteating whore!" he roared. Then he calmed suddenly, but his eyes blazed. "I was just telling your girlfriend here about the experiments I'm going to perform. I was going to start with minor flesh wounds. Work my way up. But now I'll tell you about what I'm looking forward to. I want to know how fast your limbs grow back. If I stick one of your fingers in a cup of human blood, can I grow more of you? I'm going to cut off more and more of you until I find out when it ends. What's the least amount of you that can grow back? Head and torso? Maybe half a torso? Just your head and a clavicle, maybe? We're going to find out."

"Wait!" Lena shouted. "I thought we were negotiating. You jumped to the torture part, but aren't there other things we can discuss? Maybe some limited freedom? Put us in a cell, chain me to a chair with a typewriter, and see what I make for you? I've done it before. That's how the warlock Erdogan got the first book from me."

The King snorted. "I know you're stalling for time. But I don't know why. And I don't know why you would tell that particular lie."

"What lie?"

"It wasn't Erdogan. It was Matteo Bern. Now, maybe you think I don't know Erdogan is dead." The King stepped away, still holding his hand pressed against his ear, purple blood running down between his fingers. He looked at Egg standing at the base of his throne. "So maybe she thinks we'll waste a bunch of time trying to track down Erdogan and postpone slicing and dicing her girlfriend. Makes sense. But why direct us to a warlock at all?"

Egg shrugged.

"Unless! Unless she really didn't know it was Matteo Bern, her friend, so she didn't even think she was being sneaky." He spun and faced her. "You didn't know, did you?"

Lena said nothing.

The King snatched the silver knife from the troll who had freed their heads, then stomped back across the stage toward her. He put the knife's blade against her throat to keep her from biting, then pressed his crown against her forehead once again. "You didn't know Matteo Bern made you write the first book, did you?" he shouted. "Answer me or I'll burn into your skull, you genocidal syphilis slurper!"

"I didn't know. I didn't know, okay?"

The King stood up and pulled the knife away from her neck. "I feel like we're getting somewhere."

Both the King and Lena were surprised when they heard Bel's voice. "Was Matt working for Nigel or Cassius or Apraxis?"

"She can speak!" the King shouted. "Now see, that wasn't so hard, was it? You know, if you tell me where the books are, I won't have to start cutting up your girlfriend to get you to talk when you're nothing but a head."

"Yes, I can talk." Bel smiled. Purple blood dribbled down her chin. "I just had to spit some of your meat out of my mouth first. Talking with your mouth full is unladylike. So, tell me, was Matt working for Nigel or Cassius or Apraxis?"

"Oh, you think you're so clever. You think I'm the one being interrogated here. You don't know shit. Apraxis? That little flying weasel? He can't accomplish much of anything because he can only lie. He's good at hiding it, but no one should ever work with him. Which means, if Cassius thinks Apraxis took care of your golem friend, he didn't. Cassius is a sucker for trusting him. And you're an idiot for asking me questions and thinking you're going to learn anything helpful. I have you, not the other way around. I could tell you anything. I could blow your mind with what I know. About Cassius. About your Archduke. About Tisina. Oh, just wait until you learn about her. Because it won't matter. Sure, maybe you'll outlive me if you can grow back from a finger I flush down the toilet, but you're going to be my prisoners for as long as I'm the King of the trolls!"

Bel looked at Lena. "I suspect he's right about that." Then she looked beyond him at the little trolls near his throne. She didn't say anything, and four of them quailed in her glare. But Egg's eyes went wide, and then he looked away, considering.

"Oh, you can take your empty threats and shove them into the empty sockets I'm going to leave when I rip your arms and legs off." He held up the silver knife. "Know what? I think we can start now. Boys, which would you prefer to eat in front of her girlfriend, a leg or a wing?"

"Wait!" Lena shouted. "I have a deal for you. This is a negotiation after all. Let's deal. Offer on the table."

The King continued to approach Bel, knife outstretched, ready for her to bite again. "You know what?" He held the blade near Bel's throat, then grabbed her right ear, pulled it away from her head, and sliced, leaping back with it in his hand before she could bite him again. He stepped in front of Lena and wiggled the ear. "I'm listening."

"Okay, here's an offer. I can't just tell you where the books are. You wouldn't be able to get them. And obviously you can't let me leave. But I'll tell Bel where I hid the books, and you can send her up to get them. She'll come back with them to trade them for me. You know she will. And then you'll have the books or me. You'll get to decide."

Lena knew the King would believe he could recapture Bel and have both. And the King knew Lena knew that. But he raised one of his pierced eyebrows, considering it anyway.

"Don't do this, Lena," Bel said.

Lena guessed the trolls had hearing far better than any humans, considering the size of their ears, and she didn't know if it was better than the supernatural hearing of vampires, so she chose her words carefully and whispered, "Better one of us than both."

Chapter 14

When Torreblanca first woke up, she examined the world through a haze of pain so thick, she couldn't clearly identify her surroundings. A heart monitor beeped gently on the left side of her bed, and an aluminum pole holding clear bags of liquid stood to her right, plastic tubes running down beneath the line of sight, making their way under her blankets and back up into needles in her arms. The walls did not look like any hospital room she'd ever seen. There were no windows, and the plain, wooden door was closed.

The walls themselves weren't standard drywall painted white. They were the same rich wood as the door, but even if Torreblanca had possessed all her faculties, she wouldn't have been able to identify it as agarwood from the Aquilaria malaccensis trees, a wood so rare and precious that the trees themselves were critically endangered. Agarwood was almost never used in building construction. If the wood produced a specific resin in response to a specific fungal mold, the tree was harvested (illegally) for incense and perfumes. But this agarwood had been cut down hundreds of years ago and masterfully converted into parquet panels for these walls. The resin protected it from the predation of time, and the smell dissipated over the centuries, so now it only produced the slight hint of what an expert might describe as "very soft fruity-floral" smell characterized by a "sweet-balsamic" note and "shades of vanilla and musk." Torreblanca was not an expert in perfumes, but she could tell the room didn't smell like "strong notes of antiseptic cleaners" with hints of "old people" and subtle notes of "hand sanitizer" and "piss," so it was unlike any hospital she'd ever visited.

As she rose to consciousness, she noticed the most striking difference. The ceiling was the same wooden parquet as the walls. Instead of the sickly glow of fluorescent tubes Torreblanca would expect in a hospital, the room was lit by flickering radiance from rectangular lampshades, three vertical feet long, hung in each corner of the room. Each held something that looked like a candle, but the flame was larger, dangerously large for the thin lampshades, and producing light but no smoke. A mirror hung on the back of the room's closed door, but she couldn't see herself in it from her position, just another angle of one of the strange lanterns in the corners.

Her heart monitor started to beep a bit faster as she thought about the lampshades catching fire in the enclosed space. The room seemed to get warmer and stuffier, but that was only her nerves. Torreblanca decided it was time to get up, but when she tried to sit, the pain in her stomach flared with such intensity she gasped and fell back onto her pillow, staring at the ceiling and breathing like she was practicing Lamaze.

The door to her room opened, and a man entered. He wore a long white garment, almost like a labcoat, only somehow simpler and more formal, made of some kind of woolen fabric, with no pockets, and closed with a series of oblong, white jade buttons. He was tall, thin, clean shaven, his hair a bit on the long side for a doctor, and his features were the slightly androgynous variety popular among Korean and Japanese pop stars. Torreblanca didn't think he was Korean or Japanese, though she couldn't quite identify his nationality. She wouldn't have been able to recognize him as a member of the Khon Isan of northern Thailand, and that might have offended a true Isan person, but it wouldn't have bothered him a bit, since he wasn't really Khon Isan anyway. Torreblanca did immediately identify him as handsome in a way that was simultaneously calming and thrilling, and the heart monitor didn't know what to make of the effect he had on her.

"Lieutenant Torreblanca," he said, "I'm glad to see

you're awake." His voice was deeper than she expected, and he had a clear British accent with a slight hint of Cantonese underneath, an accent she'd heard before in Hong Kong. Only, Torreblanca thought she'd heard this particular voice somewhere else, too. Somewhere she'd been more recently. She couldn't quite place it, though.

"I know you probably want to get up, but you're going to need to stay in bed for a while longer while you heal. You are very lucky to be alive. Your injury would have been fatal in any normal circumstances."

"Where am I?"

"I'm sure this is all very disconcerting," the man said. "It's important that you remain calm. I can answer all your questions, but please promise me you will do your best to keep your breathing and heart rate as steady as you can, alright?"

Torreblanca nodded and discovered even that movement tightened her abs and caused a flare of pain.

"It's okay," the man said. "You have lots of time to heal, so we're in no rush." He took a chair standing against the wall and pulled it over near the bed. "Here," he said, "I'll tell you what. When you start to feel anxious or feel any pain, you can squeeze my hand until you calm down again. Are you comfortable with that?"

She made a much smaller nod, and the man took her left hand in both his own. His hands were soft and bony. Torreblanca thought she might break them if she squeezed too hard.

"Okay, so the answer to your first question might frighten you, but I want you to know you are safe here, and we're going to get you all healed up and back on your feet, okay?"

Torreblanca gave the man's hand a gentle squeeze, and he returned it.

"When we found you, you were very near death. We could not take you to a normal hospital. You would certainly have died. They would not have had the necessary … skills to save you. So we brought you back here, to my home."

Torreblanca frowned. "Okay, where is your home?"

The man squeezed her hand again, this time more tightly than she expected, and she liked that. "I want to assure you I am not trying to be cagey or secretive or … what do they say now? 'Sus'? We are in Cambodia. I can be more specific, but that is a much longer story, and we have the time, so I will tell you how my home came to be here, but before I launch into that very long tale, what other questions do you have?"

"Who are you?"

The man sat back in his chair, but he didn't let go of her hand. When he exhaled a long sigh, Torreblanca noticed all four candles in the corners of the room flickered. "Well, that's a difficult question also. Again, I'm not trying to be reticent to share information. I'm worried you might react negatively, and that could impinge on your recovery. First, Lieutenant Torreblanca, may I call you Anahí?"

Torreblanca was a bit surprised the man pronounced her name correctly. She had an aversion to people butchering her name, but she now found she also didn't like it when English speakers said it correctly. It felt wrong to her somehow, like they were trying too hard and showing off. Normally she just told people to call her Torreblanca. But for some reason she couldn't quite identify, she didn't want this man to feel so remote. She suspected it was the handholding which she'd come to think of as his bedside manner.

"Call me Ani," she said. She immediately felt strange about her choice. Only her mother and sister called her Ani. Even her father and older brothers called her Anahí. And she'd pronounced Ani in Spanish, the way her mother and sister said it.

She frowned, and the man said, "Are you sure," as though he knew this was strange.

Torreblanca made another of those tight nods.

He squeezed her hand. "Alright, Ani," he said. "Now, I'm going to need you to stay calm, okay? My name is Long."

"Lung?" she asked.

"Almost. Think of the word 'long' and the word 'lung,' and find the place halfway in between. Then tilt it up at the end like you're asking a question in English."

"Lóng?" she said. "Lóng. Lóng." She repeated it until he nodded and smiled.

"Yes, that's close enough. Better than most, Ani. Now, do you remember…"

Before he could finish his sentence, she frowned. He stopped and waited. The surprise blossomed on her face like a time lapse of a flower opening to the morning sun.

"Okay, remember to stay calm. You're safe here."

She tried to sit up, and the burst of pain roared behind her belly button then shot upwards toward her heart. She reached out with her free right hand to push herself into a sitting position, but when the pain came, she could only grab a fistful of the blanket and hold on. Long held her other hand up off the bed so she couldn't grab hold.

"Breathe," he said softly. "You're safe. Just breathe."

"You're…" She gasped and writhed, pulling herself to the right, then back in the direction of his hands around her left. He didn't squeeze too tightly, but his arms didn't move. "You're a … one of the … a monster … we …"

"Yes, we met in Canada not too long ago. Pardon the pun." He smiled at his accidental joke. "And we worked together in Las Vegas. You remember."

"And they said… Esau said you were a dragon."

"Yes. Not to be pedantic, but I am still a dragon."

"You, um, looked different before." Torreblanca blushed, but her heart rate slowed on the monitor.

"Yes. That was a disguise."

"Is this the real you?"

Long shook his head. "No, this is a disguise as well. I thought you might feel more comfortable with this one."

"I … I like this one better, but I'm still scared of the real you."

Long nodded. "That's reasonable. But I assure you, you are safe here. I personally guarantee your safety. I have worked quite hard to keep you alive, Ani. Your survival was unlikely."

Torreblanca looked down at the blankets over her wound. "Thank you."

Long squeezed her hand. "It was my pleasure."

She looked up into his eyes. The black pupils were lost in black irises. His smile was warm and seemed genuine, the slightest hint of crinkles at the corners of his eyes dimpling his smooth skin. She felt an urge to reach over and place her hand on his face, to run a thumb over the crinkles to see how they felt. When she lifted her free right hand and crossed her body, her stomach screamed again. She settled for resting her hand on top of his which still held her left. "Thank you," she said again.

And then her door opened.

Matt Bern leaned into the room, holding the frame with one hand. "Oh, she's awake!"

"Yes, and in good spirits, but in a good deal of pain, too, I think," Long said.

"And what have you told her?"

"She knows who we are and what we are, and I told her we're in Cambodia, and I promised to tell her the whole story of my home, but we haven't gotten to that just yet. If you'd like to stay here with her for a second, I will go get her something to eat. Ani, do you prefer pho or chicken noodle soup?"

"Either sounds good. I'm pretty hungry, now that you mention it."

"And thirsty, I expect. I'll get you some water, but is there anything else you'd like to drink?"

"What do you have?"

Long cocked his head in Matt's directed but didn't break eye contact. "Between the two of us? Absolutely everything."

"In that case, a cold Tecate."

"You're in Cambodia and want a beer made in Mexico but owned by a company in Holland," Long said. He turned to Matt. "She's testing our powers."

Matt chuckled, came into the room, and pulled up a second chair on Torreblanca's left side.

Long stood. "Don't upset her," he said, and though his face was impassive, his eyes flashed. Literally. Liquid gold fire filled up his eyes and spurted out the sides before vanishing as though it had never been there.

Matt raised his hands defensively. "I wouldn't think of it."

Long left the room, his long white coat whipping around him and falling slowly back in a way that made Torreblanca think of some creature in flight.

"I sometimes upset humans on purpose," Matt explained. "Quite a bit, truth be told. But I don't need to do that to you because you are just a roiling mass of emotions right now. Like those barrels full of eels you humans used to have all over. Before your time. You know, they used to use them as currency in England. It's true. 11th century to the 16th. People ate more eels than freshwater and saltwater fish combined."

He paused.

"Okay?" Torreblanca said.

"I'm just reminded because your feelings are like that right now."

"Gross."

"Maybe a little bit. But also vibrant and lively and valuable and constrained in this really unnatural way. I know this is all very confusing. You are quite committed to killing monsters, and here you are, saved from death at the hands of a fellow monster hunter by two monsters."

"It feels like you're trying to upset me."

"I don't always do it on purpose. Believe it or not, I'm trying to calm you down by offering to be helpful. But I acknowledge I have a tendency to be showy, and I haven't had an audience other than Long for some time. You were unconscious, and he's a bit on the stoic side. So, if you have any questions, especially if they would require a dramatic explanation, maybe with some amusing singing and dancing, I'd really love an opportunity."

Torreblanca shook her head a bit. "Sorry. I'm pretty tired."

"I completely understand. Still healing up. I'll tell you what." Matt leaned forward and clapped his hands together gently. "I'll tell you a long, boring story, and I promise not to be at all offended when you fall asleep, and that way I get an audience, and you get a deep voice droning on to help you slip off to la la land."

Torreblanca thought about it, and the thought made her yawn. She laughed, then winced. "Yeah, I guess that would work."

"Well, seeing as you are having conflicted romantic feelings about a dragon … now, now. Don't deny it. I can read you humans like a book. And I get it. This new Long is quite dashing. But thinking about him is not going to help you sleep, so instead, let me tell you the very boring story of a princess who lived in a city under the ocean and only wanted one thing in her entire life, and then she got it, and it was her undoing. Tragic, yes, but really she was a boring princess. In fact, her name meant "silence" because, at birth, she didn't cry, but even when she grew up, she was very quiet, and it fooled people into thinking her head was full of devious plans, when she really only had one plan all along."

Torreblanca was already asleep. Long came back with a steaming bowl of soup and a bottle of beer cold enough to sweat profusely in the Cambodian humidity. Before he could speak, Matt put a finger to his lips and whispered, "See? I didn't upset her."

Long snorted a silent laugh. "Good."

"I didn't get to tell her anything about her role in all this before she fell asleep," Matt said. "I started to tell her about Tisina, but I took the long way to let her doze off, so I didn't get to Lord Varr."

Long set the soup and beer down on the end table by Torreblanca's bed, then sat back down and laid a hand on top of Torreblanca's. "That's alright," he said. "There's plenty of time."

Chapter 15

The emissary paused suddenly. "Come to think of it, you could plug in a whole monologue by that Matt Bern character to fill the viewer in on Tisina's backstory there. They might need that."

Kim, surprised by the abrupt departure from the story, looked to Joyce, then Carol, then back to the presenter. "But he said that story was boring."

"True," the emissary said. "And it is, sort of. Until the ending with the whole conception and birth of the world-destroying kaiju. But that Matt Bern character is very charismatic. So if the story gets at all confusing to test audiences, have him do some voice-over narration."

"Ugh," Carol said. "I hate voice-over narration. It's bad exposition, and it always feels insulting and lazy. Dislike."

Joyce shrugged. "But maybe as a kind of transition, from a diegetic bit of dialogue into a flashback or a new location?"

"Maybe," Carol said, not wanting to directly contradict Mr. Joyce but not wanting to give too much ground on her sincere distaste, either. "It might just be me."

"No, I hear what you're saying," Kim said. "They should be avoided if possible."

"Alright," the emissary said. "I was just spit-balling. Tangent. Sorry."

Mr. Joyce raised a hand. "Wait, before we jump back into the pitch, we just had a conversation in a dark room in … What was it? Cambodia?" He looked to Carol. "We could probably change that to China, right?" Before she could answer, he looked back to the emissary. "And before that was a tense interrogation, so that's good, but before that it was like… a weird phone call? Terrible on film. We need some action pretty soon."

The emissary's eyes flashed. Figuratively. He stuck his hands out, fingers splayed. "Oh, you'll love this next scene. Violence and guns and blood."

"Okay, but not more torture, right?" Kim said. "I thought that Torreblanca woman might get tortured, too, and I just am not down with the torture porn."

"Exactly!" the emissary said.

Kim didn't know what the man meant, and they did not find it reassuring.

Joyce was obviously interested again, though. He sat forward in his seat, leaning on his elbows. "Okay, gimme this action scene."

"It starts with a dolly," the emissary began.

"Like, a creepy toy doll?" Kim asked.

"No, like one of those handcarts with two wheels and the lip for lifting things so one person can pick up a bunch of boxes. Only, in this case, it's kind of a comic shot because we see the dolly first, and then we see that it's being operated by three trolls. Two are trying to push it, and one is managing them, only they're all too short to maneuver it correctly, so he's shouting at them in that way trolls do…"

"We live in such an age of chatter and distraction. Everything is a challenge for the ears and eyes."

-Rebecca Pidgeon

Chapter 16

"Left! I said 'left,' you scrotum wrinkles! No, more left," Egg shouted.

The pair of trolls rolled the dolly toward the stairs to the stage where the King's throne sat. Only they were veering too far to the right and would miss the stairs entirely and smash into the front of the stage itself. Egg wanted to hurry up and get this plan moving because he worried if he gave the King too much time, his monarch might change his mind, and Egg suspected this was his only chance for the next hundred years.

"Okay, stop, just stop!" he shouted.

The trolls made an effort to bring the dolly upright,

almost got it, let it slip forwards so the handle on top smacked one of them on the head. The other caught it, and righted it again, this time pointing too far to the left so it would miss the stairs the other way.

"Hey, morons, what are your names?" Egg asked.

"I'm Bubwan, Mr. Egg, sir," the first said.

"I'm Bubtu," reported the second.

"One and two, eh? What are your real names?"

"I'm Cum Bubble Number One," said the first, then hooked a thumb at his partner, "and he's Cum Bubble Number Two. We're twins and accidents, and our mom was mad at whichever troll is our dad for not sticking around—"

"She had to give birth to us at her desk, and no one helped. They just laughed and threw flaming shit on top of her desk while she was underneath it, cranking us out, so she was kind of in work mode and angry at all the other trolls—"

"Angry at everything and everybody. Our mom is like that pretty much all the time," Bubwan said.

"-and so she named us Cum Bubble One and Cum Bubble Two."

"She wanted to name us Fucking Piece of Shit Cum Bubble One and Two, but those were too long."

Bubwan shrugged. "She tried, but she'd keep adding more words, and then she'd get confused, and then—"

"She's not a good mom. Even for a troll."

Bubwan looked at Bubtu. "She lacks skills."

"Don't make excuses for her."

"She's doing the best she can with the skills she has."

Bubtu shook his head. "Fucking Susan."

"Your mother's name is Susan?" Egg asked.

"No, Susan is my therapist," Bubwan explained.

"You have a troll therapist?"

"Human. Online." He turned to Bubtu. "And Susan's right; every child has different parents, even twins."

"Mom's nicer to you because you make excuses for her bad behavior. You enable her, and I deal with the consequences. It strains our relationship. Tell that to Susan."

"Okay, Bubwan, you take the right side, and Bubtu, take the left," Egg said. "We'll talk about you unburdening your soul to a human later."

The trolls managed to roll the dolly to the base of the stairs with Egg yelling, "More, Bubwan! No, slow up. Bubtu, stop. Pull back. Now push." But when they ran into the bottom of the stairs with a thump, all three were flummoxed for a moment. "Okay, I've got it!" Egg announced. "Bubtu, turn it around. No, Bubwan, the other way. Other way, you idiot! Okay, now stop. Stop! Both of you pull back. Pull it back! Now lift it up. Keep pulling it back. Good, morons!"

Eventually, they got it up onto the stage, then nearly lost it in an attempt to turn it around, made a more-than-360-degree turn, and wheeled it up behind Bel's chair. Egg pushed the chair up onto its two front legs, and the twins tried to put the lip under both back legs, but the dolly was thinner than the chair. Egg shouted at Bubtu and Bubwan for a while.

Bel and Lena shared a glance, and both rolled their

eyes in unison.

Finally Egg figured out the problem, scurried off the stage, and came back with a piece of wood a bit wider than the chair. He ordered Bubwan and Bubtu to push the back legs into the air again, slid the board under, and then told them to push to dolly under the board.

They tried. The board was pushed forward by the lip of the dolly, and Bel clanked heavily onto the stage.

Bel frowned. "If you unlock me, I could just walk."

Bubwan and Bubtu leaned around her and looked to the King, their thick unibrows raised.

"No, you nimrods. The second those chains come off, we're all dead."

Bel shrugged. "Not all." And when the King wasn't looking, she shot a quick glance at Egg.

He noticed but had no idea what to do about it, so he called another pair of trolls, and they lifted the back legs of the chair while he placed the board, then lifted the board while Bubtu and Bubwan got the dolly under it. Then Egg and his two new compatriots pushed Bel back as Bubtu and Bubwan caught her on the dolly, but not before Bel caught Egg's eye again. He made the facial equivalent of a shrug, an unpleasant expression on a human face and revolting on a troll's, but Bel knew she was making progress. Outside, there might be the space to start to hatch a plan.

Egg and his crew needed to get Bel to the elevator on the far side of the room. And it was a giant room. They could have taken her down one of the three aisles running lengthwise perpendicular to the nearly two hundred rows of desks where the trolls on the floor did their work, but they all knew their brethren were hard to control, and even with the King's shouted commands, it was unlikely they could roll a target through the aisles without someone deciding to throw something at them. That would lead to a frenzy, and even if the first troll only tossed an empty Doritos bag or a drained can of Red Bull, soon all the trolls would be loading their favorite ammunition, their own feces, which, by dint of their troll magic and the popular diet, was delivered into their hands (yes, directly into their hands) already on fire and ready to hurl as burning, stinking projectiles. Bel would have weathered this without much physical damage, but Egg and his crew, despite their own ability to briefly hold their own flaming shit like hot potatoes, would be painfully burned if they were caught in such a barrage.

Instead, they planned to wheel Bel to one of the doorways on either side of the stage which contained a short, concrete two-flight stairway up to the catwalk that ran around the room suspended from chains anchored in the ceiling. The workers below would still make an effort to pelt them, but the distance would protect them, and if they pushed her along fast enough, they might get most of the way to the elevator before the workers noticed and flung their digested lunches.

But the group of five had only managed to lower Bel, still in her chair and bumping down each step, to the bottom of the stars in front of the stage and were engaged in an argument about which staircase to the catwalk was closer (they were exactly equidistant), when the elevator bell dinged in the back of the room.

Despite the crown that made him three times the size of a normal troll, the King's vision was not enhanced, and though trolls saw better in the darkness than humans, they didn't see much farther, so when the elevators doors opened, he could see only a rectangle of light widen to a square of light against the cavern's distant rear wall. The trolls didn't get many visitors, but the elevator was used enough that he could tell this was off. Normally, the occupant would cast a smudgy shadow in the middle of that square of light. In this case, he could see only the glow, then two small flickers at the edges.

The King couldn't identify the two arms tossing grenades, then reaching back into the hidden space just to the left and right of the elevator's open doors, grabbing more, and tossing those. Then the grenades started going off.

The rules of The Convention prohibited monsters from killing other monsters. After keeping monsterdom secret from the human population, that was The Convention's secondary raison d'etre. But the rules sometimes got fuzzy. They allowed for self-defense, so in a fight between monsters, CimBim often had to make a judgment call about which party was initially using lethal force, and which party was merely responding with lethal force. Also, if no one was actually killed, The Convention hadn't technically been violated. Lena and Bel's assault on Cassius' office had exploited this loophole when the werewolf pups from Nando's community leapt on Cassius' guards and ripped their limbs off. Bob and Augy were merely incapacitated, not killed, so that was legal. Bel and Lena's capture by the King also fell into this permissible side of the ledger. If the grenades had been of the standard explosive variety, they certainly would have killed many trolls, but these released either tear gas or smoke. The assailants could credibly claim that, at least at the beginning of the incursion, no lethal force had been employed.

Some trolls were seriously injured in the first minute of the attack because they panicked. Some ran for the columns leading up to their rooms. Because of the screeching of the panicked trolls, many of those sleeping above during their off-shift woke up and started coming down to see what was going on, and when the escapees met the looky-loos on the sheer faces of the columns, many of the climbers fell back down. Other trolls decided their best defense was a good offense, but they had no clear sense of their targets, so they hopped up onto their desks to try to see above the smoke, looked for the locations of the explosions themselves, couldn't see much of anything through their stinging, tear-filled eyes, then squatted, shat into their hands, and started throwing flaming globs of sticky goo blindly in whatever direction they thought best. The fireballs set desks ablaze, melted computers, and stuck to other trolls who filled the cavern with new kinds of screams.

The chaos made for an indecipherable light show for the King on the stage in the front of the room. Balls of light arced through the smoke, and fires from burning desks glowed inside the clouds rolling across the floor.

In the midst of all the screeching and hollering, he couldn't hear the clinking of the chains or the clicking of claws on the metal catwalks, and he didn't notice the blurs of dark shapes racing down the catwalks at 35 miles per hour. In all the chaos, not a single troll threw poo at the shadows racing at their ruler.

The smoke and teargas rolled toward the stage, and the wave of escaping trolls moved at about the same speed, clambering over the rows of desks, leaping onto one another, heedless of whether they were clawing and stomping on one another's heads as they ran. The King didn't even know what to shout at them. On instinct, he did what came naturally, grabbing one of the members of the upper management team on the stage, lifting him over his head by the smaller troll's thigh and shoulder, and shouting, "Get back to work, you little shits!"

This had zero effect.

"Back!" the King tried feebly. "Back!" Then he whipped the smaller troll in a circle like a bolo. "I said 'back'!" He threw the manager into the center of the mob.

This had slightly more impact, but only on the manager and exactly ten trolls knocked down like bowling pins. The rest of the horde kept coming.

Two werewolves in their half-wolf form, eight feet tall, covered in muscles and nothing else, squeezed through the standard-sized doorways on either side of the stage, ducking under the six-and-a-half-foot header jamb and turning their enormous shoulders slightly to pry through the three foot width. One was obviously male, the other obviously female and also noticeably pregnant. They threw their arms wide, raising their heads to their full heights, long snouts pointed to the cavern's ceiling, and howled before dropping to all fours and snapping at the coming trolls, saliva flying, lips curled back to reveal their perfectly deadly teeth.

This worked.

The mob doubled back on itself, those closest to the stage deciding teargas and trampling sounded positively delightful compared to being the first to reach the werewolves. Some reconsidered the potentially deadly climbs up the columns to the sleeping quarters, now braving the bodies falling down on one another. Others, completely flummoxed, ran back into the gas, then in circles, screaming and blind and smashing into one another and whatever remained of the desks and computers.

In the midst of this chaos, Egg poked his head up into Bel's sightline, smiled uncertainly, and hung an open padlock on the loop of chain wrapped around her middle. Then he disappeared, ducking behind her, racing back up the stairs onto the stage, to a narrow space between the stage and the rear cavern wall, a space he'd used before to escape the King's view during tantrums. He leapt headfirst into the space, got stuck briefly with his legs sticking straight up against the wall, then wriggled, his heels kicking the stone, until he fell down onto his head into the relatively safe darkness under the stage itself.

Bel didn't understand immediately, but when she looked down at the padlock hanging above her bellybutton, she watched it slide down under its own weight, and she realized the chains were no longer held fast by anything. A quick glance to each side revealed none of her movers were paying her any attention. She began rocking her chair back and forth, not enough to tip over, but enough to wiggle it off the board supporting the back legs. When it fell the inch and a half to the ground, the impact caused the chains wrapped around the burlap sack to slip into a neat ring around her feet. It took a few more seconds to use her sharp nails and some super-human speed to slice through the bag, and then the burlap fell away. She was free.

Her moving crew had backed close to her, all their attention on the werewolves on either side of them and the mob running toward them. Bel gently tapped Bubtu on the shoulder. He turned and looked at her, stopped screaming, then went right back to staring at the werewolves and screaming again.

She extended her lower jaw and released her real teeth, then tapped Bubwan. When he turned to face her, he stared directly into a mouth that looked like a hybrid of a lamprey's and an angler fish's, only each tooth was moving independently, begging his flesh to enter and be sucked dry. His agitated hooting turned into a tea-kettle whistle-scream, and that got the attention of the others who turned, saw she was free, and bolted, some leaping halfway onto the stage, catching their stomachs on the edge and kicking frantically, while the others went running in the only direction not occupied by werewolves or a vampire, which meant directly into the oncoming cloud of teargas and smoke.

Bel turned her attention to the stage, ignoring the two scrabbling trolls trying to climb onto it, and darted up the stairs toward Lena. To her amazement, Lena didn't shout, "Bel!" Instead, Lena shouted, "Napoleon!"

The skeleton slipped out of the door behind Lucia. He'd taken off his stuffed costume that let him blend in with the humans to a limited degree, preferring to have his full range of motion for his part of this battle. He wore only one thing: A backpack. He raced up the stairs onto the stage, whipped the backpack off by removing his left arm with his right, swinging the bag around so the strap left his left shoulder and arced over his spine, reattached his left arm, and caught the swinging bag when it came around in front of him. The ridiculous move shaved a fraction of a second off the normal time it would have taken him to remove a backpack in a human way, but he enjoyed the flourish. Before the left arm was back in its socket, his left hand was already pinching the zipper tab and yanking it. Everyone on the stage, including the King, stopped to see what he would pull out of the bag.

He tossed the first object directly to Bel, then pulled out a second and approached Lena while Bel turned it around in her hands, figuring out what she'd been thrown. Napoleon maneuvered the straps of the gasmask over Lena's hair with an obviously loving concern for her dignity and the position of her curls, then tightened it against her face.

Bel yanked hers on, heedless of the top strap parting her pink mohawk in two, then faced off against the King, claws out at her sides, her hiss only partially muffled by the pane of round plastic.

Napoleon threw a gasmask back to Lucia, who was changing into her human form as she ran up the stairs onto the stage. He fell onto all fours, elbows up at insectile angles, and crab-walked sideways to the edge of the stage where he winged a pass to Nando who was running up the other side. The human-shaped werewolves put on their gasmasks and held their positions at the top of each flight of stairs, ready to keep any brave trolls from attempting an assault on higher ground or any cowardly ones from trying to escape down the stairs.

Cardinal rule of the internet: There are no brave trolls.

The cowardly ones on the stage did not care enough to try to run for the stairs. They leapt straight off the middle of the stage, crashing into the managers' desks at the front of the room, landing on top of one another, and then scurrying into the smoke and gas which were now reaching the stage. Only the King remained.

He held the silver knife, the one he'd used to cut off Bel's ear. He climbed up onto the seat of his throne, compensating for his tiny legs and becoming proportional to his giant head, shoulders, and arms. He swung the knife back and forth in a slow arc, aiming it at all of them. "Come and get it! None of you fleabag mangy giant chihuahuas or suckface human-juice lickers want a taste of silver, and I plan to give you— Oh, goddamn! That stings! Mother fu—" And then he could only make choking, retching sounds because the teargas and smoke were so overpowering. Every time he tried to open his eyes, he'd see briefly through the protection of his tears, and then the sting would return like he'd been jabbed in his pupils by white-hot needles. Almost worse, his own snot, copious to begin with, now ran freely from his nose but also down his throat, choking him. Every time he'd gag and cough, he'd breathe in more of the gas and smoke. He kept his wits about him enough to continue swinging the knife back and forth, but now he couldn't see far enough to locate Bel, Nando, or Lucia, and could only assume Lena was still chained in her chair.

The knife was dangerous enough to keep Bel, Nando, and Lucia at bay. They came together at the foot of the throne but had to keep ducking and weaving as the knife made its potentially deadly passes. Bel could more easily survive a stabbing than Nando or Lucia, who would have died if pierced by that blade, but the King was so strong, a swipe might have been able to decapitate her, and that would have killed her as well. All three rocked back and forth on the balls of their feet, waiting for an opening, trying to keep an eye on the knife as it faded in and out in the smoke.

The King got to the end of one swing, this one to his right, and as he came back to the left, the blade was caught in a hand. Not by a hand. Inside a hand. Specifically, between the metacarpals of Napoleon's palm. The blade passed through without damaging the bones or puncturing any flesh, since Napoleon didn't have any, and then Napoleon turned his hand sideways, pinching it more tightly. The skeleton was no match for the giant troll's strength, but he had a second in which the blade was captured before the King could pry it free or bash in Napoleon's skull with his other hand.

The King couldn't see Napoleon clearly, but he felt the knife sticking in something and reacted on instinct, jerking the knife towards himself to snatch it back. This had two effects: Napoleon was yanked forward so fast, his feet left the ground. As he flew toward the King, he threw a punch. Since the troll was standing up on his throne, the aim was off, but Napoleon's momentum multiplied the skeleton's supernatural strength with the King's even more astounding might. Napoleon slammed his bone knuckles squarely into the King's dick.

Unfortunately, the momentum also pulled Napoleon's head toward the King's hand. The knife's blade which poked back through his own hand drove directly into Napoleon's skull. His body went limp immediately, and the remainder of a corpse hung suspended, his feet a foot above the stage.

Lena screamed Napoleon's name. The King doubled forward, crouching in pain and an attempt to maintain his precarious balance on the throne. Bel saw her opening and lunged forward. Her hand shot up, sharp nails swinging at an angle. They entered the King's throat next to his Adam's apple on his right side, but because of her speed and momentum, they came out just to the right of his spine. The King was thrown back and tripped by the back of the throne itself. As he slid into the thin space between the throne and the stone wall behind it, his head was bent down against his chest, and then the full weight of his body came down on his neck. That body, magically enlarged by the silver diadem, snapped his spine. It sounded like a waterlogged, moldy stick broken over someone's knee, a wet grinding series of cracks as all that weight tore and tore the tissue.

But they were all monsters after all, so death was not so obvious. "Did that finish him?" Nando asked. His voice through the mask sounded like he had a cold and a bad phone connection, but Bel could understand her friend.

She peered around the throne, holding up her hands in their fighting posture, ready to strike again. The King's body slumped to the side, his shoulders rolling out of the way so she could get a good look at his head. The head was still attached, but it rolled in the opposite direction farther than should have been possible. And then the silver diadem fell off.

"Yep," she said. "He's done-zo."

A small troll's hand snaked up from behind the stage, patted around until it found the diadem, grabbed it, and slid back underneath. Bel waited. Then she heard a loud bump and saw the three tines of the crown pierce through the wooden surface of the stage.

"Ow," groaned Egg.

The three tines disappeared back into the stage.

"Let's go before the smoke clears and the trolls come back," Lucia said. She looked beautiful and alien, a visibly pregnant woman, completely naked except for a gas mask.

"Agreed," Nando said. "But how will we carry Lena?

None of us can touch those chains for that long."

Two much larger fingers rose up in the crack behind the stage, their hand now too large to fit. Pinched between them: A stubby key.

Bel plucked it carefully and said, "We walk. You live."

The two fingers receded, a thumb rose. Then it sank back, also.

Bel walked behind Lena and found the lock. "I've got you, Honey," she said.

To which Lena replied, "Napoleon!"

Napoleon stood up. He'd fallen in a heap in front of the throne when the King let go of the knife as he toppled backwards, and he had to manually assemble himself a bit, but when he was fully constructed, he turned to Lena, reached up, and pulled the knife from his eye socket. The blade had cut some of the sphenoid bone, the butterfly shaped bone inside his skull making up the back of the eye sockets, and the shock of the impact had also damaged the temporal bone slightly. That, in turn, had shaken the bones of his inner ear enough to take away Napoleon's balance. When he pulled the knife out, it irritated these bones again, and he stumbled to one side like a drunk, dropping the weapon. Nando and Lucia dodged the clattering knife. Each caught one of Napoleon's shoulders, and they held him up. He gently rubbed the metacarpals of his palm on the top of his skull until he felt better, then stood up on his own. When he looked at Lena again, she could see the bones at the back of his eye socket healing up.

"Napoleon, you might be as immortal as Bel and me,"

Lena said in Spanish.

Nando spoke to Lena in Spanish. She wasn't used to that, and it wasn't a conscious choice on his part, just a reaction to hearing her. "Is he one of the ones from Paris? One of Nigel Marion's?"

"We'll fill you in later," Bel said. She unlatched the padlock, twisted it off carefully, then pinched the chain in some of the burlap to try to loosen the chain without touching it.

Napoleon stepped over next to her and gestured for her permission to try. Bel stepped away, and Napoleon grabbed the chain without any undue effects and began unlooping it. Once he'd dropped the chain on the floor around her feet, he picked up the silver knife and cut a slit so the neck hole fit over Lena's shoulders. She stood, and the bag dropped away.

Lena hugged Bel, then grabbed Nando and Lucia in a quick embrace, too. "How did you find us?"

Nando shook his head. "Let's get up to the parking garage first. It's a long story, but that's okay because we have a long drive ahead of us."

"Words have no power to impress the mind without the exquisite horror of their reality."

-Edgar Allan Poe

Chapter 17

Gabe didn't want to think too much about the family dynamics which had brought him to this precise moment in his life. He wished he were the kind of person who could just enjoy being where he wanted to be, doing what he wanted to do. But one of the benefits and curses of their voyage was it forced them to have time to reflect. Gabe's dad talked about it like that was a lot of the point, but Gabe wasn't so sure his dad wanted to reflect honestly or deeply.

He didn't know the details of his parents' divorce. They'd done a decent job of keeping that from him and Esther. Gabe's older brother, David, claimed to understand it better. He may have, since. he was living with their mom. Gabe couldn't be sure because David was also an asshole who acted like he knew everything. Esther, only 10, thought the debate about sailing around the world was the heart of the conflict between their parents. She knew their mother did not want them to go, and she knew their father did. From a kid's perspective, that seemed to explain everything, and Gabe could understand that playground logic. But he was 14, and he knew it was more complicated.

Sure, their dad had been talking about this round-the-world sailing adventure since they were really little, and yes, their mom had always opposed it, but their dad didn't get really serious about it until after the divorce, so it wasn't the cause. This was the effect. And Gabe had always sided with his dad in the debate. He didn't particularly care about sailing around the world. He just knew, even when he was much younger, that he got to spend more time with his dad when they were out on the boat, and he got to be visible to his father because David didn't like to sail. Gabe didn't even mind so much when Esther started coming along on their trips because their dad elevated Gabe as Esther's teacher of all things nautical, and Esther, a total brat at home, suddenly became a good pupil on the boat.

So he should have felt good about everything. He was getting to sail with his dad and sister around the world. But when the wind died like this, when nothing moved and even the sound of the waves against the side of the boat receded to a gentle clapping, Gabe would look out over the emptiness of the water, without land in any direction since they left Tinian in the Northern Mariana Islands headed for The Philippines, blue horizon meeting a dome of cloudless blue sky, and it gave him time to miss his mom. And when he did that, he thought maybe she was right about some things. Not the part about how they would all die at sea and she'd never see them again. That was just her being a worrywart, as far as Gabe was concerned. But her contention that all this time away from school, away from their friends, away from any people besides the three of them, that this might be bad for them… That had seemed absurd to Gabe when she'd been begging him not to go. He wanted this time with his father. He wanted this adventure. So he convinced himself she was wrong about everything. And he could mostly maintain that belief. Until these still moments. The stillness was dangerous.

In the quiet, when the boat wouldn't move, before his dad would reluctantly give up on the wind and fire up the motor, burning some of their precious gas "just till we get a breeze we can work with," in the silence made by that stinginess, Gabe would consider what David said, that their dad was selfish and didn't care that the trip was dangerous because he just wanted to run away from his problems, and that running away was what caused the divorce, and that he'd run away from his children someday, too.

Gabe's eyes stung at his own doubt, but he blinked hard and blamed the salt in the wind, even though there was no wind. When he peered off at the horizon again, he saw something. It was a distortion of some kind, a place where the horizon wasn't flat, a bump in the surface of the water.

"Hey, Esther?"

"What?" She said it as though his existence irritated her, but she'd read something strange in Gabe's voice, some weary uncertainty, so she rose from her place at the table in the cabin and stepped out on the back deck with him.

Gabe pointed. "Can you see that?"

"Where?"

"It looks like a hill. In the water."

"An island?"

"No, like the water is up higher in a spot. Like a hill of water."

Both Esther and Gabe turned when their dad stepped out of the cabin, too. He was yanking on his baseball cap, a sure sign he was just waking up because he only took it off when he was sleeping.

"Sorry. Didn't mean to wake you up," Gabe said. They had to do some sleeping in shifts, and their dad didn't really trust Esther to be the only one awake, so he tried to grab a chunk of sleep during the afternoons and then again in the early evenings since Gabe was more of a night owl but liked to sleep in late in the morning. His dad said that was a teenage boy thing, and Gabe was pretty proud of that.

"No prob. I was up," Frank said. He was lying. Gabe's calling to Esther had woken him. But it wasn't the volume. Frank heard the same uncertainty Esther had identified. "So, what is it?"

"Gabe found an island made of water," Esther said. "See it?"

Both kids were pointing, and Frank used his height advantage to triangulate. He was still taller than Gabe by a head, though maybe not for long. His son was growing so fast. "Oh, yeah. What is that?"

The kids could tell their father was talking to himself, and they joined him in silent staring.

"It's growing," Gabe said.

"It's like the ocean has a pimple," Esther said, a near-giggle barely contained.

Frank laughed and gave her permission. "It does, kinda'," he said, putting an arm around her shoulders. "It's so weird."

Gabe was less amused. He'd found the anomaly and didn't like his sister turning it into a triviality. "Or maybe it's not getting bigger. Maybe we're getting closer to it."

Their dad looked back at the mast, the sail wrapped tight around it, even the lines still in the unmoving atmosphere. "Maybe," he said in that musing tone.

They all watched for a second, and then Frank spoke with a sternness that made Gabe and Esther start. "Gabe, let's get the engine going. C'mon." He squeezed Esther's shoulder and ran toward the wheel.

Gabe knew his dad didn't want to use the engine. Every time they had to, Frank worried loudly about the gas they were wasting, telling them they'd be taking cold showers and playing cards by flashlight before they got to The Philippines. Gabe knew it was a more direct attack on his father's pride. Frank had set out to fulfill a lifelong dream of sailing around the world, not driving a motorboat around the world. So whatever Frank had seen or suspected, it must have been more worrisome than the injury to his bucket list goal.

They ran up the half flight of stairs to the pilot's deck, a space of only a few square feet designed for one adult to stand comfortably, two to stand awkwardly, and a family of three to take comfort in one another's presence. "What do you think it is?" Gabe asked as Frank turned on the engine, pushed the throttle to full, and began spinning the wheel to port, turning them south.

"I don't know."

They watched the thing coming. It was getting closer but still looked like nothing more than a hill in the ocean.

"Okay, but what do you think it is?" Gabe pushed.

"I'm guessing it's a sub. Maybe Chinese. Only it's too high. Maybe they don't know they're that high? I just want to get out of their way."

Gabe grabbed the radio. "Should we call it in?"

Frank shook his head. "No, I don't want to piss off the Chinese. Or what if it's from The Philippines, and then they're mad at us when we get there. Or American, for all we know. Holy shit that thing is moving fast." He turned to Esther. "Sorry, honey."

"Swear jar," she said mechanically.

"It's changing," Gabe said. "Look!"

The blue hill of water became mostly white as waves formed on its surface, and the family could see its trajectory far more clearly, the waves peeling back in V shapes like arrows pointed at them. And then, at the base of each wave, something darker than the ocean came through.

"What are those?" Esther asked. She didn't sound worried, just curious, but Frank hauled on the wheel, turning the boat south-east.

"I don't know, honey," he said, and the kids could hear his fear.

"Not like any sub," Gabe said, and his father nodded.

The dark points on the hill of white froth continued to change. They rose up relative to the surface of the hill, then began to float away from it in alien, dancing motions, like moths around a light. Gabe wished he could see them more clearly, but he didn't want to be any closer to the thing. And that's when he remembered his binoculars. He ran down the stairs.

"Where are you going?" Esther cried, the first real fear in her voice.

"Just getting my binoculars!"

"Good idea," Frank called after him. Then, to Esther, "Don't worry. He'll be right back."

Gabe found them on the bench where they'd fallen off the tiny dining table in the kitchen. He snatched them up and ran back to the pilot's deck. Before looking through the binoculars, he said, "It's getting closer. A lot closer."

"I know," Frank said.

Gabe looked through the binoculars. At first the hill was a white blur above the dark blue blur of the ocean and beneath the light blue flat sky, but he focused until the dark, hovering spots became clear. They weren't moths. They were the pinchers of crabs or lobsters, opening and closing as they waved around in the air, and they looked they were floating because they were positioned at the end of dark green, blue, and purple octopus tentacles.

"It's an animal."

"What?" Frank said.

"Not man made. Tentacles and pinchers."

"Like a giant squid?"

Gabe could hear the skepticism. "No, but crab pinchers are opening and closing in the air…" His voice was dreamy.

Frank's was stern. "Describe what you're seeing. You're our eyes here, Gabe."

"It's like the claws are looking for something. There are these big claws, and they are on these tentacles. Like octopus tentacles. And the tentacles are waving around in the air, and the pinchers are opening and closing really slowly. They aren't grabbing anything. Just open and … shutting and … open like a snake's tongue and…"

Suddenly all the claws pointed right at him. It made them almost disappear, but Gabe knew. A few of them opened in his direction, and though he couldn't see the mouths inside clearly, he thought he heard a new sound over the sound of the boat's motor. A high-pitched screaming.

"It's seen us," Gabe whispered. "It's seen us." Then his voice climbed in volume and pitch. "Dad, it's seen us, and it's coming for us." It rose another octave and cracked. "Dad! Dad?"

"It's going to be okay," Frank said. "I'm turning to starboard. It's faster than we are, but we're going to get out of its path, and it will swim right by. Something that big and that fast can't just turn on a dime. We'll be fine.

Just stay close to me."

Esther wrapped her arms around her father's middle and pressed her head against his back, her eyes still fixed on the thing coming at them.

"Gabe, you're still my eyes," Frank said. "What do you see?"

"Some of the pinchers are still open, facing us, but some are pulling back into the water, and some are going back down ... down into the water, too. Now the others are closing up and pulling in. It's just that bump again."

"Pimple," Esther shouted. Gabe didn't know if she was correcting him or attempting to insult the thing, but he liked the defiance.

"Yeah, the pimple." He wanted to shout, "Fuck you, Pimple!" and knew it would feel good to get a tiny bit of revenge for his fear, but he didn't want to have to pay the swear jar.

"Okay, now what do you see?" Frank asked. "Is it ..."

"Yeah, it's still following us," Gabe said.

Frank turned the wheel to starboard so they were heading south-west. "Still?"

Gabe watched and couldn't see any change. "Yeah, still behind us and still getting closer. Can we go any faster?"

"Go faster, Dad," Esther said into his back.

"I'm going as fast as this boat can go, honey," he told her. He did not mention they were also running very low on fuel.

Gabe lowered the binoculars and grabbed the radio again. "Should we call someone? An SOS or something?"

"Maybe," Frank said. "I don't know. Jesus Christ,

what would we even say?"

Esther was crying now. "Just say something is chasing us!"

"Yeah, honey. That's right. Gabe, get on the Coast Guard band and say something is chasing us. Don't say what it is. They'll think we're crazy. Just say we're being chased."

"Okay," Gabe grabbed the dial. "What's the channel?"

"16. That's the emergency-only one. Or is it 22. Shit. I can't remember."

"Swear jar," Esther said under her breath, but it was an unconscious Pavlovian response. "Hey, is the pimple getting shorter?"

Gabe stood upright and looked back through the binoculars, but the mass of water was back to being a hazy nothing. Realizing he needed both hands, he put the radio receiver on its cradle, then turned to look back. He fiddled with the binoculars while the hill of water got closer and closer, and finally he lowered them and tried to estimate with his eyes.

"Is it?" Frank said, looking over a shoulder.

"Yeah, it's shrinking. But I don't know if it's slowing down."

Frank looked at the fuel gage. "Okay, we'll, we may get bumped, but we can't keep going at this speed, so I'm going to make as hard a turn as I can, and then we're going to stop and let it zip on by, okay?"

"But, Dad…" Esther said.

"Yeah, I know. Just hold onto me, okay kiddo?" He turned wheel hard, so hard he worried they might tip, but as he did so, he throttled down. They would have run out of gas in seconds, anyway. Better to save the gas for a final push, he thought.

The lump bore down on them. The engine still idled, but now they could hear the whoosh of the thing through the water, and there, just under both sounds, Frank thought he could hear something he'd never heard before, like a raging static, the sound of hundreds of loud clicks coming up from beneath them. He decided, if there was to be a final push, this was it. The boat hadn't come to a perfect stop. Instead, because of the turn and quick deceleration, it had begun to twist back on its original course. As the prow pointed closer and closer to the looming thing, Frank gained a clear sense of its size. Esther was right. It was sinking lower into the water as it sped up. But it still rose more than fifty feet over the surface, higher than his little boat's mast. The surface was obscured by the frothing foam it kicked up, but now, this close, he could see inside it, like spying a shark inside a monstrous wave. This was no shark. Or submarine. Or anything he could have named. In fact, even the term "sea monster" seemed so insufficient as to be ridiculous. If anything, the mass of writhing tentacles looked like something out of a science fiction movie, like a director had shouted, "Make the alien look more alien!" until they'd given up and handed her this pile of CGI garbage so discordant it would drive the audience insane and break their suspension of disbelief like a dry stick over a knee. But Frank couldn't hide from this thing by reminding himself it was just a movie.

He squinted his eyes shut and hit the throttle. The

engine roared, the teeth of the propeller catching and pulling the boat's stern lower in the water before launching it forward. Esther screamed and squeezed him to keep from falling out of the pilot deck and onto the back of the boat, perhaps out of the boat entirely.

Gabe grabbed the rail, but, like his father, he stared ahead at the hill. "Dad!" he shouted.

There was no time for Frank to reply. The hill was right in front of them. And then it was next to them. And then it was tossing the boat sideways, and all three of them were shouting again. But Gabe, even as he shouted, watched the hill sink into the surface and disappear.

The boat wobbled, the mast sinking dangerously on the starboard side, then swinging over to port, then righting itself. The engine coughed once to announce its hunger, then died.

The sea was eerily still. Even the minimal waves of a windless day were swallowed by Lord Varr's wake.

"Dad?" Esther said.

Frank looked around at the horizon as far as he could without dislodging himself for his daughter's grip, and swung his head back around all the way. Nothing. 360 degrees of empty ocean.

"Dad, should I still call it in," Gabe asked, grabbing the radio receiver?

"Um.. Yeah, let's … yeah, let's call it in. It was … something…"

"What channel?"

It would be lovely to report some more satisfactory final words, but at that moment, Lord Varr leapt completely out of the water behind the boat, his arc carrying him over them in a trajectory to clear the mast entirely and land far beyond them. As he reached the apex of his rainbow of green and blue and purple, the tentacles jabbed down like a bomber's released payload, each grabbing a single bite. One snapped the mast in two at the base while more gobbled up the top, yanking the pieces into the air. Another caught both Frank and Esther from above, severing them both so fast their four legs were still upright when they were collected. Mercifully, Gabe didn't see this. He was looking straight up when a claw removed his head and pulled it into the mouth inside.

The tentacles didn't stop at the human flesh. They grabbed clawfuls of every bit of wood and fiberglass. Railings, the oven, the small stainless-steel shower, and the guts of the engine, complete with its empty tank, were lifted out of the water because they were connected to more edible parts of the boat, and then the claws broke through the last bolts, and they fell back, hitting the surface and sinking.

Lord Varr hit the water with a thunderous crash, but a quick flick of his tentacles redirected him back down, then along his earlier course.

He was not mindless. Like his octopus cousins, Lord Varr's brain material was located throughout his arms, but unlike them, he didn't have a separate bulbous mass containing more brains and a pair of eyes. All of his brain was stretched throughout his tentacles because, aside from his claws and a stomach at his core, he was only those tentacles.

His brain didn't work like any vertebrate's, either. His

concept of self, for example, was not quite a singular "I," nor a plural or royal "we," but some amalgamation of the three no human brain could contain without sliding into madness. In fact, if Lord Varr could speak and explain his sense of himself to any human psychologist, and if the human could avoid becoming a gibbering, drooling vegetable, she would diagnose him as suffering from a host of disorders including Schizotypal (Personality) Disorder, Delusional Disorder, Obsessive-Compulsive Disorder, Body Dysmorphic Disorder, Reactive Attachment Disorder, Disinhibited Social Engagement Disorder, Acute Stress Disorder, various adjustment disorders, Dissociative Identity Disorder, Delirium, and Major Neurocognitive Disorder related to social cognition. Most interestingly, the psychologist would have to make a judgment about whether Lord Varr was also afflicted with Fetishistic Disorder since his only sexual pleasure came from eating people, Binge-Eating Disorder since he could not help but consume anything human, Antisocial Personality Disorder since he was compelled to destroy any sentient being he encountered, and, of course, Pica since he ate many things, especially humans, usually not considered food. Of course, according to the DSM-5, the psychologist would have to take Lord Varr's culture into account, and that might eliminate many diagnoses, since he was the culmination of a culture built on the monomyth of the human displacement and oppression of his entire society. But beyond his hatred of all humans, Lord Varr might still qualify as Schizotypal or delusional since he saw himself as both royalty and a god. The DSM-5 does not have any specific accounting for what a psychologist should do with an actual god, but in Lord Varr's case, the diagnostic plan is subtextual: Be eaten by him. Promptly.

Lord Varr, despite his inflated or entirely accurate sense of his own power, still thought strategically. He was, after all, bred to be the leader of an army or the army itself under the leadership of his twin brother (who he killed at birth, so that's more trauma). He could make complex plans. He knew he had to continue consuming and growing before taking on the humans as a united species. And he knew if they started to spread word of his impending arrival on their shores, they would organize against him. They couldn't help it. He saw himself as their ultimate foe, so their retaliation was inevitable. His discovery by this little group of humans in their tiny watercraft had been a fortuitous snack and a reminder to lie low. It wasn't time yet.

Lord Varr propelled himself through the water, not in spurts like an octopus or squid with their scant eight arms pulling in unison, but like an unstoppable juggernaut of motion, hundreds of massive tentacles whipping and shoving water behind him, each in their own rhythm but distinct from one another so he shot forward at a constant speed. He could stop on a dime, change his course to any direction in the 41,253 degrees in a sphere, and propel himself with enough speed to launch into the air, as he'd just shown the departed Frank, Esther, and Gabe. He could also sustain his speed without tiring thanks to his supernatural nature's refusal to be impinged upon by the plebian laws of physics he did not deign to dignify.

He lacked knowledge of the humans and their strange ways, but he was learning. So far, he was unimpressed. It seemed they operated entirely on a single horizontal plane, while he could move beneath it, through it, and above it. He filed this away as a significant tactical advantage. He'd also learned they would make a meager attempt to evade him if they saw him on that plane, but they would hold still and fail to react to his presence if he were outside of that plane. Now he traveled beneath the water. It was marginally slower and more labor intensive than skimming along the surface, but he was willing to make that sacrifice until he had eaten more humans and grown enough to do battle with them all together.

Because that belief was at the heart of Lord Varr's conception of the world: He was locked into the fate his mother had commanded. He was her army, her kingdom made flesh, her ultimate weapon. He'd already been aimed and fired. The rest was inevitability.

The Coast Guard did not receive any distress call from the little boat. The trolls did not hear any chatter about the army of Queen Tisina amassing and marching under the surface of the Pacific. No one knew Lord Varr was coming.

No one but three prescient witches and the monsters they'd attempted to warn.

And one luck dragon.

"Dying is a wild night and a new road."

-Emily Dickenson

Chapter 18

From a distance, the road trip looked almost indistinguishable from many human trips. The jeep's two bright, round headlights led the way, I80 to I90 to I94 to 6 to 11 to 55 to 155 to nowhere, toll roads to freeways to expressways to highways to logging roads, the two red taillights whispering a contented goodbye to New York City, the brighter brake lights extinguished from lack of remorse in the leaving, the white reverse lights doused by a lack of desire to return. A stalker would have noted the car only drove in the darkness, the travelers paying double to get a hotel room before dawn and leaving just after sunset. The Jeep stopped to get gas at normal intervals, but its occupants eschewed normal car trip snacks. Instead, in western Pennsylvania near the Ohio border, they stopped once when they stumbled upon a car on the side of the road being assisted by a tow-truck driver sent by AAA. The road trippers stretched their legs by frightening the couple in the car and the driver of the tow truck into the woods, then having a merry chase through the trees before eating and getting back on the road. The next night, in Wisconsin, they enjoyed what Taco Bell markets as "Fourth Meal" when they arrived at a Taco Bell at closing time … and ate the staff.

Inside the Jeep, the road trip was a party on wheels, though the kind of party changed throughout the voyage. It began as a reunion. Even before they'd left Manhattan, the friends were catching up.

"I got your text message," Nando explained, "and then a couple short messages asking for help, but in German. You don't speak German, do you?" He looked through the rearview mirror at Lena who sat in the middle, Napoleon to her right and Bel to her left.

"I know how to say "People's Car," "The Joy of Driving," and "Attention." My entire German language education comes from Volkswagen commercials and one U2 album."

"I didn't think it was you. But Napoleon couldn't reply to my replies because your phone died."

Lucia, sitting in the front seat, took it from there. "We drove to the Newark airport because, luckily, you mentioned that's where you were landing. Well, you just said 'Newark,' so we went to the big one, then a couple more before we found where you'd landed. Then we followed your scents."

"You could smell us days later when we were in a car?" Lena asked.

Lucia smiled. "It wasn't easy. We both had to stick our heads out the windows while Nando drove around. And we lost your scents on the freeway, so we'd have to do loops at the ends of each exit until we caught the smell. Luckily the Uber driver never came back for his car and didn't report it stolen to the police."

"The trolls must have threatened him with something pretty terrible."

"Maybe," Bel said. "And he saw trolls."

"Well, it's a good thing for us, because we found your suitcase and backpack right where you'd left them, and once we figured out how to communicate with Napoleon, we tracked the trolls by their scents back to the office building in Manhattan."

"That was a lot easier," Nando added. "The smell of trolls is strong and unique."

"How did you get past security to the elevator?"

"That was by smell, too," Lucia said. "We found a human who smelled like he'd been down the elevator and convinced him to take us down there."

"How?"

Lucia pointed a thumb at Nando. "You know what they say: 'Carry yourself with the confidence of a mediocre white man.'"

Nando smiled. "I just told him that his bosses had ordered him to take us down there. Plus business jargon."

Lucia put a hand on Nando's shoulder. "It really did sound like you knew what you were talking about. 'Delivering a preview of quarterly earnings reports,' and 'optimizing efficiencies across platforms.'" She looked back. "The guy was completely overwhelmed and just took us down the elevator. And he was a turbo-douche. I really enjoyed killing him."

Nando shrugged. "He tasted fine."

"Your big escape plan was pretty risky," Bel said, her tone skeptical to the point of disapproval.

"True," Lucia said, "But we did have a backup plan. It wasn't all smoke grenades and teargas. If we'd had to retreat back to the elevator, we could have held them off long enough to escape and try again. It's ridiculously easy to get guns and ammunition in this country. If we'd been pushed back to the elevator, we could have re-armed ourselves there from our bags. That's why Napoleon hung back, initially. He's a good shot, by the way. Do you know anything about his history?"

Lena shared what she knew. "He doesn't remember any of his human life, but he does understand German and Spanish. We're guessing he was a soldier during World War II."

"That would explain his comfort with guns. And why he couldn't do much with your cell phone."

"I'm glad he sent you those messages, though." She turned to her skeleton friend, "*Gracias, Napoleón.*"

Napoleon nodded and smiled at her. The smile wasn't distinguishable, but Lena understood it.

"So, what's the plan now?" Lucia asked.

"We need to find some people," Bel said. "We're going to need a crew for our next job, but to put the team together, we're also going to have to find some people I'd rather not ever see again."

"You know we'll help in any way we can," Lucia said.

The air in the car seemed a little thicker, a little more still. Lucia's offer was weighted by her guilt at her betrayal.

Nando patted Lucia's knee. "Yes," he said to the rearview mirror. "Whatever you need."

"For now, just a safe home base to collect ourselves, do some planning." Bel looked at Lena. "We might need Tina's help with some online searching."

Nando nodded. "Everyone is going to be so happy to see you, Lena. Maybe Tina most of all. Of course she won't admit it, but I think she was bothered by your death."

"Bothered, eh?"

"Yes, it molested her," Nando translated directly and incorrectly.

Lucia nodded. "Quite a compliment from a teenager, that she liked you enough to be upset when a human died."

"I'm sorry I didn't get in touch sooner. I had some adjusting to do."

"I completely understand," Lucia said, though, in truth, she resented the delay more than anyone. Her relationship with Nando had been strained by her betrayal, and she owned that, but the consequences of that betrayal had been greatly magnified by Lena's death. Maybe, if Nando had known she was alive, he would not have been so hard on her for months.

"Speaking of adjustments," Lena said, "congratulations to you two!"

"Thank you," Nando said. "We're very excited." He took Lucia's hand, squeezed it, and didn't mention their mutual excitement was a product of their reconnection during the drive out. The first day had been difficult, complete with some shouting and a lot of tears cried by both of them, and if they hadn't been trapped in a car, Nando wasn't sure they would have made it through that discussion. But what was he going to do; leave her in Wisconsin and never see his children?

"So, did you find out the gender?" Lena asked.

"Sex, not gender," Bel corrected. "A baby hasn't been taught gender yet." She tilted her head in Lena's direction. "I'm sorry. I know it's pedantic, but it's a pet peeve of mine. Every time I read about a…" She made air quotes. "'Gender reveal party' I want to scream. It's a sex reveal party!"

Lena laughed. "Yeah, but that would sound weird."

"Exactly!" Bel shouted. "Because it is weird to have a party to celebrate your baby's sex. Like, 'Our baby has a penis or a vagina, and we're going to start traumatizing the kid with all the shit we associate with penises and vaginas as soon as we possibly can, but we have to wait until the kid comes out to start brainwashing them, so eat cake with us while we plot how to fuck 'em up.'"

Lena widened her eyes and pointed at Lucia with her head.

"Oh, shit," Bel said. "Are you planning to have a gender reveal party?"

Lucia laughed. "No. It would be too risky to go to a human doctor for a sonogram. We could get a monster doctor if necessary, but everything has been healthy so far. So we know there are three by the sound of the heartbeats, but," she laughed again, "we don't know the counts of penises and vaginas!"

"Wait, triplets?"

"More common for werewolves than humans," Nando said.

"How far along are you?" Lena asked, her hesitance to cross the lines of propriety forgotten.

"Eight months," Lucia said. She watched them start doing the math. "Yes, I was pregnant when you died. I just didn't know it yet."

"You're eight months pregnant with triplets and can still run and fight?"

"You think a wolf in the wild can be on bedrest for months at a time? I'll be in fighting shape right up until delivery, and I should be back on my feet the next day, good as new."

"That's amazing."

"Good as new and with three infants to keep you busy," Bel said.

"We'll have lots of help," Nando explained. "The children are part of the pack. They are everyone's responsibility. No one raises kids on their own. That would be estupid."

"Lots of humans do," Lena said.

"Glad we're not human," Nando said. "Because that's estupid."

Lena felt some irritation at this on behalf of single parents without support networks, but she let the subject drop.

Bel made a different but related calculation, and then she decided it could wait.

Napoleon couldn't understand any of it since his friends were speaking English, but he thoroughly enjoyed the view of the city lights dwindling and transforming to moonlight forests and fields. It all felt familiar and novel, his first experience with something he had forgotten from another life.

"Well, I'm sorry our situation made you have to drive out all this way and fight pregnant. We didn't mean to put either of you at any risk. We thought we could get to Camp Bigfoot undetected."

"I'll burn the cards and phones and get some money moved around," Bel said. "I don't know how they found us, but I don't want to take any unnecessary risks." She raised an eyebrow. "It was a useful conversation with the former king, though. Did you catch it?"

"Which part?"

Bel laughed at the memory. "Right when he was telling us he was too smart to spill any information. That was when he revealed that Apraxis was behind Josef's abduction."

Lena nodded slowly, contemplating this. "I remember, but I don't know what that means to us. Apraxis was hired by Cassius. He brought Cassius Josef. And...?"

"And he always lies!" Nando said, putting it together. "I remember that from Scotland!"

"So...?"

"So," Bel explained, "unless the imp showed up to Cassius and said, 'Here's this golem I'm not really giving to you,' then he delivered Josef and made Cassius think he was under Cassius' control, but..." She made a wheeling gesture with her hand.

"Josef must be under someone else's control."

"Right! I'm guessing Apraxis' control, since imps aren't known for their generosity, but I suppose it's possible he did something different with Josef just to screw someone else even more." Bell shook her head. "Whatever he did, the King of Trolls spilled the beans that Matt Bern was involved, so he's next on my list. Let's get the imp and get our friend back."

Most of rest of the drive was a more raucous affair. Lucia and Nando liked to play music and sing loudly in the car, mostly to 80's arena rock, their voices often rising to a shared howl. Bel loved to join in. It turned out she had a pretty terrible singing voice. She acknowledged she was tone deaf, but she joked it was because she was still missing an ear. Her tastes leaned toward late 70's punk and 90's riot grrrl, so she had the car singing along to The Ramones, Bikini Kill, and 7 Year Bitch, and the music style hid some of her lack of singing talent, though it became even more obvious when she screamed and held a really flat note.

Lena decided it was her responsibility to educate all the much older people in the car about music from the current century, so she got them bopping along to songs by Beyoncé, Arianna Grande, Kendrik Lamar, Solange, and her favorite: BTS. The boy band proved divisive, but everyone loved when Napoleon started dancing in his seat to "All the Single Ladies."

The hunting breaks were fun for the vampires and werewolves. Napoleon didn't participate since he didn't need to eat, and Lena wrestled with feelings of guilt, especially when the victims were young or seemed otherwise undeserving, but she found she was feeling less and less like an abominable psychopath and more and more like a teenager who tried to become a vegetarian in an uncooperative family of omnivores. Her friends tried to respect her feelings while also rolling their eyes and completely ignoring her moral qualms, and it made her feel whiny and a bit absurd while also morally superior.

The party atmosphere quavered somewhat when Lena and Nando got into an argument about whether Lena could smoke in the car. Nando tried to say it was strictly forbidden because of the danger to the fetuses, and Lena couldn't challenge that, but Lucia took offense at being employed in that way since she knew Nando was fully aware their werewolf healing could more than compensate for the damage from trace amounts of carcinogens, and he was really making an excuse because he couldn't stand the smell that would linger in the upholstery for eternity. This made Lena angry enough at his dishonesty to motivate her to try lighting one without permission, and Bel, who normally didn't care about Lena's smoking, reached out and snatched the cigarette directly out of her mouth, tossing it out the window before Lena could blink.

"Not until you work it out with Nando, first. Laws of hospitality."

This prompted a long history lesson about Guest Rights in medieval Europe which formed the backbone of the misconception that vampires needed to be invited into a human's home. "I know it's old fashioned, but I do my best to observe the laws of hospitality."

"Since when?" Lena yelled.

"Since I was born! Sure, I make exceptions, but in general we try to follow those rules."

"Why?"

"The root is the idea that we expect other vampires to respect our space and not kill us while we sleep. It's sort of a precursor to The Convention, like the Magna Carta to the US Constitution, the idea that if vampires kill other vampires during the day while they are guests in one another's homes, the bad host or bad guest will be punished by all the living vampires for their breach of the code. By extension, or maybe just by habit, we don't invade human homes and kill them while they sleep in the understanding that, if they do that to us, they have violated the code and deserve to have all the vampires come after them, seeking revenge."

"Pretty impractical if the only humans who know vampires exist are monster hunters who wouldn't respect those rules."

"Maybe, maybe not. If some monster hunters catch us out in the open, most other vampires will shrug and say that was our fault. But if some monster hunter is going around killing vampires in their sleep, you can bet a bunch of us will hunt him down. So that's the mutual enforcement mechanism. And that's what rules are for, right? Mutual benefit if everyone follows them, supported by the assurance of mutually enforced consequences for violators?"

"So, humans got the idea you can't come in without an invitation because—"

"Because some of us, the older ones, still honor the idea that we shouldn't go around breaking into human houses if we don't want them breaking into ours. It's like a little vampire golden rule. But it extends to cars, too. Don't want somebody fucking with your ride, don't fuck with his."

Lena shook her head. "I understand the idea of a social contract, and I understand extending property rights to cars, but it's just so weird to me to honor a person's house and car but not their bodily integrity or their life. It's just such a different moral framework."

Bel shrugged. "Yep. It's different."

They all rode in silence for a moment.

"So..." Lena drew out the word. "Nando, is there room for negotiation on this? Apparently, I have to respect the sanctity of your car, but the trolls didn't let me smoke, so…"

The negotiations began, and a compromise was reached in which the group would take regular stops for Lena to smoke. Specific language was agreed upon dictating the frequency of the stops and their duration, and an enforcement mechanism was outlined allowing Nando to extend the time between stops if the stops were of excessive duration and allowing Lena to smoke in the car if stops were skipped. The terms of the agreement also allowed for modification if Nando decided he was more irritated by the stops than by the smell of cigarette smoke in his car. Everyone was equally unsatisfied which is the measure of a successful negotiation, and the party resumed.

After the first meal, Bel's ear healed perfectly. Her singing did not improve.

"The wise among them will find goodness and solace in their faith. The fools would be fools no matter what they believed."

-Brandon Sanderson

Chapter 19

The text message just said, "Contacted via email."

The odd sentence construction and unknown number made Cassius curious. Vampires get spam text messages, even on burners set aside for specific lines of communication, and the sender's message had been run through so many VPNs, Cassius never would have found the origin. Unlike the texts offering dubious human medical treatments or attention from "singles near you," this one didn't have a clear ulterior motive; no subtext, just a text with text.

Cassius found the referenced email in his spam folder. The subject line said, "Responding to your overture in Shanghai." The body didn't say much more. "We received your message of a desire to communicate directly. We are willing to consider offers of mutual assistance. Please provide details about what you have to offer and what you expect in return. We await your reply."

Cassius didn't like how this was starting. He wrote back: "I prefer a face-to-face meeting. Let's negotiate a time and place which would provide us both the necessary security and privacy to have a conversation. You will find the value of my information justifies the utmost privacy and direct diplomacy."

Esau's employer responded, "A face-to-face meeting will not be possible. If you are concerned about establishing a secure connection, we can provide software to protect your terminal from any exploitations in your server, and a secure connection to our system."

Cassius slammed a fist down on his desk. "No, you bastard," he said. "I want to look you in the eyes. I want to hear the truth or lies in your voice. I want to memorize your scent."

But that's not what he wrote. "Thank you for the offer of technical assistance. However, without a face-to-face meeting, I will not feel confident I can verify your identity."

The next email came back right away. "A face-to-face meeting would not allow you to verify our identities. You do not know us. You only know we are Captain Sullivan's employers. You could have met directly with the captain, and that can be arranged again. Captain Sullivan's arrival would prove we are his employers. But if you wish to make us an offer, you will have to do so online."

Cassius looked around the room. He sat at a desk in the middle of an unfinished basement. A large heating unit, cold and dead, took up a quarter of the space. The floor was concrete and ran down to a rusted round grate. The walls were unpainted concrete. Near the ceiling, small windows sat in spaces below ground level outside, but Cassius had ordered them covered in plywood and then buried to prevent any sunlight from getting through, so he was looking at a window with a view of plywood. He could hear the heavy footfalls of Bob and Augy clomping around the kitchen and living room as they stocked and unstocked the fridge with blood, either putting in whatever they'd set aside for him after their last kill or pulling it out for a snack while they watched the TV they never wanted to turn off.

Beyond the house, farmland stretched to the horizon, much of it acreage Cassius had owned since the Great Depression, bought cheap and rented out as a kind of passive investment until he needed a place to hide. He had locations like this around the world, places he kept off the books, safe houses in case he needed one. They were barely maintained since they didn't need to be much beyond dark holes to hide in during the day. As long as this dark hole's location wasn't on anyone's map, the safe house did its job. But it also meant Cassius felt imprisoned, not just by daylight but from the kind of social interaction which fed his need to feel he was amassing control in order to feel safe in a chaotic world. Vampires do not live by blood alone.

He decided he was already committed to this course of action. If he was being betrayed by someone within CimBim, being duped by a sting operation designed to generate proof he was collaborating with humans, he'd produced all the evidence necessary to call a tribunal and procure a Writ of Elimination. As Esau's employer had intimated, such a sting operation would have needed to be quite elaborate and would have required the cooperation of this group of monster hunters. Was it possible CimBim employed unwitting monster hunters to eliminate targets and also identify monsters willing to betray monsterdom? Possible, but unlikely; Esau's group had a reputation that didn't seem to coincide with any of CimBim's plans Cassius had worked on, and he'd been as knowledgeable about CimBim's inner workings as anyone. Had. Past tense.

His awareness of his current operational blindness rekindled his rage at his isolation. His thumbs hammered the phone's screen as he proceeded with his act of treason. Unlike a keyboard or, better, an old-fashioned typewriter, which could produce a satisfying response to his anger up to and including breaking under the weight of angry keystrokes, the phone emitted identical clacking sounds no matter how hard he pressed down. And he didn't have a second phone. And his small staff at this safehouse couldn't procure another anywhere within a twenty-mile radius.

Cassius took a deep breath and swallowed his rage.

"I am prepared to offer intelligence on an impending

attack against humankind by an army of monsters. In exchange, I want Captain Sullivan to assist me in finding and eliminating some mutual enemies. And I want your assurance that, at the end of that mission, I will be allowed to leave with two items."

The phone responded almost as quickly as the messages could travel. "Please identify the items."

"Two documents, written by a Ms. Magalena Wallace, printed out. If there are any other copies, they must be destroyed. I want your assurance I will be the only one in possession of the items at the end of this."

"Please describe the nature of the documents."

"They are of private and personal emotional significance and worthless to anyone but me," Cassius wrote.

The Ring knew exactly what the documents in question were according to Esau's report after last year's annual meeting of The Convention. Esau had described the operation to retrieve Lena's books and had received permission and transportation from Canada to Nevada. Of course, Cassius wasn't aware of the extent of Esau's employer's involvement in the events that led up to Esau shooting him in the face and setting a luck dragon loose in the middle of the meeting while someone set fire to his office suite upstairs. H just didn't want to inform Esau's employer about the true nature of Lena's books if they didn't already know.

"We know nothing about these documents, and we do not care about them. You may have them," the Ring wrote. Two thirds of this message was lies. Or five sixths. Or all of it. Most of the members of the board intended to betray Cassius and employ the second of Lena's book to eliminate all the monsters in the world, and one board member intended to betray the rest and turn the books over to Ryou-Ryou Daiō who would, in turn, betray Cassius and keep them for himself.

"Before I reveal any specific information about the impending attack on humankind," Cassius wrote, "how do you propose to assure me you will fulfill your end of the bargain?"

The Ring took a moment to respond, since the text had to be crafted collaboratively and subjected to a hasty vote. "How do you propose to assure us your information is accurate and not a means to lure our forces into a trap? We do not need to trust one another to trust one another."

Cassius read the addendum and nodded sagely. "Fair enough," he replied. He reminded himself he'd already signed his own death warrant at the beginning of the conversation, perhaps earlier when he'd sent Bob and Augy to meet with Esau, so he was pot committed, and Esau's employer had just called. He laid down his cards.

"Tisina, the Queen of the Merfolk, has been waiting for specific items to launch an attack on humanity. She acquired those items. She has since gone radio silent. Her army is on the move in the Pacific."

The Ring knew from Esau's report that Tisina had received the mystical items from Cassius himself. It had also heard the chatter in certain encrypted channels about Tisina's disappearance. She had a reputation for being secretive, but this silence was proving to be more prolonged and attention grabbing than most.

"Location of the planned attack?"

"Unknown," Cassius admitted. "I'm working on that. If you have access to satellite intelligence, you may find them before I do. I will share intelligence as I acquire it."

"Size of the invasion force?"

"Also unknown. We estimate the Merfolk population to be more than a million but less than two million. However, unlike a human country where between 5-10 of every thousand people serves in the military, the Merfolk have a religious devotion to the idea they are owed all the land on the surface and believe a messianic character will lead them to an overwhelming victory against humans, so it's possible nearly all the Merfolk have taken up arms and are moving on their target en masse. We should plan on an attack along the order of one of the top five militaries in the world making a surprise amphibious assault on some beach of the Pacific. The surprise of Pearl Harbor but on a scale ten times the size of D-Day."

The members of the board held an up-down vote on their reply. It was unanimous.

"Holy shit," they wrote.

Cassius read this and nodded again. "I believe Lena Wallace and her co-conspirators are collaborating with Tisina's army. If you will place your Captain Sullivan under my operational control, I believe his hunters can find Ms. Wallace and learn the location of the assault. She may even have knowledge of weaknesses which we could exploit to thwart the attack without bringing it to the attention of most humans."

"Captain Sullivan will not answer to you, but we can

arrange to have you embedded within his platoon until you can acquire the assets, confirm their intelligence, and provide you with the documents we've agreed upon. Is this satisfactory?"

"Fuck no," Cassius said aloud. "Yes," he typed.

"Since we do not know your geographic location," the Ring said, "please stand by for a rendezvous point. Captain Sullivan will be apprised of the situation and will be ordered to hunt Ms. Wallace and her associates and escort you to them once they have been located."

Cassius didn't like being told to wait. In this case, it served as a doubly frustrating reminder: He didn't have any choice but to work with these hunters and their higher-ups who he believed to be human. Everything about the situation infuriated him. He replied, "Acknowledged."

In the board room in Ohio, Gerald turned to Suzanne. "Esau is going to hate this." When the group got to the end of the missive they wrote to Esau, ordering him to execute the vampire and any of his entourage, then deliver Lena's books to them, Gerald conceded, "Okay, he'll like that part of the plan."

Esau's only reply to the message from his employer was, "Received. Wheels up at 16:00 hours. ETA for rendezvous: 19:00." Gerald was right. Esau hated the idea of working with Cassius and his vamp buddies, but he eagerly anticipated staking them in the back once they'd killed Wallace and her crew.

Chapter 20

The jeep rolled into Camp Bigfoot around 3am, late for the diurnal werewolves but the perfect time for a celebration for the vampires in the party. The werewolves who guarded the camp's perimeter smelled Nando and Lucia and ran at their top speed ahead of the jeep to wake the community. Nando babied the jeep's suspension on the dirt road, giving his people time to rouse themselves. When the jeep made it to the turn-around in front of the dining hall, most of the werewolves were up and standing in their human forms on the porch or in a loose semicircle in front of the building, and almost all of them had taken the time to put some human clothes on. Not Naked Steve, of course. Lena pointed him out to Napoleon. "That's Naked Steve. He knows it makes me uncomfortable that he just wanders around with his junk flopping all over, but he doesn't care. He says he's trying to help me break out of my human hang-ups."

Napoleon tilted his head and raised his hands, palms up.

"No," Lena said. "It's not working. Call me traditional. I like people to be clothed."

Napoleon pinched the lapels of his jacket, a variation on a muscle memory from his habit of wearing suspenders during his previous life.

"Yes, you look very nice in clothes, Napoleon," Lena said. "Dapper. But for some reason I don't mind it when you aren't wearing anything. I guess I'm old-fashioned when it comes to seeing exposed *skin*."

"Can I make a pun about Steve's exposed boner?" Bel asked.

"Please don't."

"Okay, I won't."

The five passengers climbed out of the jeep. Lucia put her hands on the small of her back and stuck her belly out.

"You okay?" Nando asked her.

"Sat too long. And I need to piss." She put a hand on his shoulder for support, but only so she could yank a boot off. Then she put a hand on the jeep's warm hood while she pulled off the other. She left the boots standing neatly by the passenger side front tire, but when she pulled her sweatshirt, pants, t-shirt, and underwear off, she plunked them in a pile in Nando's arms. Then she turned into a wolf and padded around the side of the building to relieve herself.

Lena and Bel pretended not to watch any of the undressing while indulging themselves with some admiring glances. They caught one another and shared a smile. "You know," Lena said, "that's something I don't miss at all. The need to pee. Think I'll ever miss that part of being human?"

"Nope." Bel shook her head. "This is progress. More and more, the uniquely human vagaries of life will feel like the inconveniences of a full bladder or an empty stomach."

Lena, always a word nerd, remembered the word "vagary" came from the Latin vagari, meaning "to wander," and she wondered what Bel, this itinerant globe-hopping vampire, might categorize as a vagary of human existence. She wasn't entirely focused when she smelled a familiar person approaching.

She'd never smelled these werewolves as a vampire, but somehow her brain must have identified a few of them with her limited human sense of smell before her death, and now she could pick them out clearly. Also, Tina's big New Rock boots made a unique sound as she stomped across the porch and down the stairs, then across the little patch of lawn, the rubber soles whumping and the many metal buckles tinkling as she came. Lena's scowl turned into a warm smile at Tina's approach, when the teenager slapped her. She saw the swing in plenty of time and could easily have ducked if her brain hadn't locked on the open hand.

"What the fuck?" said her brain.

The open palm clapped against her cheek hard, harder than a human could have hit, though not hard enough to cause her any harm or even turn her head significantly. She maintained eye contact with Tina through the impact.

"What the f—" she started to say aloud.

"That's for making me care about a human dying," Tina said flatly.

"Tina!" Nando shouted, and the crowd filled with other exclamations of surprise, most unintelligible.

Then Tina wrapped her arms around Lena, pinning Lena's arms to her sides, and Tina, taller than Lena, pressed her face to the top of Lena's shoulder. "And this is for coming back!" she said loudly enough for all to hear.

The wolves' exclamations turned into varieties of oohs and ahhs.

"Plus," Tina whispered in Lena's ear, "I wanted to see if I could slap a vampire."

Lena laughed and pushed her away, then crouched into a fighting stance and shot out her hands, gently patting Tina on the meatiest part of the thin young woman's upper arms, right, left, right, left, and a coup de grâce tap in the middle of her forehead.

Tina smiled and made a growling sound. Then the women hugged again. When they pulled apart, Tina said, "Enough of this emotional dicking around. You always bring the most interesting people. What weirdo did you bring with you this time, Baby Bloodsucker?"

Bel stepped forward and gave Tina a hug. "I'm not

weird enough for you?"

"Just because you're hot doesn't change the fact that you're older than Rita, and nobody that old can be cool."

"I heard that," Rita shouted from the porch. The wolves laughed.

"Surprised your ears still work!" Tina shouted over her shoulder.

"Love you, Tina," Rita said.

Tina made a throaty, disgusted noise. "Love you, too."

"My newest friend is a little on the old side, too," Lena said. "And young like me. This is Napoleon. He was just resurrected a couple years ago. We figure he was a human before World War II, but maybe World War I. He doesn't remember his human life, so everything is pretty new to him."

Tina stepped around Lena and shook Napoleon's hand. "Nice to meet you, Napoleon. You smell pretty good for old bones."

Napoleon nodded. He wouldn't have known how to respond to that even if he could talk. And he didn't understand English.

"He can't speak, but trust me; he's smiling at you."

Napoleon took a step back. His shoulder disconnected, and his hand remained in Tina's, his arm sliding out of the sleeve of his coat.

Tina looked at Lena, eyes wide, horrified not by the arm itself but by the social faux pas.

"It's fine," Bel said. "This happens."

Napoleon held out his left hand, and Tina gently

placed his right forearm into his palm. He tried to guide the shoulder socket back into his empty sleeve, the animated joints of his right doing their best to help despite being disconnected, but the sleeve was less cooperative, and Lena had to help him get the journey started. When they delivered the socket to the joint, they met with a satisfying wooden click.

"I like you," Tina told Napoleon.

He tilted his head and pinched up his shoulders in an aw-shucks.

"Oh!" Tina nearly shouted. She looked back and forth from Bel to Lena. "Lots of chatter in the Convention spaces about shit going down with the trolls. Know anything about that?"

"We do," Lena said.

"But keep our names out of it, if you can," Bel said. "Has anyone mentioned us?"

"Nope. I just put two and troll together," Tina said. "There was this sudden lack of content online. The bots kept humming along, but the really infuriating well-actuallys and sexual harassers and "You don't even know what AR stands for" assholes were just gone. Not the grifters, but the accounts who just post to make other people mad. Of course, people in the BIPOC and queer communities noticed first, and it took the monster community a little while to figure out the trolls were all offline. It even had an effect on Wall Street. Sudden dip in social media, no one in the comments sections of the major newspapers. The algorithms didn't know who to advertise to because 'engagement was down.' And then the trolls were back like nothing happened, screaming at people in all caps with their usual bullshit. And in the monster forums, people were posting this cryptic statement by the King of Trolls saying everything was fine."

"The new King of Trolls," Lena said.

Tina raised an eyebrow. "Oh, and which of you ganked the last one?"

Lena hooked a thumb at Bel. "Who do you think? I'll give you a clue: You would not be able to slap her."

Bel pointed at Rita and didn't raise her voice when she said, "Us old broads are tough as Roman nails."

Tina rolled her eyes. "You even make that sound old."

"To be honest, I had help," Bel said. "Napoleon distracted the King by punching him in the dick."

Tina laughed. "See? I knew I liked you!" She looked at Lena. "So, are you all here to stay this time?"

Lena shook her head. "No, we just need to regroup and figure out where we're going next. The deposed and un-alived former King of Trolls let slip a bit of information that may help us find Josef."

Lucia trotted up to Nando in her wolf form, changed back to her human form, and began climbing back into her clothes. She began speaking while her head was still making its way through her t-shirt. "So," she said, then appeared and continued while pulling the shirt over her belly, "how long do you think we'll be here before we're ready to go? Because I could use a couple of days in a hot bath."

"Um, Honey, we don't have a bathtub," Nando said.

"I've been thinking that's something you should fix. It's a good project for someone who gets to say, 'We're pregnant' but doesn't have to be pregnant."

"About that," Bel said, "please don't take this the wrong way, but I think you two should stay here."

She saw Lucia's hackles rise. Not literally, but almost.

"I'm not saying you can't fight. I know you can. But we don't know what we're getting ourselves into or how long it will take, and if we end up chained up again somewhere, I'd rather have you rescuing me than chained up and giving birth next to me. And Nando, you need to be here, too. If you missed the birth of your children because you were running around the world working with me, I'd never forgive myself. And never is a long time for a vampire."

Nando looked at Lena. "What do you think?"

"Bel's right." Lena put a hand on Lucia's arm. "You're still a better fighter than I am. It's not any commentary on your ability. I just want to make sure my little niece and nephew pups are healthy and happy." Then she looked back to Nando. "And you need to build your girl a hot tub."

Nando nodded. "Where will you go next?"

Lena looked to Bel.

"First, we're going to get Tina's help trying to find everything online about Apraxis. And then we'll go to the library."

"Are you sure that's a good idea?" Nando said.

"Wait, which part?" Tina said.

"I can think of two very good reasons you should stay

as far away from the library as possible, and they're both in Lena's backpack."

"Hold on," Tina said. "What's scary about going to a library?"

Nando said, "Not *a* library. *The* Library. The Cruentus Bibliothecae Arcanae Urbis. The great vampire library."

"Ooo, I want to go to that!" Tina said.

Nando shook his head. "No way. Vampires don't like werewolves." He caught himself. "Some. Many. Many vampires don't like werewolves. Plus, you don't even read books."

"I read lots of books. I love books!"

"On your computer. Those aren't books."

Tina looked at Lena and hooked a thumb at Nando. "Fuckin' grandpa here. If I don't get out of this camp soon, I'm going to be changing bedpans for these old turds." She looked at Bel. "Is there some kind of rule that says werewolves can't go to the vampire library?"

"Well, no, it's open to everyone in The Convention..." She looked at Nando apologetically, knowing she was not helping his case.

Tina stared at Nando. "They're taking a skeleton with them to research an imp so they can find a golem, but the werewolf girl can't go because she reads digital books? That's some bullshit, Nando."

"Nando?" Rita said from the porch. Her voice was softer than usual, not the sing-song voice she used with the little children, but not the raspy drawl she used when bickering with Tina, either.

"Yes?"

"It's time," Rita said. "She's ready."

"Ready for what?" Tina asked.

Nando sighed. "Miss Rita and I have been talking for some time about how the day would come when you would need to leave the pack temporarily to find out more about the world and more about yourself, and then come back when it's really your choice."

Tina frowned up at Rita. "You've been planning some kind of werewolf Rumspringa for me?"

Nando shrugged. "Sort of. Or maybe more like going away to college. A gap year backpacking through Europe." He smiled, and his grin was exactly what one would expect. "I just want to make sure you really want to be here when you're changing my bedpan, Tina."

"Yeah, fuck that noise," Tina said, turning away from him. Then she grabbed onto Lena's and Bel's sleeves. "Spring break, bitches! And we're going to the library!"

"It's easy to fall in love. The hard part is finding someone to catch you."

-Bertrand Russell

Chapter 21

Torreblanca climbed out of her bed carefully, taking deep breaths as she sat on the edge, collecting herself, then taking a few more after putting on the pajamas folded at the foot of the bed, then more after sliding her feet into the slippers left on the floor before standing. She was relieved to find the pain in her abdomen wasn't bad when she stood still. The first few times she'd stood, she'd only managed to stay up for a few minutes before Long or Matt had to nearly catch her and guide her back. Now she hurt with each shuffling step, but she could stand still and forget she'd been fatally shot in the stomach by someone she trusted.

She wondered if Esau ever qualified as a friend. They'd always had the power differential that comes with a platonic relationship between a commanding officer and a subordinate, but Torreblanca felt they were closer than most, a connection built on mutual respect and admiration with a hint of father-daughter concern thrown in. Now, when every step shot a searing pain into her gut, she felt the physical pain as a reminder of the deeper betrayal. Worse, she suspected he thought of her as the betrayer, and it galled her to imagine him feeling justified in his choice. Worst, she had to acknowledge the possibility that he didn't think of her at all; that he'd executed her and removed her from his memory with a few pulls of the trigger.

Yet here she was, alive and standing. The pajamas left for her were not like anything she would have worn around the house back home. The shirt was an av bar bov, a traditional Khmer sleeveless shirt, and the pants were sompot chong kben, loose fitting unisex trousers that came down to a tighter cuff at the ankle. A third garment, a sbai, was left on the bed. It was supposed to be worn over one shoulder and was purely decorative, but Torreblanca couldn't figure out how to put it on, so she skipped it. All three were made of silk and richly patterned with green, gold, and black filigree, the pants mostly green, the blouse mostly black, and the sbai adorned with gold. Torreblanca appreciated the feel of the smooth, light fabric, but it made her more than a little self-conscious about the fact that her hosts had not thought to leave her any underwear or bras, and the fit of the top, though comfortable, left little to the imagination.

Better than one of those paper hospital gowns, she thought.

She looked at herself in the mirror hanging on the

back of her room's door. The pajamas looked too dainty for her, though she did like the way the shirt showed off her arms. She was proud of her muscles and enjoyed the way they made some men uncomfortable. Those men would flex themselves sore when she walked into a room, then leave and complain about how some women were too masculine these days. Never in her presence, though. She loved that. She ran her fingers through her short, straight, black hair. She'd never liked the color of her hair, having been trained to want to be brunette or, better, blond, by the telenovelas she'd watched with her family as a kid. Instead of dying it, she'd shaved it nearly bald when she was in the army. The near baldness turned some men off, and when she was in Iraq, she found those were exactly the kind of men she didn't want to be around. She'd started letting it grow out after leaving the service, but she'd still kept it short during most of her time working for Esau, finding it more practical while they were hunting and often sleeping rough. She'd only decided to let it grow out since Vegas, and though she didn't connect those decisions, Esau's growing distrust of her had been unconsciously related to her hair. Now it was almost chin length, parted on the side and a bit longer in front than in back. Dressed in the pajamas, with her arms exposed, she felt she looked more like a caricature of an Asian man than a traditional, long-haired Mexican woman.

I've never been that pretty, anyway, she thought. And it's so muggy, I'll sweat through these in no time. That will be a look.

Torreblanca didn't want to contemplate why her appearance was forefront in her mind as she opened the door and began to shuffle down the hall to the house's dining room. She hadn't explored the house before, but she could hear two men's voices nearby, and she knew their owners. She didn't want to admit it, but she wanted Long to see her before she was a sweaty mess.

As she neared the door at the end of the hall, she could hear their voices clearly enough to make out the conversation. She wasn't intentionally eavesdropping, but she had to stop and rest every few feet, her shoulder pressed into the wall, deep breaths pulling at her healing muscles until she could calm and breathe, pain free, for a few seconds before tightening her stomach and taking three or four more small steps.

"Do you know how you'll find him?" Long was asking.

"I have a plan. It's not much of a plan, but it's something. I'll take a flight to Bangkok tomorrow, then over to Seattle, and then set sail on the *Exclamation* down the coast. I know some spells of detection that might work. It would be easier if I had a sample. But I'll try to conjure something up. The spells need a lot of juice, so I'll have to stop and charge up along the way, but hopefully I can find him in the gulf and not out in the middle of the Pacific or way up the river."

None of Matt's words made a lick of sense to Torreblanca, but Long understood.

"Alright. I'll remain here with our guest and wait for your return, hopefully with some assistance. I would wish you good luck, but you understand why I don't joke around about that. Have a safe and prosperous journey, my friend."

"Thank you, Long," Matt said.

Torreblanca heard a pregnant pause.

"Did I pronounce it…?"

"Almost," Long said, and Torreblanca could hear the smile in his voice.

She considered hurrying in to say goodbye to Matt, but one quick step reminded her hurrying wasn't part of her repertoire yet. Dizzy, she leaned against the wall. Matt closed a door somewhere further off.

Long's voice was aimed at her. "Would you like some assistance, or do you want to see if you can make it on your own?"

"I can do it," she said. Her voice was weak and breathy. She hated it. She tried again. "I can do it." She thought that was better.

"I'll get you some water. Would you like some soup?"

"I'm not … sure how … hungry … If I can eat it … "

Long stepped into the doorway in front of her. For a brief moment, the light from the room froze in the space around him, like he was caught in a spider's web covered in dew or surrounded by little LED fairy lights. The shimmer of uneven light only lasted for a second as he passed through the door, and then he stood next to her as a seemingly normal, if exceptionally handsome, human man. "I'll get you some water and a bowl of soup from the kitchen. You find a seat at the table. Take it slow." He placed his hand gently on her shoulder, then let his fingertips slide down the outside of her arm as he walked past her down the hall. Torreblanca felt another wave of dizziness, took a deep breath to let it pass, then crossed the threshold into the room where the men had been talking moments before.

An ornate table with settings for ten filled one half of

the room, clearly a dining room, but the other half held three large wingback chairs facing a fireplace in a semicircle. The walls in the dining-room half were sparsely decorated with a few tasteful paintings depicting impressionist visions of fishermen in wide, conical hats navigating rivers of speckled color or similarly dressed figures hunched over tending to rainbow rice fields of in monsoon rains of different shades. The three walls in the other half of the room were covered in floor-to-ceiling bookshelves densely packed with hardcover books and even older scrolls. The fireplace was unlit, and Torreblanca couldn't imagine it would be necessary in the slightly-too-warm, humid air, nor that it would produce enough light to aid in reading. In the corners of the room, those same odd lanterns hung, casting bright but slightly flickering white light. Like her own room and the hallway, this dining room and sitting room had no windows.

She made her way to a chair on the long side of the table so her back was to the fireplace, pulled it diagonal to the table, and sat heavily, catching her breath once again. Long returned, and as he entered, she saw that brief flash in the doorway she'd mistaken for sunlight before she found the room had none. This time she examined it more carefully and could make out a glimpse of golden scales around him in an oval as wide as the door and as tall. He slowed almost imperceptibly as he crossed the threshold. Though his human form passed evenly through the middle of the space, she realized his glowing golden aura was squeezing through.

He set a glass of water down in front of her with his

left hand, then took the finely decorated white-and-blue bowl out of his right so he could set it down at the same time he placed a matching, porcelain spoon primly next to it. Torreblanca sipped some water, cool but not as cold as she was used to, and then she dipped the spoon into the bowl. A yellow broth filled with oily bubbles steamed as the spoon revealed some white, semi-translucent noodles and pieces of onion, carrot, and some kind of meat.

"Chicken noodle," he said. "A local variety with rice noodles. The noodles were made fresh this morning. They don't keep as well as wheat noodles, but when they are fresh, they are better."

"Where are we, exactly?"

"How specific do you want me to be? We're in Cambodia. Do you know your Cambodian geography?"

"No," she admitted.

"Northwestern Cambodia. North of a lake called Tonle Sap. More specifically, we're in my home. More importantly, you are safe here."

"Am I a prisoner?"

"Absolutely not. You may leave whenever you wish, but I want to remind you that you very nearly died recently, the man who tried to kill you would not hesitate to finish the job, and the monsters he is dealing with would like to help him if they could."

"Why?"

Long pulled the chair next to her to a similar angle away from the table and sat with more grace than she'd managed. He slowly placed both his hands around her free one. When they made contact, she dropped her spoon into the bowl with a clatter. He generously ignored this and said, "That is the biggest of all questions, isn't it. May I ask you one first?"

"Sure."

"What would you like me to call you?"

Torreblanca had a brief moment where she considered a forward reply, but she relented. She didn't have the energy to flirt. "Most people call me Torreblanca. Or Lieutenant."

"But what would you like me to call you, Anahí?"

"Um, yes." She realized she was blushing and hated it.

"Anahí, then?"

She nodded.

"Anahí, as you know, I am not a human, but I have lived with humans far longer than you have. I've also lived with other monsters far longer than most of them have lived. It is possible you could find someone who has a satisfying answer to the question of why humans and monsters do what they do, but, if you will trust my experience, those people are either deluding themselves or trying to manipulate you. My honest answer, after a little less than eight thousand years of observation, is that humans and monsters have elaborate excuses for their choices, but these excuses rarely rise to the level of anything that could rightly be called reasons. The closest they come are the basest impulses. They want food and shelter and sex and safety and survival. But they really don't like to admit their reasons are so simple. They add layers of nonsense. Does that make sense to you?"

Torreblanca stared into Long's eyes, large and black and gentle and unblinking. "Mm-hmm."

He smiled warmly and looked down at her hand in

his, then back into her eyes. "Well, it doesn't make much sense to me, but I suppose I am a simpler creature. My friend Matt, who I have known for centuries, asked me to help him unravel this dangerous plot concocted by, it seems, a vampire, the queen of the sirens, and the former king of the trolls. But it started with a now deceased necromancer. And now they are trying to get your human monster-hunter friend involved. It's all unnecessarily convoluted, and I'm not convinced any of them really understand what they are doing or why. But I went because I like my friend. And because, believe it or not, I like humans. I long for community. Simple. So when we were spying on one of their clandestine meetings and saw your friend try to kill you, we intervened. And here you are, still alive. Simple."

"Do you really think being alive is simple?" Torreblanca asked. "Sure, I'm breathing. I'm slurping soup. My wounds are healing. But everything after that sure looks pretty complicated from where I'm sitting."

Long patted her hand. "Then, if I may, can I make a humble suggestion?"

To Torreblanca's surprise, Long waited for permission to give her advice.

"Sure," she whispered.

"When the future feels like too much, focus on the healing. When the healing feels like too much, focus on the soup. When the soup is too much, focus on the glass of water. And when that feels like too much, focus on the breathing. Breathing is highly underrated."

"It is easier to forgive an enemy than to forgive a friend."

-William Blake

Chapter 22

The night air was still chilly in Saskatchewan, even in late spring. The temperature didn't bother Bel and Lena. They liked sitting out under the stars in a pair of chairs they'd liberated from empty rooms in their cabin at Camp Bigfoot. The lack of light pollution allowed stars to preen in the sky, and the Northern Lights sometimes made cameo appearances, flitting through the upper atmosphere in glowing, smokey tendrils of green ionic storm. Lena liked to lean back, smoke her cigarettes, and try to exhale the smoke and steam of her breath into similar waves above her. Bel didn't care much about the stars or the light show. She just wanted to be close to Lena.

Though Bel had vast financial resources, she still liked

to be frugal. Digging in the pockets of corpses to find spare change had been her least favorite part of hunting early on, a disappointing ending to an otherwise thrilling experience, like the obligatory awkward conversation after a one-night stand. The memory of living hand-to-mouth, or, more accurately, meal-to-payday, compelled Bel to continue looking for sale prices even when compound interest had made that unnecessary. She was dinking around on her phone, searching for deals online using Camp Bigfoot's satellite WiFi.

Her pleasant mood shattered when Matteo Bern's name popped up on her phone. She would have resented wasting money on plane tickets they didn't need, so Matt's timing was actually a favor. Bel couldn't appreciate the interruption at the time, though, since Matt remained squarely near the top of her kill list.

She swiped to start the call, put the phone to her ear, and said, "You have balls of steel and shit for brains if you're calling me, Matt."

"Yes, I understand why you would be a bit peeved at me, though I'll remind you I did not shoot Lena, and she's still alive, so, if we're honest, my crime was failing to take a bullet for someone who has become bulletproof. But we'll have time to litigate that later. Just please hear me out, and then you can decide if you want to kill me."

"I don't have time for your problems or patience for your entitlement, Matt. We know you worked for Nigel Marion. We know you were the one who imprisoned Lena. Next time I see you, you're pretty well fucked, aren't you? Until then, I owe you nothing."

Matt hesitated, clearly surprised. "Ah, yes. That's … well, I can see how that is a problem. And you're right, of course. You owe me nothing. But I am currently headed off to rescue your friend, Josef, and I could use your help. I'll bet Lena would like that. Is she available? I'd like to talk with her."

Lena had already leapt out of her seat and stood over Bel, holding out a hand for the phone. Bel looked up at her girlfriend. "The stones on this obnoxious prick," she said as she slapped the device into Lena's palm.

"You know where Josef is?"

"Lena! It's so good to hear your voice. First, I'm so sorry I disappeared when Esau shot you. It was cowardly, I admit. Things with Esau are complicated, and, frankly, he scares me, but that's no excuse to have left you to deal with my mess, so I apologize."

"I don't blame you for that, Matt—" Lena began.

"I do!" Bel shouted.

Lena held the phone to her chest as though that would have any effect on what Matt could hear, but her tone was even and not the least bit conspiratorial. "Bel." It was halfway between comforting and scolding. "He dodged a bullet. You've done the same. The bullet hit the person behind him. You've done the same."

"I did it on purpose! He was part of the planning group that had been rehearsing that move the day before. He knew what we were doing to Cassius and did the same fucking thing to you. And then he dipped out. Fuck him. I see him, he's dead."

"If I may…" a tiny voice spoke to Lena's collar bone.

The vampires could hear him clearly.

"You may get bent, Matt," Bel said.

Lena turned, took a few steps away from Bel, and lifted the phone to her ear. "She's still upset about the whole experience. It was pretty traumatic for her."

"And less so for you?" Matt asked.

"I didn't say that. But I don't want to kill you. I'm not a particularly vengeful person. Even Esau. He didn't shoot me on purpose."

"No, he was trying to kill me. You'll pardon me if I do take that personally."

"Well, I'm not saying he's justified, but you don't treat your romantic conquests very well."

"This from a vampire."

She smiled. "Touche. But Matt, in order for me to get past things, I will need you to apologize for everything. Not just the one thing you don't feel bad about. The other thing."

Matt was silent for longer than Lena believed he could be silent.

"When did you learn about that? Did you know in Vegas?"

"I didn't know when we became friends. But you did, Matt."

Another pause. "I can't make excuses for that, can I?"

"No, Matt. There's no excuse."

"I'm sorry, Lena. I didn't recognize your human dignity because I'm a monster, and that's not an excuse. I own it. I bewitched you. I glamoured you. I forced you to work against your will. I violated you in that way. I recognize is unforgivable, and I do regret it. I'm sorry."

"Okay. So, you know where we can find Josef?"

"That's it?"

"What?

"You're just moving on?"

"Here's what you don't know, Matt. I was going to write the book, anyway. I'd been planning it out in my head for years. I didn't know that it would be a weapon of mass murder, but I was already planning on writing a novel that would convince the reader life isn't meaningful. So I was a monster before I was a monster. That's no excuse for what you did. In a way, that makes what you did worse, at least within the monster moral framework that humans are less-than. You unwittingly forced someone who was your monstrously moral equal to do something you didn't know she was going to do anyway. Nothing about that absolves you."

"So you're just willing to move on to finding Josef?"

"Exactly. I didn't say I forgive you. I didn't say our friendship is healed and I trust you again. I don't. But I want to get Josef back. You help me do that, and it will go a long way."

"Okay," Matt said. He sounded chastened, but Lena didn't trust him, so his tone made her more resentful, not less. "I want to help you find Josef. For you and for it. Also, I need Josef's help. I would like your help as well, but Josef's particular kind of un-kill-ability might prove essential to a certain task that's been laid at my feet."

Though she knew Matt couldn't see her, she frowned at the phone. "And that would be?"

Matt heard her frown and shrugged. "Saving the world."

Lena heard his shrug. "I knew you were going to say that. You do realize I'm the single person least likely to be motivated by altruism, right? I literally wrote the book on the subject of life being meaningless. Twice."

"And yet you've been roped into saving the world twice. One might suspect you doubt your own thesis."

"I really wish these crises would stop popping up. Saving the world hasn't gone well for me."

"Really? Two years ago, you were a lonely woman working a dead-end secretarial job at a law firm. A year ago you were sleeping on a bomb and nearly catatonic with despair. Now you're an immortal vampire jet-setting around the world with your hot vampire girlfriend. I think you've come out on top."

"Matt, I have to kill people and drink their blood to stay alive!"

"Sounds like a bad thing for them, not you. And really, is it all that different from what that corporate law firm was doing to you more slowly? Sounds to me like you're bemoaning that you're the victor instead of the victim. But what do I know? I'm a happy monster. You're a cynic."

"I just realized I've missed you, Matt."

"What can I say? I'm incredibly charming. It's magic."

Instead of flying directly to Bangkok, Lena, Bel, Napoleon, and Tina detoured to Baja California, first in the camp's jeep, then in a rented U-Haul (Tina could drive during the day with the vampires safe in the back), then a chartered private jet to Mexicali, a town on the northern Mexican border just south of Calexico, California. From there, it took another ride in a rented van to get to a tender waiting to take them to Matt's yacht, The *Exclamation*, reclining proudly at anchor in the estuary where the Colorado River met the Gulf of California, bobbling gently in the starlight under a bright moon. An island, the Isla Montegue, a wildlife preserve sat in the river's mouth. The *Exclamation* had to be anchored to the south so it wouldn't run aground in the shallows.

As the four travelers climbed out of the small boat onto the larger one, Matt came down the stairs from the upper deck to greet them, his arms open for a hug.

"The stones on this fuckin' guy," Bel muttered.

Lena stepped towards him and hugged him. It was a chilly, uncomfortable gesture for both of them, two people trying to rebuild, one not sure she should, the other not sure he deserved it. Plus, Lena wore her backpack, the green denim one that secretly carried her two blood-soaked manuscripts of mass destruction, and allowing anyone to put their arms around her and closer to her pack made her uncomfortable. But she wanted Bel to see she wasn't afraid of Matt.

When Matt stepped back, he looked at Bel. "I'm not going to hug you because I am still a little concerned you mean to kill me, but I want you to know I am available for a hug if you decide you'd like one."

"Not bloody likely," Bel said.

"Fair. What about you, Tina? Have you grown up to be a hugger, or are you still more of a flipper-off-er?"

Tina flipped him off. "You haven't fixed your old man smell problem, old man."

"I appreciate the consistency you bring into my life. And you, my new friend? What's your name? Are you a hugger?"

"His name is Napoleon," Lena said. "He can't talk and … oh! Apparently, he is a hugger."

Napoleon, freed of his human disguise, had stepped into Matt's offered embrace without hesitation. When his arms wrapped around Matt's back, the force of his embrace pulled his left arm out of its socket. He caught his left hand with his right, so when he stepped back from Matt, both arms made the trip around Matt on the right side. Matt observed this orbit of arm bones with wide eyes and shot a look at Lena. While Napoleon reattached his arm, Lena said, "It happens. He's learned to manage it well.

Napoleon shrugged. His left arm fell off again, and he caught it with his right before it hit the ship's deck.

Matt's voice dropped to its lowest baritone. "Impressive!"

"Okay, so where's Josef?" Tina asked.

"And what's this big world-ending crisis we need to solve?" Lena asked.

Matt pointed at Tina. "Not quite sure, but I think I

know how to find out." He pointed at Lena. "It's complicated, but I'll try to explain enroute." He pointed at Bel. "You're still glowering at me, and it's kind of freaking me out." He pointed at Napoleon. "You might be my new favorite. Right this way, everyone. I'll introduce you to the *Exclamation's* new captain."

Tina cocked her head in a very canine way. "What happened to Meili?"

"After our last adventure, she decided she'd had enough of monsters, and she retired. I was sorry to see her go. She'd been with us many years." He walked up the stairs and onto the main deck, continuing toward the next staircase heading up to the bridge. "It meant a nice promotion for Captain Summerfield who had been patiently waiting for the job."

When they ascended to the bridge, Matt gestured to the woman standing with her hand on the tiller. "Captain Summerfield, I'd like to introduce you to Magdalena Wallace, Jezebel Shipwright, hot lesbian vampires; Christina Sato, a Teenwolf/Wednesday Addams hybrid; and Napoleon, a reanimated skeleton, obviously."

"We've met," Lena said. "Congratulations on the promotion. I like the new hat."

Sara wore the same dark polo shirt and khaki slacks as all the other women on the crew, but she sported a ridiculously large hat, black to match her shirt, nearly pointed in the front and back and rising in a huge arch a foot and a half over her head, like a mohawk with two rows of gold piping running the length. When she shook Lena's hand, she had to pinch the front of the hat like she was about to doff it in greeting. She was really keeping it from falling forward under its own weight. "Thank you. I demanded a commodore's hat in contract negotiations. I also considered an eye patch, but it turns out those cause significant eye strain even if you remember to flip back and forth from one eye to the other on a regular basis."

Bel shook her hand next. "Lena's hot vampire girlfriend," she said.

"Welcome aboard, Ms. Shipwright," Sara said, and Bel was impressed with her memory.

Tina stepped forward next. "I prefer Tina, but Wednesday Teenwolf is actually pretty cool." She looked at Matt. "But still, fuck you, Matt."

Napoleon stepped forward to shake hands, but his left arm fell off, and he needed to use his right to catch it, so he just waved with the detached left.

"Welcome, Napoleon," Sara said, but it was almost a question.

"He can't talk," Lena explained.

Napoleon chattered his teeth to illustrate his lack of lips and tongue, then shrugged. His arm didn't fall off, and this surprised almost everyone including Napoleon.

"Captain," Matt said, "please chart a course around the island up to its northern point in the Colorado. If it gets too shallow for the *Exclamation*, drop anchor as far north as you can get her. I'm going to take our new guests down to my office and fill them in on the plan."

"Aye aye, Sir," she said, looking straight ahead and pinching the front of her hat as she nodded so it wouldn't fall forward over the wheel.

Matt led the travelers down to his quarters, a pair of large staterooms. The first was a combination of an office and sitting room where he entertained human guests, the second his bedroom where he occasionally also entertained guests, both generally in the service of causing drama among groups he brought onboard. Then he'd absorb all their emotional energy as they turned on one another. He used that to feed his magic. He was a monster, after all.

Lena could picture these private seduction sessions when she looked around at the ornate bar with different kinds of liquor in unlabeled crystal decanters, a pair of loveseats and some large, expensive chairs but no couches large enough to contain a pair at a safe distance. "Do you have any of your usual guests onboard right now, Matt?" she asked.

"No, but this is relevant and not bragging: I did do some feeding on my way here. I'm basically bursting right now. I should be exporting some of the extra energy in my usual way, but we might need every bit of it tonight." Making his magical bubbles of excess emotional energy and setting them free in the wind was a kind of Zen art project that soothed his spirit. Without this exercise, he felt jittery and anxious. "I know I have a lot of explaining to do, and I'm also aware that we have limited time. I'll need your vampire eyes to help me search for Josef tonight, so we'll only be able to search together before the sun comes up. Tina and I could continue to try tomorrow, but that will be a lot harder because we'll be looking for a faint glow in the water, and that will be hard to see in daylight."

He pursed his lips and nodded slowly, almost keeping time like a metronome. "But I promised you an explanation first. And we'll have one other task before we can start the search." He tapped the tips of his fingers together like he was about to pray or meditate, then bounced them against one another as he thought. "Okay, let's see. Where to start. Gods, this will be like charades. Okay, there's a certain someone I'm not allowed to talk about. Not allowed to reveal too much information about. No, it's not that I'm not allowed. It's a spell. I'm bewitched. But you have met him." He looked at Lena. "And when we first met him, I didn't tell you what he was. Know who I'm talking about?"

"Long?"

"You said it. I didn't. Though I'm pretty sure you're pronouncing it wrong. I can't pronounce it right, either. It's not even his real name. Just Mandarin for 'dragon.'" He looked expectantly at Tina.

"What? I'm Japanese. Half Japanese, half Canadian. I don't even speak Japanese, let alone Mandarin. Racist."

Matt held his hands up in surrender. "My apologies. Anyway, three witches sent me to find our mutual friend."

Lena brightened. "We know them!"

This took Matt by surprise. "Really?"

"Yes! We've bumped into them a couple times. Last time they said we'd need to find Josef to get ready to fight some mermaids. It was all very cryptic. But they tasked

Bel to train me to fight and said they'd be in touch about where to find Josef."

Matt nodded, excited. "They told me to find a dragon, then find Josef, then offer you all help so Bel doesn't kill me. And they said they'll come back with more instructions." He stopped. "No, now that I think about it, they didn't specifically say they would come back to tell me my other labors. They just said they couldn't tell me yet. And I'll bet they didn't specifically say they would come tell you where to find Josef. So now they have me telling you where to find Josef. Which means they may use some other means to tell me what I need to do so I don't die."

"You're going to die?" Lena asked.

"No, I'm not. They made it clear that I would die if I didn't complete four tasks. But they only told me the first two. And to provide you all with whatever material support you require. And to avoid Esau so he doesn't kill me. But those last two don't count among my four labors for some reason. It sounded like a technicality to me. I'd like credit for six labors. Six labors sounds better than four."

He shook his head, twiddled his fingers, and then started pacing. "I'm getting ahead of myself. There's an important step we need to take care of before we go looking for Josef. I'm sorry to ask this of any of you, but for our next trick, I need a volunteer.

"Which of you super-fast healers will let me cut off one of your fingers?"

"The difference between life and the movies is that a script has to make sense, and life doesn't."
-Joseph L. Mankiewicz

Chapter 23

The emissary stopped suddenly, his hands out in the universal halting gesture. "Okay, so at this point we'll need a montage. Or maybe just one dramatic long shot that zooms into a pan, sweeping from one group of men to another. But really cinematic." He swept one of his arms out to the side in a wide arc.

Kim frowned hard. "For the finger chopping?"

"No, we're not to that, yet. That will look great on film though. Extreme close up. Super-gross. No, first we need to let the audience know Cassius rendezvoused with Esau and joined up with his bunch. Maybe a Guy Ritchie-style montage, with heavy cha-chunks when a passport is stamped and a loud engine noise when a private jet takes off, and then big pdddddrrrrr when there's a helicopter on the tarmac, and then—"

"Wait," Joyce interrupted. "No dialogue? Why not?"

"Well, the audience needs to know that Cassius and his lackeys met up with Esau and his soldiers, and they all went off together, but they didn't know where to go at this point, so dialogue would probably be confusing," the emissary explained. "But a shot of all of them getting together would look cool. If you filmed it during dawn or sunset, you could have the three vampires dressed in the gear they wear to block out the sun, all covered in leather and gloves and motorcycle helmets, standing silhouetted against those heat ripples with the sun just over their shoulders. That would look cool. Or you could set it at night to show how ominous they all are, with the vampires looking half-starved because they'd been living in that hole in Kansas and surviving off bagged blood. People don't know this, but bagged blood is not great for vampires' health. But it makes them look less like humans and more like the monsters they really are. That could be neat to see under lamplight on some dark tarmac at night."

Joyce was still frowning. "Couldn't we just write in that they know where they are going, and then you could have some witty banter in this scene. Didn't you say they had been in Kansas? One of the foot-soldier guys could turn to the other and say, 'Looks like we're not in Kansas anymore.' That's a gimme. You're just going to leave that there on the table?" He looked at Kim and Carol for approval of his joke. They smiled because he was their boss, but Kim looked like they'd just smelled something bad, and Carol looked like she was trying not to cause a bad smell herself.

The emissary gazed at the ceiling. "Well, it wouldn't be as accurate if they knew where they were going at that point in the movie, but, on the other hand, I can imagine Bob saying something like that. Not the smartest character. And Augy could snap at him. It would be a nice call-back." He pointed a finger at Joyce. "Good note! We should consider that in the punch-ups."

Kim was back to their hard frowning. "Wait, did you just say 'accurate'?"

The emissary shook his head. "Of course not. I just mean faithful to the script. Which can be changed, of course. I just thought the shot would look really cool. Maybe with some really pop-y music. Like, that exciting song in the motorcycle scene in *Top Gun*. Not the sex-scene song. The other one."

"That was like 40 years ago," Carol said.

Kim shrugged. "Still a banger."

"Not that song, of course," the emissary said. "Just something that will get radio play."

"Radio play?" Carol asked. "How old are you?"

Joyce made a gesture, and Carol let it go. Then the boss made a circular motion with his wrist, and the emissary got on with it.

"Then a shot of a big helicopter, one of those ones with two huge rotors … ooh, maybe the kind with the rotors on wings that turn up in the air, the Osprey … flying out over the ocean on the way to Asia."

"Asia?"

"That's where they're headed, but they don't know that yet."

Joyce raised an eyebrow. "I like Asia. Big market."

Carol shook her head. "Yeah, but helicopters can't fly across the Pacific."

Joyce shrugged. He looked to the emissary. "Maybe they have an aircraft carrier?"

"No, they didn't." He turned to Carol. "But the audience doesn't know where they're going yet, so it won't matter."

Kim got Carol's back. "But if they leave in a helicopter, and then they arrive in a helicopter in China—"

"Vietnam," the emissary corrected.

"Even further," Carol said.

Joyce shook his head. "And not as big a market. Can we make it Shanghai? Or Hong Kong even? No, too controversial. Shanghai or Beijing."

The emissary wobbled his head back and forth and muttered, "Not how it really happened, but sure, we can make that work, I guess."

"Wait, what?" Kim said.

"Smash cut!" the emissary shouted.

"Socrates said, "The misuse of language induces evil in the soul." He wasn't talking about grammar. To misuse language is to use it the way politicians and advertisers do, for profit, without taking responsibility for what the words mean. Language used as a means to get power or make money goes wrong: it lies. Language used as an end in itself, to sing a poem or tell a story, goes right, goes towards the truth."

-Ursula K. Le Guin

Chapter 24

Lena took a deep breath. She knew if she got too excited and let her voice rise in pitch and volume, it was frightening to white people, and she still hadn't fully shed her human life of training to protect white people's feelings. Bel could teach her how to be a badass vampire, but her white girlfriend couldn't magically teach her to be a Black vampire. "Okay, did you just ask us if you could cut off one of our fingers?"

"Yep!" Matt peeped, blithely unaware of the lack of

tensile strength of the ice upon which he stood. "But allow me to explain. There's this imp. His name is Apraxis."

Lena and Bel shared one of the loveseats. Tina had another to herself. Napoleon took one of the wingback chairs. Matt paced near his desk, but Lena interrupted his movement.

"Little guy? Red? Head and body are all one thing?" Lena positioned her hands like she was holding a vertical American football. "Little wings that shouldn't be able to hold him up?"

"You've met him?" Matt was flummoxed to near-silence.

It was Lena's turn to say, "Yep!" She turned to Tina and Napoleon to explain. "Bel and I were supposedly rescued by the little bastard in Ireland, but it was a trick. He took us to Scotland and got Josef captured by a warlock." She turned back to Matt. "Yeah, you weren't the first. This Pictish warlock with blue paint on his face."

"Erdogan Ueda," Matt said. "I knew him." He looked down at the floor, ashamed. "No, he wasn't involved in making you write the book like you thought. But we both worked for the necromancer Nigel Marion."

Bel shrugged. "I killed him. Just a little nick with a knife I'd dipped in basilisk blood. Not sorry." And she looked hard at Matt to remind him he was still on her shit list.

Matt held up his hands in surrender. "He wasn't a friend of mine or anything. Just a colleague. Really more of a professional competitor who happened to be doing subcontracting work for the same employer who hired me. Not at all sorry to see him go."

"So, yeah, we met Apraxis," Lena said. "We aren't fans."

"Nor should you be," Matt said. "Here's the thing about working with imps…"

"They always lie," Lena said. "We know. He bragged about it."

"Right. Or almost always. Or always half a lie. Not enough that you can catch them in one of the old 'One of us always lies and one of us always tells the truth' logic puzzles. Because in the same way you feed on blood and I feed on strong emotions, they feed on deceiving people. But they aren't limited to humans because they're from someplace else entirely."

"Hell?" Tina asked.

"Depends what you mean by that. The bad place you go when you die? No. A different dimension that intersects with ours and has strange beings who like to fuck with us? Yes. And there are different other places. Hells. The Shadowlands of the Sidhe. Dark dimensions of different kinds. Imps and demons and yokai sometimes come to this world to stay, sometimes travel in and out. Warlocks like me try to capture them and make them work for us and straight up steal their power. They are really powerful. But they have their own agendas. And they resent being captured and put to work."

Lena slowly leaned her head to the side. "You don't say."

Matt nodded. "I'm not unaware of the irony."

Bel looked at Lena. "Is that irony, technically speaking?"

Lena shook her head.

Matt raised a finger and opened his mouth to argue, held his breath while he decided to take the loss, and moved on. "Right, so we will need to deal with Apraxis in this case because … "

"He's the one who captured Josef for Cassius," Bel said. "The King of Trolls told us. The former king. Deposed and de-headed."

All of Matt's big reveals were being stolen away like tablecloths yanked out from under decorative place settings by sleight-of-hand magicians, and he was getting tired of it. "Okay, so you also know how to summon Apraxis, right?"

Lena looked at Bel. Tina looked at Bel. Napoleon stared at the gold crown molding and wondered if it was a normal thing to find in a room on a ship. Bel shook her head, answering all their questions.

"Good thing you have a friend who is a warlock, then," Matt said. He walked over to the cabinet covered in the crystal liquor decanters, opened the bottom drawer, and pulled out a stone cutting board and an unusual knife. The cutting board was a gray rock, highly polished and nondescript. The knife had a gaudy golden handle which almost obscured the important element; the blade was made of the same gray stone, and it was serrated unevenly as though chipped by hand. "Unfortunately, this will require a bit of blood magic and the sacrifice of some flesh and bone. Got to include bone. Them's the rules. I suggest a pinky finger. Luckily for us, three of you heal very quickly. And luckily for Napoleon, he doesn't have any blood, so he's out of the running. Cleverly done, good sir."

Napoleon didn't react.

"You speak too quickly," Lena said. "He's still learning English."

Bel translated into German.

Napoleon leaned his head back with his mouth open, slapped his knee, and then shot Matt a thumbs-up.

Matt appreciated the gesture more than he liked to admit. To hide his smile, he quickly shifted his gaze to Tina, Bel, and Lena. "So, who is the lucky healer?"

Tina said, "Just being practical here. Do you have anyone willing to donate an arm or leg I could eat so I can replenish my energy? If not, it's probably easier to find a blood donor."

"I'll bet we could find you a human to feed on pretty easily, but you're right. I'm more likely to get some crew members to donate blood than to talk someone into donating a limb. The cost of the workman's comp claim would be steep on that. The blood donation request might constitute some kind of harassment. I'll run it by HR."

Lena asked Bel, "How long would it take me to grow a finger back?"

"A few hours. Less if you feed."

Lena turned to Matt. "Guess I'm giving you the finger."

Matt rolled his eyes. "Fine. Not a joke you'll get to tell very often, so you've earned it. Now, before we make our long-distance call, let's game plan what we're going to offer Apraxis. Dealing with imps is always unwise, but it would be more foolish to do it without a plan."

At the end of their strategy session, Matt set the cutting board on the coffee table, then gestured to it with the knife.

Lena placed her right hand down on the cool stone, fingers splayed.

Matt pinched at her last knuckle, massaging roughly until he found the exact spot between the bones. Then he looked her in the eye. "Ready?"

"As I'll ever be."

Bel took Lena's left hand so she had something to squeeze.

Matt set the special stone knife against the skin gently. Then he pursed his lips and frowned. "One ... two ... three ... four ... five ..."

"Oh, just—" Lena started.

He pressed forward hard, the teeth of the serrated blade catching and ripping the cartilage until the blade's point hit the cutting board, and then he yanked it back like he was slicing a rare and uncooperative vegetable in a fancy kitchen.

Lena squeezed Bel's hand so hard she nearly broke

her girlfriend's metacarpals. Her head reared back, her jaw opening, human teeth retracting almost instantly, the rows of curved syringe teeth springing out of her gums and clawing at the air and she hissed a nearly silent scream at the ceiling. She'd never transformed so fast, even in their hunting lessons. She squeezed her eyes shut against the pain, drew in a slow breath through her nose, and looked down at the wound.

The pain stopped almost as quickly as it had begun, and, as she watched, the wound closed, leaving a little lump of skin. Lena released Bel's hand like a hot potato, before she could do damage, and she lifted her injured right. She poked at the stump with the tips of the fingers of her left. It was warm to the touch, feverish and already growing back.

"Sorry about that," Matt said.

"It hurt more than I expected, but it also stopped faster than I'd expected, so…" Lena shrugged. She didn't know what else to say.

"Okay, on to the next step." Matt picked up Lena's severed pinky without any sign of revulsion, held it like a short fountain pen, and squeezed as he drew a slow circle, careful to make an unbroken ring of blood on the stone. When it connected, he set the finger down in the center.

Then they waited.

The space inside the circle lit up with a dull orange glow, like a burner inside a glass-top stove. When the orange got bright enough that it was almost white light, the circle in the stone melted, and the finger fell inside the hole. Some air whooshed in after it, as though the cavity was a puncture in the hull of an airplane, an aperture giving egress to a place with less pressure.

The five of them started at a small explosion above the stone. The space reverted to cold stone, and Apraxis settled his small feet in the circle of dried blood. "I didn't expect a call from any of you," he lied.

The imp was less than a foot tall with a barrel shaped torso that was indistinguishable from his head. He had two pointy ears and a pair of small horns, thin legs and arms with oversized, clawed hands and feet, and a prehensile tail. A pair of small, leathery wings on his back fluttered lazily. They couldn't possibly have provided the lift to hold his squat body aloft even if they'd been moving at the speed of hummingbirds' wings, so obviously he was floating via some supernatural means. And then, with a popping sound like a gum bubble bursting, he disappeared.

Or the sound came from his reappearance over Lena's shoulder, since that happened instantaneously. Lena remembered his teleporting trick and did her best not to react. "Look, I know we didn't leave things on the best of terms back in Scotland, but since then I've turned over a new leaf, and I've been trying to help you all out."

Lena almost took the bait, nearly calling him out on his lie and demanding to know how he had been helping them, but Matt caught her eye, slowly closed his own, and shook his head a fraction of an inch.

Bel leaned back on the loveseat and threw a leg over one of its arms and one of her elbows over the back, looking as much like a Viking queen as anyone had in the last few hundred years. "We are prepared to make you an offer."

"What do I have that you want?" the imp asked, grinning. His mouth widened until it was halfway around his head, and the smile curled up only slightly at the edges, a horrible expression of greedy glee.

Bel looked at the ceiling, then back at the imp. "Just a pile of dust, really. Not much."

"And what do you propose to offer me in exchange for this pile of dust."

Bel let her leg slide down and fall to the floor, and she leaned forward with careful intention, joining her hands slowly. "Oh, something much, much worse."

Once the details were hammered out, Bel rejected a handshake, and Lena sneered at the suggestion of a contract signed in blood, but the imp accepted Matt's offer of various binding wards and incantations that would prevent either side from going back on their agreement. Then Matt muttered some words they all knew were nonsense, made some glyphs in the air that glowed and said nothing, and everyone nodded solemnly to demonstrate their commitment to the farce.

The imp teleported back to the space above the stone slab, and the circle there began to glow again. "I look forward to completing our bargain in Sydney, Australia in three weeks' time," he said, and then the stone melted and pulled him back to his own dimension with the wretched, wet sound of something solid being caught and pulled through a tube made to suck liquid.

"Aw, that was nice of him," Matt said.

"What was?" Lena asked.

"His parting gift. Either he isn't really looking forward to seeing us or he was hinting that our next meeting would not be in Sydney and/or will not be in three weeks."

Lena frowned. "It's not much of a gift."

"No, but if he'd only said he was looking forward to our next meeting, that would have been the lie and an insulting one," Matt said. "He's a piece of shit, and that was as close as he can come to politeness."

"Aw," Tina said, tilting her head and looking at Napoleon.

The skeleton mirrored her affectionate gesture.

Then Tina sneered at the stone and made a fart sound.

"I think the deepest level of our freedom is being able to change our identity."

-Olga Tokarczuk

Chapter 25

Matt clapped his hands and then rubbed them together. "This is going to take some magic and some teamwork," he said. "And really, isn't teamwork just another kind of magic?""

Tina rolled her eyes. "Should I throw up over the side or right here on your boat?"

The group stood on the front deck of the *Exclamation*, peering out over the railing at the estuary where the

Colorado River ran into the Gulf of Mexico. Isla Montague, the 32 kilometer long island sitting like a bite of dry tortilla in the river's mouth, lay to their left, which Matt demanded they call "port." On their right, the coastline of Baja California rose up to scrub brush and low, distant rocks, a mottled beach that became a desert with a division as invisible as the magical line between the freshwater of the Colorado and salt water of the gulf.

"It's not a boat," Matt said. "It's a ship. Ships carry boats. Boats don't carry ships."

"But tugboats push ships and ships don't push tugboats, so which is really more impressive?" Bel asked.

"Remember that tiny tugboat pushing that huge tanker through the Strait of Gibraltar?" Lena asked. "Now that was impressive. Way more impressive than any ship I've ever seen."

"Yes, well, just more evidence that there's no accounting for taste," Matt said. "So, here's the way this will work. I'm going to cast a spell that will make Joseph glow. You all use your supernatural night vision eyes to spot the glow, and then we'll go find him. I expect he'll be somewhere here in the estuary."

"Why here?"

"I tossed him in the Grand Canyon, but he isn't there anymore. I checked. So then I went and got some advice from our magical friend, and he reminded me that magic likes liminal spaces. The gloaming between night and day. The equinoxes. Thin places in the world where other worlds can sometimes pierce through. And estuaries where rivers and oceans meet. They naturally make

326

something called a 'salt wedge' because the salt water is denser, so it's pushed up by the rising land, but the lighter fresh water rides out of the mouth of the river on top of the salt water. In the tide, it gets mixed in, but there's this space where it's cloudy and bumpy as the salinity evens out. That's on the straight physics side. Hydrodynamics? Chemistry? I don't know. The science-y side. But I'm persuaded this is the best place to look for Josef. If it fell into the part of the Colorado that runs through the Grand Canyon, maybe whatever magic of mine and magic of Josef's decided it needed to be in the river until the river isn't a river, and that's here."

"That's sound logic," Lena said.

Bel frowned. "It is?"

"'Sound,'" Lena repeated. "Like Puget Sound. A smaller body of water connected to a larger body of water. 'Sound logic.'"

Bel turned to Napoleon and spoke in Spanish instead of German so Lena would understand: "*Intraducible retruécano que no está chistoso,*" which means "Untranslatable pun which isn't funny."

Tina elbowed Matt. "These two turn into dust at dawn, so let's get this show on the road."

Matt nodded and started his incantation, a series of hand gestures and words in foreign languages that looked to Tina like a video that would make sense in someone else's TikTok algorithm. As Matt's hands continued through their motions, they began to create letters in the air in a sickly, glowing green. These weren't in any language Tina could identify, but clearly they were important because the warlock painted them in the air with precision. His frown deepened as he worked, and his concentration began to rob from the glamour he wore to pretend he was a young man. Wrinkles appeared on his frowning face which had nothing to do with the expression. His thick blond hair wavered, became transparent, and then revealed the baldness beneath, covered in liver spots and dry, pale skin. His arms and chest lost their musculature, the flesh sagging, the skin on his forearms revealing a network of blue veins. The circles under his eyes turned pale, then blue, then purple, and then fell into black pits around rheumy, bloodshot, yellow eyes.

Tina stared, entranced by the transformation, smiling mischievously at the warlock's secret revealed, his vanity punctured. She noted his concentration and bit back the urge to tease him. It would be even better later on.

Lena walked immediately to the prow, leaned over the railing, and started scanning the water below. Bel joined her, bumping her with her hip to announce her presence but otherwise copying her concentration. The water had the lumpy look Matt had mentioned, and the light of the night's crescent moon played on those indentations, but otherwise the surface was a black mirror of the night sky.

No glow.

Nothing.

Tina joined them, and once his spell was complete, Matt came up, too. The *Exclamation* moved slowly through the water. Behind them, up on the bridge,

Captain Summerfield held the wheel still and focused on the depth finder telling her how much room she had before running aground. The gulf could reach depths of over 14,000 feet, but the Colorado River was only ten feet deep in its most shallow points. The *Exclamation*, a 130-foot superyacht, had a seven-foot draft, less than people might have expected, but enough that the captain had to be careful to stay at the deepest point of the river's mouth.

The four of them looked down into the water, scanning back and forth. Each one felt her eyes catching on the reflection of the moon, the only light in the water, then chiding herself, dismissing it, and moving on, back and forth, as the ship chugged through the shallows.

Napoleon's bones clicked as he approached, but Tina, Bel, Matt, and Lena all refused to allow the sound to break their concentration. When Napoleon's dry, scratchy finger bones wrapped around the inside of Lena's upper arm, she started at the touch but continued to scan the water.

"Hey, Napoleon," she said absently.

He pulled gently.

She turned to look at him.

Napoleon pointed.

"Dammit," she said. "Y'all, Napoleon beat us to it."

The other three followed her gaze, first to Napoleon, then down the line of his still outstretched arm.

Out beyond the black water, on the patch of beach where the river curved as it made its way around both sides of the island, a 20-foot-wide circle of sand gleamed green like it was coated in the goo in the witches' glowsticks.

Matt shouted back towards the bridge. "Captain, have someone ready the tender!"

"Prepped and ready to go, Mr. Bern!"

He waved the others toward the back of the ship with excited, flapping hands. "C'mon, c'mon, c'mon," he said, then pointed at Napoleon. "Good job. Not sure how you did that without eyes, but you win, my friend."

Napoleon loved this, and he responded with a huge smile which looked just like his face all the time.

The sailor drove the tender, a heavy-duty inflatable boat with an outboard motor, right up onto the sand, just a few feet from dry land. She got out and tried to pull the boat all the way up but couldn't budge it with the weight of four complete bodies and a skeleton inside.

"It's okay," Matt said. "We can get our shoes wet. Thank you, Cecelia."

They climbed out, splashed through the last few feet, and walked over to the glowing patch of the beach.

"Do you think he'll still believe he's under orders to kill us?" Lena asked.

"I think better safe than sorry," Matt said. "Give me a second. This will be a lot to move." The warlock closed his eyes, held his hands out like he was calling for the ball on a basketball court, and muttered some words.

Then he moved his hands closer together, the basketball sized space between shrinking to a softball.

In front of them, the glowing patch lifted into a sphere floating above a pit. The shallow pit was the full twenty feet wide, but the floating ball was only ten feet across. Still, it took a massive amount of effort for Matt to hold it aloft. The ten-foot sphere contained 31,415.9 gallons of sand and weighed almost 400,000 pounds.

"He's ... heavy," Matt gasped. He levitated the sphere off to one side of the pit, not any closer to himself, but not any further. Then he let it rest on the sand by the pit, but he kept it contained in its prison. "Does someone want to knock and see if he's home?" Matt asked, the strain obvious in his voice.

Lena had been entranced by the sight, but she shook herself awake. "Sure!" She ran up to the sphere at a superhuman speed, stopped on a dime right in front of it, then rapped her knuckles on the magical surface. It had about as much give as glass and made a similar, hollow sound. "Josef? Are you there? It's Lena."

At first, nothing happened. Then the form in the sphere began to resolve into a roughly humanoid shape, though the legs ended in a single pool of sand at the base of the ball. In order to reduce its size down to its normal shape with all that material, Josef had to make itself as dense as rock. Most of its body was the normal beige, but the sandstone was striated with the green glow Matt created to find the golem. The green lines, concentrated like the rest of the sand, now shone with shocking brightness. They weren't shaped like human veins but like the uneven lines in sedimentary stone, only arranged vertically like the lines of tree bark, making Josef look slightly like a magical tree.

It also looked very angry.

Josef had no eyes, but the space where human eyes would be were filled with the strong glow, and though it lacked most facial features, its heavy brow was so pronounced, the vertical glowing lines on its surface bulged as they wrapped over the brow before straightening up its forehead. Josef stared down at Lena for a moment, then reared back and punched the interior of the sphere.

The magic held, but Matt staggered, and Bel had to catch him. The sound of the impact rolled across the empty beach, and an echo like thunder bounced back from the distant foothills of the Sierra Madres.

Lena ducked and remained crouched, worried the next punch would break through and crush her. "Josef, it's me!" she shouted. "It's Lena! You're free. We got the imp to set you free. You don't have to follow Apraxis' orders anymore. You don't have to follow Cassius' orders. You don't have to fight. We can let you free. Just promise not to kill us."

Josef reared back for another punch, then stopped. The golem froze like a statue while it processed. It felt for that external control. It rolled its shoulders, then its neck. It wiggled the three fingers and thumb of each of its huge hands. Then it reached into its chest for the tiny notebook and golf pencil it kept there. It poked around, searching, and found nothing. Without the notebook or a mouth, communication was complicated. Josef tried writing on the inside of the sphere with its index finger. The sand fell away as soon as he allowed it to leave his body, but Lena made out the letters.

"Free?" it wrote.

"Yes!" she yelled through the magic orb. "Yes, you're free. Can we let you out? Will you promise not to hurt us?"

The golem's heavy eyebrow nearly disappeared into its smooth face, and its glowing eyes widened like it would cry if it could. Josef nodded vigorously.

"Oh, thank you." Matt's voice was an exhalation of exhaustion, and he lowered his arms and flopped against Bel.

The orb dissolved like a soap bubble filmed in slow motion and popped from the highest point. Josef let most of the sand fall behind him, expelling all the glowing material which was already losing Matt's magic and dimming like green coals in a dying fire. Instead, Josef picked up some of the fresh, clean, dry sand as he strode two steps toward Lena and wrapped her in one of his huge, gentle, scratchy hugs.

"Oh, Josef, I've missed you so much," Lena said. Her throat clenched like she might sob.

Josef patted the curls on top of her head, his "Me, too."

As it held her, the golem looked over her head at the monsters who'd accompanied her. Because Bel was holding Matt, Josef knew the warlock who'd imprisoned it was no longer a threat. It recognized Tina from Camp Bigfoot and gave her a little wave. And then it saw

Napoleon. Using the same kind of spiritual echolocation it used to identify the physical world without eyes, it read the skeleton's bones and the spirit which animated them. It tried to identify the skeleton's origin, to know it in that theological way Josef knew the grains of sand on the beach.

The frown of Josef's eyebrow returned so fast it might as well have made a popping sound.

"Oh shit," Bel said.

"What?" Lena asked, turning slightly without releasing Josef from her embrace.

But before she could see the look on Bel's face, before she could identify what had caused Josef to flex against her, before she could figure out what Bel had just realized, Josef turned itself into a dust cloud, floated around her, and reconstituted itself over Napoleon.

As Josef came out of Fight or Flight Mode (which, for a golem who could turn invisible, travel as a cloud of dust, and pulverize just about anything it could punch, might better be called Fly, Vanish, or Destroy mode, but that loses the alliteration), it not only identified its friends (and former foes) on the beach, but it began to remember its own identity, as well. Tracing back further than the last battle in The Venetian Hotel and Casino in Las Vegas, it remembered the time it had spent in hiding with Lena in Costa Rica, the journey there from Paris, the hectic adventure through England, Scotland, Wales, and Ireland, its recruitment in America by the Archduke of the vampires, and the long, peaceful underwater journey trudging along the floor of the Atlantic ocean. And then it remembered the attic of the Old New Synagogue in Prague, its conjuration by the rabbis, and, once all the congregants had been taken away on the trains, its commission by the youngest Rabbi to go out and get revenge on all Nazis for the murder of the golem's people.

And now, right there on the beach with its friends, stood the reanimated skeleton of a Nazi soldier.

Josef reared back to smash the skeleton. Tina had done the math faster than Bel, and she jumped between them, her arms up. "Whoa, Josef! He's not what he seems to be."

Napoleon crouched and held his forearms up over his head protectively.

Lena and Bel rushed to either side of Josef. Bel grabbed the arm that still hung at its side and hugged it like a child with a teddy bear. Lena couldn't easily reach Josef's fist, but she put her palms to his chest and shoulder and pushed. It didn't move him physically, but it could feel the pressure, and that was enough to stall it.

Josef's rage could not be so easily contained. When it didn't punch, the anger leaked as a whirlwind. The wind on the beach swirled around their feet, and the heavy grains of sand and small pebbles pelted the vampires and the werewolf, stinging their exposed skin. Matt, who hadn't even attempted to charge Josef or capture it again with his magic so depleted, could only stumble backwards with his eyes protected in the crook of one elbow, his other hand holding the collar of his golf shirt up over his nose so he could breathe through the fabric.

Tina, the tallest of the women restraining Josef despite her age, reached up and took Josef's face in her hands. "Josef!" she shouted. "Just wait. Let's talk. Talk it out. Okay? Use our words?"

Josef remembered the SS officer it had killed in Long Island. Josef had been able to linger for a moment because the 94-year-old man couldn't have even made an attempt at an escape. Josef looked down at the cowering skeleton. On the broad, empty beach in the middle of the night, the skeleton had nowhere to run. Still, just to be on the safe side, Josef extended some of its body through the sand beneath them and grabbed both of Napoleon's feet, encasing them in conical stone pillars that rose past Napoleon's kneecaps.

Josef relaxed.

The sand in the air fell suddenly, a gentle rain-patter sound followed by silence.

Bel had a wide scratch on her cheek where she'd pressed her face against Josef's arm, and Lena had some minor scrapes on her shoulder and upper back where the space above her tank top was exposed to flying sand, but these were already healing. Matt stood up straight, removing his face from his shirt, and brushed the sand out of his hair with his fingers, reminding Lena, Bel, and Tina to do the same. Tina felt her greatest injury was the sand in her mouth that she couldn't seem to spit out.

"Goddamit, Josef," Tina said.

"No," Lena chided her. "No, thank you Josef. Thank you for trying to protect us, and thank you for calming down and listening to us."

"Yeah, and thanks a lot for the sand in my mouth, you walking dirt clod," Tina said, but her heart wasn't in it, so she took a few steps away, sat heavily, and started removing her 15-hole boots to dump out the sand inside. When even that proved frustrating, she unzipped her jeans, pulled her shirt over her head like it was on fire, and turned into a wolf so she could step out of her pants and boots more easily. Then she picked up her clothes with her teeth by placing her shirt on her pants, picking both up and biting the tops of both boots. She carried the whole pile over to the tender, leaping up to keep a dragging pant leg from touching the water. Once in the tender, she sat, looked out over the water dramatically, then laid her head down over crossed paws, sulking.

Lena continued trying to engage with Josef. "Napoleon here is our friend. We found him in Paris, so yes, he was created by Nigel Marion, but he's not fighting us. He's on our side now."

Josef squatted down, spread out his hands, and brushed a large patch of the beach into a smooth surface. Then, with one finger, he wrote, "Not Napoleon."

Bel put a hand on Josef's shoulder and stared beyond him at his missive. "Well, not the French emperor. We know that. We had to give him a name, and we found him in Paris, so Lena named him Napoleon."

Josef shook his head sternly. "Ludwig," he wrote. "German. Nazi."

"No shit?" Lena said. She turned to Napoleon. "Did you know that?"

The skeleton shrugged and shook his head.

"German?"

He shrugged again.

"It makes sense," Bel said. "He understands German and Spanish. Probably was stationed in Spain during the beginning of the civil war there, then sent to occupied France."

Napoleon shrugged again.

Lena put her hand on Josef's shoulder. "But Napoleon doesn't remember his life before the necromancer raised him from the dead. It's a fresh start. A blank slate. He's an all-new person, now."

Josef considered this, nodding its head very slowly, then shaking it. It roughly smoothed the sand, tossing out a wave of peppery dismissal. "Nazis don't get excuses," it wrote.

Bel came around the homunculus and placed a hand on the side of its face. "I agree, okay? I agree. But where is the line, Josef? If Napoleon were Ludwig, and he'd made those choices, there would be no excuses. But where is the line? Napoleon isn't Ludwig. He just has Ludwig's bones. He doesn't remember Ludwig's life, just Ludwig's languages. He's not even sure where or when he learned them. They just share some molecules. If you reconstituted yourself with the sand that had been under a Nazi's fingernails during Rommel's campaign in North Africa, would that make you a Nazi?" She sighed. "I understand the principle. The old punk quote: 'If you let one Nazi into your bar, it's a Nazi bar.' I get it. And I appreciate that you've decided not to let a Nazi decide when he's a Nazi. I respect that, too. But it's the sorites paradox, Josef." Bel reached down and scooped up some sand into her palm, then held it in front of the golem's face. "When is a heap of sand no longer a heap?" She turned her hand and dumped most of it out, then leveled it and cupped it until the few remaining grains joined, a tiny mountain just big enough to cover the space between her palm's heart line and head line. "Still a heap?" She blew into her palm until all but a few grains remained. "Still a heap?"

Josef nodded slowly.

Lena moved her hand from Josef's shoulder to the back of its neck. "None of us are perfect. I kill innocent people for food. You at least try to kill bad people. I've given up on separating the wheat from the chaff. I'm not a god of judgment, just a monster who needs to eat. So you're a lot better than I am. But you're not killing me. Please don't kill Napoleon."

The golem nodded again, still undecided, but resigning itself.

"Hey, Josef," Tina shouted from the boat. She'd returned to her human form and climbed back into her clothes, and she was in the process of banging one of her boots against the side of the rubber craft to dump the last of the sand out. "I say you pull a Dread Pirate Roberts on him."

Josef frowned, then sent her an exaggerated shrug.

"Tell him you'll most likely kill him in the morning. Then just keep telling him you'll kill him tomorrow. He's coming with us. If you get a whiff of some fascist shit, you can always crush him later."

Josef cocked his head to the side, a subconscious reaction to considering an idea provided by a canine friend, and then he stood, wheeled on Napoleon, and released the skeleton's legs from their concrete prisons. Josef pointed two of its massive sausage fingers at its own eyes, then at Napoleon.

The skeleton nodded eagerly, then stepped bravely toward the massive stone creature, wrapped his thin arms around Josef's middle, and gave the golem a hug.

"He's a hugger," Matt explained. Then he turned to Lena and Bel. "Well, now we have Josef, so …" He threw his arms wide and boomed, "'Strangers from distant lands, friends of old, you have been summoned here to answer the threat of Mordor. Middle Earth stands upon the brink of destruction; none can escape it. You will unite or you will fall. Each race is bound to this fate, this one doom.'"

"Don't," Lena pleaded.

"We shall be known as … The Fellowship of the Thing!"

"The thing?" Tina asked. "What thing?"

"The thing we need to do. Whatever this thing is. We don't know that part yet."

"Nope!" Lena declared. "I hate it. I hate it so much. Weasel words, Matt. Thing. Stuff. Might as well be 'The Group of the Event.' 'The Gang of the Phenomenon.'"

"'Phenomenon" doesn't rhyme with 'ring,'" Matt said.

"That's just a fact. You can't argue with that," Bel said.

Lena whirled on Bel. "What are you doing? Don't help

him! Didn't you want to kill him yesterday."

Bel nodded to Tina. "I'll most likely kill him in the morning." She smiled at Lena. "I had no idea weasel words bothered you so much. It's adorable."

"They're writers' bane. They cause me physical pain even if I'm the one writing them."

"'Fellowship of the Thing' it is, then," Tina said.

"You people are monsters!" Lena cried.

Matt raised a hand in the air and headed to the little boat. "Fellowship, to me! Let's away on our quest for the stuff we need to get in order to do the thing we need to do!"

Lena trudged after him. "You all suck."

Chapter 26

In the first days of Torreblanca's recovery, she rose slowly, made her way down to the dining room, ate soup, walked to the bathroom, then made it back into her bed. Other than these thrice daily rituals, she slept, and her body did all the work without her immediate supervision. But as she healed, she started to move faster. Long introduced solid food. Their conversations lengthened. In the mornings and evenings, instead of sleeping all the time, she lingered in the living room. He didn't have a TV, but he offered to read to her, and when she agreed, he got excited about the prospect of introducing her to Asian literature. It turned out he could translate so quickly, it sounded like he was reading it in English. Torreblanca, who was bilingual, couldn't imagine picking up a text in English or Spanish and reading it aloud in her other language with such fluency. Long chose passages in Mandarin, Cantonese, Thai, Malay, Khmer, Hindi, Lao, Dzongkha, and Burmese. He did have to stop, but that was to explain elements of the historical and cultural contexts necessary for her to understand the text, not to translate them. Torreblanca assumed this was a magical power rather than a skill, since no human could possibly translate so smoothly, and in a way she was correct; it had taken Long thousands of years to master so many languages, time that wouldn't have been available to the greatest of human geniuses.

Torreblanca was aware Long was a dragon. Esau had briefly described Long's intervention at the previous year's annual meeting of The Convention of Fiends. But she couldn't wrap her mind around it, and she was reluctant to ask directly. Clearly, he could change his appearance. When she'd first met him, he looked like an old, potbellied pensioner. Now he looked like a thirty-something movie star. She convinced herself the dragon part of his persona was a different illusion of some kind. It was easiest to conceive of this handsome, younger human man as the "real" Long. He was the one she saw each day. When unusual signs would hint at some other form, like the dancing lights when he'd squeeze his true self through a doorway, Torreblanca would dismiss flickering gold waves or reinterpret them as his aura. She'd never believed in auras before, but this was an easier pill to swallow.

As her stomach wound healed and the pain faded, Torreblanca developed two serious complications. One was boredom. Long's story hour was nice, but Torreblanca wanted to feel like she was doing something. Her years in the military had taught her a lot about managing hurry-up-and-wait. She'd developed routines, shows she liked to rewatch, drills to keep her senses honed, a collection of social media accounts she liked to check in on. None of those were available to her in Long's house.

Also, as a soldier, she always had the promise of action in the future. But now she wondered if she'd ever get back to the life she loved. She found herself longing for the promise of an ambush, for 60 seconds of terror and adrenaline, for muzzle flashes in the darkness. She knew this was unhealthy, an addiction she'd need to work through with a half dozen therapists once she retired, but Torreblanca was only 32 and didn't have a plan for the next phase of her life yet.

When she was in the military, she hadn't planned on dying in the sandbox, but she didn't know what kind of job she wanted when she got home. She hated the idea of law enforcement, and everything else seemed like even more of a desk job. She'd considered wildland firefighting before learning about private military contractor work. While she was in, she'd sneered at the mercenaries who did her job for the highest bidder. But the prospect of losing her sense of the family of a platoon made her reconsider. And then she'd been hired by Esau, and life hadn't been boring since. Until now.

Torreblanca' second complication nagged at her in only two circumstances: when Long was around, and when Long wasn't around. Unfortunately for her, those were her only two circumstances. Put bluntly, she was horny. This wasn't unrelated to her boredom. She'd always been sex positive and averse to commitment. When she was in the service, she slept with about half of the straight guys in her platoon, and with rotations in and out, that was a lot. The guys tended to appreciate her free-wheeling attitude until they developed feelings for her or were inconvenienced when she gave her time to someone else, and then they called her a slut and glared at her in the mess and made sure everyone knew they were there first. Torreblanca couldn't deny this hurt, but she'd learned to balance it against their sunny dispositions on the front end. When it came right down to it, if she had to be their half-favorite, half-enemy so she could get her own needs met, she could live with the hate. She knew it was sexist and unfair, but she wasn't an activist, just the kind of feminist most women she knew became eventually: Aware and exhausted and powering through the bullshit.

Torreblanca' relationship with Esau was rooted, in large part, in his ability to see beyond her gender and sexual reputation among the men. He recognized her competence and talent, and he saw her sex drive as ancillary and largely irrelevant. Their friendship was never that of peers, but it wasn't quite the hierarchical one she'd learned in the military. He outranked her, but he was a mentor, a big brother, a confidant (though always one sided since he kept so much from her). He never coddled her, and he always treated her with respect. She hadn't guessed his sexual orientation before his emotional baggage exploded in their faces the year before, but somehow she knew he would never hit on her in a way that would make her uncomfortable, and he would never hate her for having sex when she wanted to have sex. That made him a source of safety. He told her he needed her to speak her mind, to question him about his plans, to poke holes and point out flaws.

And then she took it too far. She still felt she'd made the right call, but she'd been insubordinate in a way she never had before, and she blamed herself for the outcome as much as Esau. He shot her in the gut and tried to double-tap her in the head, and she felt he'd made the right call, or at least a completely justifiable one. Now, without Esau, Torreblanca had no job, no family, no future, and part of her reaction was to long for sex. She knew she'd need another half a dozen shrinks to help her deal with that reaction, but she also felt strongly her sexuality was not an addiction like her need for danger. Sex was healthy. Sex was fun. And she generally knew how to manage her life in such a way that her sexual behavior didn't prevent her from doing her job. She maintained healthy friendships. It didn't cause financial hardship. And, in general, it didn't produce excessive distress. It simply didn't check the boxes for an addiction. The fact that it was consuming so much of her attention now, she felt certain, was that she'd been betrayed by her best friend, then trapped in a house with no windows with a dragon. Nothing about her present situation was caused by her libido.

One evening, as Long read her a story about a demon with forty arms fighting against an army of 10,000 monkey soldiers led by the great hero Hanuman, Torreblanca interrupted.

"Long?"

He looked up from the book, expecting a question about the text.

"Do you think we could read something else tonight? I'm not in the mood for a war story."

He smiled. "Of course. What would you like?"

"How about something romantic. Maybe even erotic. Do you have anything like that?"

"Certainly. Let me see." He stood and returned the Thai text to its place on the shelf, then put his hands on his hips as he scanned the shelves. "Ah, yes, this will do." He pulled a book off the top shelf and examined it. He blew off a layer of dust from the top of the book and returned to his seat.

"Been a while?" Torreblanca asked.

"Yes, it seems I haven't touched this one in many years." He opened the book and began searching for the passage he wanted.

"Is it because you haven't been interested in romance in many years, or because you haven't had the opportunity?"

He closed the book, set it in his lap, and looked at Torreblanca. "Hmm. Chicken or egg, as you say. Maybe the opportunity would have produced the interest, and maybe the interest would have provided the opportunity."

"So you have had romances in the past?" Torreblanca asked. "With other dragons, or with human women?"

"Never with another dragon. If I had, I expect we would still be together. There aren't many of us, and we tend to mate for life. Short of some tragedy, that's forever."

"Forever is always only until a tragedy, regardless of the length of time, isn't it?"

Long nodded. "That's a good point. And that has been my experience with human women. Much shorter forevers, and then tragedy. Humans do not understand luck." He looked down at the book in his lap.

Torreblanca missed the opportunity to learn about the true nature of luck because she had something else on her mind.

"Have you ever had affairs that weren't forever-until-tragedy? Trysts? One-night stands?"

Long frowned. "Well, you see, I'm a dragon. For one thing, I'm not easy to find." He waved a hand, motioning to the room. "If someone goes to the trouble to find me here, they probably don't want me to call them an Uber the next morning."

"But you could pretend to be a human and go anywhere, right?"

"I don't think it would be right to seduce someone while pretending to be a human," Long said.

"Really? I mean, no one is fully honest in the dating game. We're all wearing masks, presenting the best version of ourselves. Sure, if you were trying to find one of your forever-until-tragedy girls, you'd want to make sure to be as honest as possible, but for a one-night stand? Be whoever you need to be." Torreblanca was mostly joking.

"Perhaps that is fine for humans. Your lives are so short. You have to figure out ways to connect more quickly, I suppose. But when it comes to love, I must be a dragon. Neither I nor my partner would be very satisfied by a night with an illusion."

"Why not?"

He frowned, then smiled. Placing his hand on his chest, he said, "This is not me. You know that."

It was not a question, but Torreblanca felt the need to nod to defend her intelligence.

"The illusion has some weight, some height, some ability to reflect light. It is a fair glamour."

"Quite a handsome one, if you don't mind my saying so," Torreblanca said.

Long smiled. "Thank you. But … and I don't mean to be crass or offensive or vain, but in the act itself, this is merely a human form. Not as impressive as the body of a dragon. Imagine you were a very talented puppeteer." He held his hands out over his knees, fingers splayed, and he twiddled them back and forth, his pinkies and thumbs dancing up and down. "You have this sexy marionette on strings. And you know you can walk into a bar and entertain someone, and she will agree to leave the bar with you and come back to your home. But when she does, she will want to make love to your marionette. And, because the marionette is so small, she will not be very happy with the choice she's made for her evening.

And because the marionette is not really you, you won't enjoy it very much, either. In fact, you will probably be angry and frustrated and not like her very much if she does prefer the marionette. Would you take your marionette to the bar with you, Anahí?"

She laughed. "No, I think I'd leave the marionette at home." Then she thought about it. "Or, maybe I'd take the marionette to the bar, but only to start the conversation, and then, once she seemed interested, I'd tell her that the real me is a lot better than the puppet." She raised an eyebrow. "That might work, you know."

"Perhaps it would."

They sat in silence until it became uncomfortable. Long picked up the book in his lap. "Shall I?"

"Sure, but our seating arrangement feels inappropriate for the book. Would you mind if I sat closer?"

"Oh, of course. I mean, of course not. That would be fine." He motioned to the space next to his seat.

This was as close as Torreblanca had ever seen the self-possessed Long come to being flustered, and she loved it. She stood.

Long expected her to move her chair. Instead, she walked over to him and sat down on his lap, throwing one leg over the arm of the wingback chair and leaning into the wing of the opposite side, her face near his. She looked down at the book. "Is this alright?"

"Certainly," he said. He had to wrap his arm around her waist to reach the book in his other hand. He tried to find his place in the book.

Torreblanca examined the text as he flipped through

the pages. She couldn't even identify the language from the symbols. They had curls and dots and slashes which didn't exist in either of the languages she knew. "You know, I've been so impressed by your ability to translate so fluidly. It doesn't even seem like you need to concentrate. It just comes so naturally for you."

"Lots of practice," Long said.

"Can you still read like that when you are distracted?" Her face was very close to his, but she made a show of examining the book.

"Hmm. Distracted how?"

She looked up and placed her lips an inch from his ear. She whispered, "Like, could you still read if someone was whispering in your ear?"

"I've never tried..."

"Try," she whispered.

"'Front curls tossed in disorder,'" he read. "'Earrings scattered / beads of sweat smearing the sandal / paste on her brow — / now her eyes droop as astride her / companion she finishes...'"

"I could do more distracting things than just whispering," Torreblanca breathed. Her lips touched the outside of his ear. She slid her hand over his chest and up the side of his neck.

"'May the face of the lady protect you...'" he tried to continue.

She placed her hand against his opposite cheek and pulled his head toward her as she touched his earlobe with her tongue. He tasted like skin and salt, smelled like rosewater and green tea, and even the hitch in his breath was human, but a bit of golden light danced in her peripheral vision.

"Vishnu, Shiva, Brahma / the gods / mean nothing.'" He let the poem's end linger in the air.

She took his earlobe between her lips, then opened her mouth and inhaled a soft gasp as she ran her tongue over the edges of the folds of his ear, testing, finding.

Long turned the page. "'Tender lip bitten she / shakes her fingers alarmed — / hisses a fierce / don't you dare and her / eyebrows leap like a vine…'"

Torreblanca kissed Long's cheekbone next to his ear, signaling her trajectory as she moved into his eyeline. Her lips pinched softly at his skin, pulling, and her hand on the other side of his face sliding up into his thick hair, her nails scratching his scalp.

"'Who steals a kiss from a / proud woman flashing her eyes / drinking amrita…'" Long continued, his voice sinking to a whisper, falling an octave to a rumble Torreblanca could feel through their pressed ribs. "'The gods — fools — / churned the ocean / for nothing.'"

She kissed his face again, moving towards his lips. Long snapped the page to the next more quickly than the antique book demanded. "'Trembling with awakened love / they dart off, / then contract into two moist buds. / An instant they shamelessly stare / a moment glisten with shy indirection.'"

Long could only read out of one eye, his other obscured by her own. Her eye was closed as she kissed the corner of his mouth, and then she moved lower, kissing his chin, feeling his jaw move as he tried desperately to finish the poem.

"'Dear girl so artless — / who is it you look at / as

though the feverish spell lodged / in your heart / had rushed to your eyes?'"

She tilted her head back and kissed his neck just under his jaw, then whispered up toward his ear. "You sound like you're a bit distracted."

"A bit," he conceded.

She thought carefully about her wording as she kissed him again. Asking him to show more than his puppet might be funny, but Torreblanca suspected it would shatter the mood. And she was digging the mood. "Want to move on from the poetry?"

"Are you certain?"

She kissed his neck again. "Yes," she said, more than certain.

"We'll have to move," he said.

"Yes."

"Upstairs."

Torreblanca did not know the living quarters contained an upstairs.

"It's a lot of stairs. I can carry you, but now it's your turn to see if you can maintain your concentration."

"I'll do my best."

He stood, lifting her effortlessly, and carried her to the door opposite the one she entered each day for her meals. He held her up with only his forearm under her back, his other curled under her knees, and opened the door she'd never thought to try. Torreblanca tried to keep up on her challenge to continue kissing his neck, but she couldn't help but steal a glance into the doorway. Beyond, she caught the hint of stone steps, gray and weathered, leading up into darkness.

Long turned her and stepped through the doorway, then turned her carefully again so he wouldn't bump her head or feet in the thin hall, and he closed the door. While he was standing in one spot closing the door, he produced no light, and when the door closed, Torreblanca was consumed by a darkness so complete, she had to blink her eyes hard to feel whether they were open or not. Then Long began to ascend, and for the first time she identified the lights around him clearly. Still faint, each glimmer was a crescent shape, glowing like the pin-hole camera images of the sun through leaves during a solar eclipse. These were more evenly spaced and provided the only light in the stairway. They grew brighter against pillars on the walls and beams above holding the stone ceiling in place, then faint in the spaces between, and Torreblanca understood she was seeing some kind of reaction as Long's invisible scales scraped against the solid world as he squeezed himself through the small space. Though he carried her smoothly, she could feel the vibrations as he climbed onto each step. His sandals made velvet hisses on the dusty rocks but did not clap. She wondered if he struggled, either with her weight, the climb, or the effort to compress his true size through the hallway. If so, she couldn't read it in his pace or his breathing. She closed her eyes again, focusing on kissing him, caressing his face, maintaining his commitment to their shared cause. The gentle bounce against each step became a constant rhythm, and she fought an urge to be lulled to sleep.

Long climbed.

And climbed.

Torreblanca had no clear sense of the length of the climb, but she imagined they would either arrive at the top of some mountain the height of a skyscraper, or they'd come out on level ground, and she'd discover his home had been a skyscraper's depth below the surface. The truth was in between.

Angkor Wat's highest tower stood 699 feet above the plane in which the temple complex was built, and Long's secret exit from his lair was on the highest floor beneath that tower, more than six hundred feet up. The top floor was divided into four courtyards, the crossing intersection between them leading to the statues of four Buddhas. Long's secret stair led up to a doorway hidden in a wall near one of these enclosures, the door's face an ornate sculpture on the other side which fit together perfectly and obscured the aperture completely when it was closed. As it opened, an observer would have discovered the spaces around the sculpture's dancing characters' elbows and bent legs were not just the carving but the rough edges of the door itself. Of course, there were no witnesses; it was late at night and the temple complex was closed. Even the guards were far away at their posts near the roads leading into the complex. They like patrolling in the rain. The monsoon season was a down time for the park, and the temple was so large, the largest religious structure in the world, that no other human breathed for miles from the courtyard where Long took Torreblanca.

When he stepped out the door, they were outside the covered, intersecting halls, so the rain fell on them immediately. Even the night temperature had fallen only into the high eighties, and the rain was almost as warm as the air. It fell in large drops which bounced so hard against the stones of the courtyard that they made a haze above the ground which caught the dim light of the moon behind thin clouds. Even this was brighter than the stairway, so Torreblanca's eye made out the shape of the space, stone and square and clearly very old, some hints of the carved walls but not enough to see them clearly, and then a brief glimpse through one of the windows which only captured the roof of the jungle's canopy as a layer of black against the sky's dark purple.

"Where are we?" she asked.

"Ah, I see you can be distracted, too. We're atop Angkor Wat, the temple in what used to be the middle of the city of Angkor, the former capital of the Khmer empire."

"You live under one of the wonders of the world?"

"It makes some of the lists, yes. It's a UNESCO World Heritage Site, and they would be very angry to discover you and I are living here, but I was here before UNESCO, so I don't feel too badly about it."

She remembered her task and kissed his neck again. "This isn't, like, sacrilegious or anything, is it? Making out in a temple?"

He could hear her mischievous grin. "Oh, I'm sure it is. Are you Buddhist?"

"No."

"Hindu?"

"No."

"Then what they don't know won't hurt them. It's my house, too, after all."

"How long have you lived here?"

"Since 1644. It was almost completely abandoned at that time, just a few Buddhist monks and an occasional pilgrim, so it seemed like a good place to relocate. My previous lair was outside of Chengdu, in the hills among the headwaters of the Min Jiang river, and when the Ming dynasty fell, Zhang Xianzhong established his Great Western Kingdom and slaughtered the humans in the villages." He stopped for a moment, and Torreblanca could tell it was the wrong time to keep kissing him. "I could have fought against his armies, but I didn't see the point. My humans had run out of all their good luck." He tried to shake off the memories. "So I decided to move to a place humans had mostly forgotten and to hope to be forgotten as well."

He set her down gently in front of him, and they stood there in the center of one of the courtyards, soaking in the rain. He took her hands. "I'm sorry, Anahí. I think I've ruined the mood. I've remembered why I left humans behind. It's not your fault. It's what I do to the people I care about. I leave them disappointed in the end. I'm a luck dragon. And luck is not what humans think it is."

Torreblanca bulldozed through her second chance to learn the true nature of luck. She squeezed his hands, then freed hers and placed them on either side of his face. "Let me be the human who reminds you why you don't always leave us behind," she said. And then she kissed him.

Her lips found his stiff and surprised, then softening and pliant. Her tongue traced the inside of his upper lip until his met hers, and then their heads tilted so they could take in more of one another. As they kissed, her hands went to work on the buttons of his shirt, and when they were all unfastened, she had to yank the wet fabric over his shoulders. When his hands came free, they grabbed for the hem of hers, and that was the only cue she needed to step back and rip it over her head. Then they fumbled at one another's waistlines, undoing the cords that held the cotton trousers up, putting fingers into the hems to pull the underwear down with the pants they stepped out of.

Torreblanca stole the same moment of the poem's Indian princess, that shameless stare and shy indirection. Long's body was not the chiseled curves of many of her previous soldier lovers, nor the dad bod of a few. What is pleasing to the eye is not most pleasing to the touch, the reason humans sculpt figures to look one way and then do not sleep against those marble replicas. Long was a pleasant compromise, thin and smooth and soft under her fingers. In the darkness, she could only make out a small patch of black hair in the middle of his chest and a bit of a happy trail; most of his body was hairless, and in the warm rain his skin was smooth and just soft enough.

It was too dark to see the form of the man very clearly, and Torreblanca knew she could discover his body better with her fingertips than her eyes. She reached between his legs and insistently pulled him where she wanted him, and as she felt him prepare, she pulled away and guided him down to the stone floor. He lay on his back, and she straddled him. She leaned forward and kissed him, brushing her chest against his and pressing her knees and toes against the rough cobbles as she positioned him to enter her.

But something felt strange, and she had to assess her body at the worst possible moment to figure out what it was. It wasn't a discomfort, she realized. It was a lack of discomfort. Her knees should have scratched against the stone. Her toes as well. She pressed her palms against his chest and rose up to stare around, first at his eyes, the whites revealing his black irises in the dark, and his teeth briefly announcing a smile. He knew she was confused and looked forward to her reaction when she put it together.

Like in the stairway, the scant light on the courtyard now came from the shimmers of gold where scales scraped on stone. Only the marks were six feet beneath her. Torreblanca's knees and toes didn't feel stone because she was elevated high above the ground on the body of the invisible dragon.

"Are you ready?" he asked.

"Yes," she hissed, urgent.

"For the real me?"

"I think so, yes."

Long's human hands played against her thighs, sliding up until they found purchase around her hips, and then he pulled her down against him. She didn't feel the penetration she expected. Instead, she felt a hardened ridge running the length of most of her erogenous zones, multiple sources of pleasure instead of the traditional one or two.

And then a lot of magic happened at once.

As her wetness encompassed him, Long became fully visible to her, and he was not a man on his back on a stone floor. He was suddenly an enormous dragon, his belly pressed to the floor, his back six feet high, his serpentine form stretched across the courtyard and up the wall, his shoulders above her, his true head turned back toward her, swaying, eyes closed. She ran her eyes along his body from his true dragon head, past the point where she straddled him, and saw his back legs up on the wall behind her, his long tail wrapping around a portion of a nearby tower. Every scale glowed with that light she'd seen before. Most were gold, but the ones nearest the ridge along his back were dark, glistening, metallic red along their edges. That spinal ridge was between her legs now, momentarily still, but when she moved herself forward, grinding against him, she felt it for the first time. As he writhed in pleasure, every scale vibrated against the one beneath it. This movement produced no sound, but the vibration was intense.

Torreblanca shouted something incoherent, surprise and pleasure, and the face of the dragon wavering in front of her smiled. He didn't look like the images of European dragons she'd seen, with bird beaks and predatory eyes. Long's lips were shaped like his human ones, full and soft but much larger, and two long whiskers formed something like a mustache beneath his nose. The nose looked more like a dog's, though gold like his lips and whiskers, and then his eyes also had something of that puppy softness, their large black irises half-lidded as he felt her move. His brow ridge and ears were the same metallic red as the line along his back. His head nodded, and the movement echoed down his body in a wave, lifting Torreblanca and moving her to one side, but slowly, not threatening to buck her off. As he moved, the friction of every scale ran with the motion, so she felt the wave coming and receding like a doppler effect. And then he moved his head again, and she could anticipate the next wave hitting. As she slid up and back toward the other side of the courtyard, she pushed into it, her palms on his back a fulcrum, her spine the joist, her pelvis pressing down as each wave struck her.

The waves formed an accelerating rhythm, and as they increased in speed, the movement of Long's spine also grew, so Torreblanca was lifted higher and higher, swung wider to each side, as he writhed beneath her, always slowly, never enough to make her lose her focus and worry about flying off, but enough that it slightly changed the direction of the impacts of the drops of rain against her bare skin, adding another source of pleasure. She threw her head back and let the rain pelt her face as she pushed herself back and forth, back and forth. The rain hid her tears, but she could feel them, her body unable to contain all the sensation, her brain converting it to emotion and expelling it as joy through her eyes.

When Torreblanca came, her back spasmed so hard, she suspected the spot where she made contact with his spine would feel bruised later, but that couldn't stop her in the moment, and she continued, holding it, gasping, then almost choking as her throat produced a high pitched sound she didn't recognize. She smiled, laughing at herself, and even that couldn't stop her, another spinal contraction slamming her again. The waves down Long's ridge began to slow, and he rested his belly on the courtyard floor again, letting her catch her breath.

She fell forward, her arms hanging limply on either side of his body, her cheek pressed against his back.

"That was …" she breathed. She tried again. "That was …" Words disappeared.

Then she remembered a question which hadn't seemed particularly relevant seconds before. She propped her head on her hand, her elbow on his back and stared forward at the face of the dragon twisted back and looking at her. "Does it feel good for you, too?"

In response, Long closed his eyes very slowly, then said, "Hmmmmm."

The vibration flowed back and tickled her awake. "Hey!" she said, laughing. "Seriously, does it do anything for you?"

"Oh, yes," the dragon said. "Just wait. You'll see."

"Wait for what?"

"The next time."

"When will that be?"

The dragon smiled. "As soon as you're ready, Anahí."

"Really?" She shot him a look with a dangerously raised eyebrow. "There's more than that?"

"Oh, so much more."

"Okay, I'll bite. Show me what you've got."

"Are you sure you're ready?" Long asked. The smile in his voice exceeded the seriousness of the question.

"Yes," she said, and it came out somewhere between a laugh and a scream.

Long closed his eyes slowly, nodded, and then turned away from her, his head climbing up the face of the wall. This motion started the vibrations of the scales again, and Torreblanca gasped. Then Long turned and followed the inside of the wall, his forearms carefully finding purchase in windows and along the roof so they wouldn't scratch the sculptures. With each movement, the vibrations began. Torreblanca could feel them starting ahead of her, racing toward her, and then passing back to Long's tail. She found the rhythm and joined in, pressing against each wave as it struck. Long, in turn, felt her pressure and warmth, her knees pressing into his flanks, her palms caressing as she pulled away and then pushing in as she leaned forwards again.

But this time, instead of moving her side to side as he undulated beneath her, Long moved her up and down. She was too focused to notice the effect at first, but with each movement, he ascended a bit off the cobbles of the courtyard. He began to circle within the space, his long, thin body encompassing the entire open room and doubling back over his own tail. Torreblanca didn't even realize she was leaning slightly inwards towards the center of this gyre because Long carefully aimed his own spine in line with her gravity, feeling her thrusts and measuring the angle he needed to keep her so the centrifugal force wouldn't toss her out of the spiral, and the centripetal force wouldn't drop her into the middle. All she could feel were the waves, but in addition to the vibrations they brought with them, each seemed to leave her higher. With barely any frame of reference in the rain and darkness, Torreblanca didn't become fully aware of the effect of these changes in elevation until her peripheral vision caught the roof of the temple and the dark forest canopy below. She looked over the side of Long's body and realized his arms and legs were no longer grabbing at part of the temple to maintain his motion. Instead, they clawed out into the wind like swimmers' hands attacking and pulling back at water. The dragon had no wings, but he didn't need them. With each undulation, he climbed higher on the air. Torreblanca was riding a dragon, and the dragon was flying.

"Don't stop," she screamed into the rain and the night. "Don't you dare stop!"

He didn't, and she didn't either.

Chapter 27

Matt rented a private jet and got them all to the airport before dawn, so they were safely ensconced, window shades down and duct-taped, before the first rays of sunshine hit the plane on the tarmac in Mexicali. The airport in Mexicali wasn't technically called the Mexicali airport. It was the Aeropuerto Internacional General Rodolfo Sánchez Taboada. Taboada was a controversial figure honored because of his success later in his career as the longest serving governor of the state of Baja

California, but dogged by the suspicion that as a young man he may have participated in the plot to assassinate Emiliano Zapata and may have even been the one to pull the trigger, killing the iconic leader of a peasant revolution. The airport was the opposite of controversial, but Matt wanted to change that, if only for a moment.

He felt wrung out by the effort to discover and then restrain Josef. He needed juice. His favorite way to produce the kind of emotional energy he liked best was to welcome tourists onto his yacht, then manipulate them until they all resented one another. Resentment is an incredibly powerful fuel because it burns slowly. Rage flares and fizzles, but if Matt could get a meal of unexpressed jealousy, suspicion, and repressed indignation, he could power his magic for months.

Sometimes he could generate a decent amount in a single evening in a bar or nightclub, charming his way into a group of friends, then innocently asking them to introduce themselves and creating a series of false hierarchies which made them suspect they were each the least valued member of the group. So many humans carried around suspicions their friends didn't really like them, and Matt found it very easy to activate these. Still, he preferred to have the time to really dial these up to eleven on the ship. The wrong friend group in a bar could leave him feeling the magical equivalent of stomach pangs if the friends couldn't be divided by a random charming stranger. The groups he brought into the confinement of a ship at sea didn't stand a chance.

Without the luxury of time, Matt needed a meal

quickly. For resentment, suspicion, and indignation, an airport was an all-you-can-eat buffet. While the rest of the Fellowship of the Thing waited on the plane, Matt went into the airport itself. He chose his mark, an older woman traveling with her son and daughter-in-law and their two young children. He set his plan into motion almost immediately. It barely took any effort at all. He had to change his glamor to look like someone else for the cameras. He picked a heavy-set man with dark, curly hair and a thin mustache, not exactly like the son of his target, but similar enough that the description would produce suspicion. Then he sauntered by the old woman and took her small, rolling suitcase. Instead of walking out of the airport, he went deeper in, walking around the line for security and nearly to the agent who glanced at passports before people stepped through the metal detector. Matt set the bag down and kept walking without breaking his stride. A few people were already sneering at him as he walked past them, the beginning of the resentment he could taste, and some of them noticed his strange deposit, though none called out immediately.

He turned back into his normal, charming, false face as he walked up to the ticket gate for one of the major airlines. In heavily English-accented tourist Spanish he said, "Excuse me, ma'am, I don't know who to talk to about this, but a man just left a bag by security, and I think it's a bomb. Who should I talk to about that?"

The woman's eyes went wide, and she grabbed a walkie-talkie on her desk, barked a name, and then said some code words. A police officer nearly ran to the desk and asked Matt to repeat the accusation.

Matt pointed at the security line, described the son of the woman he'd stolen the bag from, and explained why he thought the bag was a bomb. The officer told him to wait there and started toward security, already talking into his walkie talkie.

In minutes, the people in line were being moved back. The woman identified her bag, but that just led to more questioning. The son got angry. The kids were frightened. The man's wife tried to calm him. He got angry about that. The mother tried to explain further to defend her son. The police tried to move them away from the bag while they called in the bomb squad. The woman refused to be moved without her suitcase. The travelers all started to worry this would make them miss their planes. Some felt the woman's bag should simply be returned to her, and that the police were mishandling the whole situation. Others felt the family was suspicious, and the bag making it to the head of the line needed to be investigated. People became irritated by their fellow travelers' reactions, even their own family members.

Matt absorbed all these strong feelings until his proverbial tank was proverbially full. Then he walked out to the cab that ran him the short distance to the private entrance leading to the runway for private planes.

"That didn't take long," Lena said as he stepped aboard. Her voice was muffled because she'd thrown her sweatshirt over her face so she wouldn't get singed by the indirect light coming through the plane's door. When he closed the door, she pulled it down into her lap, making her curls quiver as they popped back into place. "Everything go okay?"

"Better than I expected, but we should get going before the whole place gets locked down." He knocked on the cabin door, gave some instructions to the pilots, then found a seat.

Tina held up a finger. "Wait," she ordered. She'd made her phone into a hotspot and was downloading shows to watch onto her laptop.

"What is it?" Matt asked.

"Wait," she repeated. She clicked through some tabs, checking the progress of different streaming services. Satisfied, she said, "Okay, all good."

"But what was it?" Matt asked.

"Nothing. Gawd." She looked at her screen and flapped her hand toward the cockpit. "Mind your business and get your little plane going," the teenager teenaged.

"Well," Matt harumphed, rolling his eyes to Lena and Bel, "this will be a fun trip."

Bel shrugged. "We're flying west, so we'll land in … what?... three days?"

Matt nodded. "It will feel longer."

The flight from Mexicali to Seattle took 10 hours. Refueling at SeaTac took less than an hour because Matt had the money to buy a spot further up in the line. The flight to Osaka took 13 hours. Another hour for refueling. Then 6 hours to Bangkok. In addition to the 31 hours in the air, the world beneath them rotated another 15 hours away, so they left after sunrise and arrived just before dawn two days later. By the time they climbed into a cab to take them from Bangkok's Suvarnabhumi Airport to their hotel downtown, despite their supernatural powers, most of them needed showers and time apart. Matt got them checked into the Sindhorn Kempinski Hotel, an opulent 5-star establishment with striking, curved architecture on the front of the off-white concrete 20-story skyscraper, contrasting with the elegant dark wood paneling in the lobby and bar on the first floor. They climbed into the elevator, Napoleon hidden in Bel's rolling suitcase, Josef transformed into a few cups of sand and voluntarily contained in a two-liter bottle in Lena's backpack along with her punctured, bloody manuscripts.

As the elevator door closed, Tina muttered, "I'm so hungry I could eat half the Thai national soccer team."

"Why don't you go get yourself a bite to eat while we sleep?" Lena asked.

"I don't feel like it."

Bel pulled her phone out of her back pocket and tapped at the screen.

Lena felt a vibration in her pocket and examined her phone.

"She doesn't want to hunt alone. Young wolf. New city," Bel's message read. "Needs pack."

"Tell you what," Lena said aloud. "If you can wait until sunset, the three of us girls will hit the town and find some people to eat, okay?"

"Red light district," Bel said. "Johns are easy marks

for three hot women who aren't going to charge them."

"Sound good?" Lena asked.

"Yeah, I guess," Tina said.

"Can I come?" Matt said. "Lots of drama for me to feed on in bars."

"Let's split up for the evening," Bel said. "Make it a girl thing for Tina."

Matt nodded. "I will pretend not to be hurt and offended."

Tina put a hand on his shoulder. "Please, Matt," she said, "don't pretend."

He pouted. "I am hurt and offended."

"Thank you."

Once in their room, Bel and Lena blocked the windows by leaning the two queen-sized mattresses against the curtains and stuffing the pillows into the space between where any sunlight might peek through. Then they enjoyed a nice, hot shower together and slept perfectly comfortably in one another's arms on the floor.

Tina tried to watch TV on the big screen in her room, but most of the offerings were in Thai or Hindi or were sports or news in English, and she wasn't interested. She used the hotel WiFi to download some more anime episodes from Crunchyroll and sulked while her stomach rumbled.

Napoleon and Josef shared a room with Matt, one Bel had insensitively referred to as the "boys' room" despite one of the occupants being nonbinary. Matt, Swiss by birth, spoke fluent German, and both Napoleon and Josef could write it, so they passed around notepads and carried on a long conversation. Napoleon couldn't remember any music he'd liked as a human, and Josef liked classical music, especially pieces that placed a heavy emphasis on stringed instruments. Matt asked Josef if they should attempt to offer Napoleon the foundation of a musical education, and Josef liked the idea very much, so the warlock and the golem spent the entire day walking the skeleton through the history of European art music, rarely veering far from the composers of that continent but finding the best examples of their work recorded by symphonies from São Paulo, Guiyang, and Cleveland.

The sun set at 6:30. Bel and Lena knocked on Tina's door.

"Ready to go?" Bel asked.

"I guess," Tina said. She was wearing her boots, a long black skirt made of light cotton, and a high-necked, long-sleeved top that showed off her belly. She'd spent almost an hour on her makeup, getting advice on her eyes from three different TikTok videos. She would never admit how much she was looking forward to the evening out.

"You look great," Lena said.

Before Tina felt she had to respond, Bel said, "Let's get a tuk-tuk and hit the Red Light district."

Tina smiled. "What's a tuk-tuk?"

"Local kind of cab. A motorcycle with a metal body that adds a couple wheels and some seats in the back. You'll see lots of them. Fun way to travel." She leaned close to the younger woman. "And the drivers will take you wherever you want, including secluded places where no one can see them. Meals on wheels."

They came out of the elevator and saw people walking into the lobby with umbrellas. The doorman accepted a few from returning guests and offered them to the women as they approached the door.

"Thank you," Bel said, accepting one.

"No, but thank you," Lena said. She was an Oregonian, and the idea of carrying an umbrella challenged her sense of self.

"Nah," Tina said.

Bel gave the man a few US dollars. He thanked her and waited until the women had left before examining the bills. Wrinkled, torn, or vandalized currency couldn't be used in Thailand, and American currency was the worst.

Outside, tuk-tuk drivers lined the semicircular drive in front of the building, and one pulled up for them before they could even step out from under the awning. As they walked around to climb in, heat lightning flashed in the sky, and all three women caught the briefest glimpse of something above the skyscrapers across the river.

"Um..." Lena said.

"Did you two just see that?" Tina asked.

"What ... the ... fuuuuuh," Bel breathed.

Lena was surprised to hear her girlfriend's reaction. "What did you see?"

"I saw a gold dragon, and ..." she looked from Lena to their teenage ward. "... and something else."

Tina raised an eyebrow. "Oh, could you see the naked

woman on the dragon's back having an orgasm in the sky?"

"I mean, maybe she was …" Bel said.

"Oh, definitely," Tina said. "Like 90% sure she was not faking."

Bel stepped away from the tuk-tuk, out into the rain, and stood there, staring, her umbrella hanging at her side.

Lena joined her. "Have you ever seen that before?"

"Nothing like that, ever. And I've seen a lot of weird shit."

"Do you think that was Long?" Lena asked. "I mean, what are the odds?"

"There aren't that many dragons in the world, so, maybe," Bel said.

"The old guy with the potbelly?" Tina asked. "Gross." She shrugged and climbed into the back of the tuk tuk. "And good for him," she muttered to herself. "Get your game on, old guy."

Bel, in passable Thai, asked the driver to take them to the Déjà Vu A Go Go Club. The driver was impressed by her knowledge of the language and the city and didn't try to come up with a longer route to raise the price. Bel hadn't been to Bangkok in twenty-five years, but she'd visited the Soi Cowboy street the last time and remembered the Déjà Vu A Go Go Club and was pleased to find it still existed.

When the tuk-tuk driver dropped them off at one edge of the street, the night was still young, and many of the dancers and other sex workers weren't out yet, but the crowd was already beginning to grow as the lights came on. Bel led the way, holding Lena's hand casually. Lena hooked her other arm in Tina's, and while Bel stalked toward their destination with aplomb, the other two women looked up at the lights and scanned the clubs with open fascination. Music already thumped out of the clubs, battling for volume dominance as they passed each entrance.

"Yeah, this place kicks ass," Tina said.

"It's fun," Bel acknowledged, almost indifferent. "Now, a noob move is to hire one of the dancers, let her take you back to a private room, and eat her there." Bel had to raise her voice slightly so the superhuman ears of her compatriots could pick up the sound of her voice over the music, though it would have been impossible for a human to make out her words clearly. Still, Lena balked at the brazen way she talked about hunting in public.

"That's a bad move," Bel explained, "because they watch the doors of those like hawks, and there are even hidden cameras in some of them to make sure the girls don't get roughed up, don't pocket the proceeds and pretend they got stiffed, and don't get murdered. You can ask them to come back to your hotel, and some will, but they have to clock out, so that creates a witness. There are other working girls who hang out in the clubs looking for johns, but the clubs are watching for them, too, because they are actively trying to steal business, so they're only slightly safer. Your best bet is to be a customer, watch the dancers, throw some money their way, and then start chatting up a john and invite him to come back to your place for free. Dollars to donuts he comes with you, you take him wherever you want, drain him there, and you can still come back for more if you're feeling peckish."

"More than one feeding in a night?" Lena asked.

"No, not really," Bel said. "No need, and every extra kill just increases the risk. Greedy vampires become dead vampires. But hunt like you want to be able to walk back in without any suspicion at all."

"Makes sense," Tina said.

"It may be trickier for you," Bel told Tina. "You'll have to find your clothes, and you can't come back into the club or back to the hotel with blood all over you."

Tina frowned. "I know how to hunt."

"True. Sorry. Here." She handed Tina a card, one she'd brought from the room with the name and address of the Sindhorn Kempinski Hotel. "In case we get separated, show this to any tuk-tuk driver and give them whatever Bhat they ask for. They'll probably overcharge you if you're alone and don't speak Thai, but it won't be too much. Just a little foreigner surcharge."

Bel wedged her fingers into the front pocket of her jeans and pulled out a stack of Thai Bhat. "This is ten times what you'll need, so see if you can break it for tips for dancers, and don't give it all to a tuk-tuk driver.

They're pretty honest here, as a general rule, and you don't haggle, just pay what's asked."

"Gotcha," Tina said. She didn't thank Bel for the money, not because she was ungrateful but because she wasn't sure if Bel might be one of those super-rich monsters who hated talking about money because they never had to think about it anymore and considered it an unworthy human game, or one of those not-rich monsters who hated talking about money because they had to think about it all the time and resented having to play human games.

They were welcomed into Déjà Vu A Go Go by a blasted rendition of a song in which a rapper complimented a woman for wearing a specific brand of jeans produced by another rapper. The referenced woman was also wearing boots with fur and sweatpants and name brand tennis shoes. So she may have been a centaur. Lena and Bel and Tina did not question this because they were occupied with their hunting. Also, Bel had met centaurs, so it was possible.

Because the club was mostly empty so early in the evening, the three women quickly found a table near the stage. The DJ garnered more attention at this hour than he would all night, and he waved his arms in the air, enjoying the beginning of night, but he was still outshone by the woman in the neon pink g-string and nothing else swinging around the pole.

Tina wasn't moved because she preferred men.

The dancer wasn't Lena's type. Her hair was long and dyed blond, and though she was clearly talented, the look in her eyes screamed a kind of desperation for a better shift, and she smelled like chipper morning energy. Lena was attracted to women with more chill.

Bel didn't find her particularly attractive because the dancer was so thin. Bel was self-conscious about her own lack of curves and preferred women with a bit more to hold onto. Still, she appreciated the woman's skill and eagerness, and she deposited an excessive amount of cash on the edge of the stage for her, purchasing a smile and a cute wink.

"Three o'clock," Tina said.

"Yours or mine?" Lena asked, but then she spotted them coming into the bar. The three young men wore over-priced Italian t-shirts and skinny jeans. One was tall and ridiculously muscular, another was short and stocky, and the third had thin arms and a goofy smile generally directed at the group's obvious leader.

Bel didn't hesitate. "Come sit with us, boys," she called in English, waving to them.

The one with the thin arms pointed at himself, surprised, then elbowed his tall friend and pointed. The tall one nodded like this happened to him all the time and led his compatriots toward the women's table.

"Hello, ladies," the muscle-bound one said. "I'm Won-Shik. This is my friend Dae-Hyun," he pointed at the thin one. "And this is my cousin, Min-jun."

"Call me Jun," the stocky one said, offering his hand to Bel.

Tina leaned past Bel and grabbed Jun's hand, shaking it and pulling him towards the seat next to her. "Nice to meet you, June," she said. "I'm Tina."

Eyebrows were raised and smiles flashed around the table at Tina's boldness. Bel turned back to Won-Shik and offered her hand. "I'm Bel."

Lena took Dae-Hyun's hand. "I'm Lena. Pleasure to meet you."

"Um, yes," Dae-Hyun stammered. "A pleasure!"

"Please, join us," Bel said, gesturing Won-Shik and Dae-Hyun to the other two seats at the table. These put their backs to the stage, and Lena was curious to see if they would turn to look at the dancer or stay laser focused on them. She wouldn't be offended, either way, since her interest wasn't romantic, but the question piqued her curiosity.

Dae-Hyun looked exclusively at Lena, Bel, and Tina, though mostly at their chests. Won-Shik threw an arm over the back of his chair and turned to examine the dancer, then made a show of turning back to telegraph his preference for his new friends. Min-jun only had eyes for Tina.

"Drinks are on me," Bel said. "What would you boys like?"

"Perhaps a rum and Coke for me?" Dae-Hyun said, glancing briefly toward Won-Shik to see if that was alright.

"How about shots," Won-Shik said. "Would you ladies like to do some shots?"

"Sounds like fun!" Lena lied with ridiculous glee, nearly screaming over the music.

Won-Shik looked pleased by the performance. Bel

shot Lena an amused half-smile. "All right then. Shots all around." She flagged down the cocktail waitress. "Six shots of your most expensive vodka, and keep them coming, please." Then she turned back to the young men at the table. "So, let me guess. College students from Seoul?"

"Busan," Won-Shik said.

"But Won-Shik grew up in Seoul," Dae-Hyun said.

"We attend Dongseo University."

Dae-Hyun pointed to himself. "Architectural engineering," he told Lena.

"Bio-Chemical engineering," Min-jun said to Tina.

Won-Shik nodded slowly and told everyone, "Business Administration and International Logistics."

Bel raised an eyebrow. "So, Shipping and Receiving?"

Won-Shik made sure to laugh loudly so Dae-Hyun and Min-jun knew he was not offended. "Yes, basically."

Bel leaned across the table and put a hand on his. "Would you say you prefer to ship or receive?" She winked and picked up one of the shot glasses, then leaned back and set it down in front of her.

Won-Shik picked up another, tossed it back, and said, "We'll have to wait and see, I suppose."

Dae-Hyun picked up two of the glasses and set one in front of Lena. "Are you all from the United States?"

Lena said, "I am."

"Canada," Tina said.

"A little bit of everywhere," Bel said. "I travel a lot for work. I've been to Korea many times."

"What line of work are you in?"

"We all work together," Bel said. "In the medical field. Have you heard of OPOs?"

Won-Shik looked at his friends who both shook their heads.

"Organ Procurement Organizations," Lena explained to Dae-Hyun. "Not-for-profits who arrange and transport biological material for transplants."

"You seem a little young for a sales executive," Min-jun said to Tina.

She laughed. "Oh, June, that's sweet. No, I'm doing my internship. I'm a junior at the University of Alberta in Edmonton."

"What a great opportunity," Jun said. "So what does the work entail? Networking hospitals together?"

"Less than you'd think," Tina said.

"Mostly finding the right donors and arranging transportation," Lena explained.

"Some days it feels like travel planning is all I do," Bel said. She waved to the waitress and had six more shots brought over. They were set down in the middle of the table, and Bel set two in front of each of the boys. "It's not as stressful as studying at Dongseo University. That's an impressive school."

"One of the highest rated in Asia," Dae-Hyun said proudly. "Very challenging, yes."

Tina took one of the glasses from in front of Min-jun, threw it back, and set a hand on his knee. "That is impressive."

"Oh, it's not that hard," Won-Shik said, punching Dae-Hyun on the shoulder softly enough to seem friendly and hard enough to make his friend wince.

"Still, I'll bet you boys have earned a relaxing long weekend off."

"Yes, I thought we should come down here, have some drinks and some fun," Won-Shik said. He picked up another shot and drank it. "Party, you know?"

"I like your thinking," Bel said. She waved over six more shots. As they arrived, she looked squarely at Won-Shik. "You know, we're looking to party, too. It's our last night in Bangkok, and we don't want to waste it. Would you three like to join us somewhere more private?"

Lena placed a hand on Dae-Hyu's. "Why waste time, right?"

"Yes, I agree," he said, then looked at Won-Shik. "Right? You guys want to go?"

"Sure," Won-Shik said, pretending to be almost indifferent.

"Hell yes," said Min-jun, and he jumped to his feet.

"Don't let these shots go to waste," Bel said. "And another round for the road."

The men each downed the shots in front of them. Bel stood just as the next round was arriving. "Okay, you guys down those, and we'll get out of here."

The young men stood, then did as ordered. They weren't wobbly yet, but Lena and Tina shared a glance, knowing it would hit them soon. They each took an arm and herded the college students out of the club.

The six of them walked to the end of the street. As they passed a different club, the sound of a K-pop song leaked out the door and caught Dae-Hyu's attention just as the alcohol gave him enough courage to sing. He began to mumble the words quietly, and then Min-jun and Won-Shik heard him and joined in. Soon they were all shouting the lyrics, off-key and out of rhythm. The group climbed into an extended cab tuk-tuk, and Bel gave the driver directions to a nearby hotel far from their own. The driver smiled at the three singing men, either enjoying it or pretending to in order to appease Bel. She decided to tip him well as an apology, but not so well he'd remember the fare as extraordinary.

Still, a witness was a witness, and Bel decided it would be best to put a little distance between the place the driver dropped them off and the location they'd end up, so after the driver left them, Bel turned to Won-Shik. "Crap. This isn't the right hotel. We're a block over. C'mon. We'll walk."

"Sure!" he said more loudly than he meant to. "I can walk fine."

"Me too," Dae-Hyun said, honestly believing Won-Shik would find this impressive. When Won-Shik didn't react, Dae-Hyun turned to Lena. "I can walk," he informed her.

"That's great," she said. "And then we'll see what else you can do."

"Long division in my head," Dae-Hyun said. "And sex stuff. I can do the sex stuff."

"He does that in his head, too," Won-Shik said, elbowing a laugh from Min-jun who hadn't been listening but knew the cue.

"Let's cut through here," Bel said, pointing down an

alley between a bank and a travel agency, both closed for the night.

Once Lena was certain no one else could see them, she said, "Can we stop for a second? I want to have a cigarette before we get to the hotel." She pulled the pack out of her pants pocket. A small lighter was hidden inside along with the remaining cigarettes. Before anyone could voice an opinion, she lit one and leaned on the wall. She scanned back and forth. Dumpsters on either end of the alley hid her from the view of anyone on either street. "Do you smoke?" she asked Dae-Hyun.

"Just at parties," he said.

"It's a very bad habit. Unsafe. C'mere and have one with me."

As Dae-Hyun followed her into the shadows, Bel took Won-Shik's arm, turned him, and pushed him gently to the wall. "We don't have to wait for the hotel, you know. Or wait on these slow smokers." She ran a hand over his chest and back down toward the button of his skinny jeans. "You don't want your friends to beat you to anything, do you? You like to be first."

Tina stepped into the shadow of the dumpster, sat down, and started taking off her boots.

Min-jun didn't know what to do. "Should I...?" He motioned to his shoes.

"Just wait a sec," Tina ordered.

"Okay, I..."

She kicked her second boot off, then pulled her shirt over her head and dropped it on her boots so it wouldn't get dirty. She stood and beckoned to him with a finger.

As he stepped toward her, she hooked her thumbs in the waist of her skirt and shimmied it down, stepping out of it, brushing some dust off the hem and the seat, and then folded it over her arm and placed it carefully on her shirt. When she straightened, Min-jun found she had not been wearing anything under the skirt. She took a long stride toward him and pressed her body against his. Too drunk to pretend to be patient, he grabbed her ass cheeks with both hands and tried to kiss her, but she dodged slightly, placing her head next to his, and whispered into his ear.

"I want you to do two things for me, June. First, look at your friends."

Min-Jun turned his head and saw Win-Shik and Dae-Hyun were making out with Bel and Lena. Both young men's heads were thrown back in pleasure as the women kissed their necks. But as Min-jun's eyes adjusted to the deeper darkness, he noticed the whites of their eyes. They were both wider than he expected, and the expressions on their faces looked more surprised than pleased. For a sluggish, drunken few seconds, Min-jun thought both his friends had ejaculated prematurely and simultaneously while they still had all their clothes on. They were quivering and breathing erratically, but neither looked pleased with his performance.

Then Bel and Lena, almost in unison, grabbed their dates' hair and repositioned their heads as the young men went wobbly at the knees and needed to be held in place so they wouldn't fall into heaps on the ground. As the women leaned away from them briefly to pin their heads to the concrete wall, Min-jun saw the fist-sized, jagged holes in their necks. Blood gurgled out to the rhythm of their slowing heartbeats.

And worse, when the women pulled away, he saw their mouths, the unhinged, extended jaws, the rows upon rows of thin, needle teeth questing for more. And then the women dove back in, their lips forming better seals so they could catch every drop.

Min-jun's scream started as a low whine and rose in pitch and volume, but he was still not screaming at his full volume when Tina pressed her hand to his mouth. "No, I didn't tell you to scream, Jun. The second thing I need you to do is to run as fast as you can."

His voice disappeared as she took her hand off his mouth and stepped away from him, then fell forward. He wasn't sure which way to run, so he was still standing there when a thick coat of black fur sprang from her back. From all fours, she looked up at him, and her upper and lower jaws jutted out in a lurching, uneven motion that made a crunching sound before they resolved into a snout which joined her elongating nose.

Tina peeled back her lips and growled at Min-jun. He decided the best direction was directly away from her, so his first steps launched him into a gallop that sent him bouncing off the alley's far wall before he straightened out.

He made it to within twenty feet of the road, close enough to be visible if anyone had been looking, before the wolf leapt onto his back and sunk her teeth into the muscle between his shoulder and neck. Her speed and momentum kept her going forwards, but her teeth held, so she spun around him as he fell. Without dislodging her fangs, she shook him once, so hard his head hit the asphalt, and he saw stars. Too dazed to scream, Min-jun could only groan as the wolf danced sideways and began dragging him back into the alley.

As Tina neared the dumpsters, Min-jun recovered enough to begin to make too much noise, so she released his shoulder, let him scramble up onto his hands and knees, and then she sank her teeth into his throat. She shook him again, this time tearing more flesh, effectively silencing him, but Min-jun was still alive when she rolled him over, placed her paws on his shoulders, and began biting his abdomen, yanking out feet of intestine with one bite, driving deeper to pull out the lower part of his right lung with the next, chewing a cavity toward his still beating heart, her favorite part of a meal if she could get there soon enough. Min-jun wasn't conscious when she'd consumed enough of his entrails to get there, but his young, healthy heart still made its last feeble effort, and she was more than satisfied by her dinner.

Matt and Napoleon were startled by the loud knock on their hotel room door, but Josef had expected it and finished writing its reply to Matt's contention that Dvořák's contribution to classical music was just as significant as Mozart's. Josef found this absurd to the point of being offensive and kept flipping the pages of the little hotel notepad as it composed multiple pages of examples of Mozart's influence. The little golf pencil Josef carried wasn't up to the task, and Josef stored it away in its chest, replacing it with the hotel pen which seemed to only release ink out of one side of the ball, meaning Josef's essay was written as divots and valleys in the paper as much as ink.

Matt, who had completely forgotten his claim about Dvořák and Mozart and had no idea what Josef was still writing about, stood and opened the door.

The women in the hallway were glowing with satisfaction. They'd cleaned up and changed clothes, focusing on comfort. Tina wore yoga pants and an oversized Taylor Swift t-shirt. Lena was back in her Costa Rica clothes, the very same green cargo shorts she'd been wearing the day he met her, and a simple ribbed tank top. Bel didn't modify her style for the Bangkok heat, wearing her normal black jeans, boots and punk t-shirt, this one advertising the Alkaline Trio. All three looked happy and sated.

"Get your shoes on, kids," Bel said. "It's time to go to the library!"

Chapter 28

The MBK Center, a mall in the heart of Bangkok, nestled between office towers and a stop for the elevated train. Eight stories tall and containing 2000 stores, it was the largest shopping center in all of Asia when it was built. A cavernous atrium beneath an enormous glass ceiling softened the blinding equatorial sun to a cream-colored light. A hundred thousand people visited each day. That was a major part of the reason The Convention of Fiends decided to build the mall in the first place. If a shopper or two went missing at the mall, it wasn't that noticeable. The guests had no idea they were visiting a fast-food restaurant attached to a much larger institution.

The construction of The Great Monster Library began in 1784, shortly after King Rama I decided to move the capital to the small hamlet that would become the megalopolis of 11 million people. The Convention of Fiends chose the location because Thailand seemed likely to remain stable, had a growing population to keep the staff fed, and had the kind of weather lots of monsters enjoyed. The heat and humidity kept the jungles lush just beyond every tilled rice field, and those dense forests provided the preferred homes and hunting grounds for many kinds of monsters. As the city grew, the library attracted staff who preferred an urban environment. It also continued to acquire books and other documents important to monsterdom. When Bel first visited in the mid-1800s, the library already sank seven stories into the ground, a remarkable feat of architecture, engineering, and magic in a country where the water table not only flooded basements but frequently flooded the streets as well.

Bel led The Fellowship of the Thing to a restricted employee entrance into the MBK mall, then to an elevator guarded by a troll glamoured to look like private security. After enduring some obligatory and half-hearted insults from the troll (who really couldn't help himself but didn't get anything out of it if a monster, rather than a human, were outraged by his slurs), they climbed into the stainless-steel box and dropped 26 stories down into the muddy earth. The doors opened on the bottom floor (though construction was already underway on three new floors below). The group walked out beyond the overhanging balcony ringing the second floor (the 25th from the surface), and the monsters looked up. Those who could speak gasped audibly. Napoleon's jaw fell open and hung there as his ocular cavities widened to the exact same size they always were. Even Josef looked awed. Though the golem had no mouth or nose, its thick eyebrow ridge rose higher on its forehead, and it blinked its sandstone eyelids over its sandstone eyes.

The rings of each story were perfect circles, each with a perimeter greater than two football fields. A floor contained only a single row of bookshelves running all the way around and from floor to ceiling, with ladders on tracks making the higher books accessible on each. The shelves, each holding an average of seventy books per foot, were made of a dark local teak, so a polished ring of darkness marked the interior surface of each floor. The ceilings and floors, all polished white marble reflecting the lights in the ceiling, filled each ring with a bright glow. Each floor held roughly 91,000 books. Though a few human libraries had larger collections, when Lena, Bel, and Tina looked up with their superhuman vision at the 25 stories above them, they could see the spines of more than two million books, more than any human library had on display from a single vantagepoint. The ceiling was decorated with a fake glass skylight in front of electric lights, creating the illusion of the same glowing, cream colored ceiling the mall above enjoyed during the day, even though it was 3am.

In addition to the staggering sight of so many books,

the central space of the library was decorated with an inverted fountain, a waterfall of four streams of water coming in from the four points of the compass, arcing out from apertures near the ceiling above the 26th floor and curving down toward the center of the colossal space, then twisting in ways that defied gravity, spiraling around one another like water manipulated into unnatural shapes by intense sonic waves, only without any sound at all. The rivulets of water changed slowly, spiraling around one another, then curving out to create round and diamond-shaped designs, then changing course again to land in the center of a wide, shallow reflecting pool. No human library would have dared to risk an art installation involving water so close to precious, ancient books, but monsters had the benefit of magic protecting the books, even managing the room's humidity, and the effect of the piece was stunning.

The group of newcomers walked out into the main atrium, and the four who possessed noses were struck by the scent. The mixture of the fountain and the books created a variation of petrichor and old books. If such a smell existed in the human world, it would precede the smell of moldering, ruined books, but because of the magic of the library, this unique smell could exist in perpetuity.

All six of them walked in looping paths while they stared up at the rings of light and darkness and books upon books upon books. Bel, Lena, Matt, and Tina breathed like bellows, taking great lungfuls through their noses while they spun around. It took a monumental distraction to produce a rare event wherein someone could sneak up on hyper-sensitive superhuman monsters.

"It's actually even more impressive than it looks," a quiet voice said.

The six of them spun on the speaker and her two colleagues who had approached without making a sound.

"Holy-shit-you scared me!" Bel said. "Dammit, Lydia." And then she beamed and reached out to give the woman a hug.

Three women stood shoulder to shoulder before the awestruck gawkers. All three were shorter than Lena, the shortest of the Fellowship. Two wore glasses, while the third had a pair on a chain around her neck. All three were strikingly beautiful. Lydia, the one in the middle, looked like she was the tallest, but that was just because her afro, currently picked out and dyed hot pink, made her a few inches taller. Lena identified all three women as vampires because of the perfection of their skin. Tina pegged them as vampires by smell. Matt knew by some magical art. Josef knew because he could feel the way their muscles vibrated, taut and ready to spring, while they stood perfectly still. Napoleon had no idea.

Lena also suspected Lydia was a lesbian and might have had a previous relationship with Bel because of the way the women held one another. She thought it would make sense and might reveal a bit about Bel's type, since Lydia was Black and a little on the thicker side just like she was.

Bel stepped back to introduce them. "Lena, this is Lydia. Lydia, this is my girlfriend, Lena."

"Nice to meet you," Lena said, offering her hand. Before Bel could introduce the other two, Lena decided to ask, if circuitously. "Were you two …?"

"Don't worry. We're a throuple, and we were already together when we met Bel," said Kate, the white woman to Lydia's right. She was the one whose glasses hung from a chain on her neck. None of them needed the glasses to see, of course, but they liked leaning into the aesthetic of the hot librarians.

Lydia's glasses had bright orange frames that clashed with her matching pink hair and lipstick. She'd ascended to that level of punk.

Jacqui's cat's eye frames were black, like her hair. She was more apple-cheeked than her partners, and when she looked at Bel, her right cheek pinched her eye in a wink that repeated a few times, then stopped. She looked at Lena, winked in the same way, and then said. "I'm not winking … (twitching)… at your girlfriend." Her head ticked to the side and back. "I have Tourette's. I might be winking at you, though… (hot) … You're hot."

Lena didn't know how to respond to that at all. She considered offering some kind of expression of condolences, like the woman had revealed she had cancer, and then she realized that was impossible for a vampire. "But…"

"Yeah, I know. Vampire with Tourette's You're thinking … (awk) … (ward) … thinking it should have cleared up when I was … (bite) … turned. I thought so, too, and I was pretty pissed about it for like twenty years … (piss) … and then I finally understood that turning just makes you into the most attractive version of yourself so you can hunt … (feed) … effectively. I'm the hottest lesbian vampire librarian with Tourette's in the world, and I've ack … " She halted and twitched again, then finished, "accepted that."

"Frankly, that's rad," Lena said.

"Right? … (rad) … (closet)," Jacqui said.

"Yes," Bel said, "we never dated, but there was one night. Do you all remember that?"

"How could we forget?" Lydia laughed.

Kate crossed between Lydia and Bel and put her hand on Lena's forearm. "It was not a big deal. Nothing romantic."

"We'd been hunting, and it was fun, so we were all a little, you know," Bel said.

"Twitterpated?" Lydia tried.

"Aflutter?" Jacqui said.

"But we'd left a bit of a mess, and may have been spotted, so we had to hide in a closet," Kate recounted.

Jacqui twitched and said, "(Janitor)" under her breath.

Lydia swung her hand around at the wrist. "Yes, a big janitor's closet, but still a small space for four people to hide. And one thing led to another, and…"

"And some of us are not very good at staying quiet in certain situations," Kate admitted.

"And not just the one of us with Tourette's," Jacqui said. "I'm a talker. Kate's a screamer."

"So, as you'd expect, the janitor opened the door," Bel said.

"Not what he expected. I will never forget the look on his face," Lydia said.

"Like three seconds. Shocked and then considering

and then all-in," Kate said.

Jacqui nodded. "Like he'd died and gone to heaven."

Lydia shrugged. "I mean…"

"He just got the order backwards," Jacqui said.

Lydia nodded sagely. "Good times. So, what brings you all to the Library of the Convention of Fiends?"

"Lydia, we interrupted introductions with our nostalgic tales of yore." Kate said. She turned to the others. "I'm Kate."

"I'm Jacqui."

"We're the librarians. As Lydia was alluding to when she startled you all, we're really the most impressive thing about this marvelous institution."

"No matter how many pieces … in the collection, a library is only as good as its librarians," Jacqui said.

Lydia agreed. "We have a huge collection of materials, but you'll find we are the ones who make this place useful, accessible, and welcoming. So, welcome." She looked at Tina.

The young woman wasn't sure how to respond. "Thank you," she said. "I'm Tina. Werewolf. Canadian."

Kate shook her hand, then turned to Matt.

"Matt Bern. Warlock. Originally from Switzerland."

Jacqui shook Josef's hand, then waited patiently while it pulled the notepad out of its chest, wrote with its little pencil, and showed her.

"Josef. Golem from Poland," she read to her colleagues. "Welcome, Josef."

Lydia took a step toward Napoleon. He gave her a hug.

"Oh, okay? Hello. Nice to meet you," she said.

Josef handed the notepad to Napoleon. The skeleton drew a line beneath Josef's introduction, then scribbled his own and handed the pad to Lydia.

"Napoleon. Skeleton. Origin a subject of some debate," she translated his German. She looked up into the skeleton's sockets. "Oh, is that why you've come to us?"

Napoleon looked to his compatriots.

"No, we have an issue that's a bit more pressing," Matt said. "Napoleon's identity is less of a mystery and more of an ontological question, and we have a quandary with more immediate consequences. Potentially. Maybe. You see, we are The Fellowship of the Thing, and we are on a quest."

Lena rolled her eyes and made a choking noise.

The librarians caught Lena's reaction, looked at one another, and Kate asked Matt, "A quest to find what?"

"The Thing," Matt said. "We don't know what it is. That's why we're here."

Kate looked at Lena and raised a skeptical eyebrow, but Jacqui clapped her hands together and then rubbed them up and down. "Ooo, this sounds like my kind of puzzle!"

Matt looked at the others. "May I?"

"Do your thing," Lena said.

The warlock leapt up onto the marble bench that ringed the fountain in the middle of the atrium. "Story time!"

"The trouble with life isn't that there is no answer, it's that there are so many answers."
-Ruth Benedict

Chapter 29

The emissary suddenly lowered his hands. "At this point we'd have an expositional monologue that reminds the viewers about how this group got together and what they're after. So you're going to need to get a really charismatic actor to play the part of Matt. Someone sexy enough that people would want to watch him with the sound off. And the writing will have to be punchy. Lots of jokes. Focus group, A-B tested editing. That kind of thing."

Carol looked at her boss. "Do we even need it?"

Mr. Joyce shrugged. "He's probably right. The

average viewer will need a reminder."

Kim said, "Hell, I need a reminder."

"The three witches," Carol said. "They sent Matt."

Joyce frowned. "Not the same as the librarians."

"Totally different characters." Carol looked at the emissary. "Can they be joined? You have a lot of characters for people to keep track of."

The emissary looked at the ceiling. "The Weird Sisters McElroy as the librarians in The Great Monster Library? I hadn't thought of that."

Kim shook their head. "I like the lesbian vampires."

Joyce turned to them. "Could they replace the witches?"

Kim tossed that to the emissary with a questioning stare.

The emissary shrugged. "Vampires can't teleport onto a yacht in broad daylight, so it would take some re-writing, and you'd lose the cinematographic shots of the sun on the water and the magical bubbles floating over the ocean…" He looked at the producer's expressions. "But sure, we could workshop that. But then we lose the librarians helping to solve the mystery."

"What's the mystery, again?" Joyce asked.

"Well, at this point, The Fellowship of the Thing—"

Joyce interrupted, turning to Carol. "Is that going to be a copyright problem?"

"Should be fine. Satire law supersedes some elements of copyright."

"The Fellowship of the Thing," the emissary continued, "still thought Tisina was going to attack with an army, and they still thought their job was to stop the invasion."

"Tisina is the queen who died at the beginning," Joyce reminded himself.

"Yeah, she gave birth to the big monster and then sent it to attack the humans, and then her people turned on her for offering them up as sacrifices to her larger plan," Kim said.

"People do hate that," Carol joked. Joyce didn't laugh, so she got serious. "Audiences will approve of her murder."

"But there's also the bad vampire," Joyce said. "What's his name?"

"Cassius."

"Right. And the human bad guy."

"Esau isn't exactly a bad guy. He's just passionate and heartbroken and manipulated," the emissary said.

"Tragic backstory. Got it."

The emissary frowned. "I don't know if I'd call it tragic. Relationships are complicated, and they don't always work out. Every couple is a system, and when one party is a monster, that doesn't necessarily mean anyone is to blame..." He caught their expressions again. "But yes, sad, and it turned him into a super-duper-monster killer, so, tragic backstory."

"And he's with the Cassius guy now, and there's a dragon who is having sex with a human. It seems like a lot of threads."

"Ah, yes, but it's all starting to come together, thanks to Hanuman, the monkey soldier."

"Who?" Carol asked. "Have we met that character before?"

"No. Hanuman is fictional. Doesn't exist. But the librarians figure out the connection. Come to think of it, maybe we could plug in an animated sequence when they tell the whole story. Something really artsy. High quality but not done in a realistic style. Or maybe a dramatized flashback, I don't know. Even with CGI, that could be expensive. Anyway, the librarians take some time to do their research, and so maybe a montage or some dissolves or something, and then they're right back at the fountain with the findings."

Carol caught Kim's eye and tapped her watch. Kim pointed to Joyce with an eyebrow.

Joyce leaned forward. "I like it. What did they find?"

"There is no real ending. It's just the place where you stop the story."

-Frank Herbert

Chapter 30

The Fellowship of the Thing spent hours wandering around the library, but they didn't accomplish much. Lena, the only writer in the group, spent her time admiring the early editions of the portion of the collection written in English, including a first edition of *Pride and Prejudice*, one of her all-time favorites, and a bound stack of pages which must have been Mary Shelley's original draft and notes for *Frankenstien* because they were handwritten, brutally marked up, and hastily scrawled in a young woman's looping, severely angled cursive. Whole paragraphs were struck through with multiple vertical lines leading to horizontal ones where the writer wanted her original to continue. Lena admired the strategy and discovered newfound respect for a book she'd always considered flowery and overwritten.

Bel could read so many more languages than her partner, so she wandered through different levels, pulling down books about life in far-flung cities she'd visited, reminiscing about the social intrigue that seemed all-important to the long dead writers and was now, judging by the light layers of dust on the books, only of interest to an 800-year-old vampire. She didn't find anything related to their current quest, but then she didn't even know where to start, so she indulged in a walk down memory lane as she sauntered around level after level of the library.

Josef, predictably, sought out texts of Talmudic scholarship. It was disappointed to find the library concerned itself more with cabalistic magic than Biblical exegesis, but it found an interesting volume on methods of textual analysis, squatted down so its lower half was a conical pile of sand, and read diligently while the others explored.

Matt recognized an opportunity and went straight to some of the magical tomes located on the top three floors. He found a copy of one of his favorite texts, *Δημήτριος' τις οδηγίες του όχι πολύ ωραίου τύπου για να μάθεις απαγορευμένα πράγματα*, the title of which roughly translated to *Dimitrios the Not-Very-Nice-Guy's Instructions to Learn Forbidden Things*.

To increase his own sales, Dimitrios had made sure

the spells in the book only worked properly if a warlock had a copy of the book in hand. The ancient wizard was very clear about this in the forward, but many a magic users over the ages had tried to ignore the warning and recite the incantations without holding the book. The curse started with a painful stomachache and diarrhea, but if that didn't stop the careless wizard, the results worsened until the wizard did to himself what J. K. Rowling did to her legacy. Magic and wisdom are not universally concurrent. Matt carried the book open in one hand as he recited the spell, as Dimitrios instructed. Other books floated out of their shelves towards him, opened, and revealed spells which, thanks to Dimitrios' incantation, Matt instantly memorized for later use. This was the brilliance of Dimitrios' cursed text: It allowed the user to memorize spells but couldn't be memorized itself. Without Dimitrios magic tome, the spell-gathering spell wouldn't work.

Using the book inside the library was a stroke of brilliance. The books with forbidden and useful spells came from all around the atrium, on different floors, and floated to Matt as he walked around a single ring. Unfortunately for the librarians, when Matt was finished with each one, it fell behind him, leaving a trail of discarded books they'd need to reshelve in their proper places. Unfortunately for Matt, the center of the atrium was occupied by an ornate waterfall fountain, so when the books floated to him, one of them passed directly under a stream of water. The brief interruption caused a break in the interlacing threads as they fell and a splash of water which missed the pool 23 stories below. The librarians, who were engaged in research on various floors, all stopped what they were doing and ran to the railings to look up at him. Their jaws dropped, their rows of spiney teeth popped out, and they hissed like pissed-off cats.

"Sorry," Matt shouted. "Um, my bad. I have a spell that can repair the wet book. I'll get on that right away. Sorry. Sorry!"

Matt then spent the rest of the time repairing the book he'd damaged and using magic to discover the proper locations of the other volumes he'd dropped behind him, and he still wasn't certain this would prevent the vampires from killing him when they'd finished their work.

Napoleon tried to do some research on necromancy and the relationship between reanimated skeletons and their former human selves, but he couldn't find a single story of a skeleton remaining animated and autonomous after the necromancer was killed, so no one had been able to make even the most casual observations of a monster like him, let alone perform any kind of rigorous study or do any interviewing. He did uncover some entries about the Priory of the Brothers of Saint Quentin of Amiens, the monastery where the monks had all turned into necromancers in the 1300s. This, Napoleon surmised, was where Nigel Marion, the necromancer responsible for reanimating him, had lived and trained before venturing out into the world in search of a way to wipe out most of humanity to keep the priory a secret.

Napoleon figured they must have learned how to deal with necromancers dying in the past and would know what happened to their skeletons after a brother of the priory kicked the bucket himself. He figured Bel and Lena could take him there and get some answers, maybe with the help of the rest of the Fellowship, but he knew that was a pursuit for another day.

Tina found some manga written and illustrated by monsters, for monsters. She sat down with her back against the shelf and started to read one. To her surprise, the series had very little gore or sex. Instead, it focused on a group of monsters of various kinds struggling to form romantic relationships with one another while remaining hidden in the human world. It was instantly her new favorite book ever. She sped through the first in the series, grabbed the second, and was just starting the third when the librarians called them all to gather by the fountain on the bottom floor. Tina brought the book with her in case the conversation got boring.

The librarians brought three chairs over from a nearby reading table, set them in a semicircle, and motioned to the visitors to sit on the bench surrounding the fountain.

"Okay, I think we figured it out," Lydia said.

"Really?" Matt gawped. "That's amazing!"

Kate shrugged. "We're librarians."

"We can do amazing things when people aren't soaking our books… (asshole)," Jacqui said. She stared at him. Her cheek ticked eloquently.

"Sorry. I got it all dried out good as new. I mean, returned to exactly the condition it was in before I arrived, not a bit newer or younger."

"Anyway, have you all heard of Hanuman?"

"The monkey guy on the beer?" Bel asked.

"That's him." Lydia turned to the others. "Hanuman is a famous and popular character here. Super strong and powerful. There's a beer named after him."

"He's like the local Superman," Kate said.

Lydia gave her girlfriend a skeptical look. "More like Thor. Modern character based on a mythological character."

Kate nodded. "I can see that."

"Hanuman is a character from ancient Hindu mythology. He's in lots of stories and does all these incredible things. He's a deity himself, and he's revered because of his devotion to Rama."

"He's first mentioned in a song written between 1500 and 1200 BCE," Kate said. "But in that version, he's just a silly little monkey, not a great hero. That will be important later."

"Hanuman has crazy powers," Lydia continued. "He can grow to the size of a mountain and shrink down to the size of an ant. He's immortal. He's super-strong, so strong he picks up the Himalayas at one point. He carries an army in his mouth once. He can heal any disease. And he's a shapeshifter. He's way over-powered. Like all the X-Men and Avengers in one guy."

"So we need to find Hanuman?" Lena asked.

"No," Jacqui said. "Totally fictional."

"There are lots of monkey men characters in lots of Hindu stories," Kate said, "and Hanuman himself is worshiped by Hindus and humans of other religions, as well. But from what we can find, there aren't any monkey soldiers and never have been."

"No weremonkeys," Jacqui said. "Kind of a bummer."

"Okay, so no Hanuman," Bel said.

"Right!" Lydia said, getting excited. "Now, have any of you ever heard of Suvannamaccha?"

"A what?" Matt asked.

"A who. She was a mermaid princess. So, in the story of Suvannamaccha and Hanuman, this goddess, Sita, is kidnapped, and her husband, Rama, asks his best pal Hanuman to build a bridge from India to Sri Lanka so they can attack the island and rescue his wife. So Hanuman gets a bunch of monkey soldiers together."

"They're called the Vanara," Kate added.

"Right, so the Vanara start throwing giant boulders into the ocean to build this bridge," Lydia said. "And they keep doing that for days, but the bridge isn't rising to the surface because something under the water is moving the rocks."

"So Hanuman swims down into the water to see what is going on, and he watches as a bunch of mermaids take the most recent boulder to fall on the seafloor, and they move it somewhere else."

"The story doesn't say where they move it," Jacqui interjected. "Not in any version. I checked."

"So our superhero, Hanuman, watches this operation, and he notices the mermaid who is in charge," Lydia continued. "That's Suvannamaccha. And she's beautiful, of course."

"And a boss, which is hot," Kate said.

"Right. So he swims over to her, starts chatting her up, asks for her digits or whatever, and they get together. And they hook up, and he gets her pregnant. And then, after they have been pretty intimate for people who have not revealed their identities to one another, he finds out she's the daughter of the demon who did the kidnapping, and she finds out he's the right-hand man of the god trying to rescue his wife."

Jacqui picked up the story from there. "And Suvannamaccha isn't down with kidnapping. She just thought she was protecting her father's land from an invasion of hostile warriors. So when she learns what's really going on, she not only promises to stop stealing dude's rocks, but she orders the mermaids to put them all back and build the bridge."

Kate shook her head. "We never hear the mermaid workers' feelings about this, but I would have been pissed. 'Wreck this bridge. Nope, changed my mind. Build this bridge.' I'd demand a raise, personally."

"So they build the bridge, Hanuman and his army rescue the goddess Sita, and Hanuman and Suvannamaccha part on good terms." Lydia made a yadda-yadda gesture. "She later has a son, Macchanu, and he's a superhero, too, but that's irrelevant to your situation here."

"Okay," Lena said. "You said there was no Hanuman, no monkey soldiers, so is any of this story true?"

"All myths are true and false," Lydia said. "The X-Men are about marginalized communities. Superman is about an immigrant trying to assimilate and bring what is valued to his new home without frightening them with what is foreign to them. Iron Man is about the superficial strength of physical might and wealth compromised by hidden interior fragility. Those are all true stories and fictional, right?"

"Lydia's go-tos are always comic book examples," Jacqui said.

"I'm a Blerd! Never tried to hide it."

"But the same relationship between truth and lies is in any good story," Kate said. "Herakles is about the tension between obeisance to the gods while also striving for immortality, about atonement for sins, about attempting to do the seemingly impossible."

Matt nodded sagely. "Labors to atone for sins. I completely identify with Herakles."

Bel rolled her eyes. "So what is the Hanuman story really about?"

"Well, human scholars had lots of theories, but ours might be a lot more one-to-one. Remember when I said the first reference to Hanuman was a poem where he was just a silly monkey? Then we start to see images of Hanuman where he has four distinct faces and a human body. So we got to thinking, instead of representing Hanuman's shape-shifting abilities, what if this was a way to represent a real shapeshifter."

"And one of those faces is pretty clearly a dragon," Lydia said. "So, a dragon with a human body could be a representation of a dragon in its human form."

Tina sat up straight, closing her manga novel in her

lap. "Like Long?"

Lena told the librarians, "We know a dragon. He seemed human when I met him, and he introduced himself as Long."

The librarians laughed out loud. When she'd composed herself, Kate said, "Lóng is Mandarin for 'dragon.'" She pronounced the word correctly.

"Yeah, but I didn't know that at the time."

"So here's our theory, based on some other sources we were able to piece together. The human scholars didn't know dragons exist, and they didn't know Merfolk exist, so they were not likely to see the connections. But there are dragons, and sometimes they take on a group of people and protect them. And we know the Merfolk hate the humans because they feel entitled to the surface world. According to Merfolk mythology, at some point a mermaid princess was seduced by a human and betrayed the Merfolk, giving the human the magic of the Merfolk, and preventing them from taking the land until some future Merperson would complete a prophecy, give birth to a messiah, and that great leader would reclaim the magic that was stolen and use it to retake the surface world."

"So the human who took the magic wasn't human!" Tina said.

"It makes a lot more sense that it was a dragon, right?" Jacqui said. "A dragon could be in human form or in its dragon form and go into the ocean. … (monkey) … And then the people who forgot the details would take a character from another story, a silly monkey, and turn him into that dragon."

"Hence, Hanuman. Dragon headed dude becomes monkey headed dude becomes the monkey from the poem but with superpowers."

"So there's an army of Merpeople heading to attack Long?"

"Maybe, but I don't think so," Kate said.

"I'm not convinced of this theory," Lydia said.

"What's the theory?" Matt asked.

"Merpeople politics," Lydia said. "We looked up the prophecy, and it's vague about some things, as all prophecies are, but it's very clear about others. It says that the queen of the Merfolk has to get these two magic items, and then she has to put the beautiful one under her bed and she'll have this perfect messiah, but if she puts the ugly one under her bed, she'll have a monster, and if she puts both under there, she'll have both."

Kate said, "But in the prophecy, it's very clear that the queen is a direct descendent of the mermaid princess who was seduced by the human—"

"Who we now think was a dragon," Lydia interrupted.

"Right, but there's all this text about how the mermaid queen will be the kind of virtuous character who would choose to only use the good spell. Tisina, the current queen of the Merfolk, isn't even a mermaid. The nation of the Merfolk is composed of a coalition of the gorgons, the Merpeople, and the sirens. There's been a lot of backstabbing and coups and wrangling for the throne. By all accounts, Tisina is ruthless and unhinged."

"See, this is why I disagree with this theory," Lydia said. "For one thing, if we can accept that a human in one story and a monkey in another is really a dragon, why can't a mermaid really be a gorgon? Also, this whole part about the mermaid queen being virtuous to balance out the betraying mermaid sounds to me like the Eve/Mary, virgin/whore dichotomy. And how much of the reputation Tisina has is just men deciding that a woman who manages to stay in power must be cruel and crazy because she does the very same things that would be accepted if a man did them?"

"Fine, let's game it out," Kate said. "Maybe you're right, and Tisina is the character from the prophecy, and the details about her being a gorgon don't matter, and she is only described as virtuous because that's the sexist trope they wanted her to fill. So she is what, leading the army herself? Or she only conceived the messiah character, and that person is leading an invasion force? Or she conceived both, and there's a monster and some great military general leading an army of Merfolk?"

"She had the benefit of the prophecy," Jacqui said. "I can't imagine she's that stupid … (dumbass)... she'd risk conceiving both if she knew better?"

"People aren't always rational. Who knows what she's thinking? If the prophecy is so specific about the queen needing to be a mermaid rather than a gorgon, maybe she wasn't able to conceive at all. It might be Tisina herself who comes ashore. The key is that we think we know where she's headed."

"Where?" Matt asked eagerly.

"There's a dragon living under Angkor Wat. Not sure which one, but based on our research, it's a dragon who has previously taken on villages of humans as its protectorate, once in eastern China, and, get this, once in Rameswaram."

"Where's that?" Tina asked.

Lena was grateful to have a young friend who hadn't had hundreds of years to learn geography and languages because she'd never heard of Rameswaram, either.

"It's the area of India that's on one side of the bridge to Sri Lanka."

"That bridge is real?" Lena asked.

"Not built by monkeys or dragons or mermaids, but it exists now, yes. Built in the early 1900s by humans. But still, if there was a conflict with Merfolk, and if the story says it happened between India and Sri Lanka, and we've got a dragon who once lived right there, and that dragon now lives in Angkor Wat, it stands to reason that's where Tisina is headed."

"Or, at least, it's the best lead you've got."

"Any sense of a timeline?" Bel asked. "Some prophecy that says it will be on the third full moon after the second Tuesday of whenever?"

Jacqui shook her head. "No, nothing like that."

"So this could be years from now." Bel looked at Matt. "Cassius was just wheeling and dealing with Tisina last year, right?" Then, to Lena: "The King of Trolls said we'd meet her, but he didn't say when. If she just had twins, they're babies, right? She's not going to invade with an army led by two babies. We have time."

"Maybe, but we don't know that. The witches made it sound like this was imminent," Lena said. "I think we need to get over to Angkor Wat and see if we can find this dragon, ASAP. Especially when we might find out it's not the right dragon and we have to find another. Or the dragon wasn't a monkey soldier after all. No offense, but that's not guaranteed."

The librarians acknowledged this in their own ways. Kate smiled and nodded. Lydia frowned and shrugged. Jacqui twitched and hid whether she was offended or not. She'd grown very talented at using her uncontrolled reactions to control her reactions.

Matt raised his hand, but only as high as his chin, a sheepish gesture.

"What?" Bel asked, irritated.

"We know who lives under Angkor Wat."

"We do?" Lena asked.

"We know because I know. I'm prevented from saying who it is, but you know that, so you know who it is, too."

"Ah," Tina said. "Clever. Okay, let's go find the dumpy old Chinese guy who is having dragon sex in the sky with the human."

The librarians looked at one another, and then Lydia leaned forward. "When you are finished, I'm going to need you to come back and tell us that story."

Jacqui added, "You know. For research."

"The temptation, as I write this, is to go back, put you there in that shelter, / to that first moment of unconscious breath and before the last, // to imagine you there with the sky in no hurry / and the palms and frost // and how it might, finally, go on forever this way, / with you here. // Christ, just one more breath, I would say. / I would say."

-Joshua Robbins

Chapter 31

The city of Vũng Tàu, on the coast of Vietnam, was part industrial port, part tropical paradise. Ships laden with cargo passed beyond its wide, Pacific-facing beach, just within sight of the admiring vacationers, then turned around the horn at the edge of the isthmus to head into the industrial shipyard and heavy port on the other side of the city facing the mouth of the Mekong delta. It would have been a slightly shorter trip if any of them could have climbed up onto land, crossed through the city, and docked on the back side, but ships don't have that option.

Lord Varr did.

The six-year-old blond girl ran up the beach, her four-year-old sister following close behind. "Daddy, look at that boat!"

"Liv, how do you run like that in this heat? You're so fast!" Oliver Johnson said. Even hiding under the umbrella and sipping a sweating beer out of a bottle, he felt like he might faint, but his daughters seemed to have infinite energy. "Remember to drink some water, okay, girls?"

"I'm fast, too!" Charlotte said.

"You're very fast," Oliver said. "You've earned some water." He handed his younger daughter a plastic bottle, and she tossed it back, spilling it down her cheeks.

Oliver turned to his wife. "Maybe we should always have Char eat and drink in a swimsuit outdoors. No cleanup."

Victoria Johnson laughed at the implication her husband regularly took part in cleaning up when the girls made messes, but Oliver thought she appreciated his joke. Victoria was grateful Oliver had brought them all on this holiday, even if he wasn't going to win Father of the Year. They'd argued about the wisdom of visiting during the monsoon season. For one thing, it meant taking Liv out of school for two weeks. Oliver said that didn't matter much in grade 1, and Victoria thought that was a terrible message to send about the importance of education. She also thought they'd spend the entire time trapped in their hotel room watching Vietnamese TV while it poured outside. Oliver assured her it only rained for an hour or two each day, and the costs of the flights and hotel would be so much cheaper, it made the minor inconvenience worthwhile. Not only was he right about the length of the daily downpours, but she had to admit she found it refreshing to get rained on at the hottest time of the day each afternoon. The girls were at an age when they could entertain themselves on the beach all day. Victoria doled out sunscreen and drank daiquiris. So far, she'd read an excellent romance novel, a thoroughly mediocre literary novel a friend kept recommending, and was now making her way through a BritLit classic she'd pretended to have read during university. She hadn't been looking forward to the trip, and now she wished they could postpone their return to suburban Brisbane for a few months.

"Daddy, look at the boat!" Olivia shouted again, this time with a hint of frustration. "It's sinking!"

"What's that?" Oliver looked out the way his daughter was pointing. "Which boat?" He saw a variety of boats out on the water, some small fishing vessels, a dining cruise vessel of some kind, and, further out, some tankers and cargo ships. He couldn't clearly distinguish those. He just knew they were the big ones. He figured Olivia was referencing one of the smaller boats near the shore, and he scanned them. They all looked fine to him, but he noticed some fisherman standing very still in their boat, poles hanging at their sides, staring out toward the horizon. "Vicky, do you see what Liv is talking about? Your eyes are better than mine."

Victoria suspected Oliver was trying to redirect the girls to her, and she lowered her book reluctantly, but when she looked over at her husband, he was scanning the horizon in a way that wasn't designed to humor the girls. She followed his eyes, trying to see what they were all talking about.

One of the ships looked off. While it should have been a roughly horizontal rectangle resting just below the horizon, the front half of it seemed to be angled slightly up out of the water. Worse, Victoria judged the angle to be increasing, like the ship was bending at the middle.

"Do you see the boat, Mommy?"

"Yes, Liv dear. I think I see the one you're talking about," she said.

"Which one?" Oliver asked. They were all staring, now.

Victoria leaned sideways toward him and began to point, but before he could sight down her arm, the ship grabbed his attention when its center lowered fully into the water, and its prow and stern rose up like the wings of a V. Then, just when it seemed impossible it could remain in that position, like it must plunge into the water as an arrow pointed to the sea floor, or the sides must break off because they were cantilever skyscrapers with no support, the oil inside the tanker caught fire, and the center exploded, pushing each half of the ship away. The sound, a loud, low, wet whump, reached the beach a second later. One half of the ship sank immediately. The other skipped on the top of the water, then plunged more slowly, some air needing to escape from its tanks before it could complete its journey.

Eyes wide, Oliver looked up and down the beach to see if other vacationers had caught the same sight. The sound had roused everyone. People laying on towels climbed to their feet, shaded their eyes, and looked out to sea for the thunder's origin. The few who had witnessed the sinking pointed and tried to explain.

"Blimey," Oliver said, and he was surprised by his own conversational tone. Some part of his brain told him he ought to be screaming, and he looked at his wife for confirmation.

Victoria returned his wide-eyed stare. She reached forward and pulled both the girls closer.

"What, Mommy?" Charlotte asked.

"I don't know, dear," Victoria mumbled.

"And what's that?" Olivia said, pointing again.

This time Oliver trusted his daughter's vision and insight more than his own. He dropped a knee into the sand, leaned his head over Olivia's shoulder, and peered down her arm. "What do you see, honey?"

"That bump," she said.

He recognized the elevated area, a distended hill moving on top of the water in front of the explosion. With no additional pressure to keep the fuel contained, the bulbous clouds of fire had collapsed into a flat patch of flame on the surface, nearly invisible at their distance, just a reflection of the sun on the water in the wrong place and time for the hour of the day. Even the thin wisp of smoke barely gave away the position of the explosion, but it created a frame of reference for the bubble passing in front of it. Oliver thought it was moving slowly north of them.

"Blimey," he repeated. "Vicky, do you see it?"

"The bump?"

"Yeah. It's moving north. See? The smoke is on its right, and it's getting further from the smoke, so it's moving north."

"It's getting bigger, too," Olivia said.

Oliver peered at it more carefully and decided she was right.

She was not.

"Bloody hell, Ollie," Vicky said. "It's not getting bigger. It's getting closer. And it's moving fast."

Oliver started to panic. He grabbed the towel on his chair, lunged for the one on his wife's, and wrapped up the book she was reading in it, throwing it all under his arm. He took Olivia's hand. "C'mon. We need to go," he said. Then he looked at his beer and tried to figure out how he could take it, too. He didn't want to drink it. He just felt compelled to grab everything before he started running.

"Where?" Victoria almost shouted.

She wasn't trying to be critical, but Oliver was in no state to tell the difference. "I don't know. Away from that. Back to the hotel."

They'd been married long enough for Victoria to hear his misunderstanding and modulate her tone. She put a hand on his forearm. "Ollie, wait. It's going toward the hotel. C'mon. Let's go that way." She pointed to the south with a tilt of her head. Then she reached down and picked up Charlotte, so he didn't have a chance to argue.

"Okay, yeah," he said, and then muttered, "yeah, yeah," as he began to pull Olivia along next to him.

Soon they were almost jogging. Olivia ran, her high, bouncy steps launching her up out of the sand while her father's heavy footfalls slowed him. He felt momentarily insane as he realized she would soon be faster than he was. He smiled, then let out a quick, hysterical laugh at the absurdity of the timing of the revelation. Still smiling, he turned back to see how far behind him Victoria had fallen. She was only a meter behind, kicking up a lot of sand as she half-ran, half-walked while carrying a lanky, frightened four-year-old. Charlotte had her face buried in the crook of her mother's neck. Victoria accidentally bonked Charlotte on the top of the head with her jaw as she mistook Oliver's look back for a glance behind her and followed his eyes. That allowed both to see Lord Varr's landfall.

Measuring animal intelligence is difficult if not impossible for humans, since they cannot help but presume characteristics mirroring their own are the pinnacle of evolution, while those they don't understand are, at best, interesting quirks, and at worst completely irrelevant. Lord Varr's intelligence could not be measured by a fill-in-the-blank test, and he might not even have passed the mirror test used to evaluate whether or not an animal could distinguish its own reflection from another member of its species. Lord Varr would have smashed every mirror, leading a human to presume he had no self-awareness. Lord Varr knew he existed and knew there were none like him. He also knew mirrors were the provenance of humans, and he had been tasked with an inviolate order which was his very reason for existence. Lord Varr wanted to destroy humanity, not just individual humans but everything which represented their dominion over the surface world. He would have smashed the mirrors, then eaten the scientists.

But he was intelligent in his own way. The humans were food, their works were heretical symbols of unholy injustice, and they all needed to be destroyed. Lord Varr was committed to the long-term quest to see to it that all humans would suffer the vengeance of the Merfolk. He also knew he needed to complete the task in stages. The people on the beach were fuel, the city beyond an obstacle, but none of them could distract him from his goal.

When Lord Varr made landfall, he didn't slither like a cephalopod out of water. He didn't even race like a crab. As soon as the water became too shallow to hide his form, he leapt into the air and came crashing down on the beach, still roughly spherical, the tentacles underneath carrying the weight, the others immediately grabbing humans who stood there, staring. His claws snapped chunks out of them, cutting some in two, removing the top third of others, the legs of the lucky few.

As the Johnsons looked back, a woman stood beneath the enormous monster, providing scale. Lord Varr was over fifty feet tall, and the midday sun betrayed his round shape as the woman fell into his shadow because she stood beneath the edge of the writhing mass. She looked up and screamed as loudly as she could, so loudly she had to squat to continue forcing air from her lungs. Then, Victoria and Oliver were struck by the sudden end of the woman's note when her head and shoulders were clipped off. Her arms fell to the ground immediately, but her legs and torso slumped sideways. They didn't reach the ground before a different tentacle opened the lobster claw on its tip and scooped up the falling body.

Oliver found his eye inescapably pulled toward the bulge that traveled down the length of the tentacle, a mouse in a snake only cartoonishly fast, and then, when the bump disappeared inside the knot of tentacles, the one which had eaten grew with equal speed, its width increasing at its base and then traveling outwards like a clown's long balloon being inflated. The medium sized tentacle became one of the largest, but another, having just eaten, was growing at a similar rate. And another. And another. The largest tentacles curled under the ball, the smaller ones whipping out at the remaining beachcombers from the top. Victoria and Ollie realized it was rolling forward, up the beach, toward the resort hotel.

Oliver wanted to shout, "Run!" at the tops of his lungs to warn the people in the monster's path. An equally powerful impulse demanded he stay perfectly still and silent so the creature wouldn't turn his way. It was hard to even identify the creature's destination. It was moving in every direction at once. The motion didn't look at all mechanical or graceful. Each tentacle seemed engaged in a separate project, grabbing onto a human within reach, throwing a lawn chair, wrapping around the first palm trees at the edge of the beach to haul the mass forward. The creature's center, invisible in the nest, only turned over itself in that the tentacles that had been on the top became those on the bottom. But as Lord Varr crossed the beach and had more to grab onto, he sped up, using the trees for leverage but leaving them undamaged. In contrast, when he came across a golf cart used by hotel staff, he picked up the thousand pound conveyance and tossed it, very intentionally, at a group of people running away across the hotel parking lot.

Lord Varr reached the front of the hotel itself, picked up two parked scooters in a pair of tentacles, and swung them like the heads of hammers at the awning over the entrance. Though both were smashed and the awning cantilevered downwards, hanging on by only one of its supports, the monster recognized the scooters, with rubber tires on each end, made inefficient weapons. In another sign of its rapidly evolving intelligence, it tossed the scooters away at screaming pedestrians while grabbing the awning's remaining pillar with a different tentacle and wrenching it free. The pillar had a decorative stone facade around a metal beam core, and when pulled free, most of the stone broke away, but the brick-red steel beam, 14 feet long and over 1600 pounds, yanked away from the building, then whipped back. The tentacle flicked at the last second, sending the head of this new club crashing into the second story. The impact on the second floor pressurized the rest of the building, causing the large windows in the sliding glass doors on each room's private balcony to explode outwards. The eight-story building was taller than Lord Varr, though his height was impossible to measure accurately since the tentacles were all moving and growing with each consumed human. The glass caught the sunlight like salt shaken onto food. For a moment, Lord Varr sparkled as he took a second swing at the building, this time at the south corner. When the beam struck, the glass on Lord Varr fell away. The dust from the smashed concrete billowed out, and the monster seemed to slide into a cloud.

From down the beach, Victoria and Oliver, walking backwards, mouths agape, watched as half of the monster disappeared. Charlotte and Olivia were trying to watch, also, but Victoria covered Charlotte's eyes with a hand as she pressed her daughter's face into her chest and neck. Oliver wrapped an arm around Olivia and pulled her into his side, then remembered to block her view as well. They couldn't protect their daughters from the sounds, and even though their ears still rang from the thunderclaps of the impacts to the front of the building, they could hear screaming coming out of the dust cloud as Lord Varr's tentacles poked through the hole in the side of the hotel, sought out the people cowering in their rooms, and snapped them up, adding their mass to his tentacles' girth. All the tentacles were different sizes and lengths, some enormous and bloated, some stringy and short, each with one of those pinching claws on the end, each with a hungry mouth inside. The gestalt was so horrifyingly unnatural, Oliver and Victoria's brains couldn't make sense of it. Their eyes wanted to slide off the sight, to examine the building with its right angles and straight lines, because even in its destruction the hotel seemed more real and comprehensible than the metastasizing thing attacking it.

The tentacles snaked through the building's hallways, smashed doors, sniffed human meat, and found people under beds and in closets. On the sixth floor, Bảo, a member of the cleaning staff, crouched behind her cart of supplies in the middle of the hall. She heard the guests screaming, then silenced one by one as the inexplicable horror approached her. She remained as quiet as she could. A small claw, only a foot long and six inches high, slid past her cart, its sharp bony point a rusty red from past feedings followed by nodules of blue and green and iridescent purple like a parking-lot oil slick. Bảo trembled but held her breath as the claw passed only a few inches from her head. Then the claw opened so the mouth inside could taste the air.

The claw swung toward her. Bảo screamed and pushed away from it, her hand instinctively hammering the closest object for purchase, the corner of her cart. The sticky caster on one of the wheels saved her life, slowing one wheel enough that the front corner pinched the tentacle against the wall. The tentacle smashed the cart away, swinging over Bảo as she rolled on the thin carpet, scrambled to a crawl, then a run. She sprinted down the hall faster than she'd ever run, faster than she'd been able to move before her three children were born, faster than she'd run on the playground, faster than playing with her sisters and cousins in her grandfather's rice field. She felt wind in her hair even in the contained space of the hotel hallway. But she knew the tentacle was faster, and she had nowhere to go.

At the end of the hall, she slammed a shoulder into one of the locked guest room doors. It didn't budge. She turned and watched as the claw shot like an arrow, the tentacle floating above her overturned cart. The serrated upper and lower portion remained fixed open as it flew at her, the points aimed like flying knives. She could see the pink mouth inside, not a human mouth but an aperture surrounded by muscle tissue that could only grip and swallow meat and bone cut off by the claw. And then the claw snapped closed right in front of her face. And stopped.

It opened again, clapped shut, tried a third time, and then began snipping wildly as it was dragged backwards, the bulk of Lord Varr moving on, leaving the hotel behind. The claw swung, slamming into the right side of the hall, bouncing into the left, then up where it shattered a light fixture as it was dragged through the hole of an unhinged door and down the stairwell. Bảo heard a series of receding clanking sounds as the claw banged against the metal stair railing, then silence. Then she experienced a brief moment where she seriously considered going over to her upended cart to get a clean guest room towel to sop up the small pool of urine she'd left at the end of the hallway.

As Lord Varr left the hotel behind, he picked up cars on the road in front of him and tossed them at nearby targets. Scooters vastly outnumbered cars in normal circumstances, but the people on scooters had been able to escape on their conveyances, while the people in cars had to leap out of them and run for their lives. Lord Varr's tentacles managed to grab the slower of the escapees, but he had better luck poking claws into the windows of the office buildings across the street, grabbing employees who'd heard the commotion and come to watch what was going on below. Behind him, a huge chunk of the hotel, destabilized by the hole he'd left in the building, cracked and slid away, leaving a pile of girders and concrete, but most of the building remained standing, hollowed, empty, and filled with horror.

Hollowed, empty, and filled with horror, Oliver and Victoria looked at one another as Lord Varr receded into the city and out of sight. The monster's nearly perfect linear path took it partway into an office building, then through the center of a high-end department store, then over a gas station. The eruption of the tanks didn't slow the monster any more than the explosion of the oil tanker, but when the bright yellow clouds of light appeared over the smashed buildings, Oliver and Victoria flinched back, remembering the tanker blast and fearing the monster's return. Then they stood up straight again, stiff, immobilized by shock.

Charlotte rescued them. "Mommy, I want to go home."

Oliver stepped toward his wife, still holding Olivia against his hip, and placed a hand on the back of Charlotte's neck. "I want to go home, too, love."

"But all our things are in the hotel." Olivia was very pragmatic.

"You're right, dear. Our things are in the hotel," Victoria said. Her voice was far-off, almost dreamy.

Oliver's was clearer. "Yes, but honey, I don't think we'll go back there just yet. Let's just wait here on the beach, okay?"

"For how long?"

"I don't know, honey," Oliver said. "I don't really understand … much of anything, I guess."

When Lord Varr reached the industrial docks on the other side of the city, the people had already evacuated, but by then he'd eaten enough humans that he'd nearly doubled in size, the bulk of his tentacles reaching the height of a ten story building, a few lashing even higher into the sky. And because he was roughly spherical, the path of destruction beneath him spanned the width of a city block. Fires from gas lines and exploded cars were sprinkled among the rubble, but most buildings in Vũng Tàu didn't have heating systems or need gas for their AC, so the line of destruction looked less like the product of a war and more like the product of an earthquake, if that earthquake only affected a straight line through the heart of the city.

At the docks, Lord Varr's anger at the absence of people to eat was redoubled by the discovery of ships, some of which floated in the harbor, but many of which were dry docked for repairs and basic maintenance. To Lord Varr, these were reminders of the human disregard for his domain, his mother's empire, the territory the Merfolk were allowed when the humans claimed all the land above, a sovereignty humans defied every time they sailed one of their crafts onto the sea anywhere in the world. Enraged, Lord Varr grabbed these ships, regardless of their size, and threw them back at the city, tossing them over his shoulder and shoulder and shoulder and shoulder. Some he flicked out at great speeds, knocking down towers which had been lucky enough to avoid his direct path of destruction. A hurled ship can topple multiple high-rises before coming to a stop. Others Lord Varr threw high into the air, catapulting them into parabolic arcs that rained enormous artillery down on other parts of the city. These did less structural damage than the skipped stones of iron and steel clipping the lower floors of high towers, but when they landed, the shrapnel spread death and ruin over huge areas. The survivors of Vũng Tàu looked out of the windows of their homes at the hulls of huge ships in residential neighborhoods and thought those were the strangest sights they would ever see. They didn't see Lord Varr himself, and they never would.

Within seconds of his landfall, the operatives of CimBim were scrubbing the internet of every cellphone video, every security camera glimpse, every satellite image of the monster. The destruction couldn't be hidden, and eyewitnesses would need to be cowed to silence or eliminated, a monumental task when the monster violating The Convention was 100 feet tall and not making any effort to hide himself. Cover stories were mocked up and layered on top of one another in a tapestry of misinformation. The truth could never be entirely removed, but it could be buried under enough lies that any individual human recounting what they'd seen would be dismissed as a kook, a nut trying to blame the results of a devastating natural disaster/foreign attack/crashed satellite on a raging ball of tentacles.

The day after Varr's attack, a werewolf who looked like a large human in a uniform and carrying official looking paperwork and an official looking gun came to Bảo's house and told her the Vietnamese government would greatly appreciate it if she didn't tell anyone what she'd seen, and it would be proportionately *un*appreciative if she whispered a word of it to anyone. She took the hint.

Officials in Vũng Tàu had to reach out to the Australian consulate in Saigon to get the Johnson family's passports replaced so they could return home.

432

Those documents were delayed enough that The Convention's story was firmly in place and the family's tales of a giant monster would never be believed when they returned home. CimBim didn't even have to slow the paperwork. The massive, tentacled monster of government bureaucracy moved at a glacial pace in the best of times. Lord Varr was already heading directly through Saigon, and he'd bring it all to a sudden stop.

Chapter 32

Matt had to pay so much in "coffee money" to expedite a trip by private jet to Seam Reap, Cambodia, that if the Thai and Cambodian officials had put their bribes together, they could have started their own cafe. Then he rented a Hyundai H1 passenger van which came with a chauffeur. The Fellowship couldn't tell the driver to take them to the temple at night, so they took him far enough outside the city that they felt comfortable, asked him to get out of the van (which made him very uncomfortable), then had Tina chase him into the forest and eat him, making his comfort or discomfort a metaphysical question.

With that obstacle overcome, they doubled back and drove to a spot outside the park surrounding Angkor Wat temple, left the van on the side of the road, and hiked in on foot, keeping an eye out for security staff who might be patrolling the park looking for humans who might have lingered after the visitor hours had ended. Lena, Bel, and Tina could see well enough in the darkness to step lightly through the tall roots of the resin trees. Josef and Napoleon identified them with the kind of supernatural sonar with which they experienced the world around them all the time. Matt could easily have cast a spell to provide himself with enough illumination, but it would have been a glaring beacon to any human guards, so he let Napoleon lead him by the hand.

They were most exposed as they crossed one of the bridges spanning the square moat that protected the temple, but no alarms were raised, and they made their way into the exterior walls, then to the temple itself. Matt was relieved to be on the even footpaths used each day by the tourists, but he still had trouble finding one of Long's secret entrances.

The rest of The Fellowship of the Thing, with the exception of Bel, had never visited the temple, and they walked in looping paisley patterns as they tried to take in all the intricate carvings covering the stone walls. Statues of naga serpents welcomed them up the initial stairways, and the first of the 3000 dancing girls impressed them, though these were soon so common they became boring despite each being unique.

Once inside the first layer of walls, they examined the six-foot-high bas relief wrapping around the entire temple, then found an entrance to the inner courtyard. From there, Matt's verbal directions and others' vision led them up dangerously steep stairs to the next floor. They made their way to one of the small rooms at the base of one of the towers. It reeked of bat urine, a smell so strong it pushed most humans out of the room and back into the small hallways. The vampires choked on the smell, and Tina almost vomited, her back beginning to spasm in a particularly canine way. Matt risked a spell to produce illumination, then walked straight through the most bat-vandalized portion in the middle of the tower and found the stone he was looking for on the far wall. When he pressed it, a door a bit shorter than he was and only a foot and a half wide swung into a hidden recess. Turning sideways, he edged in, then stood to his full height and rotated back around to demonstrate the more comfortable space beyond. He beckoned them with a gesture, then began to descend the staircase.

The rest of the group followed. Josef had to change its shape and density to fit through the door, then remain a cloud of sand in a gentle breeze to follow behind them, and this brought the smell of the bats along for the first half of the 40-foot descent below the temple, but by the time they reached the doorway at the bottom of the stairs, the stench had dissipated.

Matt knocked on the door. They waited. Nothing happened.

"Maybe he's not home," Bel said.

"He could be flying over Bangkok doing his girlfriend right now," Tina said.

"Maybe we shouldn't mention that inside," Matt said.

"Do you think he'd be embarrassed?" she asked. "I don't slut-shame. People can do what they want."

"It just might make him uncomfortable to know he was seen. Or maybe it will make her uncomfortable."

"Or maybe it makes you uncomfortable when I talk about it?" Tina asked.

"Maybe that," Matt admitted. He knocked again.

The door clicked and opened. On the other side stood Long wearing his movie-star human body and a black silk bathrobe. Behind him stood Torreblanca wearing a red bathrobe made of the same silk and in Long's size. Both were flushed and smiling awkwardly. "Welcome back, my friend," Long said to Matt. Then he looked past him. "Friends. Please, come inside."

"That's what she said," Tina muttered.

"Tina!" Matt scolded.

Tina shouldered past him into Long's house. "Hey, Long, I'm digging the new bod. Just so you know, we saw you two doing the mile-high club over Bangkok, and it makes Matt super uncomfortable when I mention it, so I'm just going to keep doing that to bug him. It's not personal. Nice place you got here. Classy. Not what I expected out of an underground lair."

Long motioned the others in and spoke between them to Tina who was cautiously poking a finger into the flame of one of the lanterns illuminating the room. "What were you expecting?"

"Rough stone walls. A pile of gold coins on the floor.

Maybe some stalactites." She turned to face him. "Ooh, and some slot machines. Because of the luck thing."

"Lieutenant Torreblanca, I was not expecting to see you here," Bel said. A slight edge in her voice demanded a story.

Torreblanca raised her hands defensively. "Esau shot me. Long and Matt brought me here to heal."

"Esau sucks," Tina said.

Lena turned to Matt. "Wait, you knew about her?"

Matt shrugged. "Well, since I can't talk about Long to anyone outside this house, and since I didn't know how he related to our current quest, the enemy of yours we'd rescued didn't seem like a good subject of conversation." He turned to Long. "And you have some explaining to do, too, Buster. You sent me off to find help in dealing with Esau and Cassius and Tisina, but you didn't tell me you had a previous relationship with the Merfolk."

Long didn't look as surprised as Matt expected. "Ah, you learned about that. Let me guess. The library? They know that story?"

"They didn't before. It's a new theory. Can you fill in the details?"

Long gestured to the table. "Everyone, have a seat. I'll make some soup." He looked from one member of the party to the next. "How many of you can eat soup?"

Minutes later, they were all seated at the dining table, and most were eating. Josef had turned its lower half into a pile of sand so it could squat down at the others' height without taking a chair. It didn't eat anything. Long, Torreblanca, and Matt ate the promised soup with deep spoons out of tasteful blue and white porcelain bowls resting on matching plates. Lena and Bel didn't get the same fancy bowls because the blood might stain them, but they ladled blood out of cheaper bowls with similarly shaped spoons. Tina picked meat from a plate with chopsticks. Napoleon tapped an empty spoon into an empty porcelain bowl, lifted it to his teeth, and tossed back a spoonful of nothing. It made him feel like a part of the group.

"So, you keep human meat in your fridge?" Tina said. She held a piece of meat in her chopsticks and pointed the chunk at Torreblanca. "Your boyfriend is a psycho. This is the reddest flag of all red flags." Then she put the piece of meat into her mouth and spoke with it wedged in her cheek. "Not that I'm complaining. Long. You're an excellent host. My compliments to the defroster of the human."

Bel shook her head. "No," she said, then sipped blood out of her spoon. "No, this was never frozen. I'd guess it's about 95 degrees." She put her other hand on the side of the bowl. "Yeah, the bowl is cooler than the blood, so it's not keeping the temperature up artificially. Do you have a blood donor locked away in your kitchen?"

Tina looked quizzically at the meat on her plate. "Blood and tissue donor?"

Long shook his head and smiled, but Torreblanca

recognized some sadness in his eyes. "No, no donors. Humans don't understand luck." He looked around the table. "And, no offense to my guests, but monsters don't understand it, either. You all know I'm a luck dragon. But everyone just assumes that means I'm a good luck dragon."

Torreblanca frowned. "You're a bad luck dragon?"

"No, I'm a luck dragon. I exaggerate the odds. I stretch the fabric of the universe. I open my cupboard when I have a werewolf over for dinner, and there is some human meat waiting for me because that is the absolute luckiest thing that could happen. And there is some fresh blood for vampires. And exactly the ingredients I need to make your delicious soup."

"The soup isn't already prepared?" Matt asked.

"No. I like to make soup, so prepared soup would be unlucky. But it might be prepared if I were in a real hurry."

Lena leaned forward. "So far, that's how I understand good luck."

"Yes, but good luck for whom? Somewhere in the world, someone just experienced a dramatic loss of blood pressure. Or maybe lots of people so they won't notice. Sometimes the bad luck and good luck even themselves out in convenient ways. Which is lucky. And sometimes they don't. Which might just be the universe balancing out the good and the bad."

"Do they always balance perfectly?"

"No. They don't. At least, not in my experience. And that has been distinctly unlucky for me. So maybe I am a bad luck dragon who brings others good luck. I've thought a lot about that possibility."

"Explain," Tina ordered. Even when she was interested, she tended to bark.

"Alright. Let's say you're a man who gets hit by a bus. And you're killed. Lucky or unlucky?"

"Unlucky," Tina said.

"Okay, but let's say you are the wife of that man, and he was a terrible husband, but you couldn't figure out how to escape the relationship, and then he gets hit by a bus. Lucky or unlucky?"

"Lucky."

"Right. But let's say you were the daughter of the man and woman, and you are happy your mother is free of him, but you were counting on your father for a dowry and a connection to a better family, and now you can't marry the man you were betrothed to because his parents called it off now that you're a poor daughter of a widow."

"Sounds like I might be lucky not to be marrying into such a shit family," Tina said.

"Maybe. And the next day a luck dragon flies over your village, and you win the lottery, and you can marry whoever you want. Or not marry anyone at all. And the family that rejected you all gets dysentery because, like you said, they're a shit family."

"Lucky," Tina said.

"You would think so, but are you?"

"What do you mean? Of course you are," Tina said. "You needed money. You won the lottery. You have resources and a freedom you never had before. You're lucky!"

Long looked down at the table between them. "Yes, that's how humans always see it. But it's not good luck. You now live in a town where people have to get hit by buses in order for other people to get out of bad marriages, and where you have a lot of money but there's a new outbreak of dysentery that's spreading through the populace like wildfire. It's luck, but it's not good. It's good and bad. It's out of balance. And it's going to snap back. Maybe not on you. Maybe you'll use all that money to buy a nice villa far away from the smell of diarrhea. But for the community as a whole? Did the luck dragon bring them good luck? Or did he just bring some income inequality and a higher vehicular death rate and a highly contagious deadly disease? He's no hero. He's a monster."

Long motioned to Josef. "Consider our friend Josef here. It doesn't eat people or drain their blood. It just goes around punching Nazis. Arguably, it's the most heroic of all of us, right? Except in order to need Josef, we need to live in a world with Nazis. Wouldn't we all be better off if the only monster was Napoleon, a skeleton who doesn't feel particularly inclined to hurt anyone?"

Napoleon put a skinny hand on Josef's left shoulder to assure the golem that he still thought of Josef as a hero. Josef returned the gesture, placing a huge hand as gently as he could on Napoleon's right shoulder. Josef's touch was soft enough that it didn't dislodge Napoleon's right arm, but the skeleton's left arm happened to fall off just then, anyway.

"It's important that you all understand this," Long continued, "because I expect you will be irritated with me when I tell you I cannot come fight with you against Tisina's army. As you figured out at the library, I've done that before. I wasn't trying to save the world, just a village of humans I'd taken under my wing. So to speak." He looked at Napoleon. "I don't have wings. I can fly without them." Then he turned to Matt. "I know the witches sent you to me, so you must have thought I was going to be by your side in the battle to come. But I cannot."

"Why not?" Tina asked, as annoyed as he'd predicted.

"Last time, off the coast of India, I swam down into the ocean to confront the army of the merpeople. They weren't attacking all of humanity. They just wanted to eliminate the boat traffic between the mainland and Sri Lanka."

"The bridge in the story," Lena said.

"Yes. The Merfolk felt it was a continual affront to their territorial sovereignty, and something had to be done. So they got an army together and swam up to confront the humans. This was millennia before The Convention, when humans knew of monsters and wouldn't have been as surprised to see them, but I had lived in a cave near that village for a while. Their good luck was turning into more and more bad luck. Excesses of victories for some humans over the others. Chaos. I knew, if the Merfolk attacked, it would be exactly the kind of bad luck I had brought them. They would try to fight off the army, and they would lose. So I swam down to broker a peace and promise to return to China, far from the sea. I thought, if I could beg the Merfolk to give the humans a few centuries without me, things would even out in the village, and then the Merfolk could eliminate the seafaring without compounding it with the bad luck of total annihilation of the village. I was only going to ask for a few hundred years. For dragons, this is a small amount of time. As those of you who have been human probably already foresee, this argument wouldn't work for more short-lived merpeople. Imagine if you'd joined an army and marched on a city, and a single solitary person came out of the city gates and asked you to come back in a couple hundred years. They were not inclined to be patient.

"But, of course, I was lucky. When I arrived and made my ill-fated request, it was met with derision and dismissed immediately, but the princess of the merpeople was smitten with this foolish monster making unreasonable demands. While her army swam on to attack as planned, she had me brought to her palanquin, a large tent without a firm surface on the top or bottom, just a kind of box of fabric strung between a team of four gray whales. Inside, the princess could meet with her generals in privacy or float along on this bed of pillows without having to exert her own energy even to maintain her orientation in the water, let alone to keep up with the swimming march. Inside, I pled my case, she sent her guards away, one thing led to another…" Long looked at Torreblanca. They smiled at one another as he rubbed his fingertips over her knee under the table.

"Dude," Tina said. "Bold move, flirting with your girlfriend by telling a story about an ex."

"Yes, anyway, as the story goes, Hanuman seduced Suvannamaccha. That wasn't her name, by the way. I can't pronounce it correctly out of the water, but it sounds like Kailani." He didn't say the name. He sang it, holding the vowels and humming the n for a sustained period.

"Isn't that a Hawaiian name?" Lena asked.

"It didn't used to be," Long said. "Anyway, the princess made me a promise, and she gave me a gift. She assured me the Merfolk would not press their attack further than the coastal regions where the boats could be found, preventing any more invasions of the merpeople's territory. And she gave me the merpeople's magic. Just a bit of it. It looks like a glowing stone on a simple silver chain. And it doesn't seem to do anything. But it does. With that stone on that necklace, I could have passed through the gates of her city and been received as her consort. If I did so, we would have had a child. That child would have continued her royal line."

"So, wait, you had a one-night stand and she basically made you king?" Tina said. "Good job, Long."

"Worse than that. What she didn't realize was that when she got home and word got out that she'd chosen a surface dweller as her consort, no self-respecting merman wanted to be the second choice. Her whole royal line died. The city was cursed. No one wanted to live in a palace guarded by a gate that could be accessed by a key possessed by a surface dweller. The merpeople fell into a civil war as they tried to figure out who would be the next on the throne. Eventually, the gorgons took control. They moved the capital far from the Indian Ocean, way out into the South Pacific. They told their own version of the story. In the same way I became

Hanuman in the humans' myth, I became a human demon responsible for expelling the Merfolk from the surface world. The princess became the cliche virgin/whore/betrayer figure common to so many stories, innocent because of her supposed sexual purity, guilty because of her sexual desire, and responsible for everyone's problems."

"And the key?"

"I still have it. Like I said, it's a magical keycard to a ghost town at the bottom of the ocean, now. But that's not what Tisina thinks it is. She thinks it's all the Merfolk magic in one glowing stone, and that if she had it, she'd break the seal preventing the Merfolk from conquering the surface world. When I learned she was plotting to conceive the merpeople's promised messiah character, I suspected she would come straight for me, so I left my home and traveled the world looking for a weapon that could stop her. And I was lucky. I spent a month floating in a rubber rescue boat, swirling around in the middle of the Pacific with no particular destination in mind and very little ability to maneuver the boat in my human form. I could have simply flown back home, but I trusted my luck to bring me to where I needed to be. And, sure enough, I floated right up to Matt's ship."

"Thank you," Matt said. He turned to Lena. "See? Ship. Not boat."

"But my luck wasn't bringing me to my old friend Matt. It was bringing me to you, Lena. You were carrying your manuscript which can kill monsters. I suspected it would be the device that I could use to ward off Tisina when she came for me. So when Cassius stole it, I helped you steal it back. It seemed like everything was going as planned."

"And then Esau put a hole in the manuscript and in me," Lena said.

Bel's phone vibrated. She ignored it.

"Yes," Long said, "so I figured that weapon was off the table. And that you were dead. Matt didn't know otherwise."

"Because he skedaddled right after she was shot," Bel said.

"But you are here. So maybe the weapon is your book. Maybe the weapon is you, the writer. I'm not sure. But I have the bait. Tisina will come for the necklace, and then you can do whatever it is you need to do to defeat her."

Bel's phone vibrated again.

"How are you getting cell service in a dragon's lair underneath an ancient temple?" Tina asked.

Bel frowned. "I hadn't even considered it."

"Well, answer it!" Tina ordered.

Bel fished the phone out of her back pocket. "I don't recognize the number."

"Answer it anyway," Tina said. "They called you underground. It's important."

Bel pointed at Long. "Or they're a very lucky telemarketer."

Long shook his head. "I don't tend to make people lucky at a distance. If it's a telemarketer, you are the one who is lucky to be getting the call."

"No one is lucky to get a call from a telemarketer," Bel said.

"Then it's not a telemarketer!" Tina said. "Answer it!"

Bel swiped the green dot and put the silver rectangle to her ear. "They hung up."

"Call them back!" Tina was shouting now.

Bel looked at the screen. "Can't. I don't have service."

"Oh god dammit. Give me the phone," Tina said, and she lunged over her plate to snatch it out of Bel's hand.

Because vampires are faster than werewolves, Bel yanked it away. Torreblanca, the only human in the room, couldn't even see Bel's hand move. It simply seemed to appear elsewhere. "Fine, I'll call," Bel said. She put out a hand against Tina's forehead, stiff-armed her, and sent the younger woman plopping back into her seat. Then Bel tapped on her phone twice, held it to her ear, and sounded surprised when she said, "It's ringing."

"Of course," Tina said. She motioned to Long. "Lucky."

"Maybe bad luck," Long reminded her, but by then some other voice chirped out of the phone.

"I'm putting you on speaker," Bel said.

Some more chirping.

"No, no humans in the room. Just The Fellowship of the Thing."

More chirping.

"I know. It's a stupid name. Matt made it up."

More chirping. Bel tapped another button.

"'The Thing'? Mr. Bern," the new, loud voice said. "That's not a very good name. Jeeves, doesn't that strike you as excessively vague?"

"That's what I said!" Lena shouted across the table.

A low, somber voice said, "It rhymes with 'ring,' sir. Play on words."

"Well, it's not a very good one. 'Ring' and 'thing.' Seems a bit juvenile to me," the Archduke said.

"Of course, sir," Jeeves said.

"Neither here nor there. Now, Bel, I'm calling because we need your help. I know you have been out of the employ of CimBim for some time now, but your former boss and maker, Cassius, is in charge of it, and he seems to have gone absent without leave at the absolute worst time. We have a problem on our hands. A bit of an all-hands-on-deck situation. Something of a catastrophe, really. I'm not exaggerating, am I, Jeeves?"

"Not at all, sir," Jeeves droned. "An understatement, perhaps."

"Yes, right-o. It's quite a large problem. I'm sending you some images which have been scrubbed from the human internet. Here. No. Wait. Jeeves, can you…?"

The sound shifted, and Jeeves' voice was louder. "Of course, sir. Let me."

"Yes, that one. And, no, not that one. Yes. And the… yes, you can handle the sending. Thank you, Jeeves."

"Of course, sir."

A series of bings announced photos arriving to Bel's phone. Without disconnecting the call, she pulled them up. "Holy shit. What is that?" She passed the phone around the table.

"It's a very large violation of The Convention," the Archduke said. "A … What did you call it, Jeeves? A kaiju of some kind?"

"A 'Cthulhu-esque kaiju,'" Jeeves quoted himself. "Perhaps I used the word 'eldritch.'"

"No, that wasn't it."

"Was it 'nautiloid,' sir?"

"Yes, that was the word! A hundred-foot tall nautiloid Cthulhu-esque kaiju of some kind. But with the bony parts on the ends of the tentacles instead of a shell. Or maybe there's a shell in the middle of all that. We can't tell for certain."

"What city is this? Er, was this?" Lena asked.

"Vũng Tàu, Vietnam," the Archduke said.

"We're nearby," Bel said. "Cambodia. We can get there in … I don't know. Matt, how long would it take us to get there?"

"It's not there anymore," the Archduke said. "And I'm not telling you to go fight it. It's a hundred feet tall. Not exactly something you can fight with a sword, Bel. No, I need your help with the operation to keep the humans in the dark about it. I'm calling in everyone I can, but the absence of the head of the department is making it difficult. Do you have any idea where Cassius may have absconded? He has more complete records of the whereabouts and contact information of CimBim agents around the world. Without that, we're wasting valuable time trying to track everyone down for field operations while the cyber security team does overtime shifts cleaning up references to the giant beast online."

"We know where it's going," Long said.

Everyone paused.

"Who was that?"

"Long. He's a luck dragon who lives under Angkor Wat."

"How interesting," the Archduke said, "A pleasure to make your acquaintance, Mr. Lóng." The Archduke pronounced Long's name correctly.

"And yours. Let me guess. The monster made a straight path through Vũng Tàu."

"Correct."

"And if you follow that line, it would lead directly to the mouth of the Đồng Nai River."

"That's right."

"From there he'll travel overland to the Mekong, then up to the Tonle Sap river, then to Tonle Sap Lake, and then to Angkor Wat. He could have gone straight to the mouth of the Mekong, but he wants to be bigger before he has to travel on the surface for any extended period of time. This is still the baby version. He needs to feed first."

"It's going to get bigger?" Lena asked.

"It did grow as it moved through Vũng Tàu," the Archduke said. "It almost doubled in size."

"Eating humans, I expect. So he has planned a longer route to make sure he passes through a much bigger city. I can tell you where he will surface, almost exactly. It will be the point in the river directly across from its path to overland. Then he will cut a straight line through a city of nine million people."

"How do you know?"

"He's still more comfortable in the water. That's why he went to Vũng Tàu first. It's on an isthmus, so he could surface and eat and get back in the water as quickly as possible. But he needs to eat to grow. Traveling in the rivers allows him to eat and get back into the water quickly, and then he can take his time and keep moving in this direction. And if it doubled in size in a city of a half a million humans, imagine how much he'll grow as he crosses a city of nine million. By the time he reaches us, there will be nothing anyone can do to stop him. We have two advantages. One: We know exactly where he's headed. And two: He thinks he needs the key before he starts to lay waste to all humans."

"Okay, we need to get going," Bel said.

"Yeah, but what about Long?" Lena asked. "You never finished explaining why you aren't coming with us."

"I sided with the humans last time. Like I said before, there isn't a perfect balance. Or, if there is, I'm the one who throws it off, and that always ends in bad luck. Humans have been remarkably lucky in the millennia since I took their side. Do you know how many times the Soviet Union and the United States almost started a nuclear war that would have killed most of the humans on the planet and left the rest to be food for starving monsters?"

"How many?" Tina asked.

"Seven. And that's just the nuclear wars. If Ebola had a slower incubation period, it could have spread around the world before killing most humans. They were just lucky most people died too fast to spread it everywhere. And if Covid happened to kill infants more quickly than the elderly? We know humans couldn't be bothered to take that seriously for grandpa and grandma. Do any of you think they would have taken it more seriously if it had been an existential threat to the survival of their species? They've just been lucky.

"If I go out and confront ... whatever that is, I may stretch the odds in such a way that we defeat the creature. But at what cost? Or I may turn all the luck back over to the Merfolk. Maybe it's their turn. Either way, this is not a situation that should be left up to a luck dragon.

"I'm sorry." He looked right into Lena's eyes. "As the Archduke says, you can't defeat this monster with a sword. Josef can't punch this monster to death. Matt's magic isn't going to trick that creature. This thing will be defeated by those books of yours, books written by a human, or it won't, and that's the end of the humans and the monsters who depend on them." He stood, walked around the table and over toward the fireplace, and pulled a book down from the bookshelf. He opened it, revealing a hollow interior illuminated with a soft, blue-green light. He plucked the chain out of the book-shaped box and held up the necklace. A simple, round stone hung there, glowing dully. Long walked back and held it out to Lena.

She hesitated to touch the stone.

"It's fine," Long said. "It's just a key. And a symbol. And, I hope, a kind of magical homing device the monster will sense. I don't know how, exactly, you should use this. But I believe you are the one who will use it correctly.

"And I would wish you luck," Long said, "but you are better off without it."

"I'm going with them," Torreblanca said. She hoped that would be enough to convince him to join them.

"Yes, I expected you would. I'm not sure this is the kind of monster you are trained to fight, but you are one of the most experienced monster hunters of everyone here." Long shook his head. "I wish I could bring you as much happiness as you have brought me. I never wanted to bring you bad luck, Anahí, but I fear I may have brought you the worst luck of all."

Torreblanca shrugged. "I don't believe in luck. I hope that doesn't offend you. I just don't find the idea useful. In fact, I think it's dangerous." She took his hand. "I believe in love, though."

He squeezed her hand. "Love is better than luck. I am thousands of years old, and I know love lasts longer."

The group rose, said their uncomfortable goodbyes, and made their way out of the opulent room into the stairway through the rough-hewn tunnel.

Long turned and walked over to his chair by the fireplace and sat heavily, not a dragon's weight, but a tired man's. He looked up at his books.

He didn't tell Torreblanca that he'd learned love lasts longer than luck because luck changes while love remains as grief.

Chapter 33

Saigon, officially Ho Chi Minh City and simply The City to residents, is home to between nine and 13 million people, depending on how one counts the suburbs. Those residents own eight million scooters. About 90% of the riders obey the mandatory helmet law. One of the side benefits of the law, besides the obvious reduction in brain injuries and deaths, is that scooter helmets are essential fashion accessories, so the number of motorcycle helmets in the city vastly exceeds the number of scooters because many people own a dozen helmets to match their outfits.

Hoa owned only one, a simple, black, utilitarian helmet he wore to his job where he, ironically, sold helmets. The shop was in an upscale mall called Takashimaya Ho Chi Minh City. Hoa couldn't afford to live anywhere near his work, so he commuted from a suburb on the south side of the city. That morning, he was stuck in traffic as usual. Three lanes were packed with scooters. Brightly colored helmets stretched out in a sea before him. He imagined the push pins with the little round heads they used to use in his geography classes to mark locations on a map tacked up to the wall, only this map was filled with thousands of the little pins.

Remembering that map made Hoa think about his daughter's class. Public school was free, but teachers supplemented their incomes by offering after-school tutoring at high prices. Students who didn't pay had a hard time in school, not because they lacked academic knowledge but because teachers were extra strict with the students who were too poor to pay for extra tutoring. Hoa knew this could be ameliorated with gifts donated to the classroom. He wondered if his daughter's teacher would like one of those high-tech air purifiers. He considered the possibility the class already had one. He tilted his black push-pin sideways as he concluded air couldn't be too clean. He hoped his daughter's teacher would agree. Or perhaps she would like some new scooter helmets to match her own outfits. He could use his employee discount.

Traffic inched along, the wide avenue curving to take in a stretch of road built over the Dong Nai River. Apartments in Saigon went for around $300 US per square foot. Families of ten frequently shared units the size of hotel rooms. A savvy community had dodged high rents for many years by living in a slum built on top of the river, but the government had forced them all into condominiums by replacing the neighborhood with roads built over the river itself. These looked less like bridges and more like freeway overpasses curving over the river, channeling the wide Dong Nai into a series of concrete aqueducts whose flow was tightly controlled to prevent flooding of the city. Hoa could barely see the water. Instead, he saw the line of slow-moving scooters ahead bunch up. And then he heard the screaming.

Scanning over the tops of the helmets, Hoa tried to make out what was happening. Some people seemed to be attempting to lift their scooters and turn them backwards, against traffic, to drive away from some obstruction, but the mass of traffic wouldn't allow it. Others were simply dropping their scooters and running. Around Hoa, his fellow drivers were grumbling, honking their horns, demanding to know what was impeding their progress to their destinations. Hoa saw a flash of color, a hot pink round push-pin head, plucked up out of the map and lifted into the air, then yanked down over the side of the road. It took him a second to remember the river flowed beneath that side and, in fact, beneath his feet.

In a slow exhalation, he breathed the Vietnamese

version of, "What … the … fu-?"

The screaming and honking noises were muted by a deafening explosion. Hoa thought it was a bomb, but it was just the sound of the concrete cracking, the rebar wrenching, and the windows shattering as Lord Varr burst through the road in front of him. The first exploratory tentacles that had grabbed samples of humans were replaced by enormous ones unfurling a hundred feet into the air above him. Claws larger than cars clicked to express their hunger, then plunged down to the road level and began snapping up commuters, sometimes taking only their top halves and leaving legs to flop to either side of their former owner's scooters, sometimes pinching all the way down to the asphalt to take victims, boots and all, leaving gouges in the road like heavy construction equipment, the front and back wheels of scooters falling, chassis sparking, like the machines themselves were in shock at the sudden loss of their mechanical torsos. Hoa picked out one of the severed legs which managed to remain upright as its owner vanished into a huge claw. A knee-high leather boot was cut so neatly, it looked like a standard mid-calf boot waiting on a bedroom floor. Then blood remembered to pool on top of the pink meat and white bone inside.

Hoa yanked on the handlebars in panic, trying to steer his scooter to the right, and smacked into the side of the scooter hemming him in that way. Then he veered to the left and discovered an opening as his compatriot in that direction made a little space, but that scooter couldn't turn around completely, and both commuters were stuck mostly facing the horror in front of them. Hoa ticked straight to his third option, leaping off the scooter (his most expensive possession), and pushing his way backwards. He had to clamber over other scooters with missing riders and push his way through a gantlet of those still on their bikes, some tilting their shoulders to let him pass, others stiff-arming him to try to retain their positions. He knocked a couple people over as he barreled past, and under his breath he mumbled instinctual apologies to the people now trapped under the weight of their scooters and the bodies of those around them. Hoa was crawling as much as running, his hands trying to find purchase on the seats of overturned scooters or the bodies of their overturned drivers, his feet stepping on wheels which turned under his weight and gripped at his ankles. The side of the road opposite the river was an eight-foot-high concrete wall. In his terror, Hoa was certain he could leap up and pull himself to safety if he could only claw his way through the impromptu junkyard/slaughterhouse.

Just over an arm's length from the wall, Hoa fell onto a scooter in front of him. It wasn't his first fall, and he didn't immediately register the challenge of rising again and continuing forward. Lifting himself up with his arms, he found his legs weren't cooperating. He turned back to see if they were stuck between scooters. They were not.

There was no scooter behind him. There was a hole in the road, more than a meter deep at its triangular point.

Everything which had been there, two scooters, a woman trapped underneath them, and both of Hoa's legs, had vanished.

A ring of gray enveloped the world as Hoa began to lose consciousness, but he had time to look up and see the claw. It reared like a scorpion's tail, hesitated for a moment above him, and a lump moved through the tentacle behind it like a mouse passing through a boa constrictor. After swallowing, the claw opened again, then struck.

All of Matteo Bern's fortune couldn't have arranged a flight from Siem Reap to Saigon in time. In fact, as they scrambled to make plans, at one point Matt snapped at Bel while hooking a thumb at Lena. "A couple white people and an American demanding to fly a plane or a helicopter from Cambodia to Vietnam over the Ho Chi Minh trail? We have a fairy story for an explanation, and they have 500,000 tons of Henry Kissinger's war crimes worth of reasons to shoot us out of the sky. Without Long, we're not getting there."

Bel couldn't argue, so she looked to Torreblanca, but she shook her head. "I do not know how we'll succeed without Long, but I am certain he won't change his mind. We have to find another way."

With the Archduke's intervention, they did. A CimBim agent in the Cambodian Army ordered them picked up by helicopter in Siem Reap and brought to a base in southern Cambodia.

The relationship between Cambodia and Vietnam is far more complex than Lena realized. Like many Americans, she thought of the countries as similarly Indo-Chinese, similarly communist, and similarly anti-American, and therefore roughly equivalent. She didn't even know that it was the communist Vietnamese who invaded Cambodia in 1979 to remove the more extreme communist Khmer Rouge which was being propped up by the U.S. Government since Kissinger wanted to use the horrific Khmer Rouge regime as a way to harm the more Soviet-friendly North Vietnamese. Though the post-Khmer Rouge Cambodian government was far friendlier to the Vietnamese government, and the countries are two of each other's largest trading partners, the people cannot forget the experience of an invasion force sweeping through their country. Resentments about disputed territory still linger, so asking the Vietnamese government to allow a helicopter from Cambodia to enter Vietnamese airspace should have taken weeks of international negotiation. Instead, through some manipulations by CimBim operatives in the Vietnamese air force, it was quietly agreed that both countries would direct their radar eyes the other way and choose not to notice the incursion.

Landing at the base near the border did waste precious time, though. Long could have flown them to Saigon in a few hours, but the wait for the helicopter, the trip across Cambodia, and the wait on the ground for the unofficial not-permission took precious time. While a certain advisor to Richard Nixon may have waved away hundreds of thousands of innocent Cambodian civilians' deaths in his Real Politique strategy to kill hundreds of thousands of Vietnamese, contrary to what one may expect based on US foreign policy, not all Americans are psychopaths. One American (who was a certified homicidal monster) paced anxiously back and forth inside the long body of the twin-propeller military helicopter sitting on the tarmac in southern Cambodia. Magdalena couldn't help but think about the innocent people of Saigon being killed by a giant monster every second they were delayed.

Bel watched Lena's pacing and read the anxiety in her girlfriend's gestures. When nervous, Lena had a habit of wiggling her fingers as though she were typing, a writer habit she'd developed searching for solace over a keyboard. Now a vampire, Lena could move her fingers at superhuman speeds, so they would have appeared as blurs of motion to a human eye. Bel could see those fingers clearly, but she couldn't read what they were typing.

"What are you thinking?" Bel asked Lena as she made one of her passes.

"I don't know. I'm just thinking of the people in Saigon being attacked by that thing."

"Okay, but remember, they're humans," Bel said. "We are going to go fight that monster for The Convention. It's a threat to all monsters, having that thing outing us and possibly killing all the humans in the world, and that's a bad thing, don't get me wrong. Very bad. But we're fighting it because it's breaking the rules and threatening our food supply. We're not rescuing those people. We're rescuing all monsters. I know it's hard, honey, but keep your focus on our job, okay? If you get distracted by your affection for your former species, it could lead to bad decision-making in the field. We'll need to keep our heads when we get there."

"I know, but…" Lena looked to Josef who sat in two of the chairs attached to the wall. "Josef, you get what I'm feeling, right? All those people?"

The golem nodded slowly, then reached into its chest for its pad of paper and its little golf pencil. Finding the pencil lead flattened, it held the pencil's back end between its thumb and one of the three fingers on its right hand and stuck the point into its left index finger. It spun the gritty sand inside its finger like the blades of a sharpener, examined the pencil, then set the pencil to the paper while the rest of the team watched impatiently. Then Josef held the notepad out towards toward its friends.

"Waiting to stop killing is killing," they read.

"Okay, sure, but we kill people all the time," Bel said. Then she looked at the expression on Lena's face and raised her hands in surrender. "But you're right. The waiting is frustrating. I get that. Just don't do anything stupid when we get there, okay? I worry about you, not them."

"I won't do anything thoughtless," Lena said. Which wasn't the same thing. Because writers care about words.

Bel knew that, too.

Measuring the fortuitousness of any choice is impossible since it depends on the consequences which cannot be foreseen and the perspective of the lucky or unlucky recipient of those consequences. One benefit of the long wait before the second leg of the journey was that it got them closer to sundown, a significant advantage to the two members of The Fellowship of the Thing who would sizzle and ultimately burst into flames in the glaring Vietnamese sunshine. Unfortunately for the people of Saigon, it gave Lord Varr a whole day to consume and grow in the heart of the city. It also gave Cassius and Esau time to move.

While the Archduke struggled to activate the CimBim operatives in Vietnam, Cassius knew just who to call to learn about the situation unfolding in Saigon, and his private plane from Hong Kong could move a lot faster than a military helicopter built in the 1980s. He landed in Saigon before The Fellowship of the Thing arrived, and his plane disgorged its unusual mixture of occupants, a small group of human mercenaries in full tactical gear and three vampires wearing motorcycle helmets and leather from collar to fingertips so they could cross the bright tarmac and get into the shade of their reserved hangar.

In the protection of the shade, Cassius took off his

helmet and turned to his new partner. "When they arrive, you get Matt Bern, I get Jezebel Shipwright, and the rest are up for grabs. Agreed?"

Esau shook his head. "It won't be that simple. You have your vampires, and I have some of my men. They have the golem. You can handle vampires and werewolves and maybe a warlock who can disappear whenever he feels like it, but that golem can take out all of us without blinking."

"It can't blink," Cassius said. "It has no eyes."

"Like I said. 'Without blinking.'"

Cassius nodded. "So, what do you propose?"

"They want to go fight a hundred-foot-tall tentacle thingy. Fine. Let that take care of the golem. Meanwhile, one of us will infiltrate their chopper and bring it back here once the golem is occupied by the giant squid. That way, all the ones we can face will be in one place, and we won't lose the books, either. Then you and I each get a copy of the books. Mutually assured destruction."

"'He who can destroy a thing, controls a thing,'" Cassius quoted.

"Right."

"So who will take the chopper?"

"Whoever can get in without getting caught. If it's still daylight, my guys can take out the pilots and replace them a lot more easily than a couple of vamps sizzling while they walk across the tarmac. But come nightfall, your boys can move a lot faster."

"How will we know we're not going to send the chopper somewhere else and try to keep the book for ourselves?"

"Well, I suspect the golem might get wary if the helicopter starts heading off in the wrong direction, but if it looks like it's coming back to base, it might stay behind to battle the tentacle monster, so we've both got that going for us. Also, we both stand better odds of taking them out if we're working together when the chopper gets back."

"True," Cassius admitted.

One of Cassius' crew, Augy, tapped him on the shoulder. "They're en route. Should be landing in a few minutes."

"Looks like your side will be the ones to bring them back here," Cassius told Esau. "Don't get killed in transit. I really need those books."

Esau shrugged. "Frankly, it's kind of refreshing that we don't even pretend to trust or like one another. I appreciate it."

"Oh, I'd make a meal of you in a heartbeat if you weren't useful to me, human. And I'm sure you'd try to throw garlic at me or wave a cross in my face if given half a chance."

"Yeah, let's just say that's what I would do."

Esau took his men out of the hangar (leaving none behind with the vampires he didn't trust), and they made their plans out under the bright sun. The Archduke and Cassius had both arranged for that portion of the military base to be conveniently deserted when The Fellowship arrived. Only a few soldiers were on duty to refuel the chopper. Esau's men shot them with tranquilizer darts, a far more generous fate than the vampires would have offered, then hid them in a different hangar to try to keep the sleeping men from serving as snacks for their new colleagues. When the chopper landed, Esau and three of his men rode out in a cart connected to the base's fuel line. The job only required one person and was generally carried out by two, but Esau hoped the occupants of the chopper wouldn't notice. While they attached the hose, Esau touched his com and whispered, "Evans and Kim, you finish up here. Nguyen, you and I will replace the pilots."

"Sir?" Nguyen asked.

"Change of plans," Esau said.

"But, no offense sir, but Kim looks the part more than you do."

"No offense to any of you, but I need to make sure this chopper gets back here one warlock lighter or you'll all die here on this airfield, and I'd like to make sure those books never get any closer to the vamps in that hangar than they already are. I know how to do both, and there's no time to explain. Plus, Kim wasn't going to fool anyone here into thinking he's Vietnamese anyway."

"Understood, sir," Nguyen said.

The two soldiers went around to the front of the chopper, ducking low as though concerned about the still-rotating blades though they were actually staying out of the sight lines of anyone in the body of the chopper. When they got to the front, they waved to the Cambodian pilots, and when the pilots opened their doors, Nguyen explained, in broken Cambodian, that they were the pilots assigned by the Vietnamese Air Force to take over in Vietnamese airspace. The Cambodian pilots gave one another suspicious stares, looked at Esau, and then explained they needed to radio home for orders. As they did so, both Esau and Nguyen kept their pistols just out of sight but ready. Esau knew, even with the silencers, any pistol fire would alert the occupants of the chopper, even over the sound of the rotors. But he couldn't let the chopper and all its inhabitants escape, even if it meant facing the golem. The sun was just setting over the treetops behind him, but the day's heat made sure his sweating didn't look out of place.

The Cambodian pilots' senior officer received his orders from a CimBim operative in the secret service, so he relayed an order to turn the copter over to the new pilots even if they were probably CIA agents and certainly weren't Vietnamese Air Force. The pilots shrugged and obeyed, relinquishing their seats to the newcomers and climbing on the back of the fuel truck to be driven away by the other pair of mercs. Once Esau and Nguyen were situated, Nguyen used the intercom to tell the passengers their new Vietnamese Air Force pilots were onboard and ready to go to the pre-ordained location in Ho Chi Minh City. He almost slipped and called the city Saigon, a name a member of the military would not have used while conducting official government business.

Bel and Matt could both hear that Nguyen's accent was a little off. Nguyen had grown up listening to his parents and grandmother speaking Vietnamese in their home in Santa Cruz, California, but he didn't sound like someone who spoke it every day of his life. Matt and Bel independently came to the conclusion their pilot might be a CimBim operative rather than a real member of the Vietnamese Air Force, and they presumed his silent co-pilot might not know that, so they didn't press the issue.

"Okay, Tina and Torreblanca, this is your stop," Lena said.

"Wait, what?" Tina shouted.

"There's nothing you two can do from the air unless you're hiding a shoulder-fired missile launcher somewhere I can't see, but we do need someone to hold this landing pad and keep it safe until we get back."

"That doesn't make any fucking sense," Tina said. "You're full of shit."

Bel put a hand on Tina's shoulder. "Yes, she is. She thinks it's a suicide mission, and you both have a lot more life left in you. Josef will be fine. Napoleon is already dead. I'm already dead. Lena is already dead. Matt is ... whatever state in between life and death that Matt is." Bel looked at Lena. "She is planning to die." When she looked back at Tina, there were tears in her eyes. "I don't plan on letting her, so you two stay here, and I'll do my best to bring her back, okay?"

"This sucks. You should have left us with Long."

"Maybe we wanted as much time with you as we could get," Bel said.

"Yeah, and maybe you want a nice goodbye, too," Tina said. "Well fuck you both. Don't die or that's the last thing you'll hear me say." Then she yanked the side door open so fast both vampires had to dodge back into the shadow near the pilot's hatch to avoid the last rays of the setting sun. Tina leapt out, her heavy boots making a thunk audible over the rotors, and stalked away, standing up straight under the whirling blades, not looking back.

Torreblanca squeezed Lena's forearm. "Please don't make her regret saying that," she said, and then she jumped down more gingerly, her stomach wound wincing a bit at the impact, and ducked her head as she jogged after her new teenage friend.

Chapter 34

The ride from the base outside the city to the heart of Saigon was less than twenty minutes. Before they arrived, Bel and Lena could hear the explosions. Josef could feel them moving the air even through the chopper's bulkhead. The chopper veered slightly to circle around the destruction, and the remainder of The Fellowship of the Thing, Matt, Josef, Napoleon, Lena, and Bel, stepped close to the windows in the chopper's large sliding door to look down.

Night had fallen, though the soft blue of the gloaming still peeked up the western sky, and the city's lights sparkled in a ring all around them, but the center of the city, generally almost as bright as day because of the multi-story plasma screens that ran twenty-four hours selling soy sauce and cell phones and the latest Chinese electric cars, was illuminated by pockets of fire that looked like candles from their height. As they got closer, they could see fires blazing in high rises, some emanating from holes smashed into the buildings, others taking up entire floors where they'd spread.

There were other light sources, too. Jets streaked overhead launching missiles which glowed briefly as they ran down city streets and struck at something the helicopter's passengers couldn't see. After each, an explosion would dance up between the buildings, a rounded glowing cloud of fire preceding the sound of thunder. Closer still, they saw other helicopters illuminated by the tracer rounds of machine guns aimed into the same spot in the middle of the city. One of these strings of light was interrupted by something dark flying back along its path. Then a car smashed into a helicopter. One or both exploded, and the helicopter spiraled out of the sky like a whirligig seedpod falling from a tree branch. The helicopter bounced off the corner of an apartment building before sinking into darkness in the streets below.

Another dark shape lashed out from between the buildings to catch the light of tracer rounds. Another helicopter was slapped out of the air, this time seeming to slide away rather than spin as it lost its vertical orientation and careened at an angle into one of the lit neighborhoods further away.

Bel grabbed a headset and called to the pilot. "Get us up higher, right over it." Then she pulled the headset down around her neck and spoke to Lena in a voice that wouldn't have carried to a human over the sound of the rotors. "Do you know what you're going to do?"

Lena grabbed the handle and opened the sliding door. She looked down at the city beneath her. At first, even with her superhuman vision, she couldn't make out what she was seeing. Gray and white rectangles marked the rooftops of tall buildings, and between them, the black asphalt of empty streets seemed alive with motion. But as she focused, she realized she wasn't seeing streets at all. It looked like a ball of breeding snakes rolling and roiling through the city. As she watched, a building beneath her collapsed, the smoke of crumbling concrete temporarily obscuring everything below, and then the dust settled, and the light of dozens of fires caught the purple and green and blue tentacles.

Lit by the dim red and orange flames, the tentacles climbed up out of the white dust, reaching out for helicopters that dared to get too low, poking into buildings where survivors still hid, each carrying a claw proportional to the tentacle's size, some now the size of large construction equipment or small houses. The claws clicked loudly but retained their high pitch, like small caliber gunfire in her ears even from a distance. The machine gun fire was lower pitched and sporadic as the last of the helicopters made their vain attempts to injure or slow the thing they could barely see, and then they were gone, the last escaping as a new volley of rockets lanced in through the streets. Those large explosions were nearly blinding against the darkness of the emptied portion of the city, but as Lena's eyes recovered, she could make out enough of Lord Varr's shape to identify its center. "A little further that way," she shouted, pointing. "Then get us lower, but not too low."

She turned to Josef. "I know it's not a Nazi, so this isn't really your bag, but if you could broaden your definition beyond your usual antipathy to anti-Semitic genocidal ideologies, I think we'd all appreciate it."

Josef stood and showed her its notepad, already filled out. "Fascists get punched," it said. Then it stepped past her and out of the chopper. The helicopter wobbled as the pilot adjusted for the sudden change in weight. Josef plummeted like … well, like a very large stone shaped like a person. It spread its arms and legs wide, briefly enjoying the feeling of wind scraping against its exterior, and then it felt the first of the tentacles reaching up to grab it. Josef turned itself into a cloud of smoke capable of moving at supersonic speed. It spiraled around a rising tentacle, arced away down a wide thoroughfare, then doubled back, reforming its upper half, one arm outstretched, its hand curled into a fist as large as its head. It slammed into the center of the tentacle with such force, the tentacle, roughly as tough on the inside as the flesh on the surface, ripped with a wet skloosh.

Far above, the car-sized claw wavered in the air, uncertain, and then the tentacle collapsed like a felled tree, bending around the gaping hole left by Josef's passing. Unlike a tree, the upper portion squiggled, limp but curving into S shapes, as it fell onto an office building, leveling it.

Josef didn't hesitate after a single success but doubled back immediately, aiming for another. This one attempted to dodge away. Josef's punch sent it whipping away into the center of a nearby skyscraper, but the tentacle recovered, shattering the last of the glass as it wriggled free and reached after Josef. Lord Varr couldn't catch it, and Josef severed a third tentacle while the second groped at its tail of smoke and sand.

More tentacles arced up out of the dusty rubble, claws snapping. Josef crushed the claw of one that got too close. Another pinched nothing but some of its comet tail. Josef felt no pain as a consequence, but it lost some matter and had to draw more out of the concrete dust filling the air. Other tentacles dodged away from its streaking form, bending as it rocketed past like men instinctively avoiding kicks to the crotch.

In the cockpit, Esau watched the golem crash through tentacle after tentacle.

Nguyen mouthed, "Now?" and pointed a thumb back toward the base.

Esau shook his head tightly. "Not yet," he mouthed back. He wanted to see if the golem would be eliminated so he'd know how much time they had to deal with the monsters when they landed. If he knew the golem was inbound, that might buy some time before Cassius tried to betray him. Also, he wanted to be able to ditch the books along the way so none of the monsters would own them and he could come back for them later.

Meanwhile, Lord Varr continued to move. From the chopper, his progress seemed slow, but he was covering the length of city blocks in agonizing seconds while poking through the buildings and eating the people who couldn't flee fast enough. Tentacles grew and new ones formed faster than Josef could cut them down.

High above, Bel couldn't tell who was winning, but Lena had already decided it wasn't Josef.

"Plan B," she shouted. Digging in her jeans front pocket, she pulled out the small round stone hanging on the thin silver chain. In Long's lair, the crystal had glowed faintly, but in the darkness, a phosphorescent bright green emanated from the center of the blue marble. "Tell the pilot to stay over the center of the thing," Lena said. "Head that way." She pointed in the direction Lord Varr seemed to be headed, roughly west, so he could cross as much of the city as possible before exhausting the human population of the suburbs and traveling through the more sparsely populated area between there and the Mekong. From there he'd be back in water, though far too large to remain submerged, and could travel in his element up to the temple where the dragon hid. Of course, Lord Varr didn't know the trophy he sought wasn't where he'd been programmed, before his birth, to seek it, but Lena wanted to reveal the stone's location and see if he'd turn around.

When she stuck her arm out of the helicopter, straining slightly to keep it stiffly in place against the force of the wind rushing past, the light emanating from the crystal flashed more brightly, beckoning to the thousands of gallons of ocean pulsing through the tentacles of Lord Varr below.

The infant prince of the Merfolk heard the call of the key to the lost capital city, the magic it believed it needed to regain mastery over the surface world. Its entire rolling bulk halted, and even over the sound of the rotors, Bel and Lena heard the shift as tentacles froze amidst the building they had been cracking open like clams. The sound was far from silence as car alarms and police sirens still blared, chunks of buildings continued to rain down, and fires kept on crackling, but the clicking of the claws disappeared momentarily.

And then the tallest tentacles launched up toward the chopper.

"Get us higher!" Bel shouted. "Higher! As fast as you can!"

"Josef!" Lena screamed.

The golem flew at the approaching tentacles, bashing and slicing the tallest as it came. They flopped and folded, obstructing the paths of their fellows as they fell, but more kept coming. Josef couldn't prevent them all. And the chopper couldn't climb fast enough.

Lena wheeled on Bel. "I'm sorry, but it's time." She unslung her backpack, pulled out the two reams of paper, bloodstained and punctured, which held the manuscripts of the two books that could end human civilization and all monsterdom.

"The books?" Bel shouted over the sound of the blades.

Napoleon, who had been strapped into one of the chopper's seats, unbuckled and rose, his gaping eye sockets filled with the fear of recognition. Matt tried to stick out an arm to reel the skeleton back into his seat, but the chopper rocked, and he grabbed the chest straps of his harness to remain in place.

"I have to," Lena yelled. "Either this will work or it won't. But if the books can kill humans and monsters, maybe they can kill this monster." She looked over the side at the array of claws reaching up for them. They were clicking again, and the sound was louder than ever, a chittering, like a horde of locusts magnified through some massive speaker system, and the dial was turning up as they rose, each click louder and louder.

Esau could hear the women's conversation coming through the headset around Bel's neck. He smacked Nguyen on the arm and pointed violently ahead of them, mouthing "Get us back to base now!"

Lena shouted at Bel. "There's no time to experiment. It's all or nothing. The books and the writer." And she stepped toward the edge of the open doorway.

Napoleon lunged for her but missed and landed on all fours. Shockingly, all his limbs remained in place.

Bel was faster. She grabbed Lena around the shoulders with one arm and hauled her back into the chopper as she tackled her to the floor. "No!" she shouted. It wasn't a cry of desperation, but an angry order. She pinned her to the steel floor, the manuscripts trapped between them. "That's stupid. You are a writer. You know better. A big heroic sacrifice when you haven't tried everything else? That's lazy writing, Magdalena Wallace, and I won't have you going out that way." Tears welled up in the old vampire's brilliant eyes. "You don't get to go without me. We are going to try everything together, okay? Everything. For as long as we can."

Lena nodded tightly.

Then Bel jerked as the first bullet entered her spine. She made a face Lena had never seen, agony and shock, and she rolled onto her back into the middle of the copter's bay. Lena raised her head and saw Esau stepping through the doorway from the cockpit, and for the second time in her life Lena looked down the barrel of a gun he'd just fired in her direction.

"Give me the books," he shouted. He stared straight at her, seeming to ignore the prone skeleton in front of him and the wounded vampire lying next to her. But he'd taken them in and was keenly aware of their positions. He couldn't see Matt buckled into the seat behind the door, but he suspected that's where the former love of his life, the source of his deepest pain, hid, cowering. "I just want the books. Don't move. She'll be fine. One bullet is only going to slow her down. But I can put more into both of you before you can get up, so hand me the manuscripts, and I'll get back into the cockpit. Then you can all jump or ride back to the base with us. Where my men are holding your friends, the ones who got out when you landed. There are no other options here, like you said." He took a step out of the cockpit toward Lena. "Just give me the books."

Matt remembered what the witches had told him. He also heard Esau's words loud and clear. There were no other options. He watched as Esau stepped carefully around Napoleon, rebalancing against the movements of the chopper as it rose away from the oncoming tentacles. Esau pointed the gun down at Bel without taking his eyes off of Lena, then reached out his left hand and gestured for her to hand him the stacks of paper. Slowly, she bench-pressed them toward him. He gripped both reams in a large hand and hauled them into his chest, then took a single step backwards.

"Esau," Matt shouted. "No glamours. No tricks. The truth. I'm sorry. I'm so sorry. But you can't do this. That monster down there—"

Esau spun and aimed the pistol at Matt. The real Matt. A husk of a man, barely more than skin and bones, with only a few long white hairs left on a bald head, scaly, covered in liverspots, his fancy polo shirt hanging on emaciated shoulders, his ribs visible where a chest should have been, and pooling on a paunch that rested on his withered, skinny legs.

Esau didn't attempt any last quip. He closed his eyes to squeeze in the tears, and he pulled the trigger.

Lena launched herself up as fast as her vampire body could go and aimed the flat of her hand at the barrel of the gun, but she wasn't fast enough to change the direction of the bullet. The impact, first of her hand against the pistol, then of her shoulder against Esau's, sent the blinking human spinning. He teetered backwards but would have found his footing, except he tripped over the skeleton who was still obeying his order to hold still on the ground behind him. As he stumbled out of the open door of the helicopter, he reached up for the skeleton hand that seemed to be reaching down to grab him.

But Napoleon caught the dislocated left arm with his usual speed and yanked it away. Esau kept both manuscripts clutched to his chest with one hand, and could only flail at open air as he watched a skeleton look down at him. The skeleton was holding onto its own arm. And the arm waved goodbye.

Nguyen's last orders from Esau had been to hold his

position, but the last ones from Bel had demanded he climb. To split the difference, he'd begun to ascend and move forward in the direction of the military base, but at a leisurely pace. The helicopter, a Z-8 designed in France and built in China in the 1980s, then sold to the Cambodian government, not only didn't have fancy rear-view cameras, but its mirrors created a distinct blind spot below and behind the vehicle. Nguyen had no idea Lord Varr continued to approach. If he could have looked behind and beneath him, he might have been paralyzed by pure terror. Lord Varr, in his desperation to acquire Kailani's gift to Long, was climbing above the streets of Saigon. Tentacles poked out sideways into the faces of tall buildings, then hauled the entire mass upwards at an angle as others gripped the tops of buildings and propelled it higher still. Some buildings crumbled under the weight, but so many tentacles gripped at everything they could reach, the creature kept rising, heedless of the claws cut down by the stinging gnat that was Josef.

Any decent reading instructor will tell you that reading is reading, whether a book's text is internalized by deciphering symbols printed on paper, replicated on a screen, or produced by some narrator's voice. Spoken words are symbols just as written ones are, and the practice of reading is decoding symbols to make meaning. Most teachers would draw the line at masticating the pulp of the paper upon which a book is printed to try to comprehend the meaning of a book, but it turns out, at least as far as monsters go, the act of consuming a book can be satisfactorily completed by literally eating it.

Lord Varr's claws, grasping toward the helicopter above, yanked at everything between them to try to gain another few feet of height, so Esau's falling body was not a target but a possible (and disappointingly useless) handhold. Still, Lord Varr detected the human meat and snapped it up instinctively. And the reading was complete. The books were consumed. They were read.

And they did their magic.

First, all Lord Varr's tentacles slumped a bit. The ones holding the giant creature aloft among the skyscrapers froze, then loosed their holds just enough that the mass of tentacles sank back down to the level of the streets below. As the mass settled on top of the rubble of cars and broken buildings and scooter after scooter after scooter, tentacles started to curl in on themselves. The tips of the claws came to rest gently against points near their bases, as though each one was Rodin's "The Thinker" touching his chin to his knuckles (and knuckles to his chin) in deep thought, because that was precisely what Lord Varr did.

The prince and heir of the sea contemplated his actions as seen in the face of his own inevitable mortality, considered whether all that energy to conquer the surface world and consume every remaining human would ultimately garner him anything of cosmic importance, acknowledged cosmic import has no meaning in a universe of inexorable decay to stasis, and simply gave up.

The body of a cephalopod requires constant muscular contraction to maintain a shape above the surface, so, if anyone could have witnessed Lord Varr's last moments down on the street level beneath the cloud of dust, he would have looked like a giant inflatable bouncy house suddenly turned off and slowly collapsing under its own weight. Lord Varr's claws, with their thick, chitinous exoskeletons, fell in upon his body and pushed the flesh of the tentacles down faster, creating indentations in the surface, but eventually the flesh of the tentacles sank below the claws into a soupy, gelatinous blanket of meat covering seven of Saigon's major intersections.

The clean-up of all that rotting meat would need to precede the reconstruction of the city because the smell would grow to be so noxious workers would require hazmat suits to get within a mile of Lord Varr's corpse, but while the copter still hovered, the pigeons and seagulls leapt to work to do their civic duty for their city. Though Lord Varr had comprehended Lena's books and lost the will to live faster than he could transport the paper of the manuscript to his core, the paper itself rotted inside the creature long before crews could uncover even a single page.

Lena's books, having done their work, were completely lost.

And the author, having resigned herself to the conclusion that ultimate meaning cannot exist, was fine with that.

Chapter 35

Lena was not fine, however, with the fact that a bullet filled with liquid silver was lodged in her girlfriend's spine. Nor was she fine with the revelation that Torreblanca and Tina were being held captive at the military base. But Matt was her first priority. Both Lena and Napoleon rushed to him. His hand pressed against a bloody hole in his chest, in the center of what would have been his left pectoral muscle if the emaciated ancient warlock still had pectoral muscles. He wheezed, but he breathed.

"Matt," she cried, crouching down and placing her hands on his knees, unsure where she could touch a creature so frail without causing more harm. Napoleon joined her, his shoulder against hers, his eye sockets staring pleadingly at the creature that now looked more like him than like her.

When Matt spoke, the blood in his mouth trickled over his lower lip. "Get me … into the …" He waved toward the front of the helicopter. "… cockpit."

Lena couldn't understand quickly enough, but she obeyed, unlatching his harness and lifting it gingerly over his head. He fell forward onto her shoulder, placed a papery hand against the back of the open door, then felt for the handle. With all his might, he pulled himself around the swinging door, but Napoleon and Lena each put an arm under his armpits and guided him in.

In the cockpit, Matt reached out and grabbed Nguyen's shoulder. The monster-hunting mercenary turned his head, expecting to see Esau, and beheld the dying warlock's face only inches from his own. He screamed, and Matt allowed himself to fall into the space between the pilot and copilot's seats. Nguyen reached for his silenced pistol in the holster that hung low on his thigh, but he'd kept the silencer on it. The specially designed holster could accommodate the silencer because the gun was held in with snaps and the barrel extended below it, but Nguyen couldn't draw it quickly without undoing the snaps. He couldn't pop them off faster than a vampire can move.

Lena, hovering in the doorway behind Matt, saw Nguyen's movement. She shot her arm forward and yanked the gun out of his hand, then unceremoniously tossed it over her shoulder and out the open door of the helicopter. Leaving a firearm around for anyone to pick up is truly monstrous behavior, but Lena was a vampire, and, luckily, the fall from almost a thousand feet bent the barrel enough to prevent any bullet from ever passing through it again, so the day wasn't compounded by another needless tragedy.

Nguyen looked up at Lena. She bared her teeth, the circular rows of hollow vampire fangs that she could extend behind her human ones and wiggle when feeding. She hissed with all her might. Nguyen saw stars as he began to pass out, and he lost control of his bladder. Beneath him he heard a voice say, "Ah, thank you for that." Blinking to retain consciousness, he looked down to see the old monster quickly turning into a handsome man with a full head of blond hair, a muscular build, and a polo shirt. It's objectively difficult to fear anyone wearing a polo shirt. Nguyen started breathing again.

Matt pushed himself up onto his knees, then sat on his feet and breathed a deep sigh. He made a constipated face while he pushed the bullet out of his chest. It fell down inside his shirt and rolled out onto the helicopter's floor. He picked it up and stuck it in his pocket as a souvenir to remember Esau. Then he looked up at Lena. "The witches said he'd shoot me on sight, and I assumed he'd kill me. I mean, it was strongly implied. But this gentleman here gave me just the boost I needed to recover." He climbed slowly to his feet, then sat down in the co-pilot's chair. "Again, thank you for that generous hit of pure terror. Strong stuff. I can do a lot with that. Now, get us back to the base before I turn you into a spider or a snake or something else you're afraid of."

Nguyen tried to say, "Yessir," but found his throat didn't work, so he made a pathetic little nod and steered the helicopter in the right direction.

Lena ran to the back of the cargo cabin and found Bel sitting on the floor with her back against the wall, breathing heavily like she was doing Lamaze.

"Are you okay?" Lena asked, crouching down and wrapping her arms around Bel's shoulders, then resting her head on top of Bel's.

"I'll be … I'll be fine … just gotta … push the … silver out … Could use … a bite to eat."

"As soon as we land you can drink the pilot. He's one of Esau's men. But you'll have to eat fast and get ready because they have Tina and Torreblanca."

"How … many …"

"I don't know. And they know we're coming. But …" She crooked a thumb at the empty space behind her. A swirl of sand flowed into the helicopter's open door, then coalesced into Josef. "… we have a golem."

Even before they touched down, they knew the situation. Cassius stood between Augy and Bob. Two of Esau's soldiers stood on either side of the vampires, their rifles pointed at Tina and Torreblanca. The captives were on their knees, fingers laced behind their heads.

Cassius and his men knew something was wrong, too. As the helicopter descended, they could see Nguyen alone in the cockpit. No one was visible through the rear windows. Nguyen must have heard some order, because he began to frantically remove his harness, but just as he grabbed the handle to open his door, a hand popped out of the cargo door, grabbed his tac vest, and yanked him into the cargo hold. He didn't scream.

"Come on out, Bel," Cassius shouted. "We trade the books for the girls, straight up. No one else has to die today."

The side door of the helicopter swung open, and Josef stepped out. "Ah," Cassius said, "I see you have a golem. Guess you think I'm pretty well cooked, eh? You win, I guess. C'mon out and watch it finish us all off."

"Um, boss?" Bob said.

"Shut up, Bob," Augy muttered.

"But that's a golem. I can't kill a golem."

"Nope."

"Boss can't kill a golem, can he?"

"Shut up, Bob."

Lena and Bel stepped around Josef and began walking toward Cassius and his crew. "Are you okay?" Lena asked Torreblanca and Tina.

Tina shrugged. "My pride got kicked in the dick, but physically we're fine. I thought about fighting them all, but they would have killed Torreblanca for sure." She looked at Torreblanca. "And me. They would have killed me, too. I admit it."

"Don't take it so hard, my little lupine friend," Cassius said. "You're about to watch Bel get a good strong kick in her pride, too. Golem, I command you to grab those two vampires!"

Bel and Lena froze, and Josef wrapped his huge hands around the backs of both of their necks. It waited until they had good, strong grips on its large index fingers, then lifted them into the air where they kicked and struggled dramatically.

"See, this was always your problem, Bel," Cassius

said. "You didn't trust me enough. Look at Bob and Augy. They do whatever I say without question because they know I've thought everything through five steps ahead. I'm playing chess, and you're playing checkers. And Bob is playing tiddlywinks, but he knows better than to think he's playing chess."

Bob nodded.

"But you thought you could go off with your girlfriend and make your own plans and I wouldn't catch up with you. And then you had me shot in the face. And you think I'm just going to let bygones be bygones. Because we're family, right? Because I made you who you are."

He stepped up to the women dangling from Josef's outstretched arms. Then, faster than Lena could move, faster than even Bel, he punched Lena in the stomach. She could feel her organs crush and rupture, her intestines sliced against her spine. The blow would have killed most humans immediately, and the unlucky few who would have survived would have bled out internally in minutes or died from sepsis in agonizing days. Lena's body immediately began to heal, but she felt all that pain, an agony she'd never experienced before in her short life.

"See, I'm going to beat your girlfriend nearly to death while you watch. But I won't kill her because she can give me those books." He looked back to Lena. "Or write me new ones. Maybe better ones. More deadly. Or more targeted. Bunker-buster nukes of books. Whatever I want." He looked back to Bel. "And she'll write me all the books I want. Hell, I may cut her legs and one arm off. I just need her brain and one writing hand, right?

And you won't be able to save her because after I'm done torturing you by beating on her, I'm going to finish you off tonight. Because you are dangerous, Bel. That's what I made you. Dangerous. A dangerous disappointment. Golem, turn her this way to make sure she watches. Bob and Augy, if she tries to close her eyes, cut off her eyelids, okay?"

"You got it, Boss," Augy said.

"Yep," Bob agreed.

"You're right!" Bel called out.

That got Cassius' attention.

"What was that?" he asked, hoping to hear it again.

"I said …" Bel made a choking sound, then kicked her legs some more. "I said …" Now she only whispered. "You're right. I'm …"

Cassius got closer. Not close enough she could kick him, but enough that all his attention was focused on her. "Are you sorry now?" he asked.

"No … I'm … I'm dangerous." And then she stiffened and held out her left hand, fingers splayed. But instead of five fingers, she held up four and a ragged stump where her pinky should have been.

Lena couldn't move as fast as Cassius or Bel, and she expected Bob and Augy would be quicker than she was, too, but she didn't need to be the fastest. When the other vampires saw her drop out of Josef's hand and crouch down on the ground behind their employer, they sprang into action like experienced bodyguards, expecting her to attack Cassius from behind. They were running full speed toward her, fangs bared, their claw-like nails ready to slice into her, when Josef swept an arm out and punched both with a single blow. Cassius saw them

490

sailing away before he turned all the way around and beheld Lena's work.

At that same instant, Torreblanca and Tina vanished. The monster hunters didn't know what to do. They looked to one another for direction, then to Bob and Augy landing in ragged heaps on the tarmac, then to Cassius.

The old vampire spun on Lena, but it was too late. Between them, she'd crouched down and used Bel's pinky like sidewalk chalk, grinding a jagged, bloody circle only four inches in diameter. The space inside flashed like she'd touched a flame to a small pool of napalm, and one of Apraxis' little red hands reached out and patted around the edge of the circle.

"Ha!" Cassius shouted. "He can't fit!" He looked into the hole at Apraxis. Only one of the demon's eyes was visible, appraising the vampire. "You thought you could betray me, too. All of you thought you could outsmart—"

Apraxis pointed a tiny finger up at the vampire. Iron manacles on chains flew out. Cassius tried to dodge them like bullets, but the manacles swerved and found the vampire's throat, wrists, and ankles.

"No, you can't!" Cassius shouted. The manacles pulled him down onto the concrete and dragged him toward the hole. "I won't—"

Cassius didn't have time to mansplain the physical impossibility of pulling a normal-sized vampire through a four-inch hole before Apraxis' chains proved him wrong. A lot of Cassius remained on the tarmac, but all the important bits were hoovered up by some suction in the place where Apraxis lived.

When he was gone, Bel looked down into the hole. "So, a deal is a deal. Good doing business with you."

"I was never going to betray you if you'd let me out of here, and I'm really glad you're so clever," Apraxis said, then raised his little hand into our world in a one finger salute before closing the portal behind him.

The four human monster hunters remained in their positions, their guns now trained on Bel and Lena. Unsure what to do, they dared a look back to where Augy and Bob lay. The two vampires stood up, flexed, assessed the damage, and then Augy shouted, "Humans, attack them!" Then he grabbed the shoulder of Bob's jacket and pulled as he started to run away.

"You can run away, too," Lena said to the monster hunters. "It's been a difficult night."

To their credit, two of them did run away. They were caught by Vietnamese authorities who aren't too keen on men running through their streets carrying machine guns. And they were accused of perpetrating a terrorist attack that killed thousands of people in Saigon and left much of the city covered in seafood. They received the death penalty and still fared better than the two who chose to fight. Before those could pull their triggers, Matt made Tina reappear, and she recovered some of her lost pride.

Chapter 36

The hall was louder than usual. The representative of the delegation of the sirens was at the mic, trying in vain to make a formal apology on behalf of her people. Since she wasn't allowed to use her own voice on the floor of the annual meeting of The Convention of Fiends, she had to hold a cellphone up and let it read her prepared statement in a tinny, robotic voice. The vampire delegation booed. The werewolves shouted. The gremlins laughed. The Archduke, serving as the presiding officer, banged the gavel and called for order. The gremlins laughed louder.

When the pre-recorded message ended, the siren bowed her head and slinked back to her table among the Merfolk and gorgons. It would have been clearer if a merperson or gorgon had spoken, since they were allowed to use their voices, but they'd decided any resemblance to Tisina would be worse than sending a person who looked like a human woman holding a cell phone. And they were right. The monsters expressed their displeasure at the Merfolk delegation for a few more moments, then got over it.

Next, the Archduke talked about plans to reorganize CimBim to prevent any single monster from being a bottleneck the way Cassius had been. The mention of the dead vampire garnered as many boos and shouts as the Siren had, even louder from the vampires who wanted to publicly distance themselves, but these dissipated more rapidly. After all, technically speaking, Cassius hadn't broken any rules of The Convention. If anything, his attempt to acquire Lena's books had been in keeping with two previous New Business Items. But the rumor mill had attached him to the public display in Saigon, and rumors supersede technicalities. Plus, he was a douchebag with a lot of enemies, so it was easier to blame him than excuse him.

Then the Archduke announced the opening of the debate on that year's New Business Items. "With everyone's permission, and recognizing we passed this year's agenda with flexibility, I'd like to move NBI 4 up to the top of the order so we can thank a certain monster."

Bel tapped Lena's leg. "This is your big moment," she whispered. "Do you know what you're going to say?"

"Yep. Watch this."

"... the monster most responsible for bringing the catastrophe in Saigon to a quick end and averting what could have been a much bigger disaster for all of us, Ms. Magdalena Wallace, vampire, North American delegation."

Lena stood and waved as the room burst into applause. Nando had organized the werewolf delegation into a strong, unified voting bloc, and he used some of that authority to make sure his friend got a standing ovation. Bel had given up her position in CimBim temporarily so she could serve as a delegate and then do some traveling, so she got to sit among the vampires for a change, and when the other vampires saw Bel stand in support of Lena, they jumped to their feet. The trolls were wary of Bel and Lena and decided hearty applause looked better than any kind of defiance, so they jumped up on their tables and waggled their naked privates in their culturally appropriate show of appreciation. The Merfolk were genuinely appreciative since they had more reason to hate Lord Varr than anyone in the room. The gremlins, ever the contrarians, made raspberry noises, but their hearts really weren't in it.

"Ms. Wallace, please step to Microphone Six to present your NBI," the Archduke said. The applause died down as she shimmied sideways between the long tables, then made her way down the aisle to the microphone. Her image was captured by the video crew and projected up onto the two screens behind the stage, so she looked up at two huge versions of herself squinting uncomfortably in the bright lights.

"Ms. Wallace, would you like to speak to your NBI?"

This was her big moment. She brought all her rhetorical strategies, eloquence, and writing skill to bear for maximum persuasion.

"Nope," she said.

The vampires laughed nervously. The gremlins cackled. The werewolves howled with delight. It was perfect.

"Alright then," the Archduke said. "We are now in debate." He scanned the crowd as Lena made her way back to her seat. "Seeing no one rising to the microphone, I'll- Oh, yes, there on Microphone Two. Speaking for or against?"

Lena didn't recognize the monster, a human-looking white woman with red hair. "Clodagh Lynch, Banshee, European delegation." The Banshees, unlike the sirens, were allowed to speak because the sirens could conceivably manipulate monsters with their magical voices, while the banshees could only kill them with their screams, and that would be fairly obvious to everyone. "Rising to ask a point of information. This NBI is really long. It's like thirty bloody pages. Has anyone actually read ta' whole thing, then?"

The gremlins to Ms. Lynch's right booed and started throwing candy wrappers and balled-up napkins at her. She wheeled on them and inhaled, considering some light murder. The gremlins cowered, then snickered as she turned back to the microphone. "Well, have ya'? Anyone?"

The Archduke cleared his throat. "Points of

information can only be made to the chair or through the chair to the maker, but I'm going to rule this one out of order on the grounds that it's a rhetorical question."

"It's not!" Ms. Lynch cried. "I'll put the question to you, then, Mr. Chair. Have you read it?"

The Archduke leaned sideways as the new parliamentarian, a Japanese Namazu wearing a human glamour, whispered in his ear. Then he straightened and spoke into his microphone. "I'm sorry, Ms. Lynch, but your first question was already ruled out of order, and according to the rules, you cannot ask a second until you get out of line and we get through a full round of debate with one speaker for and one against."

She waved at the microphones. They all stood silent and alone.

"And, seeing no one rise to speak in favor or against, I will put the question to the body," the Archduke said.

Ms. Lynch stamped her foot and went back to her seat, stalked by more laughter.

"All those in favor of Ms. Wallace's NBI 4, say aye."

The room filled with a lowing of ayes.

"All those opposed, say nay."

A few monsters, including Ms. Lynch, shouted performative nays, but the vote was nearly unanimous.

"The ayes have it. We've passed NBI 4. Now let's return to the order in your handbook, beginning with NBI 1 on page 34…"

A few hours later, Lena and Bel sat down in a booth

across from Torreblanca in a 50s-style retro diner across the Strip from The Venetian.

Lena beamed. "It passed. Tomorrow, you can go in and sit in the back."

"Really? What was the vote?"

"Nearly unanimous," Bel said. "We'd organized most of the groups beforehand, and then Lena gave this really amazing speech.

"Really?"

"Nope," Lena repeated her speech. "I just kept it short and made them laugh, so they liked that. I didn't want to give anyone a reason to look too closely. The first few pages are just junk about reorganizing CimBim."

"They aren't junk. They'll be really important now."

"Sure, but they were filled with jargon and didn't make much sense until you got about three quarters of the way through. Then it all becomes clear."

"Yep. Human beings are now officially members of The Convention," Bel said.

Lena gave her girlfriend a sidelong glance for stealing her thunder, then smiled at Torreblanca. "That's right. You people are monsters now."

"So, what all does that mean? Monsters can't eat us anymore?"

"No, that was the big compromise I had to make to get the thing passed. In the fine print after your official inclusion, there are these carve-outs that allow monsters of other kinds to continue feeding on humans as long as they do so in a responsible way which will not diminish the human population too much or reveal the existence of The Convention of Fiends to the general population."

"Wasn't that already the rule?"

"Yeah, it mostly maintains the status quo which was the way to get the more conservative delegates on board, but this will prevent anything like Nigel Marion's NBI from passing in the future. If some monster decides to propose an NBI that will wipe out a large portion of the human population, it would be ruled out of order. So we keep the normal feedings, and you all get to avoid the genocides."

"It's an improvement, I guess."

"It's a start," Lena explained. "Because now that you're members, the language at the beginning about reorganizing CimBim applies to humans, too. So now they'll have to incorporate some humans into the branch of The Convention that enforces the policies made at the annual meeting. Turns out there's a yokai who has infiltrated a certain secretive group of monster hunters who once employed you. He thinks he can get them to work with CimBim eventually." She looked at Bel. "When he talked about how he might have to knock some heads to get it done, I got the distinct impression he was being literal."

"Same," Bel said.

"Wait, so you found out who Esau was working for?"

"This demon guy did."

"Who was it?" Torreblanca asked, almost bouncing in her seat. "I'm not sure if Esau even knew."

"Just a bunch of old monster hunters. And the monster mole this yokai has on the inside."

"I fuckin' called it. Hot damn!"

Lena turned back to Torreblanca. "Well, now we're on the same side anyway. They just don't know it yet.

Just imagine: Monsters and humans working together to make sure monsters don't overstep."

Bel inclined her head. "And monsters and humans working together to make sure humans don't wipe themselves off the face of the Earth."

"Yes, that's important, too," Lena agreed. "If some human billionaires decide to burn down the planet for a profit, or if some human dictator decides to nuke the whole world rather than go on trial for war crimes in the Hague, they will find that CimBim agents now have jurisdiction to protect the human population. Imagine vampires and humans sent to make sure some tycoon doesn't kill off a few third world countries so he can mine rare Earth metals to make a gazillion dollars. Those millions of humans now have recognized worth in the eyes of The Convention and an enforcement agency dedicated to protecting them, even from other humans."

"Because we're food," Torreblanca said.

"Because you're valuable food," Lena said. "You might not like being valued as food, but being valued is an improvement, and if that's offensive, it should be. Yes, it's fucked up that vampires and werewolves care more about humans than humans do, but here we are."

"And," Bel said, "you've been nominated by a certain delegation of vampires to be one of the first human agents of CimBim, if you'll take the job."

"Can I think about it for a while?"

Bel looked at her watch. "Tomorrow's meeting starts at 10pm. I suggest you call your monster boyfriend and get his opinion about whether his human girlfriend can partner with monsters to save monsters and humans."

"I see your point," Torreblanca said. She stared through the window into the Vegas night. The tourists with kids were mostly off the streets, but the crowds were as thick as ever, some people headed purposefully from one casino to the next, others stumbling along already drunk, others pointing at fountains and glowing signs as they ambled by. But one person stood on the sidewalk staring in at them. He wore a black sweatshirt that said, "Angkor What?!" And he had no skin, just a skull.

Torreblanca waved at Napoleon. He waved a gloved hand back, then caught his other arm as the bare bones slid out of his sleeve.

"He kinda looks like the grim reaper dressed like that. But cute. He doesn't look that scary. He … he looks kind of goofy."

Lena nodded. "That's where I am with death at this point, too. Like Napoleon, it's not scary. Or it doesn't have to be. It's absurd and silly and … lovable. Believe it or not, you can live with death. You can find someone you love." She took Bel's hand under the table and squeezed it. "And you can both live with death, just hanging out, just there with you. With a time limit of unknown duration." She looked at Bel. "No dramatic heroics. I understand that now." Then she turned back to Torreblanca. "You can choose the monster you want to be. And death can become your friend."

"These are your choices, choices you have been fortunate to have been given, so don't waste them while you have them. Don't look back in years to come and wish you had grasped a fleeting opportunity. Grasp now with both hands. Live. Strive. Love."

-Sir Terry Pratchett

Chapter 37

"...and fade to credits," the emissary said. "Or maybe zoom in on Napoleon's face first, then fade out. Director's choice. So, what do you think?"

Joyce looked at Kim, then at Carol. "I see some promise, but it's confusing. Like, what does it mean?"

Carol frowned and stared at the emissary. "Is this really what you believe? That understanding our mortality would lead to the downfall of civilization, so we all need to embrace death? That's a pretty grim day at the movies."

The emissary nodded. "I guess it depends on what you mean by 'civilization.' If, by 'civilization,' you mean patriarchal, white supremacist, heteronormative, hierarchical hyper-capitalism, then yeah, I think that is in direct conflict with accepting our own mortality. That kind of society is rooted in the idea of legacy and passing on wealth to maintain itself, and the central motivation is amassing wealth to aggrandize oneself into perpetuity. If people fully understood death, that would all fall apart. Why try winning at capitalism if it won't matter the next day? You have to believe you'll put your name on a new university library and matter to people a generation later. Do you remember the name of your college library?"

"I think it was Cooper. Thomas Cooper. Something like that."

"And do you care about Mr. Cooper?"

"Nope."

"How many people did he have to climb over to get his name on that library? Sure, he may have helped a lot of people, too. I don't know anything about Thomas Cooper. Did he own slaves?"

"Well, it was University of South Carolina, so, probably."

"Regardless, he cared about his legacy. And for what? So you could walk under his name every day and not care a bit about him."

"Thank you for presuming I went to the library every day in college," Carol said. She turned back to her boss. "Mr. Joyce, I just can't imagine anyone paying to go see a movie about how all their hopes and dreams are pointless. Worse, I can't imagine them paying to see it twice, and we are not in the business of making little arthouse films people watch once. It's a no for me."

Joyce turned to Kim.

They shrugged. "I admit I kind of disagree, Carol. I see your point. The whole metaphysical part of it is a giant bummer. But the monster part could sell tickets. We can downplay the reasons behind it." They turned to the emissary. "Though I do like the anti-patriarchy stuff. But we'll keep it subtle." They turned back to Mr. Joyce. "The whole pivot to people becoming monsters? That's got some Lady Gaga vibes I like a lot. I think we could sell that."

Joyce leaned back, pushing his feet into the carpet until the chair squeaked. "I just… I think I'm going to have to pass." He looked at Kim. "I don't know how we can do the monster stuff without the death stuff. Especially with the skeleton guy. What was his name?"

"Napoleon," the emissary said. "But he was only named that because of the hat. That could be changed."

"Yeah, no, it's the whole death thing. No one wants to think about it. Being a monster sounds cool. But being a monster in a world where we're all going to die? Death in movies is a plot device, not an existential reality. It breaks the whole magic illusion if the characters are speaking honestly about death. I'm sorry, but we're going to pass on this one."

The emissary either maintained his composure or genuinely didn't care. "Okay, but can I ask you all one question? Who was your favorite character?"

"Lena," Carol said.

"Bel," Joyce said.

"Josef, of course," Kim said.

"Dammit!" the emissary shouted. "Anyone else you liked?"

"The skeleton guy," Joyce said. He'd already forgotten the character's name.

"Oh, and the little troll dude," Kim said.

"I felt bad for Nguyen," Carol offered.

"Damn. Fine. I'll work on that," he said, then turned and stormed out.

When he stepped out of the office, three women stood between him and his car. "How did it go," the youngest asked.

"You already know they turned it down," Matt said.

"Maybe you aren't trying hard enough," the oldest said.

"Now Justinia, that's not nice," the middlest said. "I like it. It's funny. But it's not nice."

"So how many more of these do you have to do?" Garifinia asked.

"How many more production companies are there in Hollywood? And New York? And Bombay? And then I'll have to start pestering directors, probably. And individual movie stars. I don't think it will ever end."

"It does sound like a pretty Herculean labor now, doesn't it?" Justinia asked. "Not so fun being a genuine hero."

"It's not just the labor thing. Lena added it to the fine print of her NBI. Part of her plan to soften up the masses and prepare them for the idea they are monsters who should stop slaughtering one another so there's more left for her to drink. Just between us, I think this is revenge for causing her to get shot. Which was not my fault at all. And she said she forgave me."

"Oh Matty," Garafinia said, placing a hand on his forearm, "I'll bet you are no fun at parties anymore. I should just start hanging out with that skeleton guy. What's his name?" She smiled and winked.

"Okay, tell me the truth. How many times have you two watched my pitch just to laugh at me?"

"Truly?" Justinia asked.

The sisters shared a glance, then replied in unison. "Twice."

Matt turned and shouted at the office building. "See, Carol from Racist University? People *will* watch it twice! See?"

Laughing, the four of them got into Matt's car.

Or maybe they all froze in awkward poses like a movie from the 1970s.

Or maybe the witches teleported back to Scotland, and Matt drove off by himself into the California sunset.

Reader's choice.

The End

About the Author

Benjamin Gorman is an award-winning former high school English teacher, political activist, author, poet, publisher at Not a Pipe Publishing, and host of the *Writers Not Writing* YouTube show/podcast. He is now an author-in-exile living in  Barcelona, Spain with his favorite wife, bibliophile and guillotine aficionado Chrys, his favorite daughter Franke, their small dogs Merry and Pippin, and their dire wolf Havoc. He is proud to be the father of his favorite son, Noah.

9 781956 892703